MURDER IN STEEPLE MARTIN

This is a tale of engaging misfits and muddlers in a Kent village, whose theatrical endeavours rouse the long arm of the past with murderous consequences. Artist Libby Sarjeant's fresh start in a picturesque Kent village includes a new romance in the form of Ben, but who's complaining? She just isn't expecting ingredients three, four and five: mystery, intrigue, and the shadow of old murder...

MURDER IN STEEPLE MARTIN

Murder In Steeple Martin

by

Lesley Cookman

Magna Large Print Books
Long Preston, North Yorkshire,
BD23 4ND, England.

British Library Cataloguing in Publication Data.

Cookman, Lesley
 Murder in Steeple Martin.

 A catalogue record of this book is
 available from the British Library

 ISBN   978-0-7505-3622-6

First published in Great Britain in 2006 by Accent Press Ltd.

Published in Large Print 2012 by arrangement with
Accent Press Ltd.

Magna Large Print is an imprint of Library Magna Books Ltd.

Printed and bound in Great Britain by
T.J. (International) Ltd., Cornwall, PL28 8RW

In memory of Brian Cookman

Acknowledgements

There are many people I have to thank for helping this book to see the light of day, so here they are, in no particular order. Hazel Cushion of Accent Press, Jenny Hewitt, who saw the original version years ago, the wonderful Hilary Johnson, without whom… Bernadine Kennedy, who nagged me, all my friends in The Romantic Novelists' Association, especially Jenny Haddon and Katie Fforde and, finally, my fantastic children, Louise, Miles, Phillipa and Leo. Thank you all, very much.

Chapter One

Libby sat on a plastic chair in the middle of what would be the auditorium of the Oast House Theatre and considered mass murder. Her feet were cold, her hands were cold, she was thirsty and it seemed to her that every single person on the stage – and behind it – was going out of their way to do exactly the opposite of what she wanted.

'Bloody hell,' she muttered as a member of the cast ran to the wrong corner of the stage *again* and then stopped and looked for a prompt.

'Other way, Emma,' she called, just refraining from adding, 'You silly cow.' What was the matter with the girl? She was behaving like a rank amateur. She *was* an amateur. Oh, bloody hell again.

The rehearsal wore on. The partially constructed hop garden at the back of the stage was showing an alarming tendency to become part of the action and was constantly being propped up by nervous actors; the back-stage team were having a violent argument at a pitch the actors could only dream about and the plastic chair was getting harder and harder.

'That's it,' said Libby standing up suddenly and dislodging a pile of the lighting technician's notes. 'Let's all go to the pub.'

Silence fell and bewildered faces turned towards her.

'But we haven't done scene three,' came a

plaintive voice from the back of the set.

'We haven't done scenes one and two, either, have we? Not properly. Not so's you'd notice.'

'What?' People began looking at each other, shrugging.

'That's a bit unfair, Libby,' said the plaintive voice.

'On me, yes.' Libby walked forward, gathering her long cardigan around her. 'Now don't get me started, or I shall bawl you all out and you'll hate me. So, let's go and have a sociable drink and forget it for tonight. We'll put in an extra rehearsal tomorrow...'

Howls of protest met this remark, as she'd known they would.

'I can't make tomorrow–'

'I haven't got a babysitter–'

'It's my late night–'

'But tonight was extra! I only said I'd do a Sunday as a favour–'

'Try.' Libby was firm. 'Everybody who can. We go up in less than two weeks and this – not to put too fine a point on it – is a shambles. Pull your socks up and I'll see you here at seven-thirty tomorrow night.'

She watched the cast gather their belongings together and mutter their way towards the back of the theatre.

'Libby, darling,' came a voice from behind her, 'you must meet my dear mama.'

Libby turned the full force of her smile upwards at the severely coiffured head of the woman standing next to Peter Parker.

'How lovely to meet you,' she said. 'Peter's told

16

me so much about you.'

Peter acknowledged this patent untruth with a lift of an eyebrow and turned to his mother.

'Mum, this is Libby Sarjeant–'

'With a J,' interrupted Libby automatically.

'With a J,' Peter continued smoothly. 'You've heard all about Libby, haven't you?'

'Of course.' Libby detected a faint twang of something other than Home Counties in the nasal voice. 'You're the lady who's come to help Peter with his little play.'

Libby saw Peter suppress a wince and fumbled for his hand to administer a solidarity squeeze.

'Not exactly come *specifically*, Mum. She lives here already.'

'Yes, dear.' Peter's mother inclined her head. 'Where was it now? I'm sure you told me.'

'Allhallow's Lane, yes, Mum.' Peter was clearly getting impatient. 'We're all going for a drink. Would you like to come with us?'

Millicent Parker's face showed a certain degree of horror at this suggestion and she moved towards the back of the auditorium.

'No, thank you, dear.' She bestowed what she obviously thought was a smile on Libby. 'But thank you for asking me. I'll just pop off home.'

'She didn't even say what she thought of the play,' said Libby wonderingly, gazing after the retreating figure. 'I thought she wanted to come and see it.'

'She did. She asked. Wanted to make sure it was suitable for her little boy to be mixed up with.'

A tall figure in pink shirt and leather trousers, blond hair flopping over his brow, emerged from back-stage as Peter was closing the door. 'Who was that?'

'My mother.' Peter flung himself onto Libby's abandoned chair.

'Oh, 'er. All padlocked knickers and spray polish,' said Harry. 'We going to the pub?'

Libby sighed. 'I don't really feel like it, if you don't mind,' she said.

'I don't, but I think your stage manager might be miffed. He's already gone.'

Peter reached over and patted him firmly on the bottom. 'Make us a cuppa, then, love.'

'Oh, make it yourself,' grumbled Harry, but disappeared into the kitchen nevertheless.

Libby sat on the edge of the stage and found her cigarettes. 'So that's your mama.'

'That's her. All M&S pretties and hair like a middle-aged Barbie.'

'She doesn't look like a farmer's wife.'

'Well, it's the old East End, isn't it? Not county born and bred.'

Harry came in with a beautiful decoupage tray and assorted chipped mugs. 'Sorry about these. We've used all the decent ones.' He handed a mug to Libby, pulled up another plastic chair beside Peter, sat down and lifted Peter's feet on to his lap.

'I'm not sure I understand your family,' said Libby. 'It's very complicated.'

'That's because you have a sweet, simple nature, you old trout.' Peter sipped his tea. 'Like us. That's why you fit in here.'

'The theatre or Steeple Martin, do you mean? I wonder. They don't really know anything about

18

me.' Libby frowned into her mug.

'They know you're divorced and you've got children.' Harry shrugged. 'Probably know how often you wash your sheets and whether you've had the change yet, I shouldn't wonder.'

Libby nodded, acknowledging the omniscience of villagers.

'Anyway, I like it. I love the cottage. And it'll be lovely to have the theatre.'

'If we ever get the bloody thing off the ground.' Peter said, absent-mindedly resting his mug on Harry's crotch.

'Watch the goods, dear,' said Harry, gently moving it aside.

Libby looked up. 'I thought we *were* getting it off the ground. The theatre's nearly finished, we've only got two weeks until we open – what's the matter?'

'Oh, I don't know. I'm just filled with doom and despondency the further into it we get. Who's going to come to a converted oast house in the depths of Kent to see an unknown play performed by amateurs?'

Libby stood up. 'Publicity, that's what we need. Something to make it stick in people's minds, so that they say – "Oh, yes, The Oast House. That's where they did that terrific–" well, I don't know, but terrific something. Harry's caff's doing OK. And that was good opening publicity, wasn't it? And people remember the name.'

'I wish I could forget it,' said Harry gloomily. 'Pink bloody Geranium. What a name for a caff.'

'Didn't you name it, then?' asked Libby, surprised.

19

'No, it was already the Pink Geranium. I thought it sounded good for a vegetarian restaurant,' said Peter, 'but a ponced-up caff is hardly the same as a theatre, is it?'

Harry came over and pulled Libby off the stage.

'Oh, come on. Let's go to the pub after all. A game of darts might cheer the old sod up.'

'I really won't come if you don't mind,' said Libby swathing herself in blue wool. 'I need to think what to do with them tomorrow. And I've got to get back to Sidney.'

'Have you got to go and feed that walking stomach of yours?'

'Sidney is a very well-built cat,' Libby defended.

'Spoilt rotten and completely dictatorial. I wonder you didn't call him Hitler,' said Peter.

'And I need to go and be nice to the crew. If they're still here.'

'Most of them. Stephen went because you said you were going,' said Harry.

'Yes,' Libby sighed. 'Never mind.'

Peter grinned at her. 'That was telling 'em, though, ducky. Needed a nuclear device up the jacksie tonight, didn't they?'

In the unfinished emptiness of the auditorium, she made her way round back-stage to soothe the ruffled spirits in the workshop. A hand fell on her shoulder, making her jump.

'Stephen! I thought you'd gone.'

'I thought you were going to the pub, but Harry and Peter said you were still here.' Stephen's light, pleasant voice sounded slightly petulant.

Libby picked her way carefully between new

ropes and stage weights, feeling in front of her with an outstretched hand. 'I wasn't really in the mood. Sorry, Stephen. You go.'

'No, I'll walk you home. You shouldn't be out on your own at this time of night.' He held the door to the workshop open for her.

'In Steeple Martin?' She laughed. 'Can't see anything happening to me here.'

The remaining two members of the back-stage crew were putting on their coats and switching lights off.

'You OK, you two? I wasn't moaning at you, earlier, by the way.'

They both grinned and assured her they were immune to moaning.

'Can you come tomorrow?'

No, they couldn't they said, or their wives would have their guts for garters, but they'd be there the day after.

'I can't either, Libby,' said Stephen as they walked back through the darkened theatre and he turned to lock the doors behind them.

'Never mind. It's the actors who need the rehearsal, not back-stage.'

'Yes, but I'm stage manager. I ought to be there.'

'It's fine. Pete'll be with me. And we won't move anything on set, just work round it.'

Stephen took her arm and frowned at her as they walked down the drive to the High Street. 'Peter's always here. Does he need to be?'

Libby looked up, surprised. 'He wrote it, it's his baby. Of course he wants to be here.'

'So why was his mother here tonight?'

'The play's about his family. She just wanted to

see what's going on.'

'She didn't look too pleased.' Stephen smiled grimly.

'No, she didn't, did she? Don't know why, she was only a baby when it all happened.'

'The main character's her sister? Peter's aunt?' asked Stephen, as they turned into the High Street.

Libby closed her eyes and hung on to her temper. 'Did you not read the script, Stephen?'

'Of course!' He sounded surprised. 'But the script doesn't say who the real people were. And I haven't had much discussion with you since you asked me in to take over back-stage.'

'Sorry,' said Libby remorsefully, 'I know I've taken advantage of you.'

Stephen was resident stage manager at the Little Theatre where, over the years, Libby had made a name for herself as an actor and director. Now, faced with the challenge of a new theatre and inexperienced but willing stage crew, Libby had persuaded him to come and take charge. A divorcee like herself, he had interpreted her request in a somewhat more intimate manner than Libby had intended, but she was managing to keep him at bay so far, with the help of Peter and Harry, whom Stephen quite obviously resented.

Allhallow's Lane led off the High Street, an indeterminate huddle of cottages of varying ages, which petered out in a half-hearted manner in front of what could have been a green.

'Well, you could tell me now,' Stephen said, as they approached the green. 'I could come in for coffee?'

'I'm tired, Stephen. That's why I didn't go for a drink. And you've got half an hour's drive home, don't forget.'

She saw him open his mouth to reply, and knew he was going to suggest that he stayed. She hurried on.

'It's really very simple. Peter's Aunt Hetty came down here to Manor Farm as a hop picker with her mother and sister, who is Peter's mother Millie. One weekend when their brother, Lenny, was down here with their father, a tallyman was killed and their father disappeared. Eventually Hetty married Greg, the owner of Manor Farm.'

'So they're all still alive?' asked Stephen, coming to a halt by his car, parked on the verge opposite Libby's cottage.

'Yes, and they all live here, except Lenny. Even Hetty and Greg's children, Susan and Ben, are local.'

'And Peter? Does he have any brothers or sisters?'

'One younger brother, James. He lives in Canterbury.'

Stephen frowned down at the car keys in his hand. 'And none of them married?'

Libby shot him a surprised look. 'Eh? Well, Hetty and Greg obviously are. Millie's husband died, Ben's divorced and Susan is married to a local doctor. And Peter...'

'Is married to Harry.' Stephen raised an eyebrow. 'More or less.'

'And they're very happy.' Libby tightened her lips.

Stephen laughed. 'Don't jump to their defence,

23

Lib. I wasn't criticising.'

'You don't like them.'

'Peter always seems to be there when I try and talk to you. I think it's more that he doesn't like me rather than the other way round.'

Libby let herself relax. It was probably true. 'Well, I'm sorry. I'm sure he doesn't mean it.' She reached up impulsively and kissed him on the cheek. 'Off you go. I'll see you the day after tomorrow.'

Chapter Two

The following night's rehearsal was marginally better, although not as well attended by either crew or cast, but, nevertheless, Libby felt able to go and have a drink with the cast, if only to deprive them of the pleasure of talking about her behind her back.

The pub, much beloved of calendar photographers, rested wearily against an upright Georgian house in the middle of the High Street. One day, Libby was convinced, its hanging baskets would slide right in through the windows next door. She pushed open the door and battled her way through bucolic humanity to the side bar where the cast and crew who were allowed to stay out after ten o'clock had gathered in a dismal group. Peter put a pint of lager into her hand.

'A pint? I can't cope with these big glasses.'

'Oh, shut up, do. Come on, someone, give

Auntie Libby a seat.'

One of the younger women stood up. 'Here you are, Libby. I can stand.'

'So what's the gossip, then?' asked Libby, as she squeezed into the vacated seat.

'Uncle Lenny's back.'

'Who?'

'Uncle Lenny. My Uncle Lenny. Bert in the play.'

Libby squinted up at the tall figure beside her. 'I thought he didn't visit?'

'Apparently, he heard all about our little play. He just arrived. This afternoon. Turned up as large as life on Aunt Hetty's doorstep. She wasn't tickled pink, I can tell you.'

'I bet she wasn't. How long's he staying?'

Peter shrugged. 'Until he's seen the play, anyway. My mama is devastated.'

'Is she?' Libby was interested. 'Why?'

'I don't know. Bit of a puzzle, really. She doesn't remember anything about our real life drama, she was too young at the time, so it's a mystery. Started telling me on the phone that I shouldn't ever have written the play. That it would drag it all up again. I said it was a bit late for that. It's already been dragged.'

'Did she object before?' asked Libby. 'Or was it just because she came to see it last night?'

'Not much.' Peter shrugged. 'More than anyone else did, funnily enough. Aunt Het told her not to be a fool, hardly anyone round here remembered it, they weren't born then. And nearly everyone who would remember was dead. No, it's the murder which bothers Mumsie. After all,

25

it was her dad who disappeared leaving behind the mouldering corpse.'

'Wasn't he ever found?' piped up the woman who'd given Libby her seat. A chorus of groans answered her, and Peter turned patiently towards her.

'Paula, do you know the story of the play, dear?'

'Well, yes–' Paula giggled. 'Sort of. I mean, I'm only in bits of it, aren't I? There's no point in reading all of it.'

Taking in Libby's stunned expression, Peter hurried on.

'Well, here you are then, dear. Potted version coming up. Best that you know it all, in case you're called on to take the lead.'

Paula gaped.

'Hetty and her mum were hop pickers who came down to Kent from London every year, right?'

'Yes, I know all that bit. And Hetty's friend, Flo. Me,' beamed Paula.

'That's right. And Hetty fell in love with Gregory, who was the son of the squire. He got her into trouble, the tallyman from the hop gardens told her drunken old sot of a father when he came down for the weekend with her brother Lenny, and then lo and behold, nasty old tallyman is found dead, daddy disappears, Greg marries Hetty and all is tickety-boo.'

'But he doesn't marry Hetty in the play.'

A collective sigh went up.

'No, dear, because he did that a bit later, after the baby was born, so we've just ended it on a note of hope and explanatory notes in the programme.'

'Oh. I see,' said Paula, clearly not seeing. 'So why–'

'Enough,' cried Peter, clapping a hand to his head and spilling a good deal of his drink. 'I'll bring out a book.' He looked round the bar. 'Anybody seen Harry?'

'He went to see your cousin,' somebody said, 'before the rehearsal.'

'And he's not back?'

Peter's frown boded ill for the absent Harry, not to mention his cousin, thought Libby, her brain conjuring up an unlikely picture of Harry entwined with grey-haired, genial Ben, whose adventures with the fair sex were legendary, if Peter's stories were anything to go by.

'He said he'd be in later,' the barman leaned over and called through, 'when he came in earlier.'

'Came in earlier?' Peter's frown turned into a scowl.

'Oh, come on, Pete. Give the boy a bit of freedom. He slaves away in his caff every night.' Libby tipped up her glass and was surprised to find it empty. 'Come on. I'll buy you another sweet sherry.'

'Get one in for me, ducks,' said a voice in her ear as she stood at the bar waiting to be served. 'And one for me friend.'

'Harry.' Libby turned round as far as she could. 'You're for it. Going off to play fast and loose with other men. Hallo, Ben.'

Harry pulled a long-suffering face and began to move towards the small bar. 'Make mine a double, then,' he muttered.

27

'And how are you, Libby?' Ben Wilde moved into the space vacated by Harry. 'Haven't seen you for ages.'

'No.' Libby's smile was forced. Cousin Ben always made her feel slightly uncomfortable. To her relief, the barman materialised before them.

'Oh – er – half of lager, please, half of bitter–' she looked doubtfully across to where Harry and Peter were deep in conversation. 'Do you really think he wants a double something?'

'Give him a Pils. And a pint for me, Jim,' said Ben, laying a note on the bar.

'Oh – I was getting these–' Libby, flustered, was wrong-footed.

'I insist.'

'Oh, all right,' she said ungraciously, and immediately felt ashamed.

They carried their drinks through to the other bar and Libby handed Peter's over. He took it without a word and turned away to speak to someone else.

'Oh, dear, Harry.' Ben grinned at the eloquent back. 'Shall I speak to him for you?'

'Oh, let him stew.' Harry leaned elegantly against the bar. 'Even married couples have some time off.'

'Some more than others,' said Ben.

'Well, we all know about you, you old reprobate. South-east England wasn't safe after your divorce.' Harry chucked Ben playfully under the chin.

'Don't give the lady a bad impression, Harry boy. She disapproves of me already.'

'Old Libby?' Harry gave an incredulous squawk.

28

'She doesn't know the meaning of the word. Do you, ducks?'

Libby cast around for something to change the subject. 'Have you seen Uncle Lenny yet?'

'Of course. He's in the second-best spare bedroom, next to me,' said Ben.

'What's he like?' asked Harry.

'Gruesome.'

'Gruesome? Ugly?'

'Just gruesome. He cackles.'

'Oh, dear.' Libby watched her vision of a well-built upstanding man dwindle away.

'We're none of us as we used to be, Libby.' Ben was watching her face and it annoyed her that he had apparently read it so accurately.

'So have you talked to him?' asked Harry.

'You can't avoid it. He keeps waylaying you and saying he could tell a thing or two if given the chance.'

'Oh, heavens.' Harry put a hand to his mouth, delighted. 'I must meet him. Hey, Pete. Uncle Lenny's being an embarrassment.'

Peter rejoined the group, laying a possessive arm across Harry's muscular shoulders.

'So butch,' he murmured, a tacit sign that all was forgiven.

'We have *got* to go and pay a call on Uncle Lenny.' Harry leaned against Peter's arm. 'Tomorrow. It'll be a hoot.'

'I've got to go to town tomorrow, you know that.'

'When you get back then.'

'The caff'll be open.'

'No bookings. Donna'll cope.'

29

'Oh, all right then. Do you want to come and meet Uncle Lenny, Lib?'

'I've called a rehearsal,' said Libby regretfully. 'I can't back out now.'

'I know,' Harry turned to Peter, his eyes alight, 'let's bring him to rehearsal.' He turned to Ben. 'Can he walk? He hasn't got a Zimmer or anything?'

'No, he can walk. He's a bit slow, but he can walk fine. He's only seventy-seven, for goodness sake. Not in his dotage.'

Harry, all of twenty-seven, looked doubtful, but said nothing.

'That's settled, then. How's the play coming, Libby?' Ben shifted comfortably, changing the subject.

'OK,' said Libby, without looking at him.

'It's bloody terrible, Ben,' said Peter. 'I'm beginning to think it's my script.'

'Oh, surely not.' Ben raised one eyebrow and looked sideways at Libby.

'Of course it's not his play. It's the bleedin' actors. Not a brain between 'em.' Harry patted Peter's cheek. 'Libby's good, Pete's play's good, the theatre's bloody marvellous – we can lick this bunch into shape.' Harry was trying to be bracing, but Libby sensed a degree of unease beneath the bravura.

'Anything I can do?' Ben looked at Libby.

'I don't think so – is there, Pete?'

'Get him to organise that lot back-stage. Few ideas.'

'Stephen might not like that.' Ben shook his head. 'You called him in, didn't you, Libby?

Where is he, anyway?' He peered round the bar.

'Over there with Paula and Emma,' said Libby, 'I don't suppose he can hear us, if that's what you're worried about.'

'If you did it gently? You know, the "...How would it be if," sort of thing, and then let him think it was his idea,' suggested Peter.

'If you think–' he looked at Libby again. What does he want me to say? she thought. Or do? She settled for nodding.

'I'll come down tomorrow. Tell you what–' he turned to Harry. 'I'll bring Uncle Lenny down.'

'Oh, fabe!' Harry crowed and subsided into giggles as everyone in the bar looked round.

'What is?' asked a new voice.

'James!' Paula appeared magically between Harry and Peter. 'Where've you been?'

Peter looked amused. 'Yes, baby brother. How dare you go off on your own concerns?'

James, younger, darker and altogether bigger than his brother, grinned. 'Can't call my life my own, can I?'

'Drink, James?' asked Harry.

'I'll get them. Anyone else?' James looked round at Libby and Ben, who both declined.

'There's something going on there,' said Peter, as Paula pushed in beside James at the bar.

'No!' Harry struck an attitude. 'How did you guess?'

'I thought they'd split up?' Libby watched as Paula laughed up winningly into James's face.

'James told me he was going to end it.' Peter turned away, frowning.

'Dump her? Doesn't look as though he has,

31

does it?' said Harry.

'Perhaps she didn't want to be dumped,' said Libby. 'Perhaps she talked him into staying. I just wouldn't want to see him caught up with her, though. She's too old for a start.' Libby finished her drink.

Ben looked surprised. 'Too old?'

'She's nearly forty.'

'Come off it, Lib.' Peter laughed. 'She's thirty-five and looks twenty-five. James is only four years younger. Hardly toy boy territory, is it?'

'She's after him. Her clock's ticking,' said Libby stubbornly, 'I just hope he realises it. She's such a little cow.'

'And such a crap actress,' added Peter gloomily.

'Oh, I don't know,' said Harry, watching Paula coax a smile from James. 'She's acting the sweet little innocent well enough now.'

The bell rang for last orders and Ben offered Libby a lift home.

'I've only had one pint, you're quite safe.'

'No, it's not that.' Libby dithered, pulling her cape round her, adding to the protective bulk. 'I like walking. It's not far.'

'Sure?'

'Yes, thank you.' I sound like a prim schoolgirl, she thought, annoyed with herself.

'OK, I'll see you tomorrow, then.'

'With Uncle Lenny.' Libby offered a tentative smile.

'Indeed, with Uncle Lenny. Well after rehearsals have started, yes?'

'Might be better.' She nodded. Then hesitated. 'Ben–'

'Yes?' He turned back from the door of the car.

'Why is Millie bothered about Uncle Lenny?'

Ben shrugged. 'She's grown up classy, hasn't she? Uncle Lenny might let the side down.'

'You think that's it?' Libby was relieved.

'Positive. Sure you don't–' he gestured towards the car and she shook her head.

'Right. See you tomorrow.'

Stupid bloody woman, Libby berated herself as she marched down the High Street towards All-hallow's Lane. What's the matter with you? You're behaving like a teenager. She almost stopped dead as the shock lurched under her rib cage. No. It couldn't be. She couldn't *fancy* him, could she?

The cold began to seep through her cape and she started off again at a slower pace. Good God, she must have softening of the brain. Fancy a reprobate like Ben Wilde? Scourge of the under thirty population of Canterbury and all points east? An explosive chuckle escaped her. And that was the whole point. Ben Wilde hadn't been known to go out with anything over thirty since his divorce. He would hardly be interested in an over-weight, vertically challenged middle-aged female, who, as Peter so succinctly put it, was dressed by Oxfam and coiffured by Garden Centre. Sleek, lean and leggy was the Wilde choice. Fat, faded and fifty didn't come into it.

Stephen, however, was another matter. Obviously, her age and style appealed to him, or maybe he just couldn't get anything better. It wasn't that he was bad looking, he was perfectly normal, if a trifle bland. He had more hair than

33

Ben, he was taller than Ben and slimmer than Ben, but in the charisma department he'd been left behind. Ben exuded sex appeal, Stephen exuded dependability. The sensible woman's choice, Libby thought, but who wanted to be sensible?

Number 17 Allhallow's Lane was in the middle of a terrace of three, red-bricked with small white-painted windows, and a step down to trap the unwary immediately behind the front door.

Sidney, a large silver tabby with an unpredictable nature, glared at Libby from his vantage point halfway up the stairs as she tripped down the step.

'All right, I know I'm late,' she said and wondered why she was saying it. There was no need to apologise, no excuses to make, nobody to placate. Not now. Not at all – not ever, if she didn't want to. But old habits died hard. After twenty years of living with other people, being on one's own came as rather a shock and not always a welcome shock at that, if she were honest. She wove her way between assorted tables and chairs, displacing several newspapers, books and typescripts as she did so and switched on the kitchen light. Sidney had been at the bread bin again.

'Listen,' she said, as he jumped up on to the table, having tried the Rayburn once or twice and suffered the indignity of burnt paws. 'You are not a vegetarian neither am I. And cats don't like bread.'

She moved the big kettle on to the hot-plate and hunted round for the half-full tin of cat food.

'There,' she said, decanting it into a chipped

Victorian saucer. 'Get on with that and shut up.'

She made her coffee, took it into the living room and sat down by the empty fireplace. The script of *The Hop Pickers* lay on the hearth, interleaved with pages of untidy notes. She picked it up and riffled through it.

She had been so enthusiastic about this project, everything falling into place just as she was in the process of buying the cottage. Peter's lovely play and the newly converted Oast House theatre had fired her imagination and given her an entree into the village community. But now her enthusiasm was ebbing away, leaving behind it a flat, uncomfortable sensation rather like thinking there was an extra step and finding that there wasn't.

'It isn't fair, you know,' she said out loud to Sidney, who spread himself out on her feet and gave a desultory purr. 'After all I've been through, this bit should go right.'

Sidney opened one eye to a slit and slowly closed it again.

Sighing, she began to read the first page of the script where the young Hetty met the handsome young squire's son Gregory. Incredible really, that this positively Shakespearean plot should be true and should actually have happened to people still living here. It really did have everything – star-crossed lovers, bullying parents, even murder. And best of all, a happy ending. Or at least in the play it was a happy ending. Looking at the protagonists today, one could be forgiven for wondering.

Libby leaned back in her chair. Was old Hetty

happy with her Gregory, even after he came back from the prisoner of war camp such a wreck? Had she anticipated having to take on the management of a hop farm when her father-in-law died because her mother-in-law was incapable? And having to bring up her young sister into the bargain.

I bet Millie was a handful, thought Libby, and yet she had met Roger Parker and married him and had given birth to gorgeous Peter and equally gorgeous James. Libby's face broke into an involuntary smile at the thought of Millie trying to come to terms with her outrageous elder son – a journalist who had set up home with the beautiful Harry, several years his junior, and not only that, but bought him his own restaurant into the bargain.

How *had* Harry taken to village life? wondered Libby. Coming from London, where he had been assistant chef in the exclusive private club Peter patronised, right in the thick of things – the right people, the right clothes, the right things to do. Libby knew what that was like, being a Londoner herself, having moved to Kent years ago when the children were small, to bring them up in a better environment. But she had been perfectly happy. Until she realised that Derek was leaving. Or rather that she was throwing him out. Still, he had a soft landing on that pneumatic Marion.

She stirred Sidney with her foot. 'Bed,' she said.

Chapter Three – 1943

'Hetty! Your mum got her letter yet?'

'Yes. This morning. You got yours yet?'

'Glad to get away from your dad, I'll bet.' Someone else put their head out of a window and winked. Hetty blushed and lifted her chin.

'Dad'll come down weekends, same as usual,' she said sharply.

'Het. Hetty. Wait.'

Hetty turned quickly and there was Flo, running up the street, cotton dress flying, bright blonde hair bobbing around her shoulders.

'You got yours?' They both shouted together, and burst out laughing.

'Hut 18, we got again. Old Carpenter's good, ain't he? Always gives us the same huts.' Flo tucked her arm through Hetty's and they strolled down the middle of the dusty street, the sounds and smells of preparing dinner wafting around them, vying with the overwhelming smell of the docks. Woman's time, it was, before the menfolk came home. Children still played on the doorsteps, grannies sat out in the sun.

'It'll never change. Not while old Carpenter's there, anyway.' Hetty gave Flo a knowing look and a nudge in the ribs. 'Go on – you like him, really.'

'Yeah. Too old for me, though. I like a bit of life in a chap. Now that pole-puller last year – remember?'

Hetty smiled, reminiscing. 'He was lovely, wasn't he? Not one of us, though.'

'Well, no. Pole-pullers are always home-dwellers.'

'I didn't mean that. He was quality.'

'From the Manor, yes. Never found out who he was, though, did we?'

'Too scared to speak, wasn't we?' Hetty laughed. 'I was surprised at you. You speak to anybody.'

'Funny though. A gent like him walking around on stilts unhooking the bines. You don't expect it, do you?'

'Perhaps he's the only one who can do it. It's quite clever isn't it?'

'Nah! He's not the only one pulling the bines. Old Carpenter had two or three doin' it,' said Flo.

'Hetty!' The shout came from the other end of the street.

'Oh, gawd. The potatoes.' Hetty's hand flew to her mouth. 'I got to go.'

'Can you come out after? Just for a chat?' Flo asked, as they turned and trotted back the way they had come in the lengthening shadows.

'I'll see,' said Hetty nervously. 'We'll be getting the box ready–'

Flo gave her a quick glance. 'Yes. I know, Het. Well, if you can. I'll come round a bit later. I won't come in.'

'No.' Hetty squeezed her friend's hand. 'Might see you later.' She whisked inside and into the scullery.

'Pleased, Mum?' she said shyly, getting the potatoes, and was rewarded with an enormous

38

bear hug.

Lillian sighed into her daughter's hair. 'I'm always worried, Het. That he won't want us again. You know why.'

'Oh, Mum. We're one of the best families, aren't we? You can pick more than anyone I know. And I'm not bad.'

'But the weekends, Het.' Her mother let go of her. 'You know. Yer dad.'

'He doesn't always come, Mum. And Uncle Alf and Lenny look after him mostly. There was only the once last year. Don't worry. Just look forward to it. Go and get the hopping box in and we'll go through it after dinner, shall we? See what else we've got to get before next week.' Hetty gave her mother a kiss and turned back to the potatoes.

Ted Fisher was in a good mood when he came in. Hetty and Lillian had made sure his dinner was ready, that Millie hadn't made a mess and that the brown envelope with the hopping letter in it was out of sight.

Hetty caught Lenny's eye and winked when he went through to wash at the kitchen sink. When their father announced he was going to the pub after dinner, Lenny didn't get up to go with him, weathering the abuse Ted Fisher flung at him for being a mummy's boy and wanting to stay with the women. They were all too used to it to worry about the abuse or the language, knowing that if they kept quiet and looked cowed, they would be spared the worst of the violence.

Lillian brought in the hopping box when Ted had gone and Millie had been put upstairs to sleep in the bed she shared with Hetty. The excitement it generated, opening it to see what was in there, that had been put carefully away all year, from last October, was like Christmas – only better, in Hetty's opinion, because Dad was drunk all the time at Christmas and upset everyone, but down hopping, they got away from him, during the weeks, anyway. And he didn't always come down at weekends with the other men who weren't away defending their country. He had other fish to fry, he said, and Lenny would look away, embarrassed.

'Het – Flo's outside.' Lenny nudged his sister and went faintly pink.

Hetty got up off her knees and went to the door. 'You can come in, Flo,' she called.

'You coming on our lorry, Flo?' asked Lenny.

'Course they are, Lenny.' Lillian was counting the tins going in to the box. 'Always have, haven't they?'

'Just checking,' mumbled Lenny, looking down at his big callused hands. Flo patted one.

'I'll be there, Lenny, don't you worry. Got to look after your sister, haven't I?'

'I reckon I'll be looking after you if old Carpenter gets after you again,' laughed Hetty.

'Warburton, more like,' snorted Flo. 'He's the one to watch.'

'Oh, him.' Lillian sat back on her heels and tucked a strand of hair back into its pins. 'He's always been a problem. Tries to get off with the women saying he'll measure them light. Nasty piece of work.'

'And do any of them go?' Hetty's eyes were wide. This was the first time she'd heard of this, although she'd always known that Warburton wasn't liked.

'It's been known.' Lillian tightened her lips and concentrated on re-packing the box. Hetty would have loved to ask who had actually gone off with Warburton, the tallyman, and where they had gone off to, and when. Life down hopping was so close that everyone knew what you were doing, and with whom. There was even a gap at the top of the walls between the huts, so, if you climbed up, you could see over the top, and you could hear everything that was said either side of you.

'Wonder if that pole-puller'll be working this year, Het?' Flo reached across and gave Hetty a poke in the chest. 'Perhaps you'll get off with him if he hasn't been called up yet, eh?'

'Flo!' Lillian and Hetty spoke together, Hetty's ready blush sweeping up her neck and into her face. She cleared her throat and changed the subject. 'When are you going to give in your notice then, Flo?'

It was understood by most of the employers in the area that the greater part of their female workforce would disappear at the end of August for three or four weeks, in the same way that the school board accepted it. They didn't like it, but when half the school was away for the whole of the first part of term, they had no choice but to submit to it. In Kent, the home-dwellers' schools understood these things better and timed the school holidays to coincide with the hop season.

But here in the East End, and even as far away as Brixton, it was a holiday, all the better for being illicit. It gave whole families time together, a smell of something other than the docks and the opportunity to breathe fresh air. Mothers took their ailing children, believing the three or four weeks of Kentish air would set them up for the harsh realities of a London winter. It was no longer an escape from the war that had been going on too long now, as Kent was in the direct firing line anyway. You could just as easily be bombed in a hop garden as in a London street.

Hetty saw Flo to the door at about ten o'clock, well before they could expect Ted to reappear. The hopping box had been repacked and Lenny had taken it out to the lean-to at the back of the privy. Lillian became quieter as the evening wore on, and Hetty knew she was bracing herself for the coming encounter with Ted. He would have to be told, he would be expecting it and would expect to visit them while they were away, but it had never stopped him behaving as though it was a major betrayal by his entire family.

In fact, all Hetty heard later that night as she lay wakeful and waiting was her father falling up the stairs and then the low growl of his voice before the creaking of the bed signalled his insistence on his marital rights. Hetty turned over and buried her head under the pillow. She hated hearing those noises. She knew, more or less, what it signified, although she had never discovered any of the details of this strange act, she only knew that thinking of her parents indulging in it gave her a funny, uncomfortable feeling inside. She knew it was what Flo had said all men were after, knew too that married women seemed to regard it with resignation rather than enjoyment, yet all the girls at work seemed to think of nothing else. As her mind began to drift away in to sleep, she wondered idly what it would be like when she began to think about it with someone ... like the pole-puller from last year. It made her want to sneeze.

Chapter Four

Libby met Uncle Lenny sooner than she had expected. As she hurried towards the butcher's shop the following morning on a quest for something succulent for Sidney, a slim, upright, elderly woman was coming out. She was holding the door open for a dapper, elderly man with a grey toothbrush moustache and the sort of jacket Libby associated with bookies.

'Hallo, Hetty.' Libby stopped, a bundle of quivering curiosity.

'Morning, Libby.' Hetty Wilde had never lost her London accent, which she refused to call Cockney, for, she said, she had not been born within the sound of Bow Bells. She glanced at the man by her side, who raised his pork pie hat and who was all but twirling his moustaches, his chest thrust out as if for Libby's inspection.

'This here's Lenny. My brother. Lenny, this is Libby Sarjeant.'

Libby was so surprised and delighted that she forgot to add 'with a J.'

'Mr–' she began and realised she didn't know his name.

'Lenny, dear,' he said, taking her hand and pressing it. 'You're the lady what's doing our Peter's play.'

'That's right.' Libby smiled. 'And you've come down to see it?'

'I have, gel, I have. Here.' He winked and gave her a severe blow in the ribs. 'I could tell you a thing or two, I could. About them days.'

'Oh, shut up, Lenny, do.' Hetty sounded weary. 'They all know all about it.'

'Do they?' Lenny looked surprised, giving his hat a flick to maintain the correct angle.

'Oh, yes, Mr er – Lenny. Peter wrote it with Hetty's full co-operation.'

'And Greg's?'

It was Libby's turn to be surprised. 'Well–' she turned to Hetty.

'Of course, you old fool. Now come along. I'm taking you to see Millie.'

'Ah, dear little Millie.' Lenny sighed fondly – and falsely, Libby was sure.

'Looked after me, she did, you know, when I come home from the war.'

'Course she didn't. She was too young. It was Mum and me who looked after you,' said Hetty, still trying to move away from the butcher's shop.

'Oh, yers, and Mum. I had a terrible war, you know, dear, terrible. I must tell you about it some time.' Lenny patted Libby's hand, gazing earnestly into her eyes.

'You old fraud. You were only in on the last knockings and even then you were on every fiddle going and a few more besides. Sorry, Libby. Got to go. Millie is looking forward to

44

seeing Lenny.' Hetty finally succeeded in dragging Lenny after her up the road. Libby watched them go. I don't think Millie is looking forward to seeing Lenny, she thought. Not after what I heard last night.

It was very cold in the conservatory that Libby used as a studio. She left the kitchen door open and pulled the calor gas heater as near to her easel as she could without danger to life and Sidney's limbs. She had lunched too well on fresh bread from the baker's and the remains of a Stilton, and that combined with the cold made her feel rather as she had felt at school in long and boring afternoon maths lessons.

The rusty tinkle of the doorbell woke her up. Who the hell is that?, she thought, passing under mental review all the likely and unlikely callers for four o'clock on a Tuesday afternoon.

'Millie. I mean – Mrs Parker.' Libby schooled her features into surprised welcome. 'Do come in.'

Millie Parker looked round as if wondering whether to make a break for it.

'Er – I hope I'm not intruding?' Her voice and appearance were a million miles from her sister's, thought Libby. What effort had it cost her?

'No, of course not,' she said aloud. 'I was just about to make some tea. Would you like some?'

'Well, if you're sure...' Millie stepped gingerly over the threshold, her high heels scraping on the quarry-tiled floor.

'Sit down. May I take your coat?'

'Thank you.' Millie handed over an expensive (real) camelhair coat and patted the sculptured

45

hair as if to make sure it was still there. Libby left her in the one decent armchair and went into the kitchen to make tea. A hasty search produced a tray and her mother's bone china teacups and, satisfied, she carried the tray through to her guest.

'Well, this is a pleasant surprise,' she lied, kneeling to put a match to the fire, which obligingly flared up immediately.

Millie looked as though her mouth wouldn't smile, so she wasn't going to try and force it.

'Milk?' Millie nodded. 'Sugar?' Millie shook her head. Libby was getting desperate. She handed over a cup and sat back on the cane sofa, which creaked alarmingly under her weight and surprised Sidney into sudden flight.

'Actually, Mrs Sarjeant–'

'Libby, please,' said Libby.

'Libby.' Millie appeared to test it out and find it wanting. 'I wanted to talk to you about–'

Here it comes, thought Libby.

'About the play.'

Ah.

'I know you've got so far with it, all the practising–' Libby winced '–and everything, but I don't know that I really think – well, that it's a good idea.'

'You don't?' Libby was not surprised. 'Why not?'

'Well.' Millie's neck was turning a rather unlovely red, the wrinkles showing up white in relief. 'Dragging things up, you know...'

'But we're not, are we? Everybody knows the story of Hetty and Greg, and if you're worried about the connection with your father – is that it?

46

Are you worried because people accused him of killing Joe Warburton?'

Millie looked startled. 'Well, yes, I suppose so.'

'Nobody ever proved it, you know,' said Libby gently.

'No.'

'And nobody is going to do anything about it now. Are they?'

'No.'

'And your sister was quite happy about it all going ahead,' persisted Libby, battling against the odds.

'Yes.'

Libby surveyed her guest in silence for a moment.

'So what is it you're worried about?' Silence. 'It's your brother Lenny, isn't it?'

Millie looked up as if it cost her an effort.

'He's a trouble-maker, Mrs, er, Libby.'

'He seemed rather a nice old gentleman to me.'

Millie's colour left her face much quicker than it had come. 'You've met him?'

'This morning. With your sister. They were on their way to visit you, I gather.'

'Yes.' Millie cleared her throat. 'Did he say anything?'

'Hallo – nice to meet you. That sort of thing.' Libby was amused.

'No one asked me if I minded, you know.' Millie stared hard at the fireplace as if suspecting it of hiding something.

'Well, you're not in the play. I mean, your character isn't. I suppose Peter thought you wouldn't mind one way or another.'

47

Millie looked affronted. 'He is my son. He could at least have talked to me about it.'

Libby looked doubtful. 'I suppose he could,' she murmured. 'But he did ask you to come and see the rehearsal last night, didn't he?'

Millie continued as if she hadn't heard. 'And they are my family. It's about my family. I have a position to keep up, you know.'

'Yes, but so do Hetty and Greg, don't they?'

'Them,' Millie said scornfully. 'Greg wouldn't have married Hetty if he'd been worried about his position in the village. And Hetty's never tried to blend in. She doesn't even try.'

Libby reflected that Hetty's non-trying was probably of more value to the village than Millie's trying, but once again kept silent.

'So you won't stop it then?' Millie transferred her gaze from her cup to Libby with a suddenness that made Libby jump.

'Well, I can't, can I?' she replied reasonably. 'It's Peter's baby. And Ben has designed the theatre. The only thing I could do would be to withdraw, and I'm sure they would be able to carry on without me at this late stage. I've done all the blocking and characterisation.'

'What? Blocking?' Millie was momentarily diverted.

'Telling people where to move and stand.'

'Suppose you told Peter it wasn't good enough to go on?'

Libby regarded her, fascinated. 'I don't believe this,' she said finally. 'Why is it so important to you that this play doesn't go on?'

The colour returned to Millie's face. 'I – I – I

just don't think it's in very good taste,' she said.

'There's nothing offensive in it, you know,' said Libby. 'No bad language or explicit sex. You saw it last night.'

The colour was deepening alarmingly in Millie's face. 'I didn't mean that,' she spluttered. A drop of spittle landed on her hand and she looked at it in horror.

'And as I said before, we have got the permission of the members of the family who were actively involved at the time. I don't think you can stop it, whatever you feel about it. I'm sorry.' Libby was beginning to feel embarrassed.

'Oh.' Millie put her cup down in a sudden clumsy rush and stood up. 'I mustn't hold you up. Thank you so much for the tea. You must ask Peter to bring you to dinner some time–'

As if Peter and I were a couple, thought Libby.

'That would be lovely, thank you,' she said out loud, 'and I really am sorry I can't help you.'

Well, what was that all about, she wondered, watching her visitor's precipitate flight down Allhallow's Lane. Why is she so afraid of Lenny? Or rather, what is she afraid Lenny might *say?* Sidney joined her at the window making chirruping noises and trying to look appealing.

'There's something more than pride behind this,' she told him severely, and he flattened his ears and cowered. 'And you can stop behaving like a whipped cur just because I won't feed you.'

The thought of Millie's uncomfortable visit kept returning to her all afternoon, until, in an effort to forget it, she was annoyed to find herself taking more care than usual over her appearance.

After a shower, she cleaned her face of the remains of the day's haphazard make-up and tried again, with not much notable success, she decided, scowling at the bags sandwiched between her eyes and what had been called her apple cheeks. She even put a jacket on over a fairly quiet roll-necked sweater instead of the collection of variegated jumpers that she normally wore, and replaced the tired Indian skirt with a plain, straight one. She tried to push her abundant and wayward hair into a neat French roll. It didn't stay there, and by that time it was too late to do anything else, so she left it loose, flying about her head in a greying red bush. Bother.

She walked up The Manor drive and paused to take in the impressive feature that was almost – but not quite – The Oast House Theatre. Its twin cones pointed proudly upwards, newly whitened, and the double doors stood open to reveal the new plate glass ones in the inner lobby. She pushed these open and was met by a welcoming wave of warmth.

'Hey!' she cried, surprised. 'The heating's on.'

Peter appeared at the top of the spiral staircase leading to the lighting box. 'Ben came in today and harried them.'

'I thought you were going to be late?' Libby squinted up at him.

'Finished early,' he said and disappeared.

To Libby's surprise, the set for the hop garden had been finished and even looked vaguely secure. Several of the actors were milling around on stage and looking a good deal more cheerful.

50

'Good one tonight, then, Libby.' The man playing the villainous tallyman hailed her.

'Too right,' said Libby. 'Anyone seen our wardrobe mistress?'

And so the rehearsal got under way.

Half-way through, Libby had to concede that there had been a hundred percent improvement since last night. Even Emma, the girl playing Hetty's character Becky, was making an effort and inspiring her stage lover to greater heights than normal.

'Right, everyone, take a break,' she called as they reached the end of a scene. 'Pickers, I'd like to see your costumes if you could put on what you've got so far, and does anyone know if we've got the bins yet?'

'Coming Thursday,' came a muffled voice from the roof space.

'Well done, Libby. You're doing wonders.'

Libby turned suddenly and came face to face with Ben. Shit, she thought as a surge of adrenalin hit her system. I'm too old for this.

'Thanks,' she said.

'Yeah, great it is, gel. Looks good, too. Just like the West End.'

Uncle Lenny had appeared silently by his nephew's side.

'Thank you, Lenny.' Libby smiled at the old man. 'Would you like to meet the cast?'

'No, yer all right, gel. All go fer a bevvy later, shall we? Ben'll drive us down.'

'Oh, it's not far. I can walk.'

'I can't though. Or not quick enough, anyhow. Ben'll give you a lift.' Lenny turned to go back to

51

his plastic chair and Libby turned her attention to the stage.

'Can we change the set to the hoppers' huts?' she called.

'Don't know whether the roof's secure yet,' came the muffled voice again.

'It should be.' Ben was still by her side. 'I was up there myself, today.'

Libby shot him a look, surprised, but said nothing and, smiling, he returned to his seat.

The hoppers' huts were set and the tin roof flown in. Libby smiled with pleasure as the scene took shape, the big hopping pot over the below-ground (and therefore not seen) fire, the pickers outside their huts while the one cut-away section revealed Emma lying on her bed of straw and faggots – or what would be straw and faggots, when it was ready. At the moment, she was lying on an old curtain and complaining about the dirt. Paula loitered unconvincingly in the background, supposedly in the next door hut.

The scene wound on, gathering pace and momentum until the climax when Becky's father arrived roaring drunk to burst in on his daughter and reveal that he knew her guilty secret. The scene closed with a blackout on Becky's screams as her father lunged towards her.

A burst of spontaneous applause from those who had been watching sent a warm glow through Libby's body. It was working.

'OK. Straight on. We've got half an hour. Let's do the fight scene.'

The lights went up as willing hands went to dismantle the huts and the wire began to raise the roof out of sight.

It swayed gently as it reached the top of its ascent. Then it fell, crushing the huts and whatever was underneath them.

Chapter Five

It seemed to Libby that the crash and the screams were simultaneous and then there was silence. She rose jerkily to her feet, her heart thudding while the dust settled on the stage and the noise broke out again.

'What happened?' she asked, running to the front of the stage. Her voice came out in a croak and she tried to scramble up, hampered by her skirt. 'Who's hurt?'

Ben was there, hauling her up beside him.

'Stay there, I'll find out,' he said plunging into the melee.

Emma was crying, her face streaked with dirt, Paula was having hysterics and being patted in-effectually by one of the older pickers. Underneath the scrambled mess that was no longer the hoppers' huts, unpleasant noises were making themselves heard. Libby stood apart, watching, not even able to think.

Ben detached himself from the crowd and came over to her.

'It's all right. No one hurt badly. Someone got a nasty ding on the shoulder and there's a few cuts and bruises. That's all. Bloody lucky.'

Libby discovered that she was shaking.

'But what happened?'

'The wire broke, apparently.' Ben was frowning. 'I don't know how. I fixed it myself this afternoon.'

'Just you?' Libby's voice was still croaky.

'No, a couple of the others who weren't at work. It should have been foolproof.'

'We could have been killed.' Emma's voice rose above all the others and they turned to look at her. 'I don't want to do this any more.'

'For God's sake, shut her up,' muttered Libby, turning her back. 'I've had enough of this.'

She sat down heavily on the edge of the stage and waited until some kind of order had been restored. Stephen came up and said they would look at the damage and the reasons behind it the following day, but he thought they had all better go home now. She agreed.

'I'm sorry, everybody.' She stood up with an effort. 'None of us knows what happened and I'm only thankful that nobody was seriously hurt.' She took a deep breath and crossed her fingers. 'It's the sort of accident that can happen at any time in any theatre, and with so much new equipment, it's not surprising that we should have a few–' she stopped and searched for the right word, 'well, minor disasters. But that's all it is. Tomorrow we'll rehearse down here in the auditorium and let the back-stage crew sort everything out without interference. OK?'

There were mutterings of both disquiet and affirmation, but gradually everything quietened down as people began to put costumes away and collect outdoor clothes.

'Drinkie-poos, petal?' Harry had appeared out of the shadows.

'I should think so.' Libby was relieved that her voice had steadied. 'A whole bucketful. Do you think we should call David?'

'Dear old Doctor David? I don't think so. No one really got hurt, did they?'

'And we want to keep it as low key as possible, don't we?' Ben came up on her other side. 'Lenny wants you to have a lift with us.'

'Where is Lenny?' Libby peered into the darkness, suddenly worried.

'In the car. He's fine. Bit shaken, but then, so were we all. Come on.'

'Go on, ducks. No arguments. You look as though you'll fall over any minute. We'll follow.' Harry patted her arm and left her.

'I ought to wait and talk to Stephen.' Libby looked back at the stage, where Stephen and his two acolytes stood surveying the mess.

'He'll come to the pub if he wants to speak to you,' said Ben. 'He knows where you'll be.'

'I'm not sure,' said Libby doubtfully, 'but I suppose there's nothing I can do.' She sighed. 'All right. I'm coming.'

Ben walked beside her in silence, holding open the plate glass door without a word, then he took her arm and steered her to the side of the building where the interior light showed Lenny sitting upright in the passenger seat of the car.

'All right, gel?' he said, half-turning with difficulty as she slid inelegantly into the back seat, thankful not to have to sit next to Ben.

'Yes, thanks, Lenny. You?'

'Bit of a shaker, that, weren't it? Nasty old business.' He turned back to the front and was silent while Ben drove them the short distance to the pub.

In ones and twos, the cast dribbled in, subdued and pale. Emma didn't appear, and Libby was relieved.

'Your mother came to see me today,' she said as Peter sat down opposite her. Ben had bought her a double brandy and she watched as the liquid clung and slipped down the side of the glass.

'My mother?' Peter took a healthy swallow of his beer. 'Good God.'

'What did she want?' Ben's voice was quiet at her left shoulder.

'To stop the play.'

They looked at her in silence, waiting for her to go on.

'That's all, really.' She shrugged. 'She wouldn't tell me why. Except that she thought it was in bad taste.'

'Always was daft, that one.' Lenny emerged from a pint of stout, froth accentuating his trim moustache. He licked it off, neatly. 'Terrible worrier.'

'But what about?' Libby burst out. 'I just don't understand what the devil's going on. Why should she suddenly be against the play?'

'Devil's right, old love,' said Peter, without a trace of his normal affectation. 'After tonight. There's a nasty old atmosphere creeping up on us.'

'Oh, come on, Pete.' Harry hitched up his chair.

56

'One accident. You heard what Libby said. It could happen anywhere – to anyone.'

'But I didn't mean it,' muttered Libby and was surprised when Ben touched her arm. She glanced at his well-kept hands – architect's hands, she thought. Clean. She pushed hers, paint-stained and chubby, into the folds of her skirt.

'Did you look at the wire, Ben?' asked Peter.

'Yes.' Ben lifted his glass.

'And?' Harry raised an eyebrow. 'I only came in at the end of the last scene. Donna had a panic. I didn't see what went before.'

'You saw the roof come down?' Libby turned to him.

'Yes, just after I came in.'

'Well, that was it. The wire gave.'

'How could it?' Peter was scornful. 'I looked at it myself when they were changing the set. It came down perfectly.'

'It didn't go back, though.'

Peter looked back at Ben. 'What's up? What aren't you saying?'

Ben shook his head and put down his glass. 'I'll look at it tomorrow. I've got the day off. I'll go in the morning.'

'Not on your own,' Libby heard herself saying.

'Why? Worried about me?' He smiled.

Oh, help, thought Libby. She picked up her brandy and the smell made her eyes water.

'Here, I'll get you a lager.' Peter stood up and went to the bar.

'I'll come with you,' she said to Ben. 'When do you want to go?'

Ben looked puzzled. 'Well I'm flattered at this

57

sudden desire for my company, but it's really not necessary, you know. I'm a big boy, now.'

'Ooh, get 'er.' Harry made a production of flinging one leg across the other and the atmosphere returned to normal with a thump.

Stephen arrived on his own just in time to get included in Ben's next round.

'Any thoughts?' asked Peter, as Stephen squeezed on to the bench between Libby and Harry.

Stephen shook his head. 'We'll have a look at it tomorrow. I'll go round straight from work.'

Ben looked at Libby as he put glasses on the table. 'Well–' he said.

'Don't worry about it, Stephen.' Libby swallowed hard. 'Ben and I are going to have a look at it in the morning.'

Stephen's face darkened. 'I thought I was supposed to be SM? Or don't you trust me?'

'Oh, God, Stephen! Of course I trust you. I was just trying to save you trouble. You hardly live round the corner, after all.'

'I'm only at the top of the drive, old son,' said Ben squeezing in the other side of Libby, so that she felt beleaguered on all sides. 'I'll have a look and report to you. Shall I take your mobile number? Then you can tell me if we need anything before you get there in the evening.'

Mollified, Stephen dictated his mobile number and Ben programmed it into his own phone.

Libby drank her lager, and even managed to finish the brandy before getting to her feet, feeling about a hundred-and-nine.

'I'm off now.' She reached for her coat, but Ben

was there before her, holding it open.

'I'll give you a lift.'

'No – it's all right–'

'Oh, don't start that again. Come on, Lenny and I are going now, aren't we, Lenny?'

'Are we?'

'I'm driving. Can't have any more.'

'Oh, all right. Got a drop back home, haven't yer?'

'Yes, you old soak, crates of it. Come on.'

'I can walk Libby home,' said Stephen. 'My car's parked there, anyway.'

'It is?' Ben sounded interested, cocking an eyebrow at Libby.

'I think I'd rather have a lift after all, thanks, Stephen,' she said, trying not to let her irritation and frustration flood out. 'Hardly worth you walking all that way there and then driving back here, is it? Anyway, you've only just got your drink.'

Stephen looked as though he realised he'd shot himself in the foot but had to give in with resignation, if not graciousness.

'I'll hear from you tomorrow, then,' he said, and reluctantly turned to speak to Peter. Harry gave Libby an outrageous wink and blew a kiss at Ben. Lenny cackled.

Libby realised that she was grateful for not having to walk home. The familiar village street looked unaccountably eerie and her very bones ached with weariness. I'm getting old, she told herself.

Ben got out to open her door.

'I won't come in,' he said with a half smile,

mocking her. 'Stephen would kill me.' She smiled uncertainly.

'I'll ring you in the morning and we can make arrangements then.' He had turned back to the car before she realised what he was talking about.

'Oh, right. Have you got my number?'

He looked up at her before he shut the door.

'Of course.'

Sidney was on his usual stair. Libby sat down on the one below and looked him in the eye.

'All right, clever clogs. So now what? I suddenly realise I fancy this bloke and then whoosh – next thing, I'm suspecting him of sabotage because of his bloody family. What do I do now?'

Hours later, unable to sleep, she wrapped herself in her patchwork quilt and went downstairs to drink copious cups of tea and work her way through the best part of a packet of cigarettes. She awoke next morning with a mouth and a head that told her she had smoked too much the night before, and the irritating trill of the telephone.

By the time she had fallen down the last two stairs and got tangled up with an irate Sidney, the answerphone had cut in and she couldn't be bothered to switch it off. She listened to the disembodied voice when her message had finished.

'Libby, it's Ben. I'm going to the theatre about ten thirty. I'll come and pick you up if you like, but I don't suppose you'll want me to, so I'll meet you there unless I hear from you. I'll open up, so don't worry about keys. See you later.'

The answerphone rewound itself and sat winking at her knowingly. She glared at it and went in to the kitchen to make tea. Before she went upstairs to dress she pressed "play" and listened to Ben all over again, and then cursed herself for being a fool.

How do I know he's going at ten-thirty? she asked herself as she hurried along the High Street towards the Manor gates. He could have been there for hours, rigging all sorts of nasty little surprises. And why? asked the other self, the one who had argued all night about Ben's putative reasons for wishing to sabotage the play. I know, she answered herself, it's his theatre, partly his idea, why the hell would he? But then, why the hell is Millie so against it? And what's Uncle Lenny got to do with it all, anyhow?

She turned into the Manor drive and tried to relax tense shoulders.

The theatre was warm, all the lights were on and the coffee machine in the foyer gurgled quietly to itself as she pushed open the door to the auditorium.

'Anybody here?'

'Up here.' Ben's voice issued from above the stage, to be followed seconds later by Ben himself. Libby went forward slowly to meet him as he came down the ladder.

'Well?' She was watching his face carefully.

He held out his hand.

'What's that?'

'Steel wire.'

'And?'

'It's been cut.'

61

Chapter Six

'*Cut?* How can you cut steel wire?' Libby sat down suddenly on the stage.

'Easy. All the right equipment's here.' He sat down beside her, looking tired.

'But who would do it? It's so dangerous.'

He nodded. 'I can only think it was a practical joke and someone didn't realise just how dangerous it would be.'

'You'd have to be bloody daft not to.'

'Well, the alternative's not much fun, is it?'

'You mean–' Libby experienced that strange phenomenon sometimes described as one's heart turning over. 'It was supposed to hurt someone?' It came out as a whisper. Ben nodded again.

'But who? Didn't they care? Just *anybody?*'

'I don't know. That's why I don't think it was meant to hurt. Nobody could have been sure who, if anybody, would have been underneath it when the wire went. So it must have been meant as a – well, as a joke.'

'Or a warning?'

Ben looked at her. 'You think that, too?'

She looked away. 'I wondered.'

'My family?'

Libby's heart began to beat faster and she felt the blood surging into her face. 'Sorry,' she muttered.

He sighed. 'Look, it's all right. Millie is behaving a bit oddly, I know, and I couldn't help wondering myself, but honestly, could you see her clambering up there into the flies with a set of steel cutters?'

Libby let out an involuntary snort.

'Well, there you are.' He stood up. 'Come and have a look round. I've taken all the security precautions I can think of.'

'You were here earlier, then,' said Libby, following him into the scenery dock.

'Yes, why?'

'No reason.' Libby tried to sound nonchalant. Ben looked at her oddly, but made no comment.

Some of Ben's precautions seemed a bit over the top even to Libby, but she had to admit he'd been more than thorough. Her suspicions gradually receded into the background of her mind.

'You seem to know a lot about it all,' she said when they finally fetched up back on the stage.

'I used to have holiday jobs back-stage in one of the London theatres when I was a student.' He tested the stability of one of the flats with a gentle hand. 'I knew one of the flymen. I acted a bit, too.'

'At college?'

'And when I was married. Didn't Peter tell you?'

'No. Where?'

'In London. A couple of the big amateur companies, and then in Surrey when we moved there.'

'Golly.' Libby always reverted to schoolgirl expressions in moments of confusion. 'Does your wife still live in Surrey?'

'Ex-wife, yes.' He looked at her, amused. 'Where's yours? Husband, I mean.'

'London. With his floosie.'

He let out a shout of laughter. 'What a lovely old-fashioned expression.'

Libby grinned. 'That's how I think of her.' He had bags under his eyes, too, nice friendly crinkly ones, nicer than hers. Hers were just ageing, his were attractive.

He leaned back against the proscenium arch, arms folded, head on one side.

'You don't trust me, do you, Libby?'

'What?' She blinked, feeling the blush start again.

'You class me with your husband – running off with a series of floosies.'

'He only went off with one – I think.'

'Whereas I didn't go off with any. Surprised?'

'Er, no, of course not.' Libby fumbled with her basket and dropped it.

'Yes, you are. But you're wrong. It was my wife who ran off. Come on.' He pushed himself away from the wall. 'The pub'll be open now. I'll buy you an early lunch.'

Libby, a prey to conflicting emotions, as she told herself, followed him out of the theatre.

They didn't sit in their usual place but at a table in the other half of the bar near the fireplace. Ben fetched drinks and the bar menu and hung her aged cape up carefully on the coat rack.

'So what now?' he said sitting down and stretching his legs to the fire.

'What now what?' Libby was cautious.

'The play. It goes ahead?'

'Of course. Why not? Nobody's going to pull the same stunt twice, are they?'

64

'Hopefully not. But don't you think we ought to try and find out why it happened at all?'

'I can't think of anything – any reason. It's stupid. And anyway, I can't go around like some half-baked Miss Marple asking leading questions, can I?'

'You could tell the police.'

'The police? Whatever for?'

'That could have been a fatal accident, you know. Not just a shock.'

Libby was silent, reflecting on the nauseating enormity of it.

'I can't tell the police,' she said finally. 'The others would never forgive me.'

'Suppose it happens again?'

'It won't.' She glared at him. 'Stephen will be all over that back-stage area like creeping ivy. He's terribly aware of all the latest Health and Safety regulations, you know. Won't let me have more than so many people on the stage at a time, and areas of responsibility and all that. He was the one who sorted out our professional insurance, didn't you know?'

'Of course I knew. I was going to do it, but Pete told me I'd been superseded.'

'Well, there you are then.'

'Supposing Stephen had something to do with the accident?'

'What?' Libby's voice rose, and several heads turned their way. 'Why on earth would he do that? You've seen what he's like with me. Why would he ruin what he hopes might become some sort of meaningful relationship?'

'OK, OK, I'm only playing devil's advocate.'

He held up his hands, laughing. 'And by the way, I ought to call him. He'll be in a ferment of jealousy by now, wondering what we're getting up to behind the stage.'

A short silence fell while Libby gazed into the sullen, intermittent flicker in the fireplace.

'Why are you always laughing at me?' she said finally.

'Am I?' He seemed surprised again. 'You do come out with the most astonishing things.'

'Well, you do. You seem to find me amusing.'

'And you don't like that? You would rather I found you dull and boring? Middle-aged and provincial?'

'Well, that's what I am.'

He shrugged. 'So am I.'

'No, you're not.'

'Not which bit?'

'All of it. There, you're doing it again.'

Ben sat forward and took her hand. 'I'm not laughing at you, I'm—'

'I know, laughing with me.' Libby withdrew her hand. 'And I'm not used to being flirted with, either.'

'Was I doing that as well? Oh, I *am* sorry.' He sat back in his chair, watching her.

'Sorry. I shouldn't have said that. No, perhaps you're not. I'm just not used to—'

'Men?'

'Well, of course I'm used to men. I've always had men friends.'

'Like Peter and Harry?'

'And ordinary married men. And their wives.'

'And Stephen, of course.'

66

'Why do you keep bringing him up? And stop making me defensive.'

'I wasn't. For goodness' sake, Libby, stop accusing me of things. I invited you out for a quiet pub lunch and it's turning into a full-scale battle.'

'Sorry.' Libby tried to breathe deeply and began searching for a cigarette. 'I'm a bit wound up.'

'Here.' He took her lighter and lit the cigarette. 'You smoke too much, you know.'

'That's not going to help the cease-fire, is it?' She grimaced. 'Sorry – no pun intended.'

'No, sorry. Forget I said it.'

'But you're right. I do. And I drink too much.'

'Do you?'

'Do you know any other women who go to the pub practically every day?'

'Lots. You don't sneak in on your own for a quiet tipple in the snug, do you?'

She grinned. 'With me fur 'at and me milk stout?'

'I can just see you in a fur hat.'

'I'll go and buy one.'

'That's better.' He reached across and patted her hand. 'Now. Let's have a look at the menu.'

After their rather tired-looking Ploughman's Platters had been delivered by an equally tired-looking young woman in an apron announcing that big was beautiful, Libby returned to the subject uppermost in her mind.

'Your family. I said to Peter the other day – it's confusing, isn't it?'

'I thought we were rather your original run-of-the-mill family. What's confusing about us?'

'Oh, dates, times, who was here when the

tallyman was murdered and who wasn't ... you know.'

Ben laughed. 'I can't see that as confusing. You're directing the play, you know who was here.'

'Yes, but your Aunt Millie was here, and she's not in the play.'

'You're really worried about Millie, aren't you?' Ben frowned at her.

Libby shifted in her chair. 'Sorry. I must sound paranoid. But she's the only one who seems to be against the play. Nobody else is – are they?'

'I think Susan was a bit uncomfortable about it at first, being a doctor's wife and all.'

'Oh, your sister. How is she? I haven't seen her for ages.'

'Fine. Wants David to retire, of course. He works far too hard.'

'But she's OK about it, now, is she?'

Ben pushed his plate away. 'Far as I know.'

'What about James?'

'James?' Ben laughed. 'Why on earth would he be against the play?'

'No idea. He hasn't been around much, that's all.'

'That's because of Paula. You saw what she was like on Monday – all over him. He's doing his best to avoid her, that's why he isn't around.' Ben sighed. 'I think he would have moved to the village rather than Canterbury if it hadn't been for Paula.'

'That would have been nice for Aunt Millie. Both her little boys round the corner.'

'Can't think of anything worse, can you?' Ben

68

grinned. 'No, that's probably half the reason for Canterbury. Millie can't quite come to terms with Pete's lifestyle, so she'd be forever trying to interfere in James's.'

'I expect she wants grandchildren.' Libby made a face. 'Most women of her age seem to.'

'Perhaps she ought to encourage Paula, then. That woman's desperate to have a baby.'

Libby's eyebrows shot up. 'How do you know?'

'You said yourself – her clock's ticking. She's nearly thirty-eight.'

'I thought Pete said she was thirty-five?'

'He doesn't know her as well as I do.'

'Oh?'

Ben looked away. 'Yes, well, not an episode I'm proud of.'

'You didn't?' Libby gasped.

He looked uncomfortable. 'Only once.'

'You can't know her that well, then.' Libby sat back in her chair.

'Once is enough. I made the mistake of walking her home after a fairly alcoholic do of some sort. She'd been coming on to me all evening, and somehow I got talked into it. Believe me, I heard all about her hopes and dreams.'

'And I hope you fulfilled at least one of them,' said Libby, squashing an inappropriate rush of jealousy.

Ben looked back at her and grinned again. 'I have no idea. I don't remember anything about it, except waking up on the sofa at four in the morning considerably dishevelled and dying for water. At which point I left.'

'What happened after that?'

'She became very coy whenever I saw her. Sharing a secret sort of coy – you know? This was in my gallivanting days, of course. After my wife went off with her male floosie.'

'There. You're laughing at me again.' Libby picked up her cigarette packet, sighed, and put it down again.

'No I'm not. Don't be so sensitive. Anyway, it was my peccadilloes we were discussing, not yours, so I'm the one who should be on the defensive.'

Libby frowned down at her plate. 'So you wouldn't want to see James tied up with her, then?'

'No, I certainly wouldn't. That woman hides a conniving, manipulative nature under all that eyelash batting. That "silly little me" act doesn't fool anybody.'

'Well, it obviously does at first. You fell for it, and so did James.'

Ben looked affronted. 'I didn't fall for it. I knew exactly what she was like.'

'You still went to bed with her.'

'You don't know that. Come to that, even *I* don't know that. We are assuming, given certain evidence.'

Libby was doubtful. 'If you say so.' She looked at her watch. 'I'd better get back. I've got a delivery to make on Friday and I haven't quite finished.'

'Framing?'

Libby blushed. 'No, the paintings.'

Ben shook his head at her. 'Too much skiving off down the pub,' he said. 'You're a terrible woman.'

Chapter Seven

Rehearsals were quiet affairs on Wednesday and Thursday. Nobody saw Uncle Lenny, or any of the family except for Peter, who was uncharacteristically subdued and disinclined to chatter. Paula didn't appear, and Libby was surprised to receive a call on her mobile half-way through Thursday from James, apologising on her behalf and muttering something about stress and nervousness.

'Does she think the perishing roof's going to fall down again?' Libby asked him. 'Because you can assure her it won't. We're not using it at the moment.'

It wasn't that, apparently, said James and bade her a hurried goodbye.

Dealing philosophically, and with some relief, with the absence of Paula, Libby stuck to her original rehearsal schedule and allowed them Friday off, but warned them that extra rehearsals might be slotted in during the following week.

'Libby?' The telephone shattered Libby's peace over toast and tea and Radio Four on Friday morning.

'Hello?' She recognised the voice but wasn't going to let on.

'It's Ben. I wondered, as there's no rehearsal to-night, whether you would like to go out to dinner?'

Libby struggled with herself.

'I'm sorry, Ben, but I've got that delivery today and I'm staying with friends overnight.'

'Oh, pity. Back tomorrow?'

'Yes. I'm going through the lighting plot tomorrow afternoon.'

'How about dinner tomorrow, then? Or we could go and see that thing at the Gulbenkian, if you fancy it.'

I ought to say no, thought Libby.

'Thank you, I'd like that. Dinner, though. I want to get away from theatre.'

'I take it you don't fancy the Pink Geranium, then?'

'I'm just not a vegetarian.' Libby was apologetic.

'Neither am I. There's a couple of decent Thai places in Canterbury, aren't there? How about one of those?'

'Lovely.'

'Pick you up at seven, then – or is that too early?'

'No, seven will be fine.' Not so long to wait and get nervous.

'See you, then.'

It was mid-afternoon before Libby was organised enough to leave. Sidney glared at her out of the front window as she loaded her bag into her ancient Renault.

'You'll be all right,' she told him. 'Mrs Next Door will be in to feed you. Stop making me feel guilty.'

'Hey, Libby.'

She turned round quickly to see Harry loping down the lane.

72

'Where are you off to?'

'Delivering paintings.'

'You workaholic, you. Listen, I was coming with a bit of news – have you got time?'

'Only just. I'm late as it is, and I'm going to catch all the traffic on the ring road now. Why didn't you ring me?'

'I did. There's a message on your answerphone, if you bothered to listen to it, and your mobile, as usual, is switched off. Anyway, it won't take long. You know what you were saying about publicity?'

'You haven't committed a murder specially for us, have you?'

'Get you, ducky. No, Pete just called to say he's organised some chap to come down from some paper–'

'*Some* chap from *some* paper?' said Libby.

'Oh, I don't know. Photo-journalist or something, I think he said. Stop interrupting. Anyway, he's coming down to do a nice little piece on the original people and the original sites and then wants shots of the cast and the sets. Isn't that lovely?'

'Great. When's all this happening?'

'Sunday. So that everybody can be around during the day.'

'Oh, hell. So I've got to call everybody, have I? But I won't be back 'til lunchtime tomorrow.'

'Oh, Pete and I will pass the word, don't worry. Chinese whispers and all that. By the time we've finished they'll all think they've got to be somewhere else on the wrong day, but I shouldn't worry.'

'Prat.' Libby opened the car door again. 'Look,

73

I've got to go. I'll give you a ring tomorrow.'

On Saturday morning Sidney welcomed her with complete indifference and the expectation of another breakfast. There were four messages on her answering machine, one from her daughter, one from Peter saying Sunday was all set up and complaining that she never remembered to take her mobile with her, and one from a member of the cast saying they were going to see Granny on Sunday. One from Stephen asking if she was doing anything tonight. Nothing from Ben.

'Well, why should there be?' she asked Sidney, 'he'll be seeing me later.'

She screwed up her courage and phoned Stephen, feeling guiltily thankful to find his answering machine switched on, after which she wandered round the cottage for a little while, trying to tidy up, putting some washing in the machine and finally coming to rest in the studio where she regarded a half-finished masterpiece on the easel with deep gloom.

'I'm going for a walk,' she told Sidney.

The walk took her, predictably, to the Pink Geranium (open for lunch on Saturdays) where she was invited to sit down. Peter was sitting at a corner table with the newspapers and pushed a batch aside for her.

'Thanks for organising tomorrow, Pete.'

'Pleasure, dear heart. Didn't get hold of everybody, I had to leave messages for Paula and Stephen.'

'Did they get back to you? I would have thought Stephen ought to know what's going on

74

at the theatre.'

'Not a dicky from either of them yet, but I wouldn't worry. Stephen's far too conscientious to ignore a call to duty. Everybody else was quite enthusiastic – made a change.'

'Even the family?'

'Well, my dear mama doesn't have to be involved does she? She wasn't involved in the original scenario and certainly isn't with the current one, so I haven't bothered to tell her. And Hetty doesn't mind. At least, I don't think she does. You never can tell with Hetty. But she's agreed to wheel Greg out for the occasion, so that can't be bad.'

'How is he?'

'Frail. I don't think anybody thought he'd last this long, frankly, but on he goes – the proverbial creaking gate.'

'Was it the war that caused all the problems?'

'Oh, yes, dear. You know he was missing presumed dead for a year?'

'No. Really? How awful for Hetty.'

'Yes, specially as by that time she was down here with Ma-in-law on the doorstep. And when Pa-in-law began to fail, she had to take over the running of the hop farm. The old girl was useless, apparently.'

'Yes, you told me.'

'Did I? Oh, yes. Well, anyway, it was Hetty who had the new huts built, you know, the proper brick ones with proper roofs. Good job they weren't there before the war when you think of what happened the other night.'

'I don't *want* to think of what happened the

75

other night, *thank* you.'

'Sorry, dear.' Peter stood up and stretched. 'Ready for a little drink? Or would you prefer coffee?'

'Coffee, please. And I think I ought to have something to eat.'

'A nice slimming salad, or something?'

'Don't be rude. No, something hot. Soup?'

'I will ask the chef, m'lady.' Peter bowed and disappeared kitchen-wards. Libby sat and looked out of the window at the wide High Street, with its eclectic mix of houses from the last four centuries bathed in unexpectedly brilliant sunshine.

'I hope it's like this tomorrow,' she said, as Peter returned with a cafetiere and two mugs.

'Course it won't be. It'll be pouring with rain, we'll all get soaked and Hetty will stomp round all tight-lipped in her green wellies.'

'Where are these photographs going to be taken?' Libby pressed down the plunger and poured coffee.

'The huts–'

'New or old?'

'Hetty had the old ones knocked down, didn't she, so it'll have to be the new ones, except that they're outbuildings now, so they don't look quite the same. Still, we'll move all the extraneous rubbish out of the way and tart it up a bit.'

'When are we going to do that?'

'How about this afternoon? Got anything on?'

'I'm supposed to be going through the lighting plot.'

'No, you're not. I forgot – I was asked to pass on the message.'

'In that case, no, not until this evening.'

Peter's eyebrows lifted. 'Ooh. Got a date, have we?'

'Not really,' Libby tried to appear cool, 'Ben and I are going out to one of the Thai restaurants in Canterbury.'

'What's that then, if it isn't a date?' Peter cackled. 'You crafty old moo.'

'I'm not. We're just both at a loose end, that's all.'

'I shall refrain from making the obvious vulgar remark.' Peter raised his mug. 'Cheers.'

Harry provided them with soup and fresh bread, a bottle of wine and more coffee and promised to join them later if he wasn't too tired.

'All the prepping up for this evening, you see, ducks. We don't just stop when we chuck the punters out.'

The new hoppers' huts were now on the edge of a paddock some distance from both The Manor and the Oast House.

'This used to be the "common",' Peter told Libby as they picked their way along the edge of the ditch that ran behind the huts. 'The Sally-Ann and the lolly-man all used to set up here. And they had a huge party at the end of the picking.'

'Lolly-man?' panted Libby, feeling hot inside her layers. 'I know the Sally-Ann is the Salvation Army.'

'The lolly-man used to come round selling sweets for the children. And the fish van used to come on Fridays – oh, a regular little hive of industry, it was.'

'Didn't they use the shops in the village?'

'Oh, no, dear. Out of the question. The villagers hated them. The hoppers used to call them "home-dwellers" and if ever they got together all hell broke loose. They say it was after one of those fights on a Friday night that Hetty's dad had a go at her.'

'How come he hadn't heard all about it until then?'

'The men used to come down at the weekends – come on, ducky, you've read the play–' he stopped and raised an eyebrow at her. 'You *have* read the play, haven't you?'

'I know that, but why hadn't he heard before if it was such common knowledge?'

'He didn't come down every weekend. According to Lenny, he had other fish to fry. Not a nice person.'

Libby struggled along in silence for a few minutes.

'There's another thing I don't understand.'

Peter raised his eyes to the skies. '*Now* she tells me.'

'No, listen. It's just struck me. How can even Hetty have known she was pregnant by that time? The hopping season was only three or four weeks in September, wasn't it? Well, even if she'd conceived on her first day here she could only just have known herself and perhaps not even then. And we know that they didn't actually *do* it until they'd been seeing one another for a couple of weeks.'

'If you'd been paying attention, Sarjeant Minor, you would have remembered that it wasn't the

78

pregnancy that caused the bit of bother – nobody knew about that then. They didn't discover it until after they'd gone back to London. No, it was the very fact that they *had* been doing it that upset the apple cart. They were funny about those things then.'

'Well, she was only seventeen.'

'And he was the wrong class. It meant as much to the lower classes as to the upper, this wrong side of the tracks business. You just did not cross over.'

'We're here.' Libby stopped. 'Aren't they small?'

They were facing a long stone building with about a dozen plain wooden doors dividing it into different sections.

'Have you never been up here before?'

'No, never. It's quite a long walk, isn't it?' She threw him a lowering glance.

'Only a mile or so.' Peter was nonchalant, opening doors and peering in.

'You could have warned me,' Libby said, trying to see over his shoulder. 'Golly. They lived in *these?*'

'And the old ones were worse. The interior walls didn't go all the way up, so you could look over into next door, like you can in the school toilets.'

'But they're so tiny. At least you can stand upright in the ones we've built for the set.'

'Artistic licence, dear.' Peter backed out. 'What we'll do is, we'll clear out one hut, so that he can get a shot of an interior, and shove all the rubbish into the others. There's nothing very heavy here. Do you want to take that horse blanket off?'

'I suppose so. I'm going to ruin my clothes.'

'Oh, I thought you'd put them on special, like.'

'Oh, shut up,' said Libby.

It took them nearly an hour to clear the hut and move some of the most obvious junk out of sight, by which time Libby was sure she had lost at least a stone, was bright red in the face and damp all over.

'There.' Peter straightened his back and stretched. 'That wasn't as bad as I thought.'

'You speak for yourself,' muttered Libby, looking in vain for somewhere to sit down. 'And now we've got to walk all the way back.'

'No, we haven't,' Peter pointed. 'Here comes the cavalry.'

A muddy four-wheel-drive was bouncing over the common towards them.

'It's your swain, come to rescue you.'

'Oh, no,' moaned Libby. 'Just *look* at me.'

'As lovely as usual, dear heart. And if you're worried about the way you look, it definitely *is* a date.'

'You dare–' began Libby.

'Hallo, folks. Spring cleaning?' Ben jumped down from the driver's seat and strolled over. 'You should have let me know. I would have come to help. Anything I can do?'

'Just in time to be too late, lucky legs.' Peter picked up his waxed jacket. 'But you can take us home again.'

'What about the other sites?' asked Libby. 'For the other shots.'

'Oh, the fight took place on the side of the ditch just along there, by the bridge where we crossed over. At least, that's where Warburton's body was found. Nothing to do there.'

'How did you know we were here?' asked Libby.

'I called the caff to find out what time the shoot was set for tomorrow and Harry told me. Do you want to come and have a cup of tea up at the house, or would you rather go home?'

'I would rather go home and have a bath, if you don't mind.' Libby surveyed her clothes and sniffed suspiciously. 'I know just how those hop pickers must have felt. Fancy not being able to have a decent wash feeling like this.'

'Oh, it was worse than this,' said Ben cheerfully. 'There was all the gunge from the hops all over everything as well. Smelt awful, stained everything, dreadful stuff. And the hops hurt your hands. They said that when the children went back to school in London the teachers all knew where they'd been just by looking at their hands.'

'You know a lot about it.' Libby climbed in to the back seat while Ben held the door open.

'Well, of course I do. I was brought up with the hop gardens. My mother virtually ran them after the war, right up until the big growers introduced automated picking and we couldn't compete.'

'So when did the last pickers come down?'

'The sixties – quite late.'

'I thought it all stopped not long after the war.' Libby was fascinated.

Ben set them bumping over the common. 'Good lord, no. And when they finally did stop, several of the old ladies who had been coming all their lives moved down here for good.'

'I'd love to talk to them.' Libby leaned forward

over Peter's shoulder.

'Well, you could always talk to my mother. After all, she was a picker herself.'

'Yes, but she went over to the other side, so to speak. What about her friend, Flo?'

'Flo married Frank Carpenter, the foreman, just after Hetty came down here. He bought the Home Farm from my grandfather just after the war. He was a lot older than Flo.'

'What beats me,' said Peter, twisting round to look Libby in the eye, 'is why, when we've been working on this play virtually since you moved in to Bide-a-Wee, you've suddenly developed this overwhelming interest in it all within the last week.'

'It's your fault. You introduced me to your mama and started to tell me all about it.'

'Come off it. You can't pin it all on me.'

'Anyway, after that there was Uncle Lenny coming down, and your mum getting uptight and–' Libby stopped.

'And other things. Yes, I know. Puts quite a sinister complexion on matters, doesn't it? Quite Miss Marple-ish, really.'

'Libby doesn't want to be Miss Marple.' Ben flicked her a glance in the mirror. 'Do you, Libby?'

Peter turned and raised an eyebrow. Libby scowled.

Ben surprised Libby by driving right behind the village and turning into Allhallow's Lane from the other end.

'I didn't know it went anywhere,' she said, surprised.

'Well, it doesn't really. It just turns into our

land, but we've never put up any keep out signs. It didn't seem worth it.'

Libby opened the door and clambered out.

'Thanks for the lift.'

'See you at seven.'

'Be good,' whispered Peter, leaning out of the window. Libby thumbed her nose at him and went inside.

Chapter Eight

Libby wore her prettiest top with her straight skirt and hoped she wouldn't get too hot. At least Ben hadn't collected her in the four-wheel-drive, or her skirt would have been up round her knicker legs.

'You're very quiet.' Ben slid his eyes sideways as he turned on to the main Canterbury road.

'Sorry.'

'You do apologise a lot.'

'S – yes.'

'There you go again. Let's change the subject.'

Libby turned her head to look at him. 'You know, you're quite different from what I've always thought. I had you down as a straightforward businessman, with perhaps a bit of golf and squash on the side.'

'I'm too old for squash, but I used to play. I tried golf, but it was too slow. Perhaps I might try again. Do you play?'

'No, I'm hopeless at sport. My ex used to say

that if I took a bit more exercise I wouldn't be so fat.'

'Nice way with words, had he?'

'Thank you for not saying "you're not fat".'

'I would have done, but you'd have thought it was flannel.'

'Hmm.'

They parked in one of the tiny back streets to the north of the city.

'So do you think you're fully *au fait* with all our background history, now? Or are there still gaps you need filled in?' said Ben as they walked to the restaurant.

'Sorry, have I been terribly nosy?'

'No, of course you haven't. Quite understandable in the circumstances. I just want to know if I can be nosy back.'

They had arrived at the restaurant and Ben held open the door. Libby didn't reply until they were seated at a table by the window.

'You can be as nosy as you like, I won't mind. I might not answer you, though.'

'I'll risk it. How long ago did your marriage break up?'

'Finally? Three years ago. It had been on the downhill slope for two or three before that. I think he waited until the children were old enough before he went.'

'Do they stay with you in the vacations?'

'Mostly, at Christmas. They spend some time with their father–'

'And his floosie.'

Libby made a face. 'But the rest of the time they swan about, working on building sites, that

84

sort of thing. Dominic's going to Europe next summer.'

'Have they been down since you've been in the cottage?'

'Belinda has. The boys haven't. I hope I can squeeze us all in if they all tip up at the same time.'

'You can always board out at The Manor.'

'That's very kind of you.'

'It isn't really called Bide-a-Wee, is it?'

'If it was I would have changed it. No, that's Peter and Harry's pet name for it. They found it for me. It was called "The search for Bide-a-Wee".'

'I didn't realise. Are you happy there?'

Libby thought. 'It took some getting used to after a four-bedroomed Edwardian terrace, but yes, I'm happy.'

'Even with all the bother at the theatre?'

'Oh, I've got that under control now. It was only one incident, wasn't it? And, you know, it couldn't have been Aunt Millie who cut the wire. Could it? I mean, how would she have got in?'

'Oh, she could have got hold of the keys from The Manor. They hang in the old pantry along with all the others.'

'So anybody could get them?' Libby looked up from the menu she was studying, startled.

'If they knew where to look, certainly. My mother never locks all the doors during the day-time.'

'You haven't told anyone else that it was deliberately cut, have you?'

'No. You didn't want me to, did you?' Ben

frowned at her.

'Certainly not. No need for everybody to worry.'

'And no need for you to worry – not this evening, anyway. Let's talk about something else.'

Somehow, Libby didn't quite know how, they did talk about something else. Several things, in fact. To her surprise, she realised when they got up to leave that they hadn't stopped talking once and had managed to steer completely clear of the play and all its ramifications.

Libby fell silent as they approached the village and discovered, as Ben switched off the engine outside the cottage, that every muscle in her body was tense.

'Thank you for a lovely evening.'

'Thank you for being a charming guest.'

'Would you like to come in for coffee–' damn. She hadn't meant to say that – 'or do you have to get back?'

'Now what would I have to get back for? My mother doesn't wait up any more, you know. And I don't have to get up in the morning.'

'Sorry.'

'There you go again. Apologising. I'd love coffee, thank you.'

Libby led the way into the cottage, forgetting to warn him about the step, which meant that he cannoned into her from behind.

'Is that meant to discourage unwanted visitors?' he asked, grabbing at the door-frame to steady himself.

'It's too late by then – they're already in.' Libby paused by the stairs to stroke Sidney. 'This is my ultimate deterrent.'

'A formidable beast.' Ben and Sidney stared at one another. 'I think I'll let him make the first approach.'

'Very wise,' said Libby, going into the kitchen and taking off her cape. 'Do you really want coffee, or something stronger?'

'Coffee, please. I'm driving and I've already had a glass or two of wine.'

'It's not far to walk,' said Libby, and could have bitten her tongue out.

'Good God, Libby. You're not actually encouraging me to stay, are you?'

'No.' Libby's face was fiery. 'I just meant, if you wanted a scotch, or something, you could leave the car here and come back for it in the morning.'

'And have the neighbourhood rife with speculation about my car being here all night?' He was laughing at her again.

'Fine. Coffee.' She turned to the Rayburn, tightlipped.

'Are you going to set the cat on me?'

'His name's Sidney.' Libby filled the kettle and put it on the hob.

'I'm sorry, Libby. I'm not making fun of you, really.'

Libby turned round with two mugs in her hands. 'I know, but you make me feel foolish. I always seem to say the wrong thing.'

He sat down at the little kitchen table and smiled up at her. 'You don't, you know. If anyone says the wrong thing, it's me.'

How he managed it, Libby didn't know, but the conversation returned effortlessly to the impersonal subjects they had been discussing earlier in the evening. Half an hour later, he took his leave and she saw him to the door.

'Sidney didn't need to leap to your defence after all.'

Sidney was still at his post on the stairs.

'No. Thank you.'

'A little self-restraint is good for us all.' He smiled at her. 'But not for too long. Don't worry, Libby, I won't rush you.' He bent forward and kissed her cheek. 'See you tomorrow afternoon.'

What do you mean, she wanted to yell after him. Does that mean you fancy me? But she didn't say anything. Just watched him reverse up Allhallow's Lane. Then she leaned back against the door and closed her eyes. The terrible thing was, she admitted, that she wanted to be rushed. Or was it just her desperate hormones? But if that was the case, why didn't she feel the same with poor Stephen? And just when had she started to think of him as "poor" Stephen?

Sunday dawned as bright and beautiful as Saturday, but by mid-day, the clouds had rolled in again and a steady drizzle was doing its best to dampen everybody's spirits. Libby met Peter and Harry for a lunchtime drink before setting off for The Manor. Peter had borrowed a four-wheel-drive from somewhere and Ben was to take his and, in view of the weather, the cast members were not required to traipse through the fields, but to meet them back at the theatre for the indoor shots.

Ben met them at the door.

'You go ahead, I'll bring Mum and Dad and the photographer. Dad's not moving too well today.'

Peter turned the vehicle round and set it at the field.

'Bloody weather,' he said.

The huts looked dismal in the rain and Libby wondered how the hop pickers had felt, stuck out here when the weather was like this. They sat huddled inside, not speaking, until they saw the other vehicle approaching.

Ben got out and went to open the rear door for his mother as the photographer jumped down from the other side.

'No wonder he wanted to bring the photographer,' said Harry, with a startled glance at Peter.

Libby was horrified to find that she actually had a lump in her throat, and an extremely unpleasant feeling somewhere under her rib cage, as she watched the tall, slim, blonde *female* striding towards them, her large black nylon equipment bags slung effortlessly over her shoulder.

'Hallo. Which one of you's Peter? Nobby couldn't make it, so he asked me to come instead. Vanessa Hargreaves – but just call me Van.'

'Oh – er – yes. Delighted,' said Peter, taking the proffered hand with a quick glance at Libby. 'This is Harry, who helps us with – er – all sorts of things, and this is Libby Sarjeant – with a J – who is directing the play.'

'Great. Are you a professional director?' Call-me-Van was fishing out a microphone and fiddling with knobs and switches inside one of the black cases.

'No,' said Libby.

'Yes. Well, she's an ex-professional. Drama

school trained.' Harry hurried into the breach.

'Oh, right. So now you're into the old am-dram, eh?'

A bitter little silence fell, while nobody looked at each other, and then Libby noticed Ben struggling alone with his three elderly relatives.

'Hang on,' she called, and sloshed through the mud towards them. 'Here, Hetty, hang on to me. Lenny, you come the other side – Ben, can your father manage?'

He turned a grateful face towards her and winked. Suddenly, she felt better.

'Right, lovely.' Van was bustling about the yard, oblivious to the mud and the rain in her leather jacket and huge boots. 'So these are the people who the play is about? Have I got that right?'

They all agreed that she'd got it right.

'OK then – if we could have you all here – in this shed–'

'It's a hut.' Hetty unclamped her lips for long enough to correct her. 'A hoppers' hut.'

'Oh, right. Well, can you all get in there, then?'

'Just Lenny and me.' Hetty took charge. 'Gregory was never in the huts. He can stay outside.'

Libby was appalled at how grey and frail Gregory Wilde had become since she had last seen him. The skin on his face seemed so thin that you could almost see the skull beneath. He raised his peaked cap to her with an unsteady hand as Ben helped him to stand by the doorway of the hut, while Hetty, dour as usual, stood inside next to Lenny, who was obviously enjoying himself.

'OK, that's lovely then, yes – one more – could

you just move out a little bit – Hetty – is that it? And Lenny, put your arm round her, dear – that's it, lovely – now, er, Mr – er–'

'Wilde.' Gregory drew himself up. 'Gregory Wilde.'

'Oh, yes, right, Mr Wilde. Could you sort of bend over a bit – perhaps look inside?'

'I think that might be too much for my father,' said Ben in a firm voice, coming forward to take his arm. 'You've got one or two of him, haven't you? I think that will be enough.'

'Oh.' Van looked nonplussed, as well she might, thought Libby. 'But I really ought to bracket these a bit – the light, you know.'

'Bracket?' Everyone looked confused.

'Hedging your bets,' explained Peter. 'They take different exposures to see which comes out best.'

'Nevertheless, my father will go and sit inside, if you don't mind.' Ben led his father away, leaving Van to do the best she could with Hetty and Lenny.

'So this is where you stayed, is it? Could we say this is the very hut?'

'No. These weren't built then. Our huts were knocked down after the war.'

Lenny chuckled. 'Hetty had 'em knocked down, didn't you, gel? Never did like those huts, our Het.'

'You be quiet, Lenny Fisher.' Hetty pushed him out of the hut.

'So where were the old huts, could we see?'

'Nothing to see. Grassed over now.'

'Oh, right. So – the murder. Hey, great, the

91

readers love a murder. So where did that happen then?'

Lenny dug Hetty in the ribs. 'Down by the bridge, weren't it, Het?'

'That's where the body was found.' Hetty gave her brother a quelling look. But Lenny wasn't to be quelled.

'In the ditch, weren't it, Het? Horrible, it was.'

'Who found the body? You?'

'Nah. Some of the kids. They used to come and look for tiddlers. Cor, they didn't half holler.' Lenny smiled reminiscently.

'Can we see?'

'Yes, we came across the bridge yesterday, so it's quite safe.' Peter gestured for her to follow him. 'You've no need to come, Aunt Het, or you, Lenny.'

'Oh, I'm coming. Wouldn't miss this for the world. You staying here, Het?'

Hetty didn't bother to answer him, but turned and climbed unaided into the four-wheel-drive beside her husband.

'You horrible old man,' muttered Ben to his uncle as he came alongside Libby and took her arm. Lenny cackled.

'Nice bit of skirt, though, in't she? Lucky bugger having her riding beside yer. Little bit of gear shifting, eh?'

'You really are disgusting,' said Ben, but he was grinning as he helped Libby over the treacherous mud towards the bridge.

'She is pretty.' Libby gave him a sidelong glance.

'Yes, she is. Why they have to wear those dreadful boots, though – and that hair.'

Libby smiled to herself

'Here we are then.' Peter presented the bridge with a flourish. 'The famous murder spot.'

'Now,' said Van juggling with cameras and recorders once more. 'Who was murdered?'

'Joe Warburton. Tallyman,' answered Lenny promptly.

'What?'

'He measured the hops.'

'Oh, right.' Van was clearly puzzled, but carried on gamely. 'And he was where?'

'Just down there.' Lenny leant forward at a dangerous angle to point and Libby and Ben grabbed an arm each.

'Can I get a shot from the other side?'

'Sure.' Peter shrugged. 'Here, I'll help you with that.'

Van trod delicately across the bridge, Peter following as bearer.

'Pete!' Harry's scream took them all by surprise. 'The bridge – careful – oh, my GOD.'

Almost in slow motion the bridge groaned, creaked and began to crack. With sounds like pistol shots it splintered and gave way. Van, squealing in terror, was already almost across, and scrambled inelegantly on to the further bank, but Peter, baggage and all, turned a somersault, grabbed vainly at the rotting railing and fell in.

With a distinct sense of deja-vu, Libby heard the momentary silence, then the explosion of sound as everybody rushed forward. A good deal of the noise was coming from Peter, who, it appeared, was not badly hurt, other than in his dignity. Van rushed up and down the opposite bank in short bursts, wailing 'My equipment. My equipment,' while Lenny seemed to be doing a little dance on the spot, encouraging Ben and Harry, who were sliding down the bank to help Peter. Libby moved to a safe vantage point, ready to reach out and take the various cases as they were handed up.

Peter emerged in a rush, covered in mud and various other unpleasant detritus, swearing fluently, 'Just like a navvy, darling,' as Harry said, admiringly. Ben was left to encourage Van down from her side, catching her as she slid awkwardly on her bottom, whereupon she clung to him so tightly that Libby began to get quite hot under the collar. With Ben behind and Harry pulling from in front, she finally landed in a heap at Libby's feet, still wailing.

'I'm so sorry,' said Libby bending to assist her to her feet. 'I can't think how it happened. It was quite safe yesterday. I'm *so* sorry.'

But Van was inconsolable. They loaded her in beside Ben, and Lenny came in the back of Peter's vehicle with Libby, with Harry driving.

'Somebody'd had a go at that bridge.' Peter broke the silence as they bumped towards The Manor.

Nobody answered him.

'I saw it. Where it split. Somebody'd had a go at it.'

'Wouldn't take much, Pete. It was rotten anyway.' Harry patted his knee.

'It took our weight yesterday – and we stood on it together,' said Libby.

'Perhaps that was the last straw, then? Whoops,

94

sorry.' Harry was contrite.

'Why would anybody do that?' asked Libby.

'Me. That's what it was. To get me.' Lenny spoke for the first time.

'You?' They all turned to look at him. 'Why?'

'Don't matter why. Just was, I tell yer,' and Lenny, for once quite serious, refused to say another word.

At The Manor, Van had already been hustled upstairs by Hetty, and Ben called out that he was taking his father up to his room.

'Kettle's on. Help yourselves.'

'I'm going fer a lie down,' announced Lenny and without looking at any of them he left the kitchen, his step considerably less springy than usual.

Libby and Harry looked at Peter.

'I want a bath,' he said.

'Come on, then, I'll take you home. Will you stay here and help Ben with Vanny Fanacapan, Libby?'

'All right,' said Libby helplessly, 'but I don't know what I'm supposed to do.'

'Neither do I, love. Stop her suing us, I suppose.'

'Oh, my God.' Libby's hand flew to her mouth. 'You don't think...?'

'Hazards of the job,' said Peter. 'Silly cow, anyway. Am-dram, indeed.'

Libby giggled, and, suddenly, they were all laughing hysterically, clutching each other. Ben came in and looked on, astonished.

'Are you going to let me in on it?' he asked.

'Release of tension, dear heart,' said Peter, his

good humour restored. 'I'm going to have a bath and Libby is going to help you stop Call-me-Van suing us.'

'Could she?' Ben looked startled.

'If she finds out that bridge was sabotaged, yes. Come on, Hal. Take me home and bathe me.'

'Sabotaged?' Ben turned to Libby when they were alone.

'Peter thinks so. He says he could see it when he went down.'

'But why?'

'That's what we'd all like to know.' Libby sighed. 'I'm getting sick of this, Ben.'

'It can't have any connection.' He came round the table and pushed her gently into a chair.

'Lenny thinks it was to get at him. He was quite serious about it.'

'I don't believe it.'

'True.' Libby looked over at the Aga where a kettle was beginning to sing. 'Shall I make some tea?'

Ben laid a tray to take upstairs and found two teapots. Libby waited for the tea to draw, gazing out of the kitchen window over fields and copses, bleached of their colour by the low cloud and rain.

'I'm going to tackle Lenny.' Ben came back into the room and flung himself into a Windsor chair by the Aga.

'Will he tell you anything?'

'I don't know. I would have thought he would want to, now, but you can't tell with Lenny. He can be an awkward old sod.'

'I can't help feeling responsible, you know.'

96

Libby carried cups to the table.

'Why? Because of the play? It wasn't your idea. That's all down to Peter and me. I'm beginning to wish we'd left well alone, now.'

'But you couldn't have known. After all, it was a family decision, wasn't it? And, from what Peter said, the story was never covered up. He's known about it since he was a child. You must have done, too.'

'That's what puzzles me. It almost looks as though whoever cut the wire and damaged the bridge must have a grudge against us – and possibly the theatre. Nothing to do with the story. Millie getting upset must be a red herring.'

'Then why does Lenny think someone's out to get him?'

'Oh, God. I don't know.' Ben leaned forward and put his head in his hands. 'You must be beginning to wish you'd never met this family.'

Libby gazed down at his bent head.

'No,' she said softly. 'No, I don't wish that. And maybe we're jumping to conclusions. Perhaps they were both accidents and we're being paranoid.'

He looked up, his eyes very bright blue in the gathering gloom of the kitchen.

'Let's put on some lights,' said Libby hastily, jumping up. 'It's getting awfully dark.'

Hetty came in to the kitchen and lowered herself into a chair by the table. She didn't look up.

'Mum?' Ben got up and went over to her. 'How are they all?'

'Lenny and your father are lying down and that

silly girl's in the bath. I've sponged off all her leather gear and she's checked her precious equipment. None of it's broke.'

'Well, that's a relief.' Libby sat down opposite her. 'Are you all right, Hetty?'

'I'm all right, girl. I'm always all right, aren't I, Ben?'

'Yes, Mum,' he said, giving her a hug.

'You'll stay for a bit of dinner, Libby?' The old lady straightened thin shoulders. 'I've got a nice bit of beef in the slow oven. Thought we'd have it tonight instead of lunchtime, what with this photo business.'

'Are you sure it's no trouble?' Libby looked from Hetty to Ben.

'No, we'd love you to stay,' said Ben, and Libby blushed.

'Can I do anything to help, then?'

'No, it's all done. Just got to put the veg on and the Yorkshire in. Have it about six, shall we? After we've got rid of that girl.'

'Better make it half-past, Mum. She might take a lot of getting rid of.'

As it happened, Van was only too eager to shake the dust of The Manor off her feet, swearing that she was fine, the equipment was fine, and yes, Nobby would write the piece if they would send him all the details. Relieved, they helped her load her car and waved her on her way.

'Ben!' shrieked Libby as they watched her car bowling down the drive. 'We forgot the cast. At the theatre.'

'Christ,' said Ben rushing inside and grabbing his jacket. 'I'd better get down there fast. If

98

they're still there.'

'I'll come with you.' Libby threw her cape around her with such violence that it nearly strangled her. 'Come on.'

But when they arrived at the theatre it was to find Stephen just about to lock up.

'Don't worry, we heard. I phoned and spoke to your mother.'

'I wonder when that was? I didn't hear the phone.' Libby looked at Ben.

'You can't hear it in the kitchen if the door's closed. Oh, well, all that rushing for nothing. Thanks, Stephen, we'll finish locking up.'

'So what exactly happened?' asked Stephen.

'Peter fell off the bridge,' said Libby. 'That's all.'

'And the photographer?'

'Well, yes, she did too, only not right into the ditch,' said Libby, wondering why Stephen was looking so suspicious.

'Why were you there, Libby? I thought it was about the family?'

Ben raised his eyebrows. 'She's the director, of course. Wouldn't you expect her to be there?'

'Not if it was only family,' said Stephen, turning away.

All three of them went round the theatre turning off lights and double-checking the set, then stopped to admire the new auditorium seats that had been delivered on Friday.

'We'll fix these in on Tuesday – you're not rehearsing then, are you?' said Stephen.

'Well, I did think I might put in an extra rehearsal–'

'Do it Friday. Better nearer the time,' said Ben. 'They'll still have two days off before the dress.'

'OK, then, I'll be off.' Stephen stood irresolute, hands pushed down into his coat pockets. 'Do you need a lift, Lib?'

'Er – I'm going back to The Manor, thanks, Stephen. Hetty invited me to dinner.'

'Ah,' he said. 'Right. See you tomorrow, then.' Without looking at either of them, he turned abruptly and went out of the auditorium.

'I don't think he's my best friend, you know, Lib,' said Ben.

'Awful, wasn't it? I don't know what to do about him. Does he really fancy me, or am I imagining it?' Libby frowned. 'He could just be being protective.'

'Was that pigs I heard landing on the roof?'

'Well, he could be, couldn't he? Otherwise I'm taking the most awful advantage of him.'

'He didn't have to do it, you know. He enjoys being needed and he knows he's good at his job. He's one of the best set builders and designers I know.'

'Yes, but now he's going to fit the seats.'

'We're all going to do that,' said Ben.

'I was going to do a without-cast technical on Friday.'

'Stop making difficulties, woman,' he turned to her in the semi-darkness and shook her gently. 'Do a with-cast tech on Thursday, instead. You've gone through the lighting and sound plots, and they've got the hang of the scene changes–'

'If nothing breaks,' said Libby.

'Oh, shut up,' said Ben, and kissed her.

100

It wasn't a very long kiss, but Libby felt as though she'd been filleted.

'Sorry,' said Ben, and had to clear his throat. 'I just wanted to shut you up.'

'You did,' croaked Libby.

'I said I wouldn't rush you.'

'Yes,' said Libby.

He turned her round and pushed her through the auditorium doors. 'Go on, you go outside. I'll just lock up.'

As they walked up the drive, Ben reached out and took Libby's hand, tucking it into his pocket. Neither of them said anything.

Dinner was served at the long kitchen table. Gregory and Lenny both came down, although Lenny was still very subdued. Gregory did his best to be a charming host, and succeeded, Libby seeing in him the young man who had bowled Hetty over and unwittingly caused the whole chain of events which, even now, were having their effect on his family. They drank a very good wine, chosen by Hetty, to Libby's surprise, and afterwards Hetty allowed them a brandy, to be taken in the sitting room.

'Let me wash up, Hetty,' said Libby as they left the table.

'Goes in the dishwasher, girl. Ben'll help you load it, but leave the pans to me. I like to do them meself.'

'Strong woman, your mother, isn't she?' said Libby as they stacked plates together.

'She's had to be.'

'Millie's not very like her.'

'No. Takes after their father, I gather. Apt to act

101

first and think afterwards.'

They both stopped and looked at each other.

'Yes, well. So Hetty takes after their mother, then?'

'Peas in a pod, so I've heard. I only remember her vaguely, but she looked just like my mother does now, I think.'

'You look like your father.'

'Do I? That's good. I've always thought of him as a remarkably good-looking man.'

Libby threw a dishcloth at him.

'Come on. Let's go and get our share of the brandy before they finish the bottle.'

Later, Ben walked Libby home – 'So that I can have something stronger, this time.'

'No rushing,' she warned him, wanting him to all the same.

But he didn't. They sat companionably by her fire, which she lit as soon as she came in, drinking the last of her precious scotch. Sidney deigned to honour them with his presence, even going so far as to forsake Libby's feet for Ben's. Ben appeared duly sensible of the honour.

When he left, he kissed her again, but gently. 'See you tomorrow?'

'Rehearsal's at seven-thirty.'

'I'll be there.'

Chapter Nine – 1943

The lorry was parked outside by ten o'clock at night and one by one the families carried out their belongings. Hetty took it in turns with her mother to look after Millie, who was infected by the excitement and the enthusiastic shouts of the other children, some of whom had been put to bed early to make up for the lost night's sleep ahead of them but had failed to stay there, escaping while their mothers and elder siblings were busy with the lorry.

It was midnight when they were ready to leave, and Ted hadn't returned home. Lillian shrugged, climbed on to the lorry and reached down for Millie. 'Best we get going,' she said shortly, and Hetty ran round to the other side to look for Flo.

'Come on. We're ready. Where's your Mum?'

'Already on, with Gran. Where's your Lenny?'

'Helping lift the kids on round the other side. Oh, don't make up to him, Flo. It makes him miserable.' Hetty paused with her hand on Flo's arm.

Flo grinned. 'Wasn't going to.'

'You can't help making up to Lenny – or anyone else. Comes natural, don't it?'

Flo regarded her thoughtfully. 'Suppose so. Like old Carpenter.'

'But not Warburton, eh?' said Hetty, and they both giggled.

The sky was just beginning to lighten in the east when the lorry lurched to a halt and Hetty sat up rubbing her eyes. Still clasping Millie, she got awkwardly to her feet, stiff and aching from the cramped journey. She clambered down in to the farm yard, aware of Frank Carpenter standing over near the oast house, already talking to Flo whose hand in her hair and out-thrust hip proclaimed her interest in the older man, however much she tried to deny it.

'Come on, Het.' Lenny jerked his head in Flo's direction. 'We got work to do even if she hasn't.'

They began to unload their belongings from the lorry and Hetty wheeled the hopping box across to what they called the Common, where the rows of hoppers' huts stood. It was a good farm. Only two years ago, the huts had been rebuilt, long stone buildings with corrugated iron roofs replacing the ramshackle wooden sheds. Hetty parked the hopping box outside number 26, hoisted Millie more securely onto her hip and made her way back to the yard to collect the hopping pot and anything else she could carry. She passed Flo carrying assorted bags and wearing a satisfied grin.

'Old Carpenter making up to you again, is he?' whispered Hetty as they passed.

'Wouldn't you like to know?' Flo tossed her head and then ruined the effect by giggling. 'I'll see you later – when we've finished.'

Hetty nodded. They had the whole day to themselves to settle in, because the other pickers wouldn't arrive until later in the afternoon and picking wouldn't start until the following day.

Lenny joined her outside the hut, and then

Lillian arrived with the padlock and key. The familiar smell of damp greeted them as they opened the door and Lenny hoisted up the roll of lino and rolled it inside.

'I got to go back with the lorry now, Mum,' he said, straightening up. 'I'd help whitewash if I could, but the lorry's got to be back before eight.'

'Go on then, son,' Lillian reached up and kissed him, ruffling his hair. 'See you at the weekend. Look after yer dad.'

'Bye, Lenny.' Hetty kissed him too, and Millie held out chubby baby arms to him. Lenny buried his face in her neck and blew a raspberry. Millie squealed with delight.

'Say goodbye to Flo for me.' Lenny looked round but Flo was nowhere to be seen. 'I'll see her at the weekend.'

Hetty began to walk back to the lorry with him. 'Don't pay any attention to her, Len. You know what she's like.'

'A flirt,' said Lenny shortly. 'She'll get into trouble one of these days, you see if she don't.'

'Ah, she knows what she's doing,' said Hetty confidently.

'No, she ruddy doesn't.' In the half light of dawn, Hetty knew her brother had coloured fiercely. 'She'll lead the wrong one on, one of these days.'

'No.' Hetty shivered in spite of herself. 'Not you, any rate.'

'No, not me.' Lenny sounded miserable. 'But I'd like to wring her neck, sometimes.'

Hetty watched as he climbed back on the lorry with the other men who were travelling back to the empty street, and waved with the wives and children as it pulled out of the farmyard. She stood watching absently as it disappeared up the rutted track while the bustle around her subsided as the yard emptied.

'Little Henrietta, isn't it?'

Hetty swung round and came face to face with a short stocky man, his dark rough jacket and waistcoat unbuttoned over his shirt, his thumbs tucked into the waistband of his trousers. His face was shadowed, but she felt a leap of apprehension as she recognised him.

'Hallo, Mr Warburton.' She edged sideways to get past him, but he stepped neatly into her path.

'Growing up, ain't yer?' His Kentish burr was soft, but Hetty heard menace in his tone. 'Pretty little thing, now.'

Hetty's stomach lurched and she found that she was shaking.

'I got to get back to help me mum, Mr Warburton. She's got the baby, you see...'

'Of course she has, Hetty – that's what they call you, isn't it? Hetty?'

'Er, yes. Me friends do,' Hetty mumbled as he fell into step beside her.

'Oh, I'm your friend, Hetty. Never you doubt that.' He laughed and spat, and Hetty shuddered. 'Never you doubt that. You tell your mum, and all. Warburton's your friend.' He swung away from her, still laughing softly, and Hetty's ears rang with the unmistakable emphasis he had placed on the last word. Wrapping her arms around herself, she ran through the chilly morning back to the hut and safety.

Chapter Ten

Harry phoned during Monday afternoon.

'Guess what.'

Libby groaned. 'Not more earth-shattering events. I don't think I can cope.'

'No, listen. Lenny's gone home.'

'Eh?'

'Yes. Apparently he came downstairs after breakfast and announced that he'd packed and was going home. Luckily, Pete didn't have to go anywhere today, so he drove him to the station.'

'Where's Pete now?'

'At his mother's. Why?'

'I just wondered if Lenny had said anything more. You know, about yesterday.'

'Well, that's obviously why he went, but I don't think he said anything. Pete didn't say.'

Libby put the phone down thoughtfully. If Lenny was gone, perhaps the incidents would stop. He had to be the catalyst. It was because he was here, because someone was afraid of what he might say, that these things had happened. Libby still didn't fully understand the relevance of the falling roof; that couldn't have been directed at Lenny, but only to damage the play. And, for that matter, why the sabotaged bridge? No one could have expected Lenny to be on it. Perhaps they were simply warnings. She went back into the conservatory and stared at a painting drying on the easel. She must stretch some more paper, she thought, but stayed where she was, staring at nothing.

If Lenny had come down for the play, big with his secret, someone must have thought that he would let it out. That someone must then have thought that it would come out anyway, whatever it was, with all the interest that was being aroused. Then yesterday, they had visited the original sites – of course. Libby stood up straight. That had to be it. It had to be something to do with the murder. But what? Hetty's father, known to be at loggerheads with Warburton, had disappeared, so where was the mystery?

Perhaps, she thought, covering the painting and beginning to collect brushes for washing, Hetty's father was still alive? And – no. That was ridiculous. He would be in his late nineties. She shrugged and went back into the kitchen.

Rehearsal that night went well. Libby was able to do a straight run, with nearly all the costumes and most of the scene changes. The roof, due to popular demand, was now to be carried on, rather than flown in. They managed to get to the pub just in time for last orders.

On the way home, Libby told Ben of her conclusions.

'Much the same as I thought myself. Lenny must have known that we would start probing, so he scarpered before we could.'

'Didn't Peter ask him on the way to the station? I hardly saw Pete tonight, and I couldn't very well ask him in the pub.'

'He tried, apparently, but Lenny clammed up.

Said it was nothing to do with him.'

Libby put the key in the door. 'Coming in?'

'People will talk.' Ben grinned.

'They are already.'

He kissed her just inside the front door before she turned the light on. Her body definitely felt as though it belonged to a teenager, she decided, and pulled away before she fell down.

'Coffee?' she asked, in a high voice.

'Coffee, tea or me? Isn't that the phrase?' He followed her into the kitchen.

'Not this time it isn't.'

'Another time? Soon?'

'Don't badger me, Ben.'

'I'm sorry. Coffee, please.'

It was even harder to break away when he left and she had to hang on to the door-frame to stop herself running after him. I'm in a cleft stick, she told herself, climbing slowly up the stairs. *I've* actually got to give *him* the green light, now I've taken the initiative away from him. How do I do that? I'm too old. I can't remember.

The next morning Libby was surprised to receive a phone call from James.

'I was wondering,' he said, after civilities had been exchanged, 'if my mother has said anything about Peter's play?'

'In what way?' hedged Libby.

'Well, she seems very worried about it. I can't quite make out whether she's worried that Peter hasn't written it well, or that it isn't going to be performed well, or what.' James did indeed sound puzzled, as if this conundrum was not the sort of thing that came up at the gym or the golf club.

'She did come to see me,' admitted Libby, slowly, 'but I think she was more worried about dragging the family name through the mud.'

'Ah. That would make sense, of course.'

'Would it?'

'Oh, yes. Ma's always been rather hot on that sort of thing. She really can't cope with Peter and Harry, you know. I think she was hoping that you would be able to drag him back on to the straight and narrow.'

'Me?' Libby laughed, and remembered Millie coupling them together. 'I couldn't compete with the beautiful Harry in a month of Sundays.'

'No,' James agreed, rather too readily, Libby thought. 'And I wouldn't expect you to. Pete's my brother and I love him as he is. Do *you* think the play's going to drag us through the mud?'

'No, I don't think so. The story's passed into local folklore, hasn't it? Everybody knows it. Your Aunt Hetty agreed to it, so did your Uncle Gregory, and surely they've got the most to lose, reputation-wise.'

'Oh, I don't think so. They've never taken much part in local social life, you see. Whereas Ma and my cousin Susan have positions in the neighbourhood.'

'And you? Don't you have a position to keep up?' asked Libby.

'Not really,' said James.

'Oh.' Libby felt deflated. 'Well, anyway. I don't think it's going to hurt anybody. Especially now Lenny's gone home.'

'Ah, yes. Ma didn't seem too chuffed about that, either. In fact, she has been a bit peculiar these last few days.'

'Has she? Do you think she's all right, James?'

There was a long enough pause for Libby to ask if he was still there.

'Yes, I'm still here.' Another pause. 'Listen, Libby, I haven't said anything to anybody yet, but you know last week when I called to tell you Paula couldn't come to rehearsal?'

'Yes.'

'Well – it wasn't just shock.' Libby heard him take a deep breath. 'She's pregnant.'

'*What?*'

'Yes.'

'Is it yours?'

'She says so.' He sighed. 'Ma will be pleased, I expect. Means I'll settle down and give her grandchildren.'

Libby spluttered. 'But I thought you'd dumped her?'

'Tried.' James sounded uncomfortable. 'My responsibility now, though, isn't it?'

'James.' Libby tried to sound authoritative and grown up. 'You're not going to marry her, are you?'

'Well, not yet, anyway. Don't know. Ma would want me to.'

'Well, don't make any hasty decisions.' Libby thought for a moment. 'Is she going to carry on in the play?'

'Yes, she says she's coming back to rehearsals. I've been helping her with her lines.'

'Good boy. Do you want me to say anything to anybody?'

'No, I'll tell Pete.' She heard him sigh again. 'I

suppose I'd better tell Ben and Aunt Het and Aunt Flo, too.'

Libby sat down suddenly on the cane sofa. 'Flo? Flo Carpenter? Is she still alive?'

'Good Lord! Haven't you met Flo? Auntie Flo, of course, as we were brought up to call her. Very much alive. Not at Home Farm any more, of course. No, she lives in Maltby Close in the middle of the village. I thought you would have known.'

'No.' Libby made a mental note to have a quiet word with Peter about this.

'I'm surprised Lenny didn't go and see her while he was down. He was always very fond of her. Or perhaps he did?'

'I have no idea.' Libby thought for a moment. 'Do you still know her well? I mean, do you think she'd mind me going to see her? She does know about the play, I suppose?'

'Oh, yes, she knows. Hetty asked her and she was tickled pink at being played by a pretty young girl, I gather. She definitely wants to come and see it. So I'm sure she'd like to see you. Hang on – I've got her phone number here, somewhere.' Libby heard rustling. 'Here we are.' James gave her the number. 'It's number six, Maltby Close. You know, those rather nice small blocks of sheltered housing.'

'Yes, I know. And thanks, James. Remember, don't make any hasty decisions about Paula.' Libby stopped short of urging him to have a DNA test. 'Sorry I couldn't be more help about your mother. If you could just put her mind at rest about dragging the family in the mud–'

112

'Oh, don't worry about it. I expect she's starting senile dementia or something. Thanks for listening.'

For the rest of the day, Libby worried and wondered alternately about James and Flo Carpenter. On James's behalf, she felt outraged fury. Peter and Ben had obviously been right about Paula, who, in turn, had read James so accurately. Trapped in a scenario that belonged in the fifties, James would no more abandon her than he would his mother. To be fair, Libby acknowledged, he had to take responsibility for the pregnancy. Whatever happened to safe sex, she wondered.

Flo Carpenter, on the other hand, might be a source of information that both she and Peter had ignored for the play and, by inference, for the two sabotage attempts. Still wondering whether she wasn't making proverbial mountains out of irrelevant molehills, at about four-thirty Libby lifted the phone and dialled the number James had given her.

'Mrs Carpenter?'

'Yes?' The voice was obviously elderly, but by no means infirm.

'My name's Libby Sarjeant—'

'Oh, the one that's doing Peter's play?'

'Yes, that's me.' Libby grinned, pleased at this ready recognition.

'I'm coming to see it, you know.'

'Yes, so James tells me. I hope you won't think we've taken liberties with you all.'

'Oh, no, dear. Hetty showed me the book – what do you call it?'

'The script.'

'That's right. Well, I read it – bit difficult to read – not like a real book – but it seemed fine to me. And that young Paula's playing me, isn't she? What can I do for you?'

'I wondered if I could come and talk to you some time? You know, get some of your impressions of those days. It would help me enormously.' Libby crossed her fingers at this bending of the truth.

'Of course, dear, but I don't see how I can help,' came the doubtful reply. 'I mean, Peter got it all from Hetty, and you've talked to her as well, haven't you?'

'Not a lot, actually. She keeps herself to herself, doesn't she?'

'Yes, that's true. Well, come any time you like, dear. I'm always glad of company. Have you had your tea?'

'Er – no–' Libby replied, visions of cucumber sandwiches floating before her eyes.

'Come down here and have it with me, then. You're not far, are you?'

'No – Allhallow's Lane,' confirmed Libby, 'but I don't want to impose–'

'Don't be silly, girl. You've got to eat. Now I've got a nice steak and kidney pudding in the saucepan, how about that? Plenty for two, with some potatoes and a bit of cabbage.'

'Well, if you're sure,' said Libby doubtfully.

'Wouldn't have asked if I wasn't, would I? I'll see you in about half an hour – all right?'

Libby agreed that it was and put the phone down, lifting it almost immediately to ring the Pink Geranium.

'Harry, is Peter home today?'

114

'Yes, dear heart, he's right here getting in my way. I'll pass you over.'

'Hallo, you old trout. Got over Sunday's shenanigans?'

'I have – how about you?'

'Oh, I'm fine. TLC from Harry all evening – and didn't I lay it on – and all ill-effects had gone. Is that all you called about, my welfare?'

'Well no, not entirely. I've just been invited to supper with Flo Carpenter – or tea, as she called it.'

'Good heavens. There's an honour. Good cook, Auntie Flo, if you're not a veggie, of course.'

'You never told me she was still alive and living here.'

'Well, don't make it sound like an accusation, dearie. I never thought about it. After all, in our little entertainment she's not exactly germane, is she?'

'I suppose not. Do you happen to know if she likes wine? I'd like to take something with me.'

'She'll have plenty – had a good cellar, old Carpenter. But she likes a drop of stout, so you could take her a bottle or two of that. Oh – and you'll be in good company, she smokes like a trooper.'

'Gee, thanks,' said Libby wryly. 'I don't know where I'd be without you pandering to my ego.'

'You'd get above yourself, that's what. Listen, Flo likes to go to bed early, so when she chucks you out come over to us for a nightcap. Harry's closed this evening.'

Libby wrapped herself in her cape after tidying herself up and trying to do something with her

115

hair, and set off for the eight-till-late to buy stout and cigarettes.

Maltby Close led off the High Street and consisted of a converted barn and several other buildings constructed in the same style. Flo lived in the original barn and opened the door immediately to Libby's knock.

'Come in, ducks, come in.' She stood aside for Libby to enter. 'Bit warm in here, so I'll take your coat straight away.'

Gratefully, Libby peeled off her cape, juggling with basket and carrier bag at the same time. It was indeed a bit warm and she felt perspiration break out in all the expected places and some unexpected ones.

'Oh, ta, dear,' said Flo, accepting the carrier bag, 'just what I like. I opened a bottle of the nice claret for you – I hope you like red?'

Libby assured her she did and was led to a modern sitting-room furnished with enough antiques to stock a couple of shops. Two overstuffed chairs stood either side of an electric fire and Flo waved her to the one on the right.

'Glass of wine, now, or would you prefer something else?'

'Wine would be lovely.' Libby subsided into the armchair amid a billowing of scarves and unwound one from her neck, while accepting a large glass of red wine from her hostess.

'So, what was it you wanted to ask me?' Flo sat down in the armchair opposite and poured stout carefully into a tall glass, giving Libby the opportunity to study her. Shorter than Hetty, she was wiry and bird-like, her plentiful grey hair twisted neatly on top of her head. Huge red spectacles dangled on a jewelled chain over an obviously expensive cashmere jumper. She put the glass down after an appreciative sip and lit a cigarette.

'What you remember of the season when the play is set, really. What was Hetty like, and Gregory – and Joe Warburton, of course.'

Flo regarded her, head on one side like the bird she resembled.

'Depends whether you want the before or after version.'

'Before what? Do you mean the murder?'

'No – before she started going with Greg. That was when she changed.'

'Did she? In what way?'

Flo settled back in her chair and took another sip of stout. 'She was always a quiet, shy sort of a girl – very helpful to her mum – good with Millie, did as she was told, you know. Me, now, I was a different kettle of fish. A bold piece, my gran used to call me, but then I'd been spoilt. I was the only one and Mum was a dressmaker, so she always had work. There were no men in our house, either, so I was used to women doing what they wanted, while poor old Het and her mum lived under Ted's thumb – or fist. Cor! – knocked old Lillian about, he did.'

'So what happened when Hetty met Greg?' prompted Libby, when Flo seemed to go off in a trance.

'Well, we'd seen him the year before, see. He was a pole-puller in his holidays.'

'Pole-puller?'

'They walked about on stilts unhooking the

117

bines from the strings strung across the poles.'

'Bines?'

Flo frowned at her. 'Bines is the hop vines. Means a climbing shoot,' she added surprisingly, 'like, you know, columbine. Anyway, when we come down this year, Frank – that's my Frank, see, he introduced us. Mr Gregory, he called him. Well, you should've seen it. One look between those two and it was like firework night. And then, Hetty, she got bolder. Used to go off to meet Greg almost every afternoon when we'd finished picking, before dinner, and sometimes afterwards. She never told me where, but I'd cover for her if I could, although I was going off to see Frank, by then. 'Course my mum and gran didn't approve of me meeting Frank – said he was too old, but he was lovely and I didn't care. He treated me different from those boys in London – all hands, they was. Frank treated me like a lady. And he had a bit put by, and a reserved occupation, of course. When we got married he brought Mum and Gran down here as well. He was a good man.'

Libby let her gaze into the electric fire for a while before asking gently, 'And Hetty? What happened?'

'She got careless. There was this tallyman – Warburton. Oh, you know about him, don't you? Well, she wouldn't have none of him and he started putting in the needle. Found out about her and Greg and told Ted. You know all this, though, don't you?'

'Yes.' Libby lit a cigarette and watched the smoke spiral up to join Flo's. 'It's a bit difficult, really. You see – Lenny came down for a few days–'

118

'Yes, he came to see me.' Flo leered. 'I don't encourage him.'

'Oh.' Libby was startled.

'Oh, he always fancied me. Then I married Frank and he went off and became a wide boy. He tries to see me whenever he comes down – not that it's very often.'

'Did he say anything about the play?'

'No, I didn't give him a chance. I was going to whist. If he don't phone first, I can't be staying in, can I?' Flo looked triumphant and Libby smiled.

'No, of course not. It was just that a couple of things have happened over the last week – accidents, you know, and it worried Lenny.' She didn't add that it had worried everybody else as well. When you took the incidents out and gave them a good hard look, they didn't amount to much really.

'Worried him? How?' Flo sat forward, frowning.

'He thought at least one of the accidents had been set up for him.'

'What? To hurt him, you mean?' Libby realised that she had shocked Flo and felt guilty.

'Yes – but I think he was wrong.' Inspiration hit her. 'That's what I wanted to ask, you see. I would like to reassure him, but he wouldn't say why he thought someone would want to harm him, so I thought you'd be sure to know.'

Flo thought for a moment before stubbing out her cigarette. 'You mean it's something from them days?'

'He thought so.'

119

Flo shook her head. 'Can't be. Everyone knew what happened – that Warburton was found dead and Ted disappeared. Clear as daylight, weren't it? Nobody blamed the Fishers – although Lillian took them all back to London straightaway. Wouldn't even stay another night. 'Course, they didn't know Hetty was expecting Susan, then.'

'Did Lenny come back when Lillian and Hetty did?'

'No, 'cause of the war, see? No reason for him to. Then when he married That Woman–' Flo spoke in capital letters '–Lillian and Millie came back again. You know all that, too, don't you?'

Libby nodded. 'So is there anybody here who Lenny might have – oh, I don't know – upset? Annoyed?'

'No. Lenny was quite a mild chap in those days. He was always more worried about Ted doing something stupid. And quite right too, as it turned out.'

'What about Warburton? Did he have any family who might have – well, wanted revenge or something?'

'He had a mother. But she was a bit doolally even then. She wouldn't have known what was going on.' Flo pushed herself to her feet. 'That pudding'll be ready now. Come and sit down.'

The rest of the evening passed pleasantly. Flo was, as Peter had said, an extremely good cook and was interested in all aspects of the play, particularly Paula who was playing Lizzie – the part of Flo herself.

'Blonde, she ought to be. I was blonde.' Flo was clearing plates in to the tiny kitchen.

'Well, she's not exactly blonde,' said Libby doubtfully.

'As long as she's pretty,' said Flo firmly. 'I was.'

'Oh, she's pretty, all right,' said Libby. 'A bit too old, though.'

'Beggars can't be choosers,' said Flo obliquely. 'I remember when she come 'ere with her mum.'

'Paula? I thought she'd lived here for ever.'

'Nah. They come about the time young James was born. She'd be about six, then. Same age as Peter.'

'He thought she was younger. Didn't they go to school together?'

'Pete didn't go to the village school. Everyone wondered about 'em. Her mum was Mrs Wentworth, but I don't reckon she was married. They used to live over the butcher's shop in the High Street.' Flo wiped her hands on her apron. 'Then they got the cottage in Lendle Lane. Don't know how they afforded that. She didn't work.'

'Who? Paula's mum?'

'Delicate, she was. Died just before Paula went to London.'

Libby thought she might have found out why Paula was so keen to settle down. And surely she didn't want to end up as a single parent like her mother.

She took her leave at about half past nine.

'I've heard as you're seeing our Ben?' said Flo as she saw her out.

Libby blushed in the darkness. 'I wouldn't say seeing, exactly. He's been helping a bit with the play, and he designed the theatre, so I've seen a bit of him, naturally.'

121

'Hmm.' Flo squinted at her. 'Well, do you both good, if you ask me. He's done enough running around with these young birds. Needs a good solid woman of his own age.'

Refusing to be insulted by this unflattering description, Libby pulled her scarf tighter and bade Flo goodnight.

Peter and Harry were wearing matching towelling robes in navy blue and white. Libby told them they looked like a shot for a mail-order catalogue. Peter poured her a large whisky and she sat in her usual subsiding chair by the fire.

'Nice din-dins?' Peter flopped back into his corner of the sofa and Harry began to massage his feet.

'Lovely, thanks. And the wine was good. Oh, and thanks for the tip about the stout. She loved it.'

'So, did you get what you wanted?' Harry swivelled his eyes sideways at her.

'Er – yes. Corroborative detail – that sort of thing.' Libby felt herself colouring up and bent down for her whisky glass.

'Come on. What is it you're after really?' Peter swung his legs down and leaned forward, elbows on his knees.

Libby tried to think of something to say while avoiding both pairs of eyes trained on her like sniper guns.

'Look, if you're trying to get to the bottom of these accidents, you might as well give up.' Peter's voice held a warning note. 'My dear mama is troubled and has now got my brother worried, and little what's-er-face who's playing Becky is

122

behaving like Mariana of the Moated Grange. I don't know what's behind it and I don't want to.'

Libby's mouth set in a tight line of embarrassment and stubbornness.

'She doesn't agree, dear heart.' Harry smiled lazily through a haze of cigarette smoke.

Peter sighed, exasperated. 'Look, Lib, have you discussed this with Ben?'

'Sort of. Last night on the way back from rehearsal. We thought Lenny must have gone back to London before we started asking any more questions.'

'Well, then. Don't you think the sensible thing to do is stop asking them?'

It was Libby's turn to sigh. 'That's all very well, but I can't risk any more accidents. Someone could be really badly hurt. If it really is someone trying to frighten us off, they won't stop, don't you see?'

Peter sat back again, scowling like a Roman emperor.

'So what did you ask Flo?' Harry stood up and went to fetch Libby an ashtray.

'I asked what Hetty and Greg were like in the old days.'

'And did you get anything useful?'

Libby shook her head. 'No. I'd heard it all before. A couple of details that were new – like how Hetty changed when she met Greg, but that was all. Oh, and Warburton had a mother.'

Harry clapped his hand to his forehead. 'That's it, then. It's a one hundred and twenty year old woman seeking revenge.'

Peter pulled at the back of Harry's robe, which

123

threatened to fall apart. 'Sit down, you tart.'

'Well, it could be a family feud, couldn't it?' Harry sat down on the sofa.

'Flo said that she was a bit peculiar and wouldn't have known what was going on, so it can't be that.' Libby gazed thoughtfully into the fire. 'What I can't get over is how Millie, who was only a toddler at the time, is so bothered by all of this.'

Peter sighed. 'Well, she's going to have something else to worry about now, isn't she?'

A small silence fell. Libby glanced furtively at Harry, who shrugged.

'Look, I know he's told you. What do you think?' Peter leaned forward again.

'Er – James? Paula?'

'Of course.'

'I'm furious.'

Peter leaned back. 'Good. So are we all. So what do we do about it?'

'We can't do anything, can we? If James really is this baby's father then he has to take responsibility for it, but whatever happened to condoms?'

'Ah,' said Peter triumphantly, 'that's where it gets even more interesting. James thought she was still on the pill, and because they were still "in a relationship" as I believe the phrase goes, wasn't using any other protection. Remember when they went away for that weekend?'

Libby shook her head. 'No. Should I?'

'Suppose not. Well, that's when it was, apparently. He wanted to dump her and she decided he wasn't going to.'

'Libby's right, though, Pete,' said Harry. 'James is a big boy now, and we can't do anything. Anyway, your ma will be pleased, won't she? Means he'll be around and she'll have a grandchild.'

'That's what James said to me,' agreed Libby. 'And Flo told me Paula's mum was a single parent, so she won't want to end up the same. Where are they now?'

'James is in Canterbury in his flat. He phoned earlier.'

'Not with Paula?'

'No, apparently she had to go out. He didn't sound too bothered.'

'He doesn't really want to be with her, love,' Harry patted Peter's cheek.

'Not much comfort, though, is it?' said Peter. 'Still, it'll keep Mum off our backs for a bit, I suppose, at poor old Jamie's expense. Never happier than when messing about with babies, my mama.'

Libby reflected on this unlikely picture of the vacuum-packed Millie of her recollection. 'Golly,' she said.

Chapter Eleven

The telephone woke Libby again in the morning. Sidney, who was playing draught excluders across her bedroom doorway, severely impeded her progress and, once more, the answerphone cut in.

'Libby, it's Hetty. Please phone me back.'

Libby seized the receiver before Hetty could cut her off.

'Hetty, I'm here. What's the problem?'

'Libby? Is that you? Not the machine?'

'No, it's me. I didn't get to the phone in time.'

'More trouble, gel. Sorry about this.'

Libby felt her heart – or something else underneath her ribcage – give an unsettling lurch. 'What's happened?' she asked, through a mouth gone suddenly dry.

'Someone tried to set fire to the theatre.'

Libby was aware of several things at once. A feeling that all the blood had drained from her head to her feet, that Sidney was nudging her arm and yowling for breakfast and that it was raining.

'It's all right. Ben saw it and called the fire brigade. It's only the back bit – and there's not much damage.'

'Oh.' Libby swallowed hard. 'When was this?'

'Early hours of this morning. It had started raining, too, so that helped.'

'What was Ben doing up at that time?' Libby blurted out, regretting it immediately.

'I don't know.' Hetty sounded surprised, as well she might, thought Libby. 'Lucky he was, though.'

'Yes. Thank you for letting me know, Hetty. I'd better get down there, I suppose. Does Peter know?'

'Yes, Ben phoned him earlier. He didn't phone you. Said he didn't want to worry you.'

After Hetty had rung off, Libby sat down heavily and allowed Sidney to crawl all over her. She desperately needed someone to talk to, but who? Peter had become distinctly unsympathetic and Ben – Libby refused to think about Ben.

126

Feeling friendless, she let herself out of the cottage half an hour later, leaving Sidney on guard. The rain was still in the air as a sort of miasma, but its earlier heavier downpour had left sinister puddles in the ruts of Allhallow's Lane and progress was slow as Libby attempted a stepping stone advance.

At the back of the theatre, she met the residue of the fire crew and a black-coated individual who turned out to be an investigator, who asked her questions with accusation in a watery blue eye.

Finally convinced that the last thing in the world she would have done was to destroy the theatre, he left her and poked about a bit more along the blackened back wall. Libby stood miserably watching him, her cape wrapped tightly round her, until one of the fireman took pity on her and told her that there was no real damage – the gentleman had spotted it so quickly. Pity she couldn't think of anybody who might have done it, but he expected it was the same crowd of hooligans who'd had a field day with local schools recently. Libby tried to keep her face expressionless and thanked him, before turning away, wondering whether she ought to go up to The Manor to see Hetty, or just go home.

Her dilemma was resolved unexpectedly by the appearance of Millie, hurrying up the drive in designer wax jacket and green wellies.

'Mrs – er – Libby.' She pulled up, panting, in front of Libby. 'I've just heard. Isn't it awful?'

'The fire?' asked Libby, cautiously.

'Yes, of course. Peter's friend just told me.'

Faint colour appeared in her cheeks at this euphemistic description of Harry. 'I am so sorry.'

'Yes, it was a bit of a shock,' Libby agreed. 'The firemen and the investigator are still there, so I thought I'd leave them to it.'

'Well, there's nothing you can do, is there, dear?' Millie turned and took Libby's arm. 'Have you had breakfast?'

Surprised, Libby looked at her and shook her head. 'No, I didn't have time. I fed Sidney, though,' she added inconsequentially.

'Sidney?' Millie withdrew her arm.

'My cat.'

'Oh.' Millie let her smile come back. 'Well, why don't you come back with me? I don't bother to cook breakfast just for myself these days but I'm sure we could both do with something.'

Puzzled, and on the point of refusing, Libby stopped. She had to get to the bottom of Millie's change of attitude somehow – what better way than this?

'Thank you – that's very kind of you. If you're sure it's no trouble?'

What stupid platitudes we do come out with in the guise of social behaviour, she thought as Millie disclaimed. Of course it was trouble to cook for somebody else – especially unexpectedly. On the other hand, Millie wouldn't have offered if, for one reason or another, she hadn't wanted to. Perhaps, thought Libby, as they started to walk, James had told his mother about Paula and the baby and Millie wanted to talk about it. Though why on earth she would want to talk to me, thought Libby, goodness alone knows.

Steeple Farm was at the other end of the village. The road wound up between banks until they could have been miles from civilisation. Millie was not a conversationalist while she was walking, but the silence, which Libby thought at first was total, was, in fact, charged with a hundred tiny, unidentifiable sounds – insects, rustling undergrowth, birdsong, far-off farmyard sounds, even, modified and gentled by distance, the sound of a tractor. A watery sun appeared between sullen black clouds, and Libby looked up at the house, some of its small-paned windows molten in the sun, two of them staring blackly from under eyebrows of thatch. Libby shivered. What should have been a picture book cottage somehow wasn't.

'Come in.' Millie opened the heavy oak door and Libby stepped into an anachronism. The hall floor, which she guessed was flagged, was covered in a thick red carpet, the walls painted cream, with gilt touches in the wall lights, switches and chain store picture frames. A teak telephone table, complete with cushioned seat and space for directories, stood by the stairs. Millie led the way into the kitchen, a magazine dream in pale wood and stainless steel, and pulled out a chair from the matching table.

'Coffee? Or tea?' she asked, shedding her jacket and going to a door at the far end of the kitchen, which proved to contain a coat lobby.

'Tea, please.' Libby tried to remove her cape unobtrusively and got one arm trapped.

'Let me take your – er–' offered Millie, coming forward revealed in smart skirt and jumper and court shoes. Libby breathed heavily and man-

129

aged to relinquish the cape.

'Bacon and eggs?' Millie was plugging in an all-singing, all-dancing kettle.

'Lovely. What a treat,' said Libby, smiling brightly.

'Yes, it is, isn't it? I find I don't eat terribly well now I'm on my own. Peter insists that I go to his friend's restaurant, but I'm not very fond of vegetarian food, I'm afraid, so I don't go often. James comes for Sunday lunch most weeks of course.'

'Oh,' said Libby, not able to think of anything else.

'It's a shame, really, because since I've had this new kitchen installed, I don't really get the chance to use it. I always wanted something like this, but Peter's father wouldn't let me change it. It's lovely now.' She looked around with satisfaction. 'So bright.'

'What was it like before?' asked Libby.

'Oh, shelves – the old dresser – no storage, really, except the larder. And that dreadful Aga, of course. Not even one of the new ones – an old cream one, it was. Terrible to cook with.' She slid bacon under a grill and broke an egg into a pan. Libby tried not to feel outraged on behalf of the old kitchen and watched as the sliced bread went into the toaster.

'I could live with just my microwave, I think, couldn't you?' Millie put a delicate translucent cup of pale tea in front of Libby, whose Assam-conditioned nose caught a whiff of Earl Grey.

'I quite like my Rayburn, actually,' Libby confessed and watched Millie's unreal eyebrows shoot up into her helmet of blonde hair.

'Really? Well, I suppose if you've never had one before they can be quite a novelty.'

'I expect that's it,' agreed Libby, chastened.

'There. You're looking much more cheerful now.' Millie smiled. 'Drink your tea. I won't be long.'

By the time Libby had battled her way through the weak, perfumed liquid in front of her, Millie had served up two antiseptic-looking plates of bacon, egg and toast.

'Terrible for the calories, of course,' she said chattily, as she sat down and shook out a snowy napkin. Libby shot her a suspicious glance but decided there was nothing untoward in this remark and picked up her knife and fork.

'So what will you do now?' Millie fixed a bright eye on Libby and chewed her toast thoroughly.

'Eh?' Libby dropped a piece of squishy fried egg back on to her plate.

'At the Oast House. What will happen?'

Libby frowned. 'I'm sorry, I don't know what you mean.'

'Will it be repaired? As a theatre? I wouldn't have thought it would be worth it. Throwing good money after bad, I'd call it.' Millie put her knife and fork together neatly and picked up her coffee cup.

'Ah.' A lot of things became clearer to Libby. Millie's astonishing friendliness, for one thing. 'I'm sorry, Millie. Harry can't have explained properly. There was a fire, but Ben spotted it and called the fire brigade before it did any real damage. We've just got rather a black wall at the

131

back, that's all.'

Millie's mouth had remained open throughout this explanation and her colour, much to Libby's interest, had fluctuated from red to white and back to red again. Finally, she closed her mouth with an audible snap and stretched it into a smile.

'What a relief for you all, then,' she said, her voice sounding like chalk on a blackboard. 'Harry's so dramatic.' She picked up her knife and fork and poked viciously at a piece of bacon.

Harry's so mischievous, Libby corrected mentally. She could just hear him giving Millie a gleefully exaggerated version of the fire. 'Yes,' she said aloud, 'it is a relief. At least it won't affect the play. We can carry on with rehearsals and nothing has been damaged.'

Millie's smile remained fixed. 'Of course,' she said, and abandoned what remained of her breakfast, pushing the plate away with a jerky movement.

Libby felt uncomfortable. 'May I help you with the washing up?' She stood and collected her plate and cup.

Millie came to life. 'No, no. It'll all go in the dishwasher. Such a boon, aren't they?' she added, with a return to her former manner.

'Oh, yes,' agreed Libby, who no longer had one.

'I shall buy one for James, of course.'

Libby's mind skittered around trying to follow Millie's quantum leap of conversation. 'Oh?' she said.

'He'll need one, won't he? Him and – the baby.'

She knows, then, but what a strange way of

putting it, thought Libby. 'Yes, I suppose it would be very handy, but the washing machine's the most essential thing with a new baby, isn't it?' she said.

'He's got a lovely washing machine in his flat. I expect he'll move it down here when he comes.'

'Oh, he's moving into Paula's cottage, is he?' Made the decision, then, thought Libby.

'Yes, I think so,' said Millie, vaguely. 'It's bound to be better than hers.'

Washing machine, not cottage, interpreted Libby, and wondered if she should offer congratulations on impending grandmotherhood. Somehow, it didn't seem appropriate.

'Thank you so much for breakfast,' she said at the door. 'It was lovely to be looked after for a change.'

'Any time,' said Millie, and Libby sensed the withdrawing into herself as Millie closed the door almost before she'd finished speaking.

The sun had retired hurt once again, and Libby sloshed through muddy puddles back to the village. Ferocious brambles caught at her cape as, more than once, she was forced into the hedge to let arrogant four-wheel-drive vehicles push past her. She found herself thinking longingly of town and metalled roads with pavements and by the time she reached the Pink Geranium, had decided what to do.

'Harry?' She pushed open the door and called.

'Hallo, dear heart.' Harry appeared from the kitchen in his leather trousers, pink shirt and an enveloping white apron. 'What can I do for you? Come for a bit of tea and sympathy?'

133

'No, I've just had that, thanks.' Libby pulled out a chair and sank down.

'Oh?' Harry raised an eyebrow and sat astride a chair opposite. 'And who was the dispenser?'

'Millie.' Libby enjoyed the reaction to her revelation and giggled. 'And it's all your fault. You told her about the fire and she came rushing up to gloat.'

'Did she?' Harry leaned his elbows on the table. 'And were you there?'

'We met on the drive, so she didn't actually see what damage had been done. She just assumed I was devastated and carted me off home for breakfast. I admit, I was puzzled at first. Then, of course, I told her that we had no damage. She was riveted.'

'I bet. So all her efforts were wasted?'

'Efforts?' repeated Libby, startled.

'Conciliating you.'

'Oh, I see. Yes. She couldn't get rid of me quick enough when she realised she couldn't gloat. Poor old Peter. Fancy having a mother like that. Did you know she ripped out a perfectly good kitchen – and an Aga?'

'Her loss was our gain, dearie.'

'Oh – I see. The dresser?'

'All of it. It doesn't fit as well in our cottage as it did at the farmhouse, but it looks better than the seventies Formica that we had before. And I adore the Aga.'

'Well, that's all right then.' Libby sat up straight. 'Look, I'm off to London this morning and I don't know what time I shall be back. Could you ask Peter if he would take tonight's rehearsal until

I am?'

'This is so sudden. What are you doing in London?'

'I'm going to see Lenny.' Libby stood up.

Harry shook his head. 'Pete won't like it.'

Libby refrained from the obvious retort. 'I can't see why not.'

'He just wants to let it lie. I think if he could, he'd give up the idea of the play.'

Libby was shocked. 'Peter? After all his hard work? Don't be silly, Harry. He's been saying that for the last week but he doesn't really mean it.'

'Well, it does seem to be fated, dear, doesn't it? I think Ben's much of the same opinion.'

'Ben?' Libby's voice rose. 'How do you know?'

'He came to the cottage. He and Pete were closeted together for ages. I was quite jealous.'

'Well, I don't care. I'm going. I was going to ask you for Lenny's address.'

'Well, that would be no good, 'cause I've not got it. Flo would have, though.' Harry got up to see her to the door.

'Thanks, Harry.' Libby stood on tiptoe to kiss his cheek. 'You're a pal.'

Back in the cottage she revised her opinion. She had just put down the phone after obtaining Lenny's address from Flo when the phone rang again.

'Libby?'

Her breathing quickened.

'Hallo, Ben.'

'What's all this about you going to see Lenny?'

That was quick of Harry, she thought. 'I thought

I would.'

'Why?'

'I thought he might tell me what he was worried about. So that we could put a stop to this stupidity once and for all.'

'Well, I think you're wrong.'

'Why? You were saying only the other night that Lenny would know what was going on. We discussed it, remember?'

Ben was silent.

'Anyway,' Libby went on, after a decent interval, 'I'm going to see Lenny. Now we've had the fire, I think it's even more important to get to the bottom of all this.'

'Do you?'

'Yes, I do. And by the way, how come you spotted the fire so quickly? Hetty said it was the middle of the night. What were you doing up at that time?'

Libby heard a quick intake of breath even as she berated herself for sounding so suspicious.

'I was coming home,' Ben replied, coldly.

'Ah,' said Libby and felt her stomach fall untidily round her boots. 'Well, I must get on. I want to be back in time for rehearsal tonight.'

'Why don't you cancel it? It would be much easier. I understand you've asked Peter to take it?'

'They need every rehearsal they can get if we're to open on time,' said Libby firmly, although her insides felt like mush. 'And now, I really must go. Goodbye, Ben.'

Resisting the urge to howl all over a protesting Sidney, Libby went upstairs and changed into what she considered appropriate for visiting London.

Not that this was exactly London, she reflected, as she negotiated Bromley's one-way system, which seemed designed to confuse the enemy and keep them well away from Bromley itself. When she eventually navigated herself into a broad tree-lined avenue she felt completely wrung out.

Coniston House was one of many large, detached Edwardian villas that stood back from the pavement protected by a broad sweep of gravelled drive. Inside, Libby sniffed surreptitiously and was rewarded by an indistinct smell of polish, cocoa and disinfectant, nothing more suspicious. She was relieved.

Underneath the curving majesty of a mahogany staircase, a little table, illuminated by a gold-shaded lamp, was enhanced by a young lady of almost greetings-card perfection.

'May I help you?' she asked Libby, with a glowing smile and in accents reminiscent of Millie's.

'I've come to visit Mr Fisher,' said Libby, wondering if she should ask whether he was at home, or whether this was superfluous.

'May I have your name?' The vision lifted the receiver of a sleek black telephone.

'Libby Sarjeant.' Libby stopped herself adding the "with a J" and waited while a number was punched into the phone.

'Mr Fisher? Oh, there's a lady in reception to see you. A Mrs Sarjeant. Shall I send her up?'

The vision listened, nodded and replaced the receiver before turning back to Libby. 'He says to go up. First floor, turn right, room number ten.'

The corridor was quiet, carpeted to a thickness hitherto untrodden by Libby, and punctuated at intervals by highly polished console tables with uniform arrangements of flowers. It didn't seem a bit like Lenny.

'Libby.' He opened the door and grinned widely. 'This is a pleasure, girl. Come in. Want a drink?'

'No, thanks, Lenny. I'm driving.' Libby sat down in a pink dralon armchair and looked round.

'All a bit prissy, ain't it?' said Lenny, going to a sideboard and pouring himself a large brandy. 'Still, it's better than looking after meself. All these things belonged to Shirley, of course. Not my taste.'

'Shirley?'

'My wife – late wife, I should say.'

'Oh. I thought she–' Libby stopped, wondering if she would ever get the hang of thinking before she spoke.

'Left me for another bloke? She did. But that was ten years ago – or more. She wore herself out, silly cow, going off with a younger man. Should've known she couldn't keep up the pace.'

'So did you never think of marrying again?' Libby knew she was being sidetracked, but couldn't think of a way to bring up the subject of the play and the theatre.

Lenny solved the problem for her.

'Oh, yes, I wanted to get married again. I always wanted old Flo.' He nodded and his eyes looked past Libby into his memory. 'Always fancied her. She was Het's best friend in London, you know. Known her all me life. Good woman, that. Bit of a flirt when she was younger, mind,

138

but a good friend. Good friend to our Het, anyway.'

'In the old days, you mean?'

'Yeah. And later on, of course, when old Greg came back from the war wounded. She helped Het run that farm along with Frank.'

Hang on, we've skipped a bit, thought Libby. Aloud she said, 'When did she actually meet Frank? When Hetty met Greg?'

'We'd all known him years, but the first time she let him come courting was that year Het took up with Greg, yeah. She was good to Het, then.' He shook his head and sat in silence for a minute while Libby racked her brains for a tactful way to ask her questions.

'So what did you want to see me about, girl? You didn't come for the good of your health, I'll be bound.' He took a healthy swallow of brandy and sat back in his chair.

Libby took a deep breath.

'I want to know what's going on, Lenny. You were there for two of the accidents which seemed directed at the theatre – or the play – or something to do with the family and then you came back home. Last night, someone tried to set fire to the theatre. Luckily, Ben saw it and called the fire brigade, so there's virtually no damage. But someone's got it in for us, and from what you said, you think you know who. And unless I find out and put a stop to it, we'll have no play – and more important, no theatre.'

Lenny sat looking down into his brandy glass for so long that Libby wondered if he'd dozed off.

'It's my fault, you know, girl. I go round saying things. Geeing people up. I don't know nothing, really, but people think I do.'

Libby regarded him balefully. 'That's no answer. Even if you know nothing, someone thinks you do. Who is it?'

Lenny shifted in his chair and fiddled with the stem of his glass. 'No idea. How could I have when I don't know what I'm talking about?'

Libby gave vent to a hefty sigh of exasperation. 'Look, do you want to see this play go on?'

Lenny looked up. 'I don't know,' he said simply.

Libby's mouth tightened. 'What?'

'I don't know,' he repeated. 'If it's causing trouble – and it is – perhaps you should call it off. It's my family, don't forget.'

Libby sat back in her chair and glared moodily at the toe of her boot. 'You're all the same. You, Ben, Peter...'

'Why, what have they done?'

'They're both warning me off, now, after being on my side to start with. I mean,' she went on, sitting forward again, 'it was Peter who came up with the idea of the theatre and the play in the first place and Ben who put them into action and saw them through. Why have they changed their minds?'

Lenny shrugged. 'Family, ducks. That's what it'll be.'

'But how do you know it's anything to do with the family? A wire was cut on a piece of scenery in the play, and a bridge was damaged when anybody – anybody at all – could have walked over it. The fire could just be mischief, as the fireman said this

140

morning. So where does the family come into it? Unless you all know something I don't.'

'What do they say about it, then?' Lenny parried.

'They won't. And yet they were both on my side, as I said – Ben was still speculating about why you'd run off home only a couple of nights ago. Then suddenly they've both changed sides. I feel like a leper.'

Lenny shrugged. 'Can't help you, girl. I don't know nothing about it.'

'Now why don't I believe you?' Libby was getting angry, a fairly common occurrence these days. 'I believed Flo. I believed everything she said to me. But you...'

'When did you see Flo?' interrupted Lenny, his eyes bright. 'Did she say anything about me?'

'Yes, she did. She said you were a wide boy and she didn't give you any encouragement.'

Lenny's face fell.

Libby relented. 'But I think she likes you.'

'Oh, yeah, she always liked me. I was too young for her at first, see? Then she went and married old Frank and that was that.'

'Well, you're both free now, aren't you? And if you want a piece of advice, next time you want to see her, let her know in advance. Make an arrangement to go down. Take her flowers. She doesn't want to be taken for granted – for you to think that she's always there whenever you want to see her.'

Lenny looked at her as though he'd seen the Holy Grail. 'You reckon?'

'I reckon,' Libby said, 'although why I should help you I can't think. You haven't done much to

141

help me.'

Lenny looked shamefaced. 'Nothing I can do, girl. I don't know what's going on. Really, I don't.'

Libby stood up, wrapping her cape and scarf round her. 'Bit of a wasted journey, then, wasn't it?'

Lenny struggled to his feet. 'No, it ain't. It's nice to see someone. I get lonely. Tell you what. It's gorn lunchtime, but how about we go out for tea? There's a lovely restaurant down the road does a smashing tea – cucumber sandwiches and everything.'

Libby looked at his eager face and grinned. 'All right, Lenny. Sounds good. As long as I get back at a reasonable time.'

The restaurant, all pale wood and pastel prints, did indeed do a smashing tea. Lenny blossomed in his role as gentleman gallant and Libby realised what a waste it was – him up here and lonely and Flo in Steeple Martin, not lonely, it was true, but able to provide Lenny with everything he wanted and needed.

'Now, don't forget,' she said, as he waited while she unlocked her car. 'Next time you come down, ring Flo and arrange to go and see her – or take *her* out for tea. Harry would do you a nice tea in the Pink Geranium if you asked him.'

'I'll give it some thought.' Lenny suddenly leaned forward and kissed her cheek. 'You're a good girl. Don't you let our Ben get away.'

Libby smiled ruefully as she climbed behind the wheel. 'I think he already did,' she said.

Chapter Twelve

Libby arrived home earlier than she expected and, due to Lenny's cucumber sandwiches and cream cakes, didn't bother with supper. After feeding Sidney she went to check the answer-phone, realising as she did so that, once again, she'd forgotten to take her mobile with her.

The number five was flashing insistently at her, and she frowned as she pressed the button. Five? No one needed her that urgently, did they?

'Libby, call me back. This is urgent.' Ben's voice.

'Lib, pick it up if you're there. Why don't you take your bloody mobile?' Peter's voice.

'Me again.' She heard Ben sigh impatiently before he put the phone down.

'Er – Mrs Sarjeant, this is, er – Detective Sergeant Cole, Canterbury Police Station. Could you call me back, please.' The strange voice gave a number and Libby's frown grew deeper. She was aware of the strange sensation under her rib-cage that she knew was an adrenalin surge – but this time which was it, fight or flight?

The next one was James. 'Libby, could you call me back? I'm at Mum's – at least I am at the moment.' There was a pause. 'Er – just thought – well, anyway, thanks.'

And then the disembodied electronic voice: 'You have no more messages.'

Oh, my God, thought Libby sinking down on to Sidney's favourite step. What's happened now?

Unwilling to find out, she pottered about, checking the studio, lighting a fire and generally pretending to be a normal, organised middle-aged woman. Eventually, aware of the fact that she was mentally putting her hands over her ears, she sat down by the telephone with a pad and pencil and reran the messages. Carefully noting the number Detective Sergeant Cole had given, she took a deep breath and punched it in.

Clearing throat. 'Detective Sergeant Cole?'

'Speaking.'

'Ah – this is – erm – Libby Sarjeant, with a J.' Pause. 'Mrs Elizabeth.'

'Mrs Sarjeant, yes. I've been waiting for your call.'

'Oh. Ah. Have you? I've only just got in. When did you call?'

'This afternoon, madam. I did come to your house, but there was no reply.'

'I wasn't here.'

'No, madam, I realise that. Mr Wilde and Mr Parker told me you were away. Have you heard from either of the gentlemen since you returned home?'

Libby's stomach was sinking so fast she had difficulty speaking.

'Something's happened, hasn't it?' she managed. 'Is it the theatre? What's happened?'

'Ah, yes, the theatre. The gentlemen told me about the incidents connected with the theatre. No, madam, it's not to do with the theatre – not exactly, anyway.'

'The children?' Libby's voice rose with a squawk and her head began to swim.

'No,' she heard from a distance. 'It's a Miss Paula Wentworth.'

'Paula?' Libby snapped to attention. 'What's she done?'

'Nothing, I'm afraid, madam. You've not heard from her, then?'

'Oh, God, she's disappeared. No, not for days. James – her, well, her boyfriend, did give me a message, but I haven't seen her since the – er, since we had a – well, an accident.'

'I heard about that, madam. No, I'm afraid it's not that. Miss Wentworth is dead.'

'Dead?'

'Yes, madam. I'm sorry.'

'No, no,' Libby began, and stopped. Her thoughts didn't seem to be in any sort of order at all. She wondered if this was the beginning of a descent into dementia. She started again.

'Paula's dead?'

'Yes, madam.'

'Was it the baby?'

'Baby?' Cole's voice sharpened. 'She had a baby?'

'No, she was pregnant. Wasn't it that?'

'No, madam.' The sergeant was speaking slowly, as if reorganising his brain. 'We haven't yet had the post-mortem results.'

'Post-mortem? What for?'

'I'm afraid she was found dead in her car this morning.' The sergeant's voice was now flat and unemotional.

'Suicide?' gasped Libby. Her pencil snapped

145

in two.

'I'm afraid not, madam. It would appear to have been a deliberate killing.'

Libby had been through so many odd sensations in the last few minutes she wouldn't have thought there was anything left, but this was entirely new. A sort of explosion of physical and mental symptoms that left her unable to speak.

'Did you hear me, madam? Mrs Sarjeant?'

'Yes,' said Libby, forcing her voice through an almost closed throat. 'Murder?'

'It looks like it, madam. I'm very sorry.'

'No, no,' said Libby again. 'No, it's all right. Murder. Oh, God.'

Sergeant Cole cleared his throat. 'Would it be convenient to come and have a word with you, madam? This evening?'

'Me? Why? Well, yes, if you need to. Whenever you like.'

'We'll be with you as soon as we can, madam. Thank you.'

It was only after she'd put the receiver down that she wondered why she'd been connected with Paula. Her mind shied away from the name.

She rang Peter, unwilling to speak to Ben.

'Lib! Where have you been? I've been trying to get hold of you.' He sounded more agitated than Libby had ever heard him.

'About Paula.' Libby took a deep breath and closed her eyes as she said the name.

'You've heard. Did Ben tell you?'

'No, the police. A Detective Sergeant Cole.'

'Ah, right. Has he been round?'

'No, he phoned. He's coming this evening.'

146

'I've cancelled the rehearsal,' said Peter after a pause.

'Oh, God, I'd forgotten that. What are we going to do?'

'I don't know. I suppose we'd better talk about it.' Libby heard him sigh. 'I really think this is the last straw.'

'You want to call it off.'

'How can we go on?'

Libby felt her throat close and tears start behind her eyes. How ridiculous, to cry over the play when there was something far more awful to cry over.

'What does Ben say?' As if I didn't know, she thought.

'He hasn't said much. Look, I must go. Call me after PC Plod's been to see you and we'll go for a drink. I think we all need one.'

'All right, if he doesn't arrest me. Has he seen you?'

Peter laughed. 'Oh, yes. He's seen all of us.'

And that doesn't tell me anything, thought Libby, as she stared out of the window waiting for the constabulary to call.

She didn't have long to wait. She saw a dark saloon roll gently to a halt just past the cottage and dropped the curtain. A moment later there was a sharp knock on the door.

'Mrs Sarjeant? I'm DS Cole. This is DC Burnham.' DS Cole flashed his ID, just like the TV, thought Libby, and indicated a young woman with pale blonde hair and glasses standing just behind him.

'Come in,' said Libby and moved into the

sitting room. She managed to clear enough space for all three of them to sit and ejected Sidney from the coffee table.

DS Cole regarded her impassively from dark eyes. His thin moustache reminded Libby of a 1950s spiv – George Cole, perhaps, in the St Trinian's films. Oh, God, his name was Cole. She vainly tried to suppress an inappropriate bubble of laughter.

'Now, Mrs Sarjeant. Perhaps you could tell me your full name and address.'

'But you're here. You know my address. And my name.'

'For the record, madam. DC Burnham will be making notes.'

Libby glanced at DC Burnham, and, sure enough, there was the little notebook that they always produced in court. ("Did you make these notes contemporaneously, Constable?"). She gave her name and address.

'And when did you last see the deceased?'

'At a rehearsal at our theatre. Last week? So much seems to have happened. Yes, last Tuesday. I think.'

DS Cole looked at his own notebook. 'And that would have been the night there was an accident at the theatre?'

'Yes.' Libby felt a blush rise up her neck. 'I suppose we should have reported it.'

'No one was hurt, were they, madam?' Cole's dark eyebrows rose sharply.

'Well, no, but we were all very shocked.' Libby wondered if Ben had told them about the cut wire. Surely not.

'No need to report it, then. And how was Miss Wentworth when you last saw her?'

'Shocked, I told you, we all were. She didn't turn up after that. James told me she wasn't well.'

'And that would be Mr James Parker?'

Libby nodded.

'How long have you known Miss Wentworth, Mrs Sarjeant?' The dark brown eyes were fixed on her again, like pools of mud with no light in them at all.

'Several years. We all belong to an amateur dramatic society near here.'

'And this is your theatre? The – ah – the Oast House Theatre?'

'Oh, no. We belong to another group. But some of us live here, in Steeple Martin, and when Peter wrote his play based on the story of his aunt and uncle, his cousin Ben decided to convert the oast house into a theatre for the local community.' Libby paused for breath. 'But I suppose you know all this already.'

DS Cole gave no sign that he knew anything. 'These gentlemen being Mr Peter Parker, Mr James Parker's brother, and Mr Benjamin Wilde?'

'Yes.'

'And did you have any closer connection with Miss Wentworth, Mrs Sarjeant?'

'Closer connection?' Libby was bewildered. 'No. She wasn't a friend, or anything like that.'

'Oh? I understood she knew all the gentlemen we've mentioned rather well.' DS Cole was watching her carefully. Even DC Burnham looked up from her notebook, light glinting off her glasses unnervingly.

149

'Well, better than I did, probably. I've only recently moved here from the other side of Canterbury.'

There was a pause.

'This accident at the theatre,' said DS Cole suddenly. 'Any chance it could have been aimed at Miss Wentworth?'

'I'm sure it wasn't.' Libby shook her head firmly. 'Anybody could have been hurt.'

'And the bridge? I understand that was sabotaged?'

God, he knew everything.

'Peter – Mr Parker – thought so. He was the one who fell in.'

'And the fire?'

'The investigator thought it might be local kids.' Libby took a deep breath. She could feel panic rising. 'That was last night. When was Paula – er – found?'

'This morning, madam. In her car.'

'Where?'

'Near her home.' Libby could almost hear him saying "We'll ask the questions", but he didn't.

'Who found her?'

'Dr David Dedham.'

'Oh, lord. Well, I suppose he was able to do anything necessary.'

'There wasn't much anyone could do, madam. Miss Wentworth had been dead some hours by the time she was found.'

'Oh.' Libby swallowed hard, trying not to imagine the body of Paula gradually stiffening, and worse, in her little blue car. 'How was she – I mean, did you...'

'Could I ask you what you were doing between midnight and six o'clock this morning, Mrs Sarjeant? Just for the record.' DS Cole's moustache was virtually twitching with anticipation as he ignored Libby's question.

'Oh, golly.' Libby tried to force her mind back to last night. 'Well, I went to supper with a Mrs Carpenter in the village, then I went to see Peter Parker and his friend Harry Price, then I came home. Mrs Wilde from the Manor phoned me to tell me about the fire at about seven this morning and woke me up.'

'And were you alone, madam?' DS Cole stared at her.

'Yes.' Libby suppressed a feeling of indignation. Who did he think he was, asking all these questions?

'Thank you,' he said, suddenly standing up. 'You've been most helpful.' I have? thought Libby. 'First of all, would you read over the notes DC Burnham has taken and sign them if you think they're correct? And if you wouldn't mind coming in to the station at some time over the next couple of days to sign a statement?'

'Of course.' Libby stood up, flicked through the proffered notebook and signed at the end of the notes. 'Does it matter when?'

'Several of your friends are coming in, so perhaps you could travel together.' DS Cole ushered DC Burnham to the door, his hand unnecessarily close to her bottom. 'Thank you, madam.'

Libby closed the door behind them and watched surreptitiously through the window as they got into the dark saloon and reversed too

151

fast down Allhallow's Lane. She reached for the phone.

'Pete? They've gone.'

'Meet you in the pub in five minutes, then. Or do you want to come here?'

'I don't mind. I just want some answers.'

'Pub, then. I'll call Ben and James.'

The pub was packed, and as Libby pushed her way towards Peter standing at the bar, she was aware of curious glances being sent in her direction. Peter turned and put a drink in her hand.

'Good timing,' he said. 'Ben and Harry are over in the corner. We managed to get a table, God knows how.'

'So what happened?' Libby squeezed in beside Harry at the small table. She looked from one drawn face to the other. 'Ben? What happened?'

Ben drew in a deep breath and looked at her briefly. 'David found her in her car.'

'I know that. The police told me. But when? Do they think it was to do with the fire?'

Ben looked up quickly. 'What makes you say that? Did they say something?'

'No, they didn't even seem very interested. Just wanted to know where I was during the night. Sidney didn't provide a reliable alibi.'

The weak joke fell flat, as she'd known it would. Harry still hadn't looked up. She touched his arm.

'Harry? I didn't think you knew her very well?'

'Well, you can think again, dear heart,' said Peter, sitting down suddenly between Libby and Ben. 'I think "very well" covers it, don't you, Hal?'

Libby stared, her mouth open. Ben caught her

152

eye and gave her a twisted grin. 'What did I tell you? Female piranha.'

'I don't know what to say.' Libby looked down in to her glass.

'There's no need for any comment, thanks,' said Harry.

An uncomfortable silence followed, while Libby wiped droplets off her glass with a fingertip, Ben drummed his fingers on the table while gazing off into the distance, Peter stared at Harry and Harry scowled at the table.

Eventually, Libby cleared her throat. 'I thought you wanted to meet up, Pete? Not much point if we're not going to talk, is there?'

Everyone shifted in their seats and looked at everyone else.

Peter sighed. 'You're right. So,' he leaned his elbows on the table and steepled his fingers, 'what did the estimable Mr Cole say to you?'

'Well, he told me David had found – er – *her*, she'd been dead some hours and he obviously knew all about you and James and the theatre. That's all.'

'That's it, in a nutshell.' Ben finished the drink in front of him. 'My poor brother-in-law is very shaken up. He found her when he was on his rounds, tucked into the woods on the side of Lendle Lane.'

'That was where she lived, wasn't it?' asked Libby.

'Yes. A no-through road. She always parked her car opposite her house under the trees.'

'So how did David come to see her? Where was he going?' asked Harry.

153

'To see a patient further up the lane, apparently.' Ben shrugged. 'Don't ask me why he stopped and looked in her car.'

'How did she – I mean, did David say–'

'How she died? No. The police didn't say, either, but I suppose there's no doubt. If it might be an accident they'd be dealing with it differently, surely?'

'So how come they got on to us?' Libby asked, after a moment.

'David told them about James and when they got in touch with Millie, she told them about the theatre and the play and all of us.'

'Thank you, Mother.' Peter looked round at the glasses. 'Anyone ready for another?'

'I'll get them,' said Ben, and began to make his way to the bar.

'Do they think this is anything to do with the theatre?' Libby chewed her lip anxiously. 'I mean, it can't be, can it?'

'They were very interested in all our little accidents,' said Harry. 'I'm surprised they didn't grill you about them more.'

'I told you, they didn't seem all that interested. Just in my movements.'

'They're more interested in our Paula's relationships, which includes James, Ben – my God, I didn't know about that one – Harry, and by association, me.' Peter looked at Harry.

'You?' said Libby.

'In case I was murderously jealous.'

'Oh.'

Harry looked up under his eyebrows. 'As if,' he said.

'Listen, this is private, between you two,' said Libby uncomfortably. 'I shouldn't be listening.'

'PC Plod knows, so why not you?' Peter said reasonably.

'And how did he find out?'

'I told him.' Harry looked away.

'What?' Libby gasped. 'Why?'

'Because they always find out in the end, and I'm sick of reading those books where some idiot keeps things to himself and makes things worse. And on telly. Stupid.'

Libby looked at Peter, who shrugged.

'Well,' she said, 'I told them about Paula being pregnant. Inadvertently. I assumed she'd died because of the baby. But they didn't know about it. They hadn't got the post-mortem results yet.'

'They wouldn't have. It's not being done until tomorrow.' Ben appeared with fresh glasses.

'I had a message from James as well. Didn't he tell them?'

'Obviously not.' Ben lifted his glass but didn't drink.

'Is he coming here?'

'No.' Peter looked at Harry quickly. 'He's with Mum.'

'Ah.' Libby looked surreptitiously at them all and decided this whole gathering was a pointless exercise. She took a swallow of her fresh drink and stood up. 'Let me know what you decide about the play. I'll have to go along with the rest of you.'

'You going?' Harry looked up, surprised.

'Not much point in staying. None of us is exactly convivial. I'd better go home and phone the cast.'

'I told you, I'd already cancelled rehearsal,' said Peter.

'I know, but they need to know what's happening in the long term,' said Libby, and saw his face redden as he looked down at his drink. 'Oh. You've already taken the decision without telling me.'

'Be fair, Lib. You weren't there to ask,' said Ben.

Libby didn't trust herself to speak and nodded. Peter stood up and kissed her on the cheek.

'See you tomorrow,' he said gently. 'I'll call you in the morning.'

Libby nodded again and turned to go, lifting a hand to the table in general. Ben lifted a hand in response, looking bewildered, and Harry winked.

Outside the pub the wind was getting up. It whipped Libby's cape backwards and brought tears to her eyes – or increased them, at any rate, she thought, feeling foolish as she started to battle up the High Street.

'Oi, wait up, petal.' A hand fell on her shoulder and she turned to see Harry grinning down at her.

'What are you doing here?'

'Thought you might like an escort. You looked a bit upset.'

'That's kind, Harry, but I'm OK.'

'Maybe, but I needed the excuse.'

Despite herself, Libby laughed. 'Getting a bit heavy in there, was it?'

'Just a bit. Might be dossing down on your sofa.'

'I've got a perfectly good spare room, and you

156

know it.' Libby grinned up at him and tucked her arm through his. 'Nice navy sheets and all.'

Sidney was waiting as usual and, after sniffing at Harry's feet, led the way to the kitchen complaining loudly that he hadn't been fed for at least a fortnight. Harry allowed himself to be convinced and rummaged round the kitchen to find some cat food.

'Don't believe him,' said Libby pouring water into mugs. 'You did want coffee, didn't you?'

'Rather have something stronger,' said Harry, peering over her shoulder. 'I'm in shock.'

'So you are.' Libby raised an eyebrow. 'Well, have this as well. Scotch? I think I've replaced it.'

'Ben drink the last lot?'

'Sort of.' Libby felt herself flushing.

Settled either side of the fire, Libby tucked her feet under her and lit a cigarette. 'I really should stop this,' she said.

'Not right now, ducks. Wrong time altogether.' Harry stared into the fire, his transient ebullience gone.

Libby let the silence drift for a little longer. Then: 'I'm supposed to be the one who's upset. Come on, you wanted a shoulder, didn't you?'

Harry looked up with a quick grin. 'Absolutely. Unshockable, that's you.'

'Oh, I wouldn't say that.'

'Oh, go on with you. Anyway, I couldn't cope with all the angst in the family. Sometimes I feel stifled.'

Libby nodded. 'They can be a bit much.'

'All for one and one for all. Even when Millie's as mad as a box of frogs.'

'That's why they all turned against me about the play, isn't it?'

Harry sighed. 'Yes, I think so. Not that Pete said, actually, but yes, it was.'

'Left us in the cold, haven't they?'

Harry sighed again. 'I deserve it. You don't.'

Libby stared at his bent head. 'Come on, then,' she said. 'Why?'

Chapter Thirteen

Harry was silent for so long that Libby thought he wasn't going to answer, until he looked up, knocked back his whisky and cleared his throat.

'It was just after you started work on the play. Remember when Pete went off up to Cumbria or somewhere?'

'Northumbria, yes,' corrected Libby.

'Wherever. Only a few months after you moved in, anyway.'

'Three,' said Libby.

'All right, all right, do you want to know or not?'

'Only if you want to tell me.'

Harry gave an exasperated sigh. 'I don't know who's supposed to be comforting who here.'

'I know, you're in shock.'

He had the grace to look abashed. 'Yeah, I know. So are you. Well, anyway, we're talking February or something, aren't we?'

'I think so. Can't really remember.'

'Well, it was cold. And Pete was away.' Harry paused and stared in to the fire. 'And one night Paula comes into the caff for dinner – on her own – and says her electricity's off. So,' he took a deep breath, 'after we'd closed up, I walked her home to check it out.'

'The fuses?'

'Yeah, and to make sure everything was all right … you know. No intruders, or anything.'

'Was this her idea or yours?'

'Well, hers, I suppose. I mean, I said I'd walk her home. After all, she does live right up at the top of the village. And that lane's very dark.'

'Yes, all right, Harry, there's no need for excuses about that. You were being a gentleman.'

Harry crowed. 'And there's freaky.'

'You can still be good mannered AND gay, surely.'

'Yeah, well.' Harry stared in to the fire again. 'Well, anyway, I went in. Flashed the torch about a bit. And then – well, you know.'

Libby smiled at his bent head. 'I expect I do know, but what I don't understand is how it came about. You were hardly likely to leap on her, were you?'

'She thought she heard a noise.' Harry didn't look up.

'Ah.' Libby smiled again. 'And threw herself into your arms?'

'That sort of thing, yeah,' said Harry looking up. 'And then she started – well, saying she could turn me. You've no idea how many women think that.'

'And she was obviously right.'

159

'Not really.' Harry leaned back in the chair and waggled his glass. 'Any more?'

Libby got up to give him a refill. 'Go on. Why was she not right?'

'I've been a bit ambivalent in the past. Wanted to try it all, just to make sure I wasn't missing out on anything. And let's face it, anything'll do for the stimulation, won't it?'

Libby raised her eyebrows. 'Maybe for men. Us women need the mental and emotional aspect, too.'

'Well, believe me, there was no emotional aspect about this. It was a straightforward shag, no frills. She knew, too. She didn't come over all peculiar next time she saw me, or anything. Didn't even think she'd had me on the turn, either.' Harry sounded morose.

'And Pete found out?'

'I bloody told him, didn't I? How stupid can you get?'

'Oh, Harry,' Libby shook her head at him. 'When did you tell him?'

'When she and James went away for that weekend. He was moaning about James getting caught up with her again and – well, it just sort of came out.'

'But you smoothed it over?'

'Just about. He hated it, on all sorts of levels, but he came round. I had to do a hell of a lot of buttering up.' Harry paused and looked up. 'Trouble is, when it happened.'

'What do you mean, when it happened?'

'Just before that weekend.'

Libby frowned. 'I don't understand...' she

began, and then she did. 'Oh. Oh, Harry.'

'Well, it could be mine, couldn't it? I mean, I don't carry condoms around with me. And I don't even have the excuse of thinking we were in a regular relationship. Oh, shit.'

'And the police know all this?'

'Not about the baby. You said they didn't know she was pregnant. I mean, she never said anything to me. It was only to James, and we all know why that was. She knew she wouldn't stand a chance with me.'

'But the police know that you had a fling? How?'

'Again, it sort of came out. When that copper came to see us. Pete went all grande dame and somehow it slipped out. And then of course, they started on both of us.'

'What a mess, Harry.' Libby stared in to the fire. 'And what about James? And Ben?'

'Well, James was obvious, and Ben owned up. Mind you, I don't think Ben actually did anything with her. He was too drunk, and he never liked her anyway.'

'According to you,' said Libby with a scowl, 'that doesn't mean anything.'

'It does as you get older.' Harry looked uncomfortable.

Libby thought for a moment. 'I don't get it,' she said eventually. 'David found the – er – the – Paula, he called the police, then what happened? Why did they start talking to everybody?'

'David said Paula was engaged to James. He didn't have James's number, so he gave them Millie's. It sort of went on from there. Ben came to ours, and PC Plod and the little Ploddette came to us after they'd seen Millie. James arrived while they were talking to her. Once she'd started they couldn't shut her up, apparently.'

'So did she tell them about the accidents?'

'Oh, yes. Full of them, she was. It was a judgement and all that.'

'A judgement? Good God. I knew she wanted to stop us, but I didn't know it was that serious.' Libby sighed. 'Well, she's got her way now, hasn't she?'

A nasty little silence fell, and slowly Libby looked up to meet Harry's eyes.

'I didn't mean that,' she said in a cracked voice.

Harry cleared his throat. 'I know.'

Another silence fell, until a log settled in the fireplace with a hiss and broke the spell. Libby got up and went to fetch the whisky bottle.

'I need more of this,' she said.

'It wasn't Millie, Lib. It couldn't have been Millie.'

'No, of course not. Why on earth would she do something like that? I don't even think she did the other things, so why this?'

Harry shook his head. 'No idea. Well ... anyway, if Millie didn't set up the accidents, who did?'

'Haven't a clue. But as Ben said – when we were still talking to each other – can you imagine Millie climbing up and cutting the steel wire?'

Harry gave a snort of laughter and then looked terrified.

'There you are, then,' said Libby. 'It's all a complete mystery, and I personally don't think there's any connection between Paula and the accidents. It must be a passing madman. That's happened near here often enough.'

'That's what they always say in the mystery stories, and it's never true,' said Harry.

'Well, we're not in a mystery story, and I have no intention of solving anything.'

'That's what you said to Ben, didn't you? I reckon you'd make a good Miss Marple.'

'Harry, this is serious. Poor Paula's dead, and although we know none of us did it, the police don't, and they're going to make our lives a misery for a while, until they catch whoever did do it. We've all got to go into Canterbury to sign statements for a start, haven't we? Have they talked to Stephen? Is he going?'

'No idea about Stephen. He didn't have any connection with her, so probably not. Pete and I are going tomorrow. You can come with us, if you like. We thought we'd have lunch while we're there.'

'It's not a jolly day out,' said Libby testily, 'but thanks, I'd like to come with you. Sergeant Cole suggested it, as a matter of fact.'

'Odd, isn't it? Wouldn't you have thought a sergeant was a bit lowly for a murder enquiry?'

'No idea. Perhaps they'll put an inspector in charge now. Anyway, I need to go to bed. And if you're staying, so do you. Or are you going home?'

Harry stood up. 'I'll go home. Make the peace.' He went towards the door, then stopped and turned. 'I do love him, you know, Lib. Really.'

'I know you do.' Libby gave him a hug. 'You're

both very lucky.'

After Harry had gone, Libby sat down to finish her whisky. Sidney reappeared, inserted himself on to her lap and purred. She stroked his head absentmindedly, gazing into the glowing remains of the fire.

Waking up this morning seemed a lifetime away. First the phone call from Hetty about the fire, then the conversation with the fire investigator, breakfast with Millie, the disquieting call from Ben and the visit to Lenny. And then...

It couldn't have anything to do with the theatre. It was just too bizarre for words. The falling scenery, the collapsing bridge and the ineffectual fire were all minor irritants and obviously directed against the play rather than the theatre, in retrospect, and despite what she'd said to Harry, Libby was fairly convinced that Millie was behind them, for reasons the family suspected. But this. There was no way Millie would do anything to harm Paula, who was carrying her first grandchild.

And the overriding emotion was horror. A stomach-churning, breathtaking horror. Libby literally had to catch her breath every time she thought of Paula, and the shaming thought of how annoyed with her everyone had been only the day before.

'She's changed everything,' said Libby to Sidney. 'She changed everything before she died and now she's changed it again.'

Chapter Fourteen

No phone call was needed to wake Libby the following morning. She had drifted into sleep somewhere around four o'clock, but when she heard the milk float whining down Allhallow's Lane just after six it became infuriatingly apparent that the ravell'd sleave of care was to remain unknitted.

After the last weeks of cold and indeterminate weather, spring seemed to have arrived. The sun shone from a clear blue sky and Libby could at last smell the lilac that tapped on the conservatory windows. In the house where she'd grown up there had been a lilac tree hanging over the fence from next door and the scent always evoked childhood and security. Now it seemed almost indecently inappropriate.

Sidney disappeared over the fence, whiskers alert for stirring wildlife, and Libby envied him his escape. At some point this morning Peter and Harry would pick her up to take her to Canterbury Police Station, and until then she had to fill her time, take her mind off things. Nothing appealed. Never at her best with housework, the thought of brushing down the stairs or mopping the kitchen floor made her even more depressed.

Eventually she settled for cutting the grass with the lightweight hover mower Harry had talked her into the last time she'd persuaded him to mow what passed for her lawn. The consequences of this decision were missing the telephone call asking her to be ready at ten-thirty and the sudden appearance of Peter in the garden, causing her to squeal loudly and drop the mower on her foot.

The inevitable delay caused by a search for something to alleviate the swelling and footwear large enough to accommodate it resulted in their late arrival at the police station, where they trooped in like a bunch of school-children hauled up in front of the headmaster. This particular headmaster turned out to be a harassed-looking, balding man with the vestiges of violently red hair lurking over his ears. He introduced himself as Detective Chief Inspector Murray, the Senior Investigating Officer, and explained that he and his colleagues would be conducting interviews with all of them separately.

Peter, Harry and Libby looked at one another in shock.

'But Sergeant Cole said it was just to sign a statement.' Libby hoped her voice had come out better than it sounded to her.

'Well, yes, Mrs Sarjeant. But I'd like to make sure we've got everything we need, if that's OK. Just a few more questions.' Inspector Murray said. 'I'm sure you understand.'

'Too bad if we don't,' muttered Harry, who received a sharp look from Murray.

'Mrs Sarjeant, perhaps you'd come with me?' Murray stepped back and waited for Libby to join him. 'I won't keep you waiting long, gentlemen.'

Libby was taken into an interview room and

offered a cup of tea. After refusing, she was left alone for five minutes before Sergeant Cole and a spiky-haired schoolboy came in.

'Mrs Sarjeant,' said Cole, sitting down and jerking his head towards his companion. 'This is DC Bulstrode. The OIC's told you what's going to happen, hasn't he?'

'OIC?'

'Officer in charge.'

'Officer in the case.' Cole and Bulstrode spoke together.

'Inspector Murray?' asked Libby.

'Detective Chief Inspector Murray,' corrected Cole solemnly.

'Yes.'

'So I'll be conducting this interview. OK?'

'I thought I was just to sign a statement,' said Libby.

'Nothing to worry about,' said Cole, 'we'll just go over the same ground we did yesterday. Ready?'

Libby answered the same questions she had the night before. DC Bulstrode said nothing throughout, but lounged in his chair and picked his nails.

'Thank you, Mrs Sarjeant,' said Cole.

'So now tell me why we had to do that instead of the statement I thought I was going to make?' said Libby, gathering scarves and cape around her and standing up.

Cole looked confused. 'Procedure,' he said, looking at Bulstrode, presumably for confirmation. Bulstrode looked at the corner of the ceiling.

'And are you going to tell me how she was killed?'

'I'm afraid I can't, madam,' said Cole, also

standing. 'I'll see you out.'

As she was ushered back into the waiting area, Libby turned and fixed Cole with a minatory glare. 'Does this mean I'm a suspect?' she asked.

'We're investigating the case, madam,' said Cole, 'we have to talk to everybody.'

'Not two interviews,' said Libby.

'Quite normal, madam,' said Cole. 'Thank you for your time. If you'd care to wait here for your – er – friends.'

Libby waited for nearly forty minutes before Peter, looking frazzled, came out to join her.

'Who grilled you?' she asked.

'That girl who came last night and another sergeant, then Murray came in and the sergeant went out.' Peter shook his head. 'Terrifying. I don't think they believed a word I said.'

'I know. But you were much longer than I was. Must have been worse.'

'Well, I'm more of a suspect than you, aren't I? And Harry's more than either of us, obviously.' Peter looked round the waiting area. 'He's still in there.'

Eventually, Harry appeared, accompanied by DCI Murray, who gave them all a curt nod and vanished back through the glass doors.

Harry swore fluently all the way out in to the street until Peter put an arm round his shoulder and shook him gently.

'Come on, love. All over now. Let's go and have a drink. I'll drive back and you can get rat-arsed.'

Harry took a deep breath and closed his eyes. 'Sorry,' he said. 'Where did Ben say he'd meet us?'

'That little pub we went to last time,' said Peter. 'They do decent sandwiches. All right with you, you old trout?'

Libby nodded, unable to say she would rather not meet Ben. Peter linked one arm through Harry's and the other through hers and dragged them both towards the underpass.

After battling their way through swathes of the inevitable French students, they turned down a side street and found the pub. Off the tourist trail, it retained a certain British integrity, Libby thought, nicely balanced by a decorative gay barman who sparkled at Harry and caused Peter to snort with laughter.

Ben rose from a table in the window.

'Hi, guys,' he said. 'This is Fran.'

Chapter Fifteen

Libby's scalp prickled and something happened to her solar plexus. The dark-haired woman sitting in the window nodded politely and smiled as Peter, after a brief but noticeable pause, leaned forward and held out a hand.

'Hi. I'm Peter, Ben's cousin.' He straightened up and waved a hand. 'This is Harry, and our friend Libby.'

Harry muttered something and looked sideways at Libby.

'What can I get you?' asked Ben, coming round the table and brushing Libby's arm. She twitched away and he looked surprised.

'Fizzy water, please,' said Peter, 'I'm driving. But I think Harry needs a treble scotch.'

Harry frowned at him and turned to Ben. 'Just a half of whatever's decent, thanks,' he said.

'Libby?' Ben looked down at her as she perched uncomfortably on a stool.

'Same as Harry, thanks,' she said, without looking up.

As Ben went to the bar a silence fell. Libby was appalled to find herself feeling all the emotions of a jilted schoolgirl, all the more inappropriate as she had no right to do so. She looked across at Fran and took a deep breath.

'Fran and I work together occasionally,' said Ben, putting a glass in front of her before she could speak.

'Occasionally?' Peter raised his eyebrows.

Ben squeezed back into his seat next to Fran, who so far hadn't said a word.

'Fran does some research for us. And for other people, of course.'

'Research? What on? Building plots?' Harry sounded derisive.

'Yes, actually,' said Ben.

'Oh.' Harry subsided and he, Peter and Libby looked at each other and quickly away again.

'I think I'm in the way, here, Ben,' Fran spoke for the first time, revealing a beautiful, deep voice. 'I'll push off. Give me a ring about that...'

'No, don't go.' Ben put a hand out to stop her rising. 'I think you might be able to help.'

'Ben...' began Peter, but Ben cut him off.

'I know what you're going to say, Pete, that this

170

is family business and so on, but I really think Fran might be able to help.'

'Why?' said Harry.

'How?' said Libby.

'Have you told her already?' said Peter.

Ben frowned. 'She is here, Pete. She can hear what you're saying.'

A faint flush stained Peter's cheekbones. He turned to Fran and smiled. 'Sorry.'

'I've told her about the incidents at the theatre and that one of the cast members has been found dead, that's all.' Ben looked at each of them. 'Anyone got anything to add?'

Libby shook her head and looked at the others. So he hadn't said anything about the intertwined relationships.

'I really wanted to know if Fran could tell us anything about the accidents, but she'd have to come and have a look, wouldn't you?' He turned to Fran, who, to Libby's surprise, was still looking uncomfortable.

'Possibly,' she said.

Eventually Harry voiced the question that Libby wanted to ask.

'But how can she help? Is she a detective?'

'Not exactly,' said Ben, 'but she does find things out for people. For my clients.'

'Look, I may be being thick,' said Libby, 'but what exactly do you find out, how and why, and why does Ben think you can help us?'

Fran pushed a strand of dark hair behind her ear. Libby put her age at roughly the same as her own, although she looked younger. Her style was smarter than Libby's own eclectic fashion statements, and altogether she looked a much better match for the urbane Ben.

'I investigate sites,' she said at last. 'And for estate agents I investigate properties and areas.'

'Oh.' Peter looked relieved. 'A sort of house detective.'

Ben grinned. 'Except that Fran uses remote viewing.'

Libby felt her mouth drop open and was aware that Peter and Harry were equally stunned.

'That's like – telepathy?' said Harry.

'In a way. Fran, aren't you going to explain?' Ben patted her hand.

If anything, Fran looked even more uncomfortable.

'I don't call it remote viewing,' she said, 'it doesn't really seem to be anything to do with me.'

Libby felt marginally warmer towards her. 'So what do you do?'

'I go and see sites where Ben's clients want him to build and just wander around. If anything comes up I tell him – or them.'

'If anything comes up?' Peter looked affronted. 'Is that all?'

'Well, that's all I can say, really.' Fran had coloured, and once more pushed the lock of hair behind her ear. Libby thought she could see a faint sheen of perspiration on her forehead. She warmed to her further, even if she was Ben's newest girlfriend, or maybe a long-standing one.

'Fran comes up with all sorts of things – unstable footings, water courses–'

'Dowsing!' said Libby.

'Absolutely.' Ben smiled at her. 'And she'll investigate streets and neighbourhoods for estate agents or private clients.'

'What? To see if murder's been committed?' Harry sounded scornful again.

'Maybe,' said Fran, looking at him curiously. 'And that's what you're worried about, isn't it?'

A charged silence fell. Harry looked at Peter, then down at his glass.

'Apparently, yes, murder has been committed. But I don't think it's anything to do with you.' Fran sat back in her chair and picked up her drink.

Peter cleared his throat. 'Yes, well, I'm sure that's very comforting, Mrs – er – Fran,' he said, 'but I don't think the police agree with you.'

Fran looked even more embarrassed and turned to gaze out of the window.

'Don't be quite so dismissive, Pete,' said Ben quietly. 'If companies like mine and Goodall and Smythe trust Fran's judgement, I don't see that you have any right to criticise, do you?'

Now Peter and Harry looked embarrassed.

'Goodall and Smythe? They're big, aren't they? Head office in London?' Libby leaned her elbows on the table, interested.

'And ads in all the glossy magazines. That's right. And if one of their clients is worried about the neighbourhood, or if anything nasty has happened in the house, or on the estate, they recommend Fran to go and have a poke about.' Ben smiled at Fran and patted her hand again. 'It all happened by accident, didn't it, Fran?'

Fran nodded, but said nothing.

'So what are you suggesting, then?' Peter

173

looked from Fran to Ben. 'Is Fran going to come and snoop round the theatre?'

'Well ... yes, I suppose so. Just to see if she can pick anything up.'

'Does it matter any more?' Libby sat back in her chair and sighed. 'After all, you've all decided that we're not going ahead with the play, so there won't be any more accidents, will there?'

'How do we know?' said Ben. 'We said it might be nothing to do with the theatre or the play.'

'You don't want it to go ahead, and neither does Peter, do you Pete?'

Peter looked at Harry, who nodded. 'Actually,' he said, 'I wouldn't like to think it was off for ever. We've all put in a lot of work on this project. But...'

'Paula, exactly.' Ben tapped his glass on the table. 'I don't think Paula's death has anything to do with the theatre or the play, but we have to be certain. We talked about it last night after you left, and, having thought it over, I agree with Pete. We've all put in too much work to abandon it.' He looked at Libby. 'You'll be pleased.'

She nodded. 'Yes, but don't hold me responsible for the whole thing. It has to be a majority decision, and it is your family who're concerned, after all.'

'Yesterday you were chasing round trying to find things out on your own. You've changed your tune,' said Harry.

'Who's side are you on?' Libby raised an eyebrow at him.

'Pete's, of course,' Harry snapped.

'Stop bickering, children,' Ben said. 'Let's just

174

see if Fran can pick anything up, then we'll decide what to do. One thing we don't want is the police sniffing around, so quietly does it.'

'When are you coming over, Fran?' said Libby. 'Can we give you a lift?'

'I'll drive over this evening, if that's OK. I can't guarantee anything, you know.'

'Not to worry.' Ben stood up. 'I'm off to be grilled now. See you all later.'

'I need to go, too,' said Fran. 'I'll see you tonight.'

Peter, Harry and Libby all watched in silence as Ben ushered Fran out of the pub, then took her arm as they started down the street.

'That his latest squeeze, then?' asked Harry.

'I don't think so.' Peter was still looking after the retreating backs. 'Just work colleagues, I'd guess. Not really his style, is she?'

'Neither's Li...' began Harry.

'Me.' Libby scowled at him. 'I know. We've already been there. But at least she's tall and beautiful.'

'And mystic.' Peter grimaced.

'Don't knock it till you've tried it,' said Libby.

'Oh, Lib, you don't believe in all that rubbish, do you?' Harry scoffed.

'I dowse all the time,' said Libby. 'It helps me not to die from salmonella.'

'Eh?'

'The old pendulum trick. You know, like they used to do over the stomachs of pregnant women to see what sex the baby was.'

'And now they've got amniocentesis,' said Peter, 'there's progress.'

175

'So how do you use it?' asked Harry.

'I ask it if the food's safe for me to eat. I don't keep my kitchen like you do, after all.'

'You're dead right there. In fact I'm surprised you haven't killed that walking stomach yet.'

'Sidney can manage the odd sparrow and field mouse, so whatever I give him can hardly hurt him, can it?' Libby finished her drink and sighed. 'And what the hell are we doing talking about cats and dowsing when Paula...' she broke off and looked away.

'I know.' Peter leaned forward and put his hand over hers. 'It's a bastard, isn't it?'

'Shall we go back?' asked Harry eventually. 'I don't feel like food, somehow. And I can always do us something back at the caff.'

'Come on, then,' Peter stood up and held out a hand to Libby. 'Let's try and get back to normal.'

'Don't forget Fran's coming this evening,' said Libby. 'That's hardly normal.'

'Neither's murder,' said Harry gloomily.

'Are we actually supposed to be there when she comes?' asked Peter, ushering them out of the pub. 'I assumed she was just going to meet Ben.'

'I thought he told us because he wanted us to be there. We've all got vested interests in the theatre.' Libby picked her way between tourists.

'Well, I suppose we'll find out if he rings us and tells us she's there. There was no mention of time, was there?'

'No, so let's not bother,' said Harry, 'and I'll do us a scrummy lunch and we can drink our way through the afternoon.'

Peter flung an arm round his shoulders.

'Harry's recipe for forgetfulness, eh?'

'And a very good idea,' said Libby firmly. 'I think there's quite a lot I need to forget.'

Chapter Sixteen

None of them was given a chance to forget, as Ben brought Fran into the Pink Geranium just after five o'clock.

Libby, replete with red wine and vegetarian lasagne, waved a languid hand.

'Find anything out?' she asked.

Ben frowned at her. 'Fran's only just arrived. She wondered if anybody wanted to go up to the theatre with her.'

Peter stood up. Despite a steady consumption of alcohol during the afternoon he appeared completely sober, although Libby was pretty sure he wasn't.

'I'll show Fran round, if you like,' he said.

'That wasn't quite what I meant, Pete,' Ben perched on the edge of a table. 'It would be just to answer any questions she had. Or to answer any that you had.'

'Coffee, anyone?' Harry pushed his chair back and folded last Sunday's Observer review section. 'Fran? Can I get you anything?'

'No, thanks. Perhaps later,' said Fran, looking very much as though she didn't want to be there, thought Libby.

'Come on, then. We'll all go, shall we? Fran,

shall I lead the way?' Libby flung her cape round her shoulders and marched past Ben and out into the High Street.

Fran fell into step with her as they walked up the drive towards the theatre. 'Can I ask you a few questions?' she said, looking sideways at Libby.

'Of course,' said Libby. 'What do you want to know?'

'Why you're so scratchy about Ben.'

Libby felt a blush rising up her neck and her scalp prickled with perspiration.

'Scratchy?' she repeated.

'I'd sort of got the impression from Ben that you were – well – an item. But you're not, are you?'

'Is that what he told you?' asked Libby, her heart thumping arrhythmically in her chest.

'No. I just thought it. Well, felt it, I suppose. Sorry.'

'That's all right.' Libby pushed a hand through her hair. 'We've been friends for years. I've known him for years, anyway. Peter's an old friend and he introduced us ages ago. I just began to see him a bit more after I moved here and we started the theatre project.'

'Oh, well, I get things wrong.' Fran shrugged. 'That's the trouble with people telling you you're psychic. You begin to think you are.'

Libby turned to look at her in surprise. 'Aren't you, then?'

Fran sighed. 'Oh, I don't know. I've always had this thing – you know – when you know who's ringing before you answer the phone, but so have a lot of people, and I don't count the times I was wrong. And occasionally I get these feelings. As

178

though I actually know what's happened, or what's going on. As though somebody's told me.'

Libby slowed down as they approached the doors of the theatre, and waited for either Ben or Peter to unlock.

'So how did you start to use it for work?'

'It happened by accident, as Ben said. I used to work for an estate agent who sent me out with buyers, and I found myself telling them stuff about the houses, or the street. When I told one lot about a violent murder, we lost the sale and I got the sack.'

'Gruesome.' Libby watched as Ben unlocked the double doors. 'So then what happened?'

'The clients went to another agent, Goodall and Smythe, as it happened, and told them all about it. They got in touch with me and offered me a job.' Fran followed Libby into the foyer. 'Hey, this is nice.' She looked around with a pleased smile.

'So, no nasties in this particular woodshed?' asked Peter, coming in behind them.

'Doesn't feel like it,' said Fran, 'but don't forget, I can easily be wrong.'

'Where's Harry?' Libby looked back down the drive. 'Isn't he coming?'

'No, he decided it was our problem and he'd stay behind and clear up, ready to have the kettle on for us when we go back.'

'He's very worried, isn't he?' asked Fran. 'More worried than you are.'

Ben, Peter and Libby all looked at her.

'About the murder, I mean. Sorry. You don't want to know about that.' Fran looked down at

179

her neatly booted feet.

'We do in a way, Fran.' Ben patted her shoulder. 'If it's connected to the theatre. Or any of us.'

'I – I don't think so. But please don't take it for gospel, Ben. I told you, I'm not sure any of this really works.'

Peter and Libby looked at each other. 'Well,' said Peter, 'I'm glad to hear Harry doesn't seem to be in the picture, in any event. Come on, let's go up on stage.'

Fran opened her mouth as if to protest, but Libby, catching her eye, shook her head. If Peter was happy believing Harry was in the clear, let him carry on believing it. She was sure no one she knew had anything to do with Paula's death, and she refused to think otherwise.

They made a tour of the theatre, in which Fran took an intelligent interest. When they finally returned to the foyer, she wandered back into the auditorium, hands thrust deep in the pockets of her coat. A very nice navy coat, Libby thought, but a bit too smart for her. She sighed, and watched as Fran detoured round the smart new seats and stopped in front of the stage.

'Honestly,' she said, turning round, 'all I can see is what's here. There's a nice feeling in the building, but you all know that. I don't suppose that's what you wanted to hear.'

'It's exactly what we wanted to hear.' Peter went towards her with a broad smile. 'It means we can carry on with the play and the opening.'

'You've changed your tune,' muttered Libby.

'I told you, we've all put a lot of work into it. And I'm sure Paula would want us to carry on.'

180

Ben came forward and tucked his arm through Libby's. She tried not to flinch. 'We could do it in her memory,' he said, 'she'd love that.'

'That's a bit tacky, isn't it?' Libby didn't look at him.

'Paula *was* tacky,' said Peter.

'She was, wasn't she?' laughed Fran, and then stopped, looking shocked. 'Sorry, I don't know where that came from.'

Ben grinned. 'I'm glad we've had it confirmed, anyway,' he said. 'Come on, let's go back to the caff.'

'I wasn't much use, was I?' said Fran, as she walked beside Libby back down the drive.

'Oh, yes, you were,' Libby assured her. 'You've single-handedly got the play going again. As long as the rest of the cast want to carry on and we can recast Paula.'

'You'll have no trouble with that, will you? In my experience there are always more females than parts for them.'

Libby looked at her. 'You've done amateur drama, then?'

'A bit. Back-stage, mostly. Where I used to live.'

'You're welcome to come and join us,' said Libby, 'although we're a bit of a rag-bag at the moment. Some of us belonged to other groups in and around the area, and some of them are brand new, just villagers who wanted to be involved.'

'It's an impressive set-up. Ben's done a lovely job on the theatre. And you used to be a professional, he said?'

'Oh, years ago, and I didn't get very far. Before I had the kids.'

'I know the feeling. I had to stop eventually.' Fran stopped suddenly, looking as though she wished she hadn't spoken.

'Acting?' Libby gasped. 'You too?'

'I'm afraid so. I wasn't going to say.'

'Oh, you must join us, then. I could do with some back-up.' Libby stopped walking and turned to face Fran. 'This is great.'

Fran smiled and looked at her feet again. 'I couldn't actually,' she said, 'I live in London.'

'London? But I thought Ben said...?'

'I don't think he did. He said I work occasionally for him and for Goodall and Smythe. But as you rightly said, their head office is in London. I just get sent to various different areas. I met Ben when Goodall and Smythe were handling one of his developments, and I've done a few projects for him since.'

'I see.' Libby turned and started walking again. 'So you won't be around to help me have a poke about in all this?'

Fran looked interested. 'Is that what you're going to do?'

'I told Ben I wasn't a Miss Marple, but I would like to get to the bottom of these incidents. Not the murder,' she said hastily, 'but the other stuff. It doesn't seem to be connected. And I'd like to put everyone's minds at rest.'

'I could, I suppose,' said Fran slowly. 'I'm freelance, so I don't have to be back for work or anything. I could take a few days off.'

'Fantastic!' Libby was excited. 'You could come and stay with me. If you don't mind cats, that is.'

'No.' Fran looked amused. 'I love cats, but I

can't have one in the flat.'

Ben and Peter already had large mugs of tea in front of them by the time Libby and Fran arrived at the Pink Geranium.

'Guess what,' said Libby, casually bumping into a table and knocking the Observer on to the floor.

'She's off,' said Peter, bending to retrieve the paper. 'You can always tell.'

'I don't know what you mean,' said Libby huffily.

'Sit down, you old trout,' said Harry. 'Tea, Fran? Or coffee?'

'Tea, please,' said Fran, sitting down next to Libby. 'Don't you mind being called an old trout?'

Libby looked surprised. 'I've never thought about it,' she said, shrugging her cape off her shoulders.

'Anyway, what's the news you are so obviously big with?' asked Ben.

'Fran's going to come and stay with me for a bit to see if we can't get to the bottom of things.' Libby was triumphant. 'What do you think?'

From the silence round the table, it was obvious that universal pleasure was not on the menu.

'Don't you think we ought to leave things alone, Lib?' Ben said tentatively.

'But you were the one who introduced Fran.' Libby was indignant.

'I know.' Ben sighed.

'If things have settled down we don't want to stir them up again,' said Peter, hooking one ankle over the arm of his chair. 'Especially for Harry.' He reached behind him to pat whichever bit of

183

Harry he could reach.

Harry scowled down at his lover's head. 'Why me?'

There was a small silence.

'Er – my fault.' Fran cleared her throat. 'I thought you seemed more bothered about – um – *things*, than the others.'

'Right.' Harry removed Peter's hand from his thigh and strode into the kitchen. Peter sighed.

'Sorry,' said Fran.

'That's all right. I should have been prepared for a few negative reactions, shouldn't I?' said Ben, looking quickly at Libby, whose stomach rolled over. There it was, that teenagerish thing again.

'So what do you think, then, Fran?' she asked. 'Do you come down anyway?'

Harry came in with mugs of tea and just about refrained from banging them down on the table.

'Er – I don't know,' said Fran, looking nervously at Harry's eloquent back.

'Let's just drink our tea, shall we?' said Ben, comfortably. 'No need to make any decisions just yet.'

'Except about the play,' said Libby.

'I think you should go ahead.' Harry turned round and swung himself onto a chair. 'You were all enjoying it until these things happened – and your bloody family got in the way,' he added spitefully to Ben and Peter.

'Harry!' said Libby.

'Don't worry,' said Peter, reaching across and patting Harry's arm. 'He's right. We'll go ahead.'

'Shall I call the cast, then?' asked Libby, after a

184

moment's thought.

'No, dear heart, I'm more tactful. Let's not put their backs up about being disrespectful to Paula.'

'Gee, thanks,' muttered Libby.

Fran leaned over to Libby. 'Give me your phone number anyway,' she said quietly, 'and I'll ring you.'

Libby raised her eyebrows. 'Do you think...?'

Fran shook her head. 'I'll ring you,' she said.

Libby delved into her basket and found a pen and an old shopping list. Writing her number on the back, she passed it over to Fran and looked round quickly to see if anyone else had noticed. Ben, Harry and Peter all seemed to be deep in conversation about the progress of the play, and she sat back and took a comforting swallow of tea. She was still confused about both her own and Fran's relationship with Ben, but somehow instinctively trusted Fran. What they would find out about the goings-on in Steeple Martin, or within the Wilde, Fisher and Parker families she had no idea, but whatever it was it had to be better than the present state of suspicion and turmoil.

'I must go,' said Fran, standing up. 'I hope I've been of some help, even if it was negative.'

Ben stood up, came round the table and gave her a kiss. 'It was a great help,' he said, 'you appear to have saved the play.'

Fran glanced quickly at Libby. 'Oh, good,' she said.

Libby smiled. 'Thank you for coming, Fran,' she said. 'I'm sure we'll meet again.'

Fran nodded and held out her hand formally to

Peter and Harry, who both ignored it and followed Ben's example by kissing her on the cheek. She blushed slightly and, before anyone could say anything else, had disappeared through the door.

'Well, that's that,' said Ben. 'Now all we've got to worry about is getting the play back on track.'

Oh, yeah? thought Libby, sitting back in her chair. That's what you think.

Chapter Seventeen

Libby went home feeling vaguely dissatisfied. Ben and Peter seemed to have completely forgotten their previous unwillingness to carry on with the play, which made her think Paula's murder had somehow negated what she now thought of as the sabotaging incidents. Which meant they assumed that the murder and the incidents had all been perpetrated by the same person and was therefore unconnected with the Family. Strange how she was coming to think of it in capital letters.

It was after ten o'clock when the phone rang. Sidney fell inelegantly onto the floor as she surged up from her chair to answer it.

'Libby? It's Fran.'

'Oh.' Libby was startled. 'I didn't expect to hear from you so soon.'

'Sorry, but I thought you seemed anxious to – well, to find out...'

'Yes,' said Libby hastily, 'I am.'

'Do you still want me to come down?' Fran sounded hesitant.

'Of course. If you want to. Does this mean that you think there is something to investigate?'

'There's something. I'm not sure what it is, exactly, but perhaps if I was down there I could make some sense of it. It might be nothing, though. You'd have to be prepared for that.'

Tempted to say anything would be better than nothing, Libby simply assured her that she would be delighted to have her to stay.

'Would tomorrow afternoon be too early?' Fran asked.

'No, not at all. I don't know yet what Pete's sorted out about the play, but if he's persuaded them all to carry on, I expect we'll have to rehearse like mad starting as soon as possible, which will probably mean tomorrow. You could come to rehearsal. If you think it would help.'

'That's great. Oh, and Libby,' Fran was sounding hesitant again, 'you needn't worry about Ben and me. There's nothing going on.'

'Oh, no, I wasn't. I mean, it doesn't matter to me. We're not – I mean – I'm not, well...' she petered out.

'That's all right then,' said Fran, sounding amused. 'So I'll see you tomorrow. About four?'

'Sounds fine. I'll make sure I'm here,' said Libby, although there was no reason why she would be anywhere else.

Sidney was sitting facing the fire, his ears down and his tail twitching.

'All right, all right, I'm sorry,' said Libby, returning to her chair. 'You can come and sit on my lap again now.'

Sidney turned his back.

'Well, you can at least listen to me,' she said, poking him with a toe. 'Fran thinks I'm interested in Ben. I must be really transparent.'

Sidney's ears twitched.

'But then, Fran's psychic – or something – so maybe it's only her.'

Sidney turned round and looked at her.

'Yes, I know,' she sighed, 'it probably isn't. I expect I look like a teenager with a crush. How embarrassing.'

Sidney stood up, stretched and walked to the kitchen. Suppertime, he said. Blow your introspective ramblings.

Libby got up early the next morning, at least, early for her, and set about getting the spare room ready for Fran. She was interrupted by the phone just after ten o'clock and, for once, wasn't expecting it to be Ben. She was therefore reduced to silence when it was.

'Just wanted to tell you, Pete's gone to town today, but he's managed to set up a rehearsal this evening. Everybody seemed keen to carry on.'

'What about Paula?' said Libby, finally finding her voice. 'I mean, Paula's part.'

'He's going to talk about it when they all get there.'

'Surely they must have asked, though?'

'Some of them did. I expect the women were a bit chary in case they sounded unfeeling.'

'How do you mean?'

'If they were interested in doing the part it

188

might have seemed as though...'

'Oh, I see.' Libby nodded at Sidney, who ignored her.

'So we'll find out tonight. Eightish.'

'Right,' said Libby, wondering whether she should mention Fran.

'And we'll put all this other business behind us, and leave Paula's murder to the police.'

Libby decided not to mention Fran.

'Fancy a drink at lunchtime?'

Experiencing the now familiar adrenalin surge, Libby blustered.

'Er, no – no thanks, Ben. I'm – er – busy. Working.' She took a deep breath. 'What about you? Aren't you working?'

'No, it didn't seem worth going in just for today. After all, it's Saturday tomorrow. Sort of thing you can do when you're your own boss. Sure you won't change your mind?'

'No, I've done far too little work over the last two weeks, one way and another. Must get on.'

Ben didn't ask her with what, to her relief, but merely said cheerfully that he would see her tonight.

Absurdly pleased that he would be there, and had wanted to take her out for a drink, Libby sat staring at nothing for several minutes. Equally pleased that she had refused, she smiled soppily to herself and gave Sidney a conciliatory stroke, before returning to the spare bedroom with renewed vigour. When she'd finished, it looked less like a store room, and, anxious not to make herself a liar, she went out to the conservatory and began to prepare some paper.

189

Although she hadn't been hopeful, she found that working distracted her from the mass of thoughts fighting for supremacy, and was quite surprised when Sidney came to remind her that it was lunchtime. After a tin of soup, she returned to the conservatory, and was still there when the doorbell rang.

Fran had dressed down today, and Libby felt a lot more comfortable to see her in jeans and a jumper. She had one large holdall and smiled rather hesitantly as Libby welcomed her with a kiss.

'I just hope I'm of some use,' she said. 'I feel as though I'm conning a free weekend away.'

'Of course not. I'm really pleased you could come,' said Libby. 'I haven't told the others, though.' She was leading the way up the stairs.

'Was that wise?' Fran manhandled her bag through the spare room door.

'I don't know,' said Libby. 'Do you think I should have told them?'

'You know them better than I do, but they weren't keen yesterday, were they?' Fran dumped her bag on the bed. 'This is a nice room.'

'Thanks. It doesn't get much use, except for the kids, and they don't come much.'

'How many?' asked Fran.

'Three. Two boys and a girl. I never know when they'll turn up, although I expect they'll come down for the play. Shall I leave you to sort yourself out while I put the kettle on?'

By the time Fran came downstairs Libby had made tea and taken it through to the sitting room. Fran introduced herself to Sidney, who traitorously demonstrated undying love and took up a place on the arm of her chair, where he periodically butted her with his head, purring loudly.

'Sorry about Sidney,' said Libby. 'He's not usually so forward.'

'I like cats, as I said. I wish I could have one, but I live on the top floor with no garden access, and I'm out quite a lot. It wouldn't be fair.'

'You work a lot then? Always the same thing?'

'Mostly. I can't really do anything else, and this has been sort of thrust on me.' Fran sighed. 'I don't really like doing it. It still seems like a con.'

'Well, if it works, it isn't.' Libby lit a cigarette. 'I hope you don't mind...'

'No, I'm a reformed smoker, but not a belligerent one.' Fran put down her cup. 'And now, tell me all about it from the beginning.'

'Hasn't Ben told you?'

'Only bits. Just the bare bones of the accidents, and the murder, obviously. I'd like to know the background.'

So Libby told her, beginning with Peter's play and the events it related, to the discovery of Paula's body and Libby's visit to Uncle Lenny. Fran listened carefully, but made no comment until Libby reached the end of her narrative.

'It sounds to me as though something happened when Hetty's father disappeared which the family have covered up. Doesn't it to you?'

'I suppose so,' said Libby. 'But what could it be? What could be worse than your father murdering someone and running off?'

'I've no idea, but there's something.'

191

'I don't think the children – that is, Ben and Peter – know anything. They were as puzzled as I am. They just suddenly seemed to close ranks.'

'Perhaps they found out what the other thing was?'

'Maybe,' said Libby slowly, 'which is why they're sure Paula has nothing to do with it?'

'Could be. But we're not going to try and find out who murdered Paula, are we? We're not television detectives.'

'No, I've said that already. I suppose I should just let things lie, really. If everyone's happy to go ahead with the play...'

'But you still want to know about the accidents, don't you?' said Fran, leaning back in her chair and stroking an ecstatic Sidney's head.

'Well, yes, it would make me feel safer.' Libby stubbed out her cigarette and emptied her ashtray into the fire.

'And that's what I'm here for,' said Fran, 'otherwise I really will feel like a spare part.'

'I'm glad you're here anyway,' said Libby, 'I've felt rather excluded the last few days.'

'So has Harry,' said Fran.

Libby was surprised. 'When did he tell you?'

'Oh, he didn't.' Fran looked embarrassed. 'Just one of those feelings. Like I said yesterday, he's more worried than the rest of you about Paula. I don't know how I know, I just do.'

'What about the rest of us?' Libby asked warily.

'Nothing. Except this feeling that there's something between you and Ben.'

'It's not just me being transparent?' Libby looked down at her hands.

'No.' Fran sounded surprised. 'Just something in my head. I got the same from Ben when he was first telling me about it. He didn't actually say anything.'

'Ah.' Libby looked into the fire. 'Then I'm not behaving like a...'

'Teenager?' Fran finished for her. 'I don't think so. I haven't seen enough of you to know. And everyone's bound to be behaving a little strangely under the circumstances, aren't they?'

Libby was silent for a moment. Then she looked at Fran.

'Does it occur to you that this is an extraordinarily intimate conversation for two people who've only just met to be having?'

'Does that worry you?'

'No,' said Libby, surprised. 'I don't know why, though. I don't normally talk to anyone about what I feel.' She thought for a moment. 'Except Pete and Harry, I suppose.'

'Why them?'

'No idea. I've known Pete for years, long before he took up with Harry. Pete became a sort of confidant, and by extension so did Harry. And they've always confided in me, at least I thought so. Until now.'

'But Harry did confide in you. About Paula.'

'Yes, but he and I are both outsiders, you've just said. And he obviously wanted to talk to somebody.'

'Do you think he might be more worried on Peter's behalf than his own?' asked Fran.

'You mean he might think Pete murdered Paula?' Libby gasped. 'Oh, no, I'm sure not.'

'Well, I'm sure he didn't do it, so there must be a reason he's more bothered than the rest of you.'

'I don't know,' Libby said uncomfortably. 'It just sounds so far-fetched.'

'I expect murder always seems far-fetched to the people involved,' said Fran. 'You always read of murderers being the last one their friends and family suspect, don't you?'

'Oh, God, don't say that,' said Libby, standing up and picking up the empty cups. 'I thought we weren't looking into that, anyway?'

Fran smiled. 'We're not, don't worry. But it's bound to come up, isn't it?'

Libby took a deep breath. 'Let's have some more tea,' she said.

They didn't return to the subject for the rest of the afternoon, but filled one another in on the trivia of their lives. Libby was astonished at how relaxed she felt with Fran, as though she'd known her for years. She still had female friends from her former life, but none with whom she exchanged confidences any more. She saved those for Peter and Harry, but there were some things she couldn't talk about even to them. She wondered if Fran's uncertain psychic abilities were at the root of this, making her somehow ultra-sympathetic.

She half expected Peter to ring before the evening's rehearsal, but the phone remained silent until they left at half past seven.

'I want to be there early,' said Libby, as they walked through the High Street. 'I only hope I can get in.'

'Should you have rung Ben and asked what

194

time he was going to be there?'

'Perhaps.'

'But you didn't want to.'

'No.'

As they walked up the drive, however, they could see lights on in the theatre, and as Libby pushed open the doors they saw Ben and Peter by the newly installed bar, deep in conversation. They both looked up, identical expressions of shock on their faces. For the first time, Libby saw a family resemblance.

'Sorry,' she said, 'I forgot I hadn't told you Fran was coming.'

Ben was the first to recover.

'Fran, lovely to see you again,' he said, coming forward to kiss her cheek. 'You didn't say, Libby.'

'No,' said Libby, looking at Peter, whose face was now perfectly blank.

Fran was blushing. 'I'm just here for the weekend, really,' she said. 'Libby said I could come to rehearsal. I hope you don't mind?'

'That's up to the director, isn't it, Libby?' said Peter. 'Nothing to do with us.'

'Well, it is in a way,' said Libby, annoyed that she hadn't thought this through. 'I just thought...'

Ben patted her arm. 'It's fine, Lib. Of course Fran's welcome.'

'So, Pete, what have you said to everybody, and how did they react?' Libby took off her cape and tried to look efficient.

Apparently recovering his normal sangfroid, Peter told her what he'd said to the cast and crew, what their reactions had been, and whom he thought could replace Paula.

'Emma was the only one who threw a bit of a wobbly,' he said, 'but I convinced her we couldn't carry on without her, and we would need her to help Paula's replacement.'

By this time, members of the company were drifting in. Most of them came up to Ben, or Peter and Libby, to ask questions, and although the atmosphere was subdued, there was a feeling of underground excitement, which faintly disgusted Libby, and made her feel guilty for wanting to carry on. Stephen arrived with other members of the backstage crew, and immediately made a beeline for her.

'Why didn't you phone me?'

'Pete said he'd do it,' said Libby, uncomfortably aware that she should have phoned him as she was responsible for him being involved. 'I'm sorry. I was entirely in their hands–'

'Whose hands?'

'Pete's and Ben's. It was up to them whether we carried on or not. I don't think they wanted to, but now they seem to have changed their minds.'

Stephen's expression told her what he thought of Peter and Ben. 'And who's this?'

'Fran. She's a – a work associate of Ben's, and a friend of mine. Down for the weekend.'

Stephen looked marginally more cheerful at this, and went off to his workshop, presumably to make the first cup of tea of the evening.

They all went into the auditorium, where first Peter and then Libby had a brief chat to explain the situation, and Peter offered Paula's part to one of the young hop-pickers, who was blushingly grateful.

196

'It means we've got to work hard over the next few days, and we'll have to put in time over the weekend,' said Libby, 'but I feel sure we can do it, and we've all put in so much work so far we don't want to waste it. And,' she said, invoking the phrase that would carry them through the next few days, 'I'm sure it's what Paula would have wanted.'

There was a murmur of assent from the company.

'And there won't be any more incidents,' said Peter, voicing the fear that Libby could almost hear rustling through the auditorium. 'Whatever, or whoever, was responsible won't try anything else. It would just be too tacky.'

A bubble of nervous laughter broke out and was quickly suppressed. Peter grinned round at them all. 'And now, let's get on with it. No mournful faces' (there weren't many) 'it will be the best memorial Paula could have.'

Libby slid off the stage and organised her troops into setting the first scene and reassuring Paula's replacement that she was going to be fine.

'Tell me you're not still investigating, you old trout.'

Peter's voice in her ear made Libby jump.

'No.' Libby turned to face him.

'No, you're not? Or no, you won't tell me?'

'No, I won't tell you. Fran invited herself down, and if she picks up any vibes or whatever, I'll be glad if she tells me.' Libby looked up defiantly. 'And so should you be. She's absolutely convinced Harry had nothing to do with Paula, no matter what the police think.'

Peter frowned, looking anything but mollified. 'They don't think he did it. Any more than they think I did. They're just casting about. I'm more worried about James.'

'But why would he do it? She was going to have his baby. They were moving in together.'

'Good enough reason, if you ask me. We all know he'd been trapped, don't we?'

Libby shook her head. 'This isn't the time to discuss it,' she said. 'Anyway, I'm not interested in the murder, only the accidents. Well,' she added, 'I don't mean I'm not interested, exactly...'

'I know what you meant,' said Peter, giving her a sudden hug. 'Now go and be a hotshot director.'

Surprisingly, the rehearsal began well. The girl now playing Flo's character had obviously been paying attention over the last couple of months, and knew the moves and even some of the lines. Libby had to acknowledge that Peter's choice had been the right one. During a scene change Libby went back to where Fran was sitting unobtrusively at the back of the auditorium.

'What do you think?'

'Good.' Fran nodded. 'Don't take this the wrong way, but better than I expected.'

'Thank you. They're all trying very hard.' Libby fiddled with a scarf. 'No – er – thoughts?'

Fran smiled. 'Nothing,' she said.

The play moved on to the difficult seduction scene, and Libby found herself holding her breath. This, after all, was the crux of the whole story, the event which set in train the tragedy to follow. She just hoped she'd got it right.

Chapter Eighteen – 1943

The mist still shrouded the gardens as they walked across the common. Flo carried Millie on her hip and Hetty clenched her hands inside the pockets of her old coat to try and warm them up.

Lillian pushed the hopping box with the billies and the thick doorsteps of bread for their lunch. Hetty was already aware of the slight tightness round her waist brought on by eating so much bread and so many potatoes over the last week and a half. And although they worked in the fresh air all day, she no longer walked two or three miles a day to and from work, the farm being comparatively small. Still, she knew she looked healthier, and a pink flush to her cheeks had replaced the East End pallor.

Lillian led the way to the middle of the row where they had finished yesterday and they spent the next few minutes establishing themselves for the day. Flo was working with her mother next to them, and in order that the two families stayed close together, Hetty used to help her from time to time, or the tally would have been too small for them to move on when Lillian had finished her row. The call came to start picking and Hetty looked up, a tingling feeling of anticipation spreading through her to her fingers and toes as she saw the tall outline of the pole puller on his stilts moving towards them.

She squinted up at him as he deftly unhooked a bine and laid it across Lillian's bin. Ignoring Flo's dig in the ribs, she moved slightly closer and met his eyes. The green tunnel receded and there were only the two of them in the world as she received the promise in the shared look of complicity. She nodded, imperceptibly, she hoped, and stepped back to let him move on.

The sun grew hot on her head as the morning progressed and her hands became inured once more to the stinging of the bines as they dried out.

'Cor, it's hot this year.' Aunt Connie struggled out of the old army greatcoat that she habitually wore down hopping. 'We ain't had no rain, yet, neither.'

'Good.' Lillian rubbed a hand across a sweating brow. 'Better tally.'

'Just as well.' Connie nodded at Hetty. 'Now Warburton's got his claws into our Het.'

'Auntie, he hasn't. Why should you think that?'

'He fancies you, duck.' Connie was matter of fact. 'And we've told you what happens then. If you give in to him, fine – but if you won't have none of him – well, pity for you.'

'Is he measuring us heavy, then?' Hetty stopped picking, an unpleasant sensation starting somewhere under her waistband and spreading down her legs. It was how she used to feel if she got called out in front of the class at school, desperately trying to think of what she'd done wrong.

Lillian shot her a quick look. 'Don't you worry about it, Het. He'll soon see he can't blackmail us. I'm goin' to report him to Mr Carpenter.'

200

'Shall I do that for you, Mrs F?' said Flo.

'No, dear. It's our concern. You got plenty of excuses to get up there and see Mr Carpenter, anyhow.'

Flo giggled and then caught sight of Hetty's stricken face.

'Cheer up, Het. Don't you worry about it.'

Hetty felt the sweat prickle under her arms and took a deep breath to subdue the panicky beating of her heart. She tried to smile. 'All right.'

The day wore on. The whistle blew at half past twelve and they sank gratefully to the floor round the bin. Hetty drank some of the cold tea which always made her wince and tried to eat a slice of bread, but her churning stomach threatened to give it straight back to her.

Flo edged over and sat beside her.

'What is it, Het? You worried about Warburton?'

Hetty gave her a quick sideways smile. 'A bit.'

'Has he found out?' Flo's voice was hardly above a breath.

'I don't know.' Hetty pushed down a renewed surge of panic. 'How could he?'

Flo shook her head.

'I know Mum said it wasn't your business – but could you ask Carpenter? ... I mean–'

'Ask him what? I can't ask him if Warburton knows about you and Mr Gregory – that'd be daft. Besides, I'm not quite on those terms with him.'

'Come on. Flo. He really likes you.'

Hetty was surprised to see her friend blush. 'Does he?' She pleated the front of her apron.

'You really like him, don't you?'

Flo looked into the distance. 'He's different, Het. Not like the boys at home. He makes me feel – I dunno – special.'

Hetty sighed. 'I know.'

Flo brought her gaze back to Hetty. 'Yeah. You would.'

During the afternoon Cousin Bet and Millie went off to buy sweets from the lolly man and the sun moved round so that Lillian's bin was in the shade. At half past four, the whistle blew again and the shout 'Pull no more bines' echoed up and down the green tunnels. Hetty pushed the box back to the huts on the return journey and went to fetch water while Lillian and Connie lit fires. Flo met her at the water pipe.

'Going for a walk, then, Het?'

'Yeah. You coming?'

'Yeah. See you in a minute.'

Hetty helped wash Millie down in the enamel bath and get the beds ready, then wandered off to the end of the row of huts to meet Flo. Without speaking, they set off across the common away from the Manor. The path forked and Flo turned right.

'See you later, then,' she said. 'No more'n an hour, mind.'

Hetty shook her head and started up the left-hand fork, which led down the stream to the lake and the ruined chapel. Anticipation bubbled under her ribcage as she picked her way along the dry, rutted track towards the rusted iron gates that hung drunkenly in their tall, crumbling gateposts. Past the dark, forbidding yew trees, over the moss-covered gravestones that stood at improbable angles, as though the dead were trying to raise them.

He turned from contemplation of the lake, ruffled now by an errant breeze, reflecting broken images of approaching grey clouds. They stood for a moment, staring at one another across the encroaching undergrowth, then Hetty stumbled forward, caught her foot in a trailing bramble and pitched into his waiting arms. She felt his warm breath on her forehead and the immediate hardening of his body that she had come to expect, before she raised her mouth to his.

Their kisses were becoming more explicit, mirroring the desires of their bodies, and he rolled her over until she lay underneath him, the breath squeezing out of her body.

'Gregory,' she gasped, as his hand searched vainly for the buttons on her dress. 'Stop. We can't.'

Hetty didn't know what it was that they couldn't do, just that since the morning's revelations about Warburton, she shouldn't be here, and the feelings that had sprung into life during the past week's meetings with Gregory were quite definitely not appropriate.

He hesitated, raising the thin, intense face above her and fixing her with ice blue eyes. 'Why?'

Hetty struggled from underneath him and raised herself on one elbow. 'Warburton has got it in for me. He might know about us.'

'Does it matter?'

'Of course it matters. You know what your folks'd say if they knew you was meeting me.'

'Oh, Hetty. Do you think I'd care?'

'Of course you would. And my folks'd say the same. We don't mix – your folks and mine. Think what the home-dwellers say about us – even if you know it isn't true.'

Gregory sat up and clasped his hands loosely round his knees. But for the well-bred, intelligent face, he could have been any other farm worker, in his corduroys tied round with string, the worn jacket and the cap that lay on the ground beside him. Hetty experienced a sudden rush of emotion and knew without a doubt that she loved him.

'Hetty,' he began, 'I've loved you since I saw you last year. I didn't know I loved you – just that you did something to me that I had never felt before. Now I know I love you, and I don't care about Warburton, my family or yours. I just know we've got to be together.'

'They won't let us, Greg,' Hetty whispered. 'And Warburton'll do anything to get back at me.'

'Why?' Gregory turned and looked at her. 'Why should he?'

'They say he fancies me.' Hetty was bright pink with embarrassment, but Gregory shouted with laughter.

'Well, I don't blame him,' he said, 'so do I.'

'But I don't like him, see. And he knows it, so he's got a down on us – me and my folks. He's measuring our bins heavy. And he'll look for any excuse to report us.'

Gregory frowned. 'Measuring heavy? What do you mean?'

'He pushes the hops down in the bin – hard.

Then when he puts his stick in it don't measure as much, so we have to pick more to get our money.'

'That isn't right.' Two pink spots appeared on Gregory's thin cheeks.

'No. He says he'll measure light for some women – if they'll – well–' Hetty took a deep breath, 'If they'll – you know.'

Gregory's eyes narrowed. 'I can guess. Does Frank Carpenter know this?'

Hetty shrugged. 'He's a good bloke. I don't suppose so.'

'We've never had trouble with our pickers. Father knows all of them, as well as Frank Carpenter.'

Hetty nodded. 'We hear all sorts of stories from other families at home, who go to the bigger farms.'

'So why is Warburton behaving like this? I'll get him turned off.'

'Oh, Greg, don't.' Hetty knelt up in a panic. 'How would you say you found out? It'd all come out – and I couldn't bear it.'

His face softened. 'All right, my beauty, I won't.' He lifted a long finger and traced the curve of her cheek. Hetty gasped and felt her breasts tighten underneath the cotton dress. She saw his eyes drop to them and watched as he turned towards her and took her hand, guiding it down his body. Excitement built quickly inside her and she collapsed beside him, her breath coming fast.

'Hetty–' he groaned as he freed himself from the constraints of corduroy and leather, his hands returning to explore Hetty's newly exposed flesh,

205

'we can't give this up.'

Then he was inside her and Hetty was beyond reply, the sensations in her body demanding all her attention as something pulled tighter and tighter inside her, aching to be set free. And then it was. Her eyes widened in shock and surprise before the sensations exploded again and a sense of unimaginable urgency took over, until they both came to a shuddering, juddering stop.

Hetty became aware of other things slowly, one by one. First, Greg's weight on her, second, the clouds scudding fast across a dull sky, then the top branches of the yew trees waving frantically in the wind and, last, something uncomfortable digging into her back. She tried to move away from it.

'Hetty.' Greg lifted a desolate face. 'I'm sorry, Hetty. I didn't mean that to happen.'

Hetty was surprised. How could he have not meant it to happen? He did it – he started it – she was only a willing accomplice.

'Didn't you like it?' she asked ingenuously.

Gregory collapsed on her, laughing ruefully. 'Of course I *liked* it. Did you?'

'It was wonderful,' Hetty breathed. 'That must be what all the other girls talk about. No wonder they get so excited.'

'Do they talk about it?' Greg lifted his face again.

'At work, sometimes. I didn't know what they were talking about. I suppose this is it.'

'Don't talk about this, will you, Hetty?' Greg's voice was urgent. 'This is ours. It's special and it belongs only to us.'

Hetty shook her head. 'I couldn't,' she said.

A drop of rain fell on her nose. 'Oh, Greg. I must get back. I told Flo I'd only be an hour.'

He rolled off, leaving her uncomfortably sticky. 'Will she be waiting for you?' He turned away while she pulled on knickers and he tidied himself up.

'Yes – by the fork in the road. She's been up to Carpenter's.'

'She won't say anything?'

Hetty shook her head again and stood up, brushing herself down. A movement beyond the yew trees caught her eye and she grabbed Gregory's arm.

'Someone's there, Greg!'

He turned round, but nothing could be seen but thick dark trunks and sombre green leaves rustling above ancient gravestones.

'There was – I swear. Oh, God – someone's seen us.'

Gregory took her into his arms. 'No, they haven't. Look, I'll wait here until you've gone past the gates. I'll see if there's anyone there.' He kissed the tip of her nose. 'Tomorrow?'

'If I can.' Hetty hid her face in his shoulder, then turned and ran, scrambling through the brambles and over the gravestones, the wind whipping at her thin cotton dress.

Chapter Nineteen

The silence at the end of the scene said it all, thought Libby. Then Emma, as always slightly embarrassed, brushed down her jeans and came to the front of the stage without looking at her Gregory.

'All right, Libby?' she called into the dark.

'Very good, Em. Both of you. Well done.' She clapped her hands for attention. 'We'll call a halt tonight and carry on where we left off tomorrow. How many of you said you could be here? I'm sorry to upset your Saturday.'

After some initial resistance born of an atavistic reluctance to have fun in the presence of death, the traditional visit to the pub was approved. Fran trailed along behind Libby, who managed to get out of the building ahead of Ben and Peter.

'Are they cross?'

'Ben and Pete? I don't think so. I still can't make them out. I know Pete's worried about his brother and the murder, but I don't know...'

'Peter's brother's James, right?'

Libby nodded and led the way into the pub.

'And Paula trapped him?'

'You wouldn't think it was possible in this day and age, would you?'

Fran shrugged. 'People don't change.'

They were settled in a corner with their drinks

when Ben, Peter and Harry joined them.

'So, Fran, did you get anything from that?' asked Peter, sitting down on the arm of Libby's chair.

Fran glanced at Libby. 'I'm not sure what you mean,' she said, 'or what you want me to reply.'

'Well,' said Peter, waving an airy hand, 'feelings. Whatever.'

Fran's lips tightened and Libby hurried into the breach. 'There's no need to be rude, Pete.'

Peter looked quickly at Harry and away again. 'Sorry.'

'What did you think of the play, Fran?' asked Ben.

Fran repeated what she'd said to Libby. 'And I thought the girl who played Flo's character–'

'Lizzie,' put in Libby.

'Lizzie, then, will be really good.'

Peter smirked. 'I said she should have had it in the first place. Paula was far too old.'

A nasty little silence fell. 'Well, you know what I mean.' He sighed. 'Sorry.'

'We can't keep not saying things just because they're about Paula,' said Ben, 'life hasn't changed completely.'

'Not for you, maybe,' muttered Harry, which earned him a look from Peter. Libby gave them an anxious glance.

'Ben's right,' she said, 'your opinion of Paula won't change just because she's dead. It won't matter to her now.'

'Anyway, I thought it was good,' said Fran. 'As I've said, better than I expected.'

Seeing Peter's expression, Libby leapt hastily

209

into the breach. 'And that's good from a professional,' she said.

Fran glared at her and Libby blushed. The whole conversation was littered with trip-wires.

'I didn't know that,' said Ben, looking interested.

'I don't talk about it. I was young.'

'Right.' Harry was looking at her speculatively.

With rare intuition, Libby knew what he was thinking. 'And the psychic ability is so *not* a theatrical trick, Harry.'

'No?'

'No.'

'Shut up,' said Peter suddenly, 'look who's come in.'

They all turned.

'Is that David?' whispered Libby.

'Sure is. He looks bloody awful.' Ben pushed back his chair.

'So would you if you'd had to attend a murder victim,' said Harry.

'That was yesterday,' said Peter, and turned to Fran. 'David is our local GP and Ben's brother-in-law.'

Fran didn't answer, but stared at the back of David's head.

Ben had reached the bar and put an arm round David's shoulders. Libby watched as he gave a tired smile and ran a big hand through his greying bush of hair. His jacket, as usual, looked rumpled and his tie was askew under the open collar of his shirt.

'Every inch the country doctor, isn't he?' said Libby, watching Fran's face.

210

'Is he genuine?' said Fran under her breath.

'Genuine? What on earth do you mean? He's a bloody doctor, you don't get much more genuine than that.'

Fran looked back at her, her cheeks slightly pink. 'Sorry. I don't really know what I meant. He just looks almost too good to be true – as you said, every inch a country doctor.'

'Central casting?' Libby was amused. 'Yes, he is. All bluff good nature, slightly shy, absent-minded and very kind.'

'Quite a paragon, then,' said Fran.

'You're not convinced,' Libby stated.

'Of course I am – you know him, I don't.'

'But you can feel something?' Libby persisted.

Fran's face took on its regular expression of discomfort. 'Oh, hell, I hate this. Everything I say is open to misinterpretation.'

Ben and David appeared at the table, David with a pint of bitter in one hand and a pipe in the other. Fran and Libby exchanged glances.

'He needs cheering up, folks,' said Ben. 'Have my chair, David.'

'Hello, David,' said Libby. 'How's Susan?'

'Oh, you know,' grunted David, squashing into Ben's chair. 'Doesn't much like this business.'

'Which business?' asked Harry.

David looked startled. 'The murder. Of that girl. You all knew her.'

'It's OK, David,' said Peter, leaning forward, 'we know what you mean. We've just had a bit of trouble at the theatre as well.'

'Oh? The theatre?'

Ben looked exasperated. 'Yes, Dave, the theatre.

211

I converted it, remember?'

'Oh, ah. Of course I remember. Millie didn't like it.' He looked at Fran as if suddenly registering her presence.

'This is my friend Fran Castle, David,' said Libby. 'Fran, this is David Dedham.'

Fran leant forward and held out her hand. 'How do you do?' she said politely.

David shook her hand and nodded. 'Fine. Nice to meet you. Staying with Libby, are you? Good. Not a nice time to be on your own.' He thought for a moment. 'For a woman.'

Libby cleared her throat. 'No, David. I agree.' She didn't look at Ben or Fran. 'I think Peter feels the same about his Mum.'

It was Peter's turn to look surprised.

'There's nothing we can do there, though, is there?' said David, taking a pull at his pint. 'She can hardly move in with Peter and Harry.'

Harry growled.

'James is with her at the moment,' said Peter, with a warning look at Harry, 'he'll be staying around for a bit.'

'James, yes.' David shifted in his chair. 'Poor chap.'

The others round the table all looked at each other.

'Yes,' said Libby.

David looked up. 'Don't you agree? Poor chap's lost his – er – his–'

'Paula. We know. And the baby,' said Peter.

'Well, I wouldn't know about that,' said David, looking uncomfortable. 'I wasn't her GP.'

'Weren't you? I thought everybody in the village

212

was your patient,' said Libby.

'No, no. I couldn't cope with everybody. Andrews and Court in Steeple Mount take a lot of the newer residents.'

'But Paula's been here longer than I have,' said Libby.

'And you've never registered, have you?' smiled David, patting her arm. 'Not that I blame you – friend of the family and all that. But you must do it, you know. If not with me, with Andrews or Court. You couldn't exactly call your old doctor all the way out here, could you?'

'I suppose not,' said Libby. She looked at Peter. 'What about you?'

'Me? Oh, am I registered? Yes. Always have been. Whole family. We were with David's predecessor, so he just took us over.'

'Really? Was that before you married Susan?' Libby asked.

David grinned, looking down into his beer. 'Yes. I had to get her registered somewhere else so I could court her.'

'Court her?' gasped Harry. '*Court* her? Good lord!'

'Shut up, Harry,' said Ben, Libby and Peter together. Fran laughed.

'Oh, well, we've always been a bit old-fashioned, haven't we, Ben?' said David comfortably. 'It suits us.'

'It certainly does,' said Ben, winking at Libby. Winking is *so* crass, thought Libby, trying not to smile.

'Not often we see you in here, David,' said Peter, leaning back against Harry. 'Did you get a late pass?'

David frowned. 'Susan's not like that. We are both free to do whatever we like. If I want a drink on the way home I pop in here.'

'On the way home? Bit late for surgery, isn't it?' asked Harry.

'House call,' said David, and drank the remainder of his pint in one go. 'Must go. Don't want Sue on her own for too long. Not at the moment.' He surged to his feet, causing seismic upheaval to all the drinks on the table. Everyone grabbed their glasses and murmured goodbye. David smiled vaguely and shouldered his way to the door, accompanied by a chorus of goodnights from the regulars.

'He's hard work, isn't he?' said Harry. 'I know he's your brother-in-law, Ben, but...'

Ben nodded. 'An upright, unimaginative salt of the earth countryman. I don't know how he got through medical school.'

'Oh, I expect he was quite different then,' said Libby. 'Rugby and rag week, I can just see him heavily involved with those.'

'Apparently, he was quite a ladies' man at that time,' said Peter. 'Wasn't there some talk of him hiding away in the country to avoid someone, Ben?'

'Come to think of it, yes. Not that I heard much about it at the time, I was only about seventeen.'

'I would have thought that was just the age to hear about all the scandal, especially jack-the-laddish sort of scandal,' said Peter. 'It was the year I was born they got married, wasn't it?'

'I think so. Can't remember your mum being

pregnant at the wedding, though.'

'I didn't realise they were so close in age,' said Libby.

'My mum and dad only got married a couple of years before Susan,' said Peter. 'Mum must be about the same age as David and four years older than Susan.'

'So your mum missed all the competition for David, then,' said Ben. 'I remember that, all right. New young doctor – the women in the village were discovering all sorts of things wrong with them. I think Susan was really surprised when he – um – came *courting*.' He grinned at Harry, who flounced back.

The bell rang behind the bar and Jim called time. Libby drank the last drop of her drink and stood up.

'See you all tomorrow, then, shall we?'

'Not me, sunshine. I'm busy in the caff all day,' said Harry.

'Well, perhaps we'll come in for a meal later, then, if you're not booked up?' said Fran. 'My treat,' she added to Libby.

Harry cheered up. 'Nine o'clock too late? Then you can have the table for the rest of the evening,' he said.

They agreed nine o'clock was perfect, said goodbye to Ben and Peter and, refusing offers of an escort home, set off down the High Street.

'Peter and David don't get on, then?' said Fran, as they turned into Allhallow's Lane.

'What?' Libby turned to her in surprise. 'What makes you think that?'

'Oh, I don't know. Take no notice. I'm going to

215

have to learn to shut up,' said Fran, frowning.

Libby unlocked the door and warned Fran about the step. Sidney looked on from his favourite stair and when he spotted Fran leapt down and tripped her up anyway.

'Coffee?' asked Libby, throwing her cape towards a chair. 'Or whisky? I've even got some red wine.'

'Tea? I'd really prefer tea,' said Fran. 'If I drink any more I'll start saying all sorts of things I shouldn't.'

'Is that what happens, then?' asked Libby, interested.

'Like just now.' Fran perched against the kitchen table. 'I say things that come into my head, without knowing why, and people attach all kinds of meanings to them. I told you, it's as if someone has told me these things. I have no spooky sensations of being spoken to from beyond, or anything like that. It's just there.'

'I wonder why Peter and David don't get on,' mused Libby, pouring water into a teapot for Fran. 'I suppose their lifestyles are so different, and Peter's young enough to be his son. But if David was a bit of a lad in his youth, you'd think he'd have some sympathy, wouldn't you?'

Fran watched Libby pour herself a whisky. 'No, that generation were raging homophobes, weren't they? In the fifties they were still putting people into clinics to "cure" them.'

'Really?' Libby poured Fran's tea and led the way into the sitting room. Sidney appropriated Fran's lap and sneered at Libby.

'Oh, yes. There were very exclusive private

216

clinics where they used to do the most unspeakable things. And David would have done his training at a time when that wasn't very far behind.'

'I've never noticed any particular disapproval,' said Libby. 'Peter makes fun of David sometimes, but very gently. Harry's more abrasive, but he's only young, and not really used to village life yet.'

'Well, it's probably nothing,' sighed Fran. 'Just my peculiar brain.'

'Doesn't matter, anyway,' said Libby, 'it's nothing to do with the theatre, after all.'

'No, of course not,' said Fran, but Libby was sure she detected doubt in Fran's voice. She raised her eyebrows, but Fran didn't look up from stroking Sidney, who was purring like a banshee.

'And there was nothing else? About the theatre?'

Fran looked up. 'I don't think so. Just the play. As I said, I don't think I'd get struck with a blinding light or anything.'

'Then how do you *know?*' asked Libby in frustration.

'I said, it's just facts in my head.' Fran picked up her mug and moved an indignant Sidney on to the floor. 'For example: you've told me quite a bit about your life, which I now know as facts. If I suddenly came out with – oh, I don't know – the fact that you had a fourth child, it would seem as though you'd told me that, but you probably hadn't.'

Libby's mouth was open. 'I haven't.'

'No, that was just an example.'

'But I had a miscarriage.'

Fran looked startled. 'I'm sorry. I really didn't

217

know that.'

'Hmm. A bit odd though,' said Libby. 'I think I need another whisky.'

Fran heaved a deep sigh. 'I think I'll join you.'

Libby looked over her shoulder and grinned. 'And then I'll wait for you to come out with something scandalous.'

Fran laughed. 'OK. I'll see what I can dredge up. How about that chap who came up to talk to you at the beginning?'

'What chap?'

'Quite good-looking, about our age. Grumpy.'

'Oh, Stephen.' Libby handed Fran her glass. 'He's another old friend imported to help us with the play. He's set designer cum stage manager, and in charge of construction. What did you dredge up about him?'

'I'm not sure.' Fran stared in to the fire. 'He seemed very angry.'

'He – ah – fancies me,' said Libby, 'at least, he thinks he does. Very jealous of Peter, Harry and Ben.'

'Well, I can see why he'd be jealous of Ben, but Peter and Harry?'

'Because I see a lot of them, I think. And he doesn't live here, which makes him feel like an outsider.'

Fran nodded. 'I'll see if anything else comes to mind.'

But nothing came up. They sat and talked for another half-an-hour before Fran said she was tired and went up to bed. Libby fed Sidney and shut him in the conservatory in case he decided to join his new friend upstairs, then turned off the lights and went up herself.

It was all very well, she thought, poking about in someone's brain to find the answers to unanswerable questions, but it looked as though there were some things that might be best left alone. David and Peter, for instance. Libby had only vaguely been conscious of the fact that they were related. Of course, she knew, if she thought about it, but David and Susan never socialised with Ben, Peter or Harry. Millicent she'd only met recently, so she had no idea whether she was on friendly terms with her niece and nephew-in-law. It would make sense if she were, as she and Susan must have been brought up almost as sisters. And what did it matter anyway? David and Susan had nothing to do with the theatre. Libby was still trying to remember whether they had any children when sleep rolled over her like a mist, shrouding her until morning.

Chapter Twenty

A note propped up against the kettle informed Libby that Fran had woken early, found the tea-towel with the rather twee map of the village and gone exploring. 'Fed Sidney,' it said, 'hope you don't mind.'

Sidney naturally lied winsomely about this, but Libby refused to give in and took her tea into the sitting room, where she sat by the window wondering how long Fran would be and what exactly she was exploring. Eventually she saw her coming up Allhallow's Lane carrying an armful of newspapers.

'I didn't know which ones you took,' said Fran, dumping them all on the coffee table.

'I don't,' said Libby, 'but if I did, I'd probably buy those.'

'Really? Oh, I am sorry. I only read the arts and review sections myself, but most people I know seem to have at least two on Saturday and two on Sunday and read through them during the week.'

'I'd never have time,' said Libby. 'Tea or coffee?'

'Tea, please,' said Fran, following her into the kitchen.

'I get my news from the radio and television. I can't be bothered with all the in-depth editorial comment. Sorry, I didn't mean to sound churlish.'

'You didn't. I got the local paper, too.'

Libby turned round from the Rayburn. 'Oh. Did it – I mean, I never thought–'

'Yes, there's a bit in there, but it must have been really close to their deadline, so it's more-or-less stop-press.' Fran took the mug Libby held out and went back into the sitting room. 'Look, there.' She held out the paper.

A small paragraph reported the finding of Paula's body, adding that the police were treating the death as "suspicious".

'I'll say,' said Libby.

'Leave it, Libby,' said Fran, 'you've got enough to think about.'

Libby nodded morosely. 'You're not kidding.'

They sipped tea in silence for a few moments.

'Tell you what I'd like to do,' said Fran. 'I'd like to go and see the bridge. If you tell me where it is, I could go while you're rehearsing this afternoon.'

'We could go this morning, then I could come with you.'

'No, it'll give me something to do later on.'

'OK,' said Libby doubtfully, 'if you're sure.'

'Sure. And I could look at the huts, too, couldn't I? How far did you say it was?'

'Quicker from the top of the lane here than the way Pete took me,' said Libby, 'but I'm not absolutely certain I could find them going that way.'

'I'll ask Ben to show me. He won't be at rehearsal today, will he?'

'No,' said Libby, after trying to find a reason for Ben to be chained to the theatre all afternoon.

'Good,' said Fran, getting to her feet. 'Oh, here's the tea-towel.'

'Where did you get to?' asked Libby, spreading it out on top of the papers.

'All the way down that way,' Fran pointed, 'past the restaurant, then back on the other side of the High Street and up to there.'

'That's Lendle Lane,' said Libby. 'Where Paula was killed.'

'Is it? I thought that was where she lived.'

'She was killed outside her house.'

'How do you know?'

Libby looked at Fran in surprise. 'What do you mean, how do I know? Her car was outside her house and she was inside her car.'

Fran stared back. 'So how do you know she was

221

killed there?'

Libby gaped. 'Good God. I never thought of that.'

'Sorry. I was being difficult again, wasn't I?'

'No, of course you weren't.' Libby slid sideways into a chair.

'It's so obvious, isn't it? Nobody said she died there, I just assumed it.'

'I expect the police thought of it, though,' said Fran, 'and they'll have gone over it with a tooth-comb.'

'I suppose it doesn't make a lot of difference where – oh! hang on – could she have been killed outside the car? Or are we saying she was killed *in* the car and then the car was moved?'

Fran shook her head. 'No idea. I didn't see the car and I didn't see any obvious police presence, either. No tape or anything like that.'

'Well, she lived round the bend in the lane, so unless you went down it...'

'No, I turned round there and came back.'

'And you didn't feel anything while you were up there?'

'No, Libby, I didn't!' Fran sighed and sat down on the arm of the other armchair. 'Don't keep asking me. If anything comes up, I'll tell you.'

'Sorry.' Libby stood up. 'Breakfast. Do you want to wait while I get dressed, or shall we have it now?'

'Can't I do it?' asked Fran. 'I only have toast and cereal anyway.'

'Oh, good, me too,' said Libby. 'I'll go and get dressed then.'

When she came downstairs, she found Fran

speaking on her mobile phone.

'Ben,' she said, as she switched it off. 'He's coming to pick me up later.'

'Oh?' Libby quelled the urgent desire to scream and drum her heels.

'To show me the sights,' grinned Fran. 'The huts and the bridge. Then he said we could meet you in the pub for lunch.'

'My whole social life revolves around food and drink,' sighed Libby, appeased.

'Doesn't everybody's?'

'Maybe. I don't know any more. I either seem to be in Harry's caff or the pub.'

'Or the theatre. Or the police station.'

'Gee, thanks. What a comfort you are.'

Libby spent the morning at the theatre with props and one of the carpenters. Happily covered in paint and glue, she was sipping a mug of enamel-scouring tea in the scenery dock when Ben stuck his head round a flat.

'I thought you were meeting us for lunch?' he said, his glance taking in her less than sartorially elegant appearance.

'What time is it?' Libby squinted at her watch.

'One-thirty. Your rehearsal starts at two.'

'Oh, bugger.' Libby put down her mug. 'Bit late now, then.'

'Never mind. I'll bring you a sandwich,' said Ben, and disappeared.

Torn between gratification that he had come seeking her out and was attending to her needs, and jealousy because he'd spent the morning and lunchtime with Fran, Libby went home to have a wash and change out of her borrowed overalls.

When she got back, she was relieved to see the lights spilling from the front doors and even more relieved when she went in and heard familiar voices declaiming from inside the auditorium. Harry appeared on the stairs to the lighting box.

'Hallo, dearheart. You're late.'

'Yes. I take it Peter's running the rehearsal?'

Harry descended the stairs, sinuous in tight leather trousers.

'Reluctantly, dear, reluctantly.'

'Oh, I hate this,' Libby burst out, flinging her cape off and catching Harry in the eye.

'Oi! Less of it.' He blinked and rubbed a delicate finger over the injured place. 'I hate it, too, but I don't get violent.'

'Sorry.' Libby peered at the reddened eye. 'I didn't mean it.'

'I know, dear.' Harry patted her arm. 'You're overwrought. Here – have a fag and calm down, then you can go in there and start throwing your weight about.'

She stood unseen at the back, looking down towards the stage, where a distinctly lacklustre performance was taking place. Peter, sunk down in the middle of the third row, was making no attempt to stop the proceedings, and as far as Libby could see was paying no attention at all to what was happening in front of him. She waited until the action had ground to a halt without any prompting from Peter and then walked forward.

'Right,' she said, going to the front of the stage and surveying the surprised faces, 'I see the general malaise has overtaken everyone.'

'Libby–' Peter's flustered voice came from

behind her.

'It's all right, Pete. I'm back. I'll take over now.' She didn't turn her head. 'Now – will you go back to the beginning of that scene, please and put some life into it.' She looked round the set.

An hour later, she conceded that there was some improvement and the new Lizzie had done very well.

'Are we still going up on Tuesday, Libby?' called a voice from the back when she'd finished giving her notes. She looked up in feigned surprise.

'Of course. Why shouldn't we?'

There was a muttering round the stage like the whisper of wind through wheat.

'We just thought–'

'Well, don't think. We've got a terrific theatre – a good play and some good publicity. We're going ahead despite any petty attempts to stop us – if that's what they are, and, as I said, we owe it to Paula.' Not that I quite see how, she thought, but it struck the right note.

There was a general murmur of approval and people began to disperse.

The promised sandwich had turned up after the rehearsal had started, handed over by Peter, but of Ben there had been no further sign. Libby had found her mind wandering from what was happening onstage to what could be happening between Fran and Ben, despite Fran's assurances that there was nothing between them.

'Pleased? Not pleased?' asked Peter, when the auditorium was empty. 'Or were you merely letting them off lightly before a rigorous workout tomorrow?'

'Something like that,' she said, climbing on to the stage.

'As long as that's all it is,' said Peter, following her behind the set.

'What do you mean?'

'You mustn't let this Paula business get in the way.'

'This Paula business, as you so delicately put it, is the reason we're rehearsing all over the weekend. And she was murdered, in case you've forgotten.'

'All right, all right, I know. I just don't want you to get mixed up in it.'

'How could I do that?' Libby turned to face him indignantly.

'You're still trying to find out who did it,' said Peter bluntly.

Libby felt herself redden. 'I don't want to do that. You know perfectly well all I want to do is find out about the accidents. Just so they won't happen again.'

'They won't.' Peter checked the back door and walked out on to the stage. 'No more accidents.'

Libby followed him back into the auditorium. 'So you're not too pleased Fran's here after all?'

'I don't think she'll find anything out. Just don't take too much notice of what she says. She might make something up just to please you.'

'She wouldn't!' gasped Libby.

'Ask yourself why she's really here, Lib,' said Peter, ushering her out into the foyer.

'She wanted a break? She wanted to help me?'

'And Ben?'

Libby went cold. 'She sees him through work.'

'But not on his home turf. And he asked her in the first place, didn't he?'

'She said there was nothing between them.'

'Of course she did. Wouldn't you have done?'

Libby's heart sank. Thought of the admissions Fran had got out of her. 'I like her,' she said.

'She's very likeable,' agreed Peter.

Libby turned to lock the doors. 'You don't like her.'

'It's not a matter of whether I like her or not,' said Peter, tucking his arm through Libby's as they began to walk down the drive. 'I don't trust her.'

This was not going well, thought Libby miserably. Pete was one of her oldest and most loved friends, and she really wanted him to like Fran.

'Maybe I'm wrong,' Peter was saying, 'just because she's turned up in this situation, where we don't need outsiders.'

'Ben invited her, not me,' said Libby.

'I just said that, didn't I? But you invited her to stay. I bet she leapt at the opportunity.'

'Don't be so rotten.' Libby pulled her arm away. 'Why don't you want her here? Why are you so bothered about people looking into the accidents?'

'I'm not.' Peter shrugged. 'I just don't want the waters muddied.'

'Peter.' Libby stopped dead, forcing him to turn and face her. 'You've been shilly-shallying about all this for the last week. Certainly since last Monday. In fact,' she added thoughtfully, 'since your Mum paid us a visit. That was when you said there was an atmosphere. What's been going on that I don't know about?'

Peter stared at her for a long moment, then turned and began to walk on down the drive.

'Pete!' Libby said. 'Answer me.'

He stopped and sighed. 'Nothing's going on. Sorry. I just don't like interference in family affairs.'

'In that case, why on earth did you write *The Hop Pickers?* You can't put your family's history and peccadilloes on show and then decide you don't like the consequences.'

'I didn't know all of the history and peccadilloes, obviously.' Peter was frowning.

'What do you mean by that? What do you know now that you didn't know a fortnight ago?'

'Nothing you don't,' he said, evasively.

'Oh, yes? And, while we're on the subject, why don't you like interference in family affairs by anyone else when you're perfectly happy about me?'

He glanced at her sideways, but said nothing.

'Oh, of course. I haven't been told everything, have I? By a long chalk.' Libby stuffed her hands in the pockets of her skirt underneath her cape and strode ahead of him down the drive. He caught her up at the bottom, just as she was about to turn left towards Allhallow's Lane.

'Lib, don't be like this.' He pulled her into his arms and rested his chin on her head. 'I'm sorry. I'm being a pig. But honestly, I can't get my head round all this. I hoped the play would take our minds off things, but now I'm not sure. I just can't help worrying about Harry, and me, and my mum.'

Libby pulled back and looked up into his face. 'As suspects, you mean?'

He nodded. 'And James most of all.'

'Not Ben?'

'I don't think the police are worried about Ben.'

'But your mum?' Libby was horrified. 'They can't suspect her, surely?'

'Yes, they can. They suspect her of the accidents, so they suspect her of the murder.'

Libby stared at him. 'And did she? Did she do them?'

'I don't know.' Peter shook his head. 'I can't see it, can you? I know she's odd, but doing all those things?'

'Ben and I said we couldn't see her up a ladder cutting steel wire. Or sawing through the bridge, come to that.'

Pete sighed. 'No. But I'd rather not know, somehow.' He smiled weakly at her. 'Go on. Go and attend to your guest. You're coming in to the caff, tonight, aren't you? I'll see you then.'

'And be polite to Fran,' warned Libby.

'I will. But you watch her, young Lib. That Ben is a right little cad in his own way. Cousin or not.'

Libby thought about this all the way home, as if she hadn't been thinking about it all afternoon, and was relieved to find Fran in the cottage alone, Sidney fast asleep on her lap.

'How did it go?' asked Fran, putting Sidney aside and going towards the kitchen. 'Can I make you a cup of tea?'

Sucking up, thought Libby uncharitably. 'So-so,' she said. 'How was your day?'

'OK.' Fran put the kettle on the hob. 'Why

didn't you come to the pub?'

'I didn't know what time you were going to be there, and when Ben came to find me it was too late.'

'Sorry.' Fran wrinkled her brow. 'He seemed to think you'd know. We got there about one.'

'How would I know? You just said lunch-time. I didn't speak to him at all.'

Fran looked up quickly. 'Oh, Libby, you're angry with me. Oh, God, I'm so crap at this.'

'Crap at what?' Libby felt in her pockets for cigarettes, realising that she hadn't had one all day. Angst was good for something, then.

'People.' Fran poured water into two mugs. 'I get them all muddled up.'

'Muddled up? How? I'm a woman, Ben's a man. Can't muddle that up.'

'No.' Fran turned round and handed Libby a mug. 'Sorry, didn't use the teapot.'

'Doesn't matter.' Libby went into the sitting room and found her cigarettes on the table.

'What I meant was,' said Fran, sitting down and lifting Sidney on to her lap, something he would never let Libby do, 'I get fixated on an idea and forget about the people concerned. I should never have gone off with Ben.'

'Why ever not?' asked Libby, feeling the now familiar blush creep up her neck.

'Well–' Fran looked down at Sidney, '–because of you. And him.'

'Fran, there *is* no me and him.'

'There is. Or you'd like there to be. And I'm sure he feels the same.'

'Look, Fran, none of us are teenagers any

more, and I'm not going to scratch your eyes out because you went off for the day with the bloke I fancy. I'm a grown-up, and grown-ups don't do that sort of thing.' Even if we want to, she thought.

'All right,' said Fran doubtfully, 'if you say so.'

'I do,' said Libby, lighting the cigarette at last and inhaling gratefully. 'So what happened?'

'Ben took me to see the huts – aren't they small? – and the bridge, then he took me to see Mrs Carpenter.'

'Did he?' said Libby, surprised. 'What for?'

'I don't really know.' Fran shrugged, and earned a baleful look from Sidney. 'He just said he ought to go and see her and did I want to come along. They talked about you, mainly.'

'Me?'

'Mrs Carpenter asked after you. "How's that Libby?" she said. Asked how you'd taken it.'

'And? What did Ben say?'

Fran shrugged again and Sidney fell off her lap. 'Said you were upset, obviously.'

'Is that all?'

'Well,' said Fran, looking uncomfortable, 'she said he should look after you. She told him off, rather.'

Libby grinned. 'I can just hear her. "You've done enough running around with these young birds. Need a good solid woman of your own age."'

Fran raised her eyebrows. 'Just about. How did you know?'

'She said the same to me. I wasn't too sure about the solid, but I took the sentiment in good

231

part.' Libby looked at the end of her cigarette. 'And what did Ben say to that?'

'Well, sort of– "I know, I know." Looked a bit embarrassed.'

'As well he might,' said Libby. 'So would I have done.'

'Anyway, that was about it. And I'm afraid,' said Fran with a sigh, 'nothing came leaping out at me at all. All day.'

'Oh, well, never mind. It was worth a try.' Libby threw her cigarette into the fireplace. 'Shall I light a fire? We're not going out until later, are we?'

'That'd be nice.' Fran smiled up at her. 'Am I forgiven?'

Libby pulled a face. 'Don't be daft.'

They spent a companionable couple of hours in front of the fire, until Fran asked if they should change before going to the Pink Geranium.

'I suppose we should look smartish. People come from all over to eat there. I tend to be there at lunchtimes or when they're closed.' Libby stood up. 'You go and use the bathroom first.'

Fran's little black jacket and tailored trousers sent Libby's heart into her boots. Her one and only silk blouse had made a return appearance, along with a rather dated pair of loose, dark red trousers. Her rusty bush of hair was tied up with a ribbon, while Fran's sleek dark bob swung provocatively over her well marked cheekbones.

'I don't know why I like you. You're far too smart and attractive.' Libby flung her cape round her shoulders and picked up her basket. 'Look at me. A reject from the hippy era.'

Fran laughed. 'I've only got these sort of clothes because I need them for work and I can't afford two separate wardrobes. And your look suits you. It's – I don't know – sort of earthy and sexy.'

'Really? Peter says I look like a window dummy from Oxfam.'

'Charity shops are really "in" these days. I get at least half my clothes from them.' Fran buttoned up her navy coat as they stepped out into Allhallow's Lane. 'This coat came from the Hospice Shop.'

'Really?' Libby stroked the sleeve. 'It's a good one, isn't it? Not my style, though.'

'No, you're more flamboyant. Your cape's very you.'

Libby smiled, a trifle smugly. Earthy, sexy and flamboyant she liked. Shame about the short fat body that went with it.

The Pink Geranium was packed. Donna, Harry's somewhat harassed young *aide de camp*, as Peter referred to her, showed them to the sofa in the window to wait until their table was ready. Peter stood behind the counter making up drinks orders and waved. A minute later, a bottle of white wine and two glasses were brought over "apologies from Pete" as Donna said.

'Apologies? What for?' Fran sat back in the sofa. Libby didn't dare or she would have disappeared.

'Oh, we had a bit of a spat this afternoon,' said Libby.

Fran looked a question.

'Can't you guess?' Libby frowned. 'Isn't it just there in your head?'

233

'Libby, please. Don't keep having digs at me. I told you I don't know much about whatever it is I've got. If facts are in my head, they're in there. If they aren't, they aren't.' Fran sighed. 'I'm not doing it on purpose, and I bet that's what the fight was about, wasn't it? Peter doesn't trust me, and thinks I'm just down here for a free ride and to get off with Ben.'

'There you are, you see. You can do it,' said Libby crossly.

'No, that was simple deduction. And obviously I'm right.' Fran looked across at Peter, who caught her eye and bowed slightly.

'Yes, you're right. I'm sorry. But he's apologised. He's just worried about his family.'

'Of course he is.' Fran put down her glass. 'You know, Libby, I'm not sure this going on with the play is the right thing to do. Is it a bit insensitive?'

'Oh, don't start that again,' groaned Libby. 'We've been going over this ever since Wednesday, you know we have. We can't renege again.'

'No, I know, and it was Peter who finally decided to go ahead, wasn't it?' Fran shook her head. 'I can't make him out, really I can't.'

'No? How do you mean?'

'He's like two different people. One minute he's being as camp as all get out, all insouciant and silly, the next he's being serious and positively angst-ridden.'

'It's being a Gemini what does it,' said Libby wriggling backwards into the sofa until her feet wouldn't touch the floor. 'Not so much a split personality as wanting to know what it's like to be different. He likes to experience all sorts of things, and it's now embedded in his personality. He really *is* serious, and cares deeply about things, but on the other hand–'

'He feels he's got to keep up with Harry?' asked Fran.

'Yes, I suppose that's it. I've known Peter for years, long before he met Harry. I always knew he was gay, everybody did, but we never knew much about what he got up to in London. When he brought Harry down here we were all surprised, but everybody said how good it was for him. He lightened up – yes, became insouciant and silly as you put it. What worries me is that Harry might run away from all this. He's not even thirty yet, and I'm not convinced he has much of a sense of responsibility.'

'I thought he told you he really loves Peter?'

'He did. But he also said he felt stifled by the family.'

Fran stared at the floor for a moment. 'D'you know,' she said finally, 'I think I know too much about you all. I'm an outsider. I shouldn't know all these intimate things.'

'But that's why you're here.'

'I know. But it doesn't seem right.'

Libby heaved a sigh of exasperation. 'Look, once and for all, Ben asked you in, I confirmed it. Whatever the rights and wrongs, you're in. If you choose to leave us to our problems – well, *them* to *their* problems, I suppose – that's your privilege, but let's not keep going backwards and forwards. Is it or is it not insensitive, are you intruding or are you not intruding. Let's just make up our minds and stick to it.'

Disconcerted, Fran sat looking at Libby with her mouth open.

'Libby, your table's ready in a minute. Do you want to order?'

Libby looked up to find Donna holding out menus.

'Thanks, Donna great. I know what I want, but Fran will need to choose.'

Fran took the menu and buried her face in it. Libby looked amused.

'Hello, you old trout.' Peter appeared at Libby's elbow. 'How's tricks?'

'Thanks for the wine,' said Libby, smiling up at him. 'A nice gesture.'

He pulled a face. 'I'm full of them. Fran, how are you this evening?'

'Fine, thank you,' said Fran, looking up and putting the menu down on the table in front of her. 'Just saying, I think I ought to go back to London and leave you all to it tomorrow. I'm only complicating matters.'

Libby and Peter exchanged surprised glances.

'Were you?' asked Libby. 'I didn't hear that.'

Fran flushed. 'Well, that's what I meant. You agree, don't you, Peter?'

Peter scowled. 'I don't know, do I?' He looked at Libby. 'What have you been saying?'

'She hasn't said anything,' said Fran. 'I just feel I'm in the way, and I can't contribute anything after all, despite what Ben thought at first.'

There was a short, awkward silence. Then Peter's face relaxed into a smile. 'Thanks, Fran. But don't feel we're driving you away. You're

236

welcome to stay if you want to get away from the rat-race.'

Libby laughed. 'In my house, of course,' she said.

'Oh, you know what I mean,' said Peter. 'Now, can I take your order? Seeing as I'm here?'

Libby and Fran were still at their table when the last of the other diners drifted out. Harry appeared, still in his checked chef's trousers and white tunic. Fran complimented him on the food and he made her an exaggerated bow.

'Pete says you're going back to London to-morrow,' he said, twirling round a chair to sit astride with his arms along the back.

Fran nodded. 'I only intended to stay for a couple of days anyway,' she said, 'and I haven't been much help.'

'You'll come back to see the play, won't you?'

'Well,' said Fran, looking at Libby, 'if Libby can put me up, I'd love to. Or are there rooms at the pub?'

'As long as you don't want to come next week-end you can stay with me,' said Libby. 'The kids are coming on Friday and Saturday.'

'I think I could only get away on Friday,' said Fran, looking disappointed.

'We'll think of something,' said Harry, 'just keep in touch with old Lib.'

Peter arrived carrying a brandy bottle and glasses.

'So, no Ben this evening, girls?' he said.

'Why should we know?' asked Libby.

Peter raised his eyebrows. 'Hoity-toity,' he said, 'I was only asking.'

'Sorry. I don't know where he is. Did he mention anything to you, Fran?'

Fran shook her head and took a sip of brandy. 'Mmm, lovely,' she said, closing her eyes.

Peter winked at Libby. 'The fruits of country living,' he said. 'The good things in life.'

Fran looked from one to the other of them. 'And I hope you appreciate them,' she said.

Peter looked taken aback and Harry snorted with laughter.

'We do, Fran, we do. But thank you for reminding us,' said Libby, patting Fran's arm.

'David and Susan were in earlier,' said Harry. 'I don't think they've ever eaten here before.'

'Must have been seeing us all in the pub the other night,' said Peter. 'Reminded him he'd got a family.'

'Reminded him that Susan has, anyway,' said Libby. 'Did he say anything?'

'Apart from "What on earth is panzanella?", not a lot,' said Harry.

'What is it, then?' asked Fran.

'Bread salad,' said Peter. 'Bog standard stuff.'

'Oi!' said Harry, giving him a poke in the ribs.

'No, I meant did he say anything about – you know. Er, Paula.' Libby buried her nose in her glass.

'Yes, he did, actually,' said Peter. 'Asked if we'd heard anything. Asked how James was and wondered if he ought to go and see him.'

'What did you say?'

'Well, I don't think James would be all that delighted to receive a visit from our resident bumbling GP, do you? He's got enough on his hands with my mum, frankly.'

'Oh, so he's still there? Is she being difficult?'

'More difficult than normal, you mean?' Peter sighed. 'Oh, I don't know. When I was round there earlier she was going on about having lost her only chance of grandchildren, which didn't go down too well with me, as you can imagine. And James looked as though he could cheerfully strangle her.' He swore. 'Sorry. That came out wrong, didn't it?'

'Why doesn't he go back home?' asked Libby.

'Maternal blackmail, I should think.'

'But it's James who's supposedly bereaved,' said Libby.

'Oh, don't ask me,' said Peter grumpily. 'We all know what we think about that situation, don't we?'

'And that's why the police are so interested in him,' said Harry.

Peter and Libby exchanged startled looks.

'Do they know about it, then? Him being trapped?' asked Libby.

'Must do,' said Harry, going pink.

Peter looked at him for a long time without speaking.

'You told them,' he said eventually.

'Not exactly,' said Harry, looking trapped himself.

Libby stood up. 'Our cue to leave, Fran,' she said.

Fran pushed her chair back so quickly it nearly fell over.

'Lovely to see you both,' she said hastily. 'Hope I'll see you at the end of the week. Good luck

239

with the play.'

Peter smiled with obvious effort, while Harry swung out of his chair and kissed Fran's cheek before giving Libby a hug. 'Wish me luck,' he whispered in her ear.

'Now I really am worried about Harry leaving,' said Libby, as they walked back down the High Street. 'Either of his own accord or because Pete throws him out.'

'Lover versus brother,' said Fran, nodding.

'Bloody hell. Why is everything so complicated?' said Libby with a sigh.

Fran stopped dead, her hand to her mouth.

'What?' said Libby. 'What is it? Fran, tell me, quick!'

Fran looked at her forlornly.

'I forgot to pay the bill.'

Libby laughed. 'Well, we're not going back. I'll take it round tomorrow. Come on, time for a nightcap.'

They were settled in front of the fire again with a bottle of whisky Fran had bought from the village shop along with the papers that morning, when Libby looked up.

'Do you know,' she said, 'we've never asked how Paula died?'

Fran looked surprised. 'I assumed you knew.'

'No. I didn't ask the sergeant – or maybe I did – but it was definitely a need-to-know situation, and he wouldn't have told me. And no one else has said anything, even David.'

'No, he didn't. But she was hit on the head, wasn't she?'

Libby stared.

'Oh, I've done it again, haven't I?' Fran sighed.

'Well, yes, I suppose you have.'

'Sorry. But I'm sure she was. And I'm pretty sure it wasn't where she was found.'

Chapter Twenty-one

Libby phoned the Pink Geranium the next morning hoping to hear Harry's voice.

'Yes, he's here,' said Donna. 'Doesn't look very happy though.'

'Hello,' came Harry's voice. 'Who's that?'

'Me. Fran forgot to pay the bill. She's left me the money.'

'Didn't even notice,' said Harry, 'under the circumstances.'

Libby tried to think of something non-confrontational to say.

'Go on, then, ask me,' said Harry, 'you know you want to.'

'As long as you're still here,' said Libby, clearing her throat.

'You thought he'd chuck me out? Yeah, so did I.'

'But he hasn't?'

'Not quite. I think the attitude is "You'd better hope they come up with the real murderer pretty damn quick." Or I'm history.'

'Oh, Harry, we all know James didn't do it.'

'Ah, but do the police? You should have seen them when I let slip about what we all felt about

241

Paula. All their little ears pricked up.'

'Is that how it happened, then? You didn't volunteer the information?'

'What do you take me for?' Harry sounded indignant. 'I told you it just slipped out. They were asking me how well I'd known Paula and how I felt about her. So I was telling them.'

'Doesn't Pete understand that?'

'If it was anyone else he would,' said Harry, 'but this is precious baby brother.'

Libby sighed. 'It's all so difficult. I wish we could just forget about it.'

'No chance, ducky. This'll be with us forever.'

Unable to settle to anything until the afternoon rehearsal, Libby found an old coat and boots and took herself off for a walk to the other end of Allhallow's Lane and on to the Manor lands. Sidney picked a delicate path behind her, but refused to go any further when she reached rougher ground by the wood.

'Chicken,' she said to him, tucking her scarf more firmly round her neck. 'You're supposed to be a wild hunter.'

But I'm not, she thought, as she tramped on along the edge of the wood. What am I doing out here taking voluntary exercise?

The answer, of course, was displacement activity. But only a couple of days ago that had been limited to stretching paper and trying to start a new painting. Something had changed. Even her consumption of cigarettes and alcohol had gone down.

An image of Ben sitting in the pub saying 'You smoke too much,' popped into her head. Was that the reason? Had she subconsciously cut down on everything to improve her standing with him? If so, it was pretty pathetic. 'All that skiving off down the pub,' he'd said. 'You're a terrible woman.' Had he meant it? Surely not, for hadn't he taken her out to dinner? Kissed her? Intimated quite clearly that he was up for a relationship? Which Libby still found surprising, being unused to even mildly lustful attentions from anybody. But then, thought Libby, what sort of relationship? He certainly seemed to have backed off since Fran appeared on the scene. Perhaps his reputation was deserved, exactly as Peter had said. A bit of a cad. Whiling away the time with her, an unlikely candidate for a flirtation, until a more suitable choice came along in the shape of Fran.

A more likely cause was the obvious one. Not only had there been the incidents connected with the theatre and the play to worry about, now there was the far more horrific reason of murder. How could anyone connected with such an event fail to be changed in some way? Although Libby felt it would have been far more in character to have smoked even more, as she normally did in times of stress. In fact, it had been the ex's defection that had started her smoking again after a gap of five years.

Something had happened to her, anyway. She suddenly felt more grown-up, an unaccustomed state, as she had firmly maintained a mental age of eighteen inside her head. Always slightly surprised to find herself with children, and worse, adult children, she was privately convinced that she was playing at coping with life, that none of this should

243

be thrown at her. One day she would wake up and someone else would have taken charge.

But not any longer. Now she was responsible. Not for the accidents, not for the murder, but just possibly for the events which had set them in train. Funnily enough, this didn't make her feel guilty, merely determined to do something to set things to rights, although no remedy came immediately to mind. She was an adult, she had to deal with things, with her life. And that meant consigning all her schoolgirl angst over Ben to the bin. She turned back along the edge of the wood to collect Sidney.

True, the play had shaped up very well, even Emma, playing Hetty's character, had pulled herself together yesterday and began to show a fraction of the talent previously exhibited, but the atmosphere in the theatre was hardly conducive to a sense of wellbeing. And then, of course, she thought miserably, there was Ben's absence. She picked up a resisting Sidney and tucked him under her chin. Up until ten days ago, Ben's absence was a fact of life, which meant nothing to her. Rather, it was his unaccustomed presence that was the problem. But since then, when she had realised that the discomfort she felt whenever he was around arose from simple attraction, things had changed. For a start, he had let it be known that the attraction was mutual and then there had been his help with the set, their dinner date ... her mind trailed off into memory and speculation, the 'what if' syndrome indulged in by romantic teenagers.

Sidney struggled and clawed her shoulder. Libby cursed and let him jump down. Time to go back and get ready for rehearsal.

While she was getting changed, Flo telephoned to tell her that Lenny had asked if he could come that afternoon instead of Tuesday to stay with Hetty as previously arranged.

'He said you'd know why,' Flo concluded, a question in her voice.

Libby frowned. 'I'm not sure I do,' she said slowly. After all, it could merely be that Libby had told him to court Flo or, again, it could be something to do with the theatre.

'Well, he's staying in my spare room. Come over and see us if you like.' Flo sounded almost embarrassed.

'I will. Thanks.' Libby was grinning as she put down the phone. If Flo and Lenny were getting together, it was one of the few good things that had happened over the past week.

When she arrived at the theatre, the front doors were unlocked and lights were already on backstage. Keen, thought Libby.

'Hallo. Anybody there?' she called, walking down to the stage. She pushed open the pass door and called again. 'Stephen? Harry? Pete? Anybody?'

'Who the hell has been in here and left the lights on?' she muttered, having completed an entire circuit of the building, lighting box and all. She went backstage to the stage door and tried the handle. It was open.

For what seemed like several minutes, but was probably only seconds, Libby stood there, listening. The only sounds she could hear were her own heartbeats, which had increased in speed until she felt almost breathless. With a sudden burst of energy, she whipped through the door and locked it behind her. If there was anyone in there, they could stay in there until she got back with some help.

'Hey! What's the problem?'

Peter was steadying her with firm hands.

'There's someone in there,' Libby panted. 'It was open when I got here.'

'Well, I expect it's one of the crew.'

'No,' Libby shook her head violently. 'I've looked.'

Peter put her aside gently and went round to the front doors. Libby followed. 'Stay here,' he said.

'No fear. I'm coming with you. You might get hurt,' she added as Peter turned a look of surprise on her.

The theatre was as empty as it had been before, the stage door shut from the outside by Libby herself.

'Are you sure it was open?' Peter folded his arms and looked down at her severely.

'Positive. All the lights were on and the stage door was actually standing open. And the front doors were unlocked. I thought either you or – or – someone had got here early.'

'Well,' Peter sighed. 'I suppose we'd better go and check that everything's in working order.'

'And safe,' Libby reminded him as she followed him back in to the scenery dock.

'Just don't tell Ben,' said Peter darkly as he began on a round of checking ropes and stage weights.

'What's going on?' Stephen appeared behind

Libby and made her jump.

'The theatre was open when I got here, but no one was inside. We're just checking that everything's OK.'

'This is getting beyond a joke,' muttered Stephen, as he went off to accompany Peter.

Nothing had been touched. The rest of the technical crew arrived, checked and double-checked, while members of the cast appeared and started showing alarmingly thespian tendencies to panic. Libby calmed them down and managed to get them all changed and on stage for a briefing. Apart from a propensity for looking over their shoulders for the first ten minutes or so, the performance began well. The new Lizzie was put through her paces until murmurs of insurrection threatened to turn into outright mutiny, short scenes were done over and over again until Libby was certain they could be performed in the actors' sleep. At the end of the afternoon, she pronounced herself satisfied.

'Dress tomorrow,' she reminded them unnecessarily, 'so only one more chance. And now I'd like to go back to the scene in the hut. Just once. We can't afford to be superstitious about it, and we aren't flying the roof now, anyway.'

The stage was set once more to the scene that represented to Libby the beginning of the problems. And, of course, the beginning of the tragedy that still, apparently, haunted Ben's family.

Chapter Twenty-two – 1943

The shouting was coming nearer. Hetty felt herself shivering as she pressed further into the bed, the straw pricking her bare skin through the thin mattress cover. Next to her, Millie was asleep, a grubby fist hanging from the corner of her mouth, her warm baby smell enveloping them both.

'Where is she?' A shattering bang on the hut door rattled the corrugated iron roof. Hetty closed her eyes tightly, her heartbeats shaking her body, drumming in her ears as she recognised her father's voice. The noise increased, and she heard other doors opening, women's voices.

'She's inside, Ted.'

Her mother's quiet voice sliced through the uproar. Hetty stopped breathing.

'Fetch her out.' Silence. Then– 'I said fuckin' fetch her OUT.'

Her father's scream was punctuated with the unmistakable sound of her mother's head hitting the door and Hetty pressed herself further into the straw and faggots, tears sliding down her cheeks. As the door was thrown open a cold draught of air chilled her through her dress and she heard the scrape of her father's boots on the floor.

'Get up.' His breath was sour as he bent down, grabbing a handful of hair.

'Cow. Slut. I said, get up.'

Hetty struggled to a sitting position, her eyes wide as she faced him, his expression wild and murderous. Without warning, her head was smacked back against the whitewashed wall and she was aware of nothing except the ringing in her ears until a warm trickle ran round her neck and under her dress. Millie was crying and Lenny supported their mother, who stood, white and silent, her eyes blank. Uncle Alf and Aunt Connie hovered in the doorway.

'Leave her now, Ted.' Uncle Alf tried to pull her father away, but he shook off the importuning hand, swearing violently, lifting his fist to strike her again. Hetty cringed back against the wall and Millie's wails renewed themselves in panic.

'Ted.' Her mother's voice was a thread, but it stayed the approaching hand. 'Leave her. Enough.'

The sudden silence seemed to reverberate in Hetty's eardrums like her own pulse beat. Then, with a disgusted oath, Ted Fisher flung himself up and out of the hut in one clumsy movement. Uncle Alf and Lenny followed him.

'Let's go down the pub, then, Ted. Give yer a chance ter cool off.' Alf's conciliatory voice could be heard as the little group moved off to the underlying accompaniment of the murmur of women's voices. In the hut, the silence was complete, even Millie had stopped crying, huddling up to Hetty's side, her thumb back in her mouth.

'Let your mother lie down, Hetty...' Aunt Connie pushed the door shut quietly. 'You go and see if the fire's still in down the cookhouse. Put the kettle on.'

Hetty moved awkwardly on the uncomfortable mattress, one arm clutched round Millie, her head throbbing and a paralysing ache in her throat. Aunt Connie pushed her mother gently down beside her and Hetty lowered her eyes.

'Hetty.' Her mother laid a cold hand on her daughter's arm. 'That Warburton. He's done this. Hasn't he?'

'Has he?' Hetty whispered, staring at her mother, confusion in her eyes.

Hetty's mother sighed and closed her eyes. 'He's told your father.'

Hetty continued to stare at her mother until Aunt Connie's voice broke the silence.

'They've gone, Hetty. Go and get that kettle on.'

Unwillingly, Hetty dragged herself to her feet, her head swimming. She felt sick, and had to lean against the wall until the nausea subsided. The long row of huts was quiet, the glow of individual cooking fires and half open doors casting tiny pools of light, while slight movements gave away the presence of interested watchers in the shadows.

'Go on, Het. They've gone now. You're all right,' someone called, and the chorus was taken up. 'You're all right, Het. Don't worry, Het. Evil bastard, ain't 'e?'

Then Flo was beside her.

'Warburton stirred it, Het.'

'Mum said.' Hetty hugged her arms round herself, shivering. 'How did she know?'

Flo shrugged. 'You can't do anything here. 'Course she knew.'

'Everything?' Hetty's frightened whisper stopped

250

Flo as they walked slowly down the line towards the cookhouse.

Flo smiled ruefully. 'I expect so, Het. Everything.'

Chapter Twenty-three

'Do as well as this on Tuesday and you won't have anything to worry about.'

A self-congratulatory murmur rustled through the cast, accompanied by a few smug smiles.

'Oh, and tomorrow the bar here will be open, so we won't have to rush.'

A ragged cheer greeted this revelation and Libby turned to where Harry lounged in the seat beside her.

'Finished up at the caff?'

'Hardly anybody in except Ben.' He sent her a sly look.

'Was he?' Libby turned her attention back to the stage, where Peter was doing a final safety check with Stephen, and stood up. 'Well, before you stir things up any more, I think we should get down to the pub.' She flung her cape round her shoulders and smiled at him sideways. 'Oh, did I miss you that time? Pity.'

Harry scowled and sauntered down to the edge of the stage.

Ben wasn't in the pub when they arrived and Libby tried not to mind. Peter bought her a drink and they settled down to organise a rota between themselves for checking on the theatre. Monday during the day was no problem as the brewery was installing the bar, but it was tonight that worried Libby.

'It's no use you going up there at night, Lib,' said Peter. 'If there is a big baddy around, he'd have you away in no time. You can prowl around during the hours of daylight, but Harry and I will have to take the night-time shift.'

'I'm just a tad busy tomorrow night, ducks,' warned Harry. 'I won't be finished till after midnight.'

'Then I'll get Ben to help.'

'No,' said Libby abruptly. 'No, you can't. You were the one who said don't tell him.'

'Stephen?' said Harry.

'He's already gone home tonight, and he doesn't exactly live locally, does he? We can't ask him to patrol the theatre in the dead of night. Although,' Peter added thoughtfully, 'he was pretty pissed off tonight. Said it meant the incidents were directed at the theatre after all, and nothing to do with Paula.'

'We know they weren't to do with Paula, though,' said Libby.

'I think he meant we should still be worried about security.'

'Well, he's right, we are,' said Libby, 'but we still can't ask him to drag out here to patrol the theatre.'

'Well, who, then? I can hardly ask Uncle Greg.'

'Lenny?' suggested Libby.

'Lenny? But he's not coming down until Tuesday – and I'd be surprised if he comes then.'

'He's already here.' Libby dropped her bombshell with a smug grin.

'What?' said Peter and Harry together, sitting upright as though choreographed.

'Staying with Flo.'

'I don't believe it.' Peter crowed with laughter. 'The old devil.'

'Well, I'm glad to hear that it's still possible at that advanced age,' said Harry, leaning back and lighting a cigarette. 'Good for them.'

'Well, I suppose I could ask him.' Peter frowned down into his drink. 'But I can't see him being keen to help under the circumstances.'

'Well, as long as we're together, I could come with you, couldn't I? I mean, the werewolf won't get me while I've got a big strong man with me, will it?'

'Depends on the werewolf, duckie,' grinned Harry. 'It might be after the big strong man.'

'Oh, shut up,' said Libby.

'Look,' said Peter, 'I think we're being a touch paranoid here. We'll pop up and do a double check now, and leave it at that. If anything's different in the morning, we'll think again.'

A quick patrol of the theatre before Harry returned to the Pink Geranium and Peter escorted Libby home to Sidney's effusive welcome sufficed that night, and the following morning the theatre was exactly the same as it had been the previous night. Peter looked smug, his expression clearly saying "I told you so". The bar was set up in the corner of the foyer and Peter, the designated licensee, had great fun sorting it out to his satisfaction.

The dress rehearsal rather fell apart after the

253

comparative slickness of the previous day, but Libby put it down to nerves and wrote an enormous cheque for drinks all round to christen the new bar, after which Stephen did a solemn check of every lock and bolt before insisting on escorting Libby home.

Uncomfortably aware that she had been virtually ignoring him over the past week, Libby acquiesced as graciously as possible.

'Did you park your car in Allhallow's Lane again?' she asked, as they walked down the drive towards the High Street.

'No, we just passed it, didn't you notice? Now the car parking area is ready it seemed silly not to use it, especially as I haven't been needed as an escort.'

Libby looked at him quickly. 'Sorry, Stephen. I haven't been ignoring you, really. It's just been a difficult week.'

'A rather puzzling one, I should say,' he said, hunching his shoulders inside his coat. 'First we're cancelling the show, then we aren't, then we don't know. Peter still doesn't seem certain.'

'It's his mum. He's worried about her, and James.'

'Why? I can understand him being worried about James, he must be shattered, but what's the matter with his mum?'

'Oh, well.' Libby squirmed. The last thing she wanted to do was be disloyal to Peter.

'She's not playing the bereaved grannie, by chance, is she?'

'I wouldn't have thought so,' said Libby truthfully, because she really *wouldn't* have thought so.

But apparently Millie was doing just that.

'I wouldn't have thought so, either,' said Stephen, grinning at her over the top of his thick scarf. 'I would have thought she'd have been quite pleased to have her baby boy's nemesis bumped on the head and seen off.'

'Stephen! That's a terrible thing to say,' said Libby, grinning back at him all the same.

'Well, she was a mess, wasn't she? A right little p.t.'

'Gosh, Stephen! I didn't realise you knew her that well.'

Stephen smiled wryly. 'And I didn't realise you knew what p.t. meant.'

'I'm a middle-aged divorcee with grown-up children, not a dinosaur. Did you know her before this?'

'This being what? The play? The new theatre? What?'

'Both. Before I invited you to help. Pleaded with you, actually.'

'I'd met her. You know what am-dram's like in a small area. Everybody knows everybody else.' He grinned again, suddenly. 'And you pleading with me was a great boost to my flagging ego. Even if you were pleading for a stage manager instead of a man.'

'Oh, Stephen. I'm sorry.'

'Hey, don't be. It's not the first time I've read the wrong signals.' His lips tightened, and Libby wondered who he was thinking of.

Feeling much more charitable towards him, she offered coffee with almost genuine enthusiasm, but was relieved when he refused.

'I can't actually see the offer as the usual euphemism,' he said wryly, 'and I'm pretty sure there's no chance of that in the future, either, so I'll just make my weary way home.'

'Oh, golly,' said Libby.

He leaned forward and kissed her cheek. 'Don't worry, Lib. I know when I'm outclassed, and I should have known it was my expertise you needed, not my body.'

Libby stared, not knowing how to answer.

'Go on, go and have a good night's sleep. Tomorrow's the big day.'

Embarrassed, guilty and relieved, Libby watched him walk almost jauntily down Allhallow's Lane.

After enjoying slightly less than the recommended good night's sleep, Libby found Tuesday was a difficult day. She went to see Flo and Lenny in the morning, amused to find them sitting either side of Flo's electric fire like an old married couple.

'Think I'm going to move down,' Lenny confided as he saw her to the door. 'Be near me family. Not that we'll get hitched or anything. Flo's not bothered about that.'

Libby leant forward and kissed him. 'Well, I think that's marvellous,' she said. 'I'll send you a non-wedding present.'

He cackled. 'And good luck for tonight, girl.' He shook his head. 'Let's keep our fingers crossed.'

Peter and Harry were unobtainable all day, and Libby loitered round the theatre on her own for a couple of hours before going home and gazing gloomily at her neglected painting.

Sidney, who had joined her, looked round suddenly and leapt lightly to the floor, padding away to the front door. Libby followed and found him investigating a large white envelope addressed in a neat and purposeful hand.

Inside was the sort of card that Libby herself always wanted to find, but never could; the sort of card that she put in a drawer and promised to frame, but never did.

'Break a leg, Libby,' it read, 'in spite of everything. Ben.'

Not "love, Ben" just "Ben", Libby thought, and had to swallow a childish lump in her throat. She had to face the fact that she was a passing fancy, despite what he had said after their dinner together. Someone in the family had annexed his allegiance and Libby was out in the cold.

'He didn't even have the decency to tell me what the problem was,' she said to Sidney, trying to work up a justifiable anger. Sidney, losing interest, strolled into the kitchen and jumped up next to the bread bin.

Fran phoned during the afternoon and, after wishing Libby luck, asked if the spare room would be available on Thursday night.

Libby felt guilty for wishing Fran wasn't coming down at all, but professed herself delighted, nevertheless.

The next phone call was from Sergeant Cole, who didn't wish her luck.

'We need to come down and interview all the people involved with the incidents at your- ah — hall. Will most of them be there tonight?'

Libby was so surprised she laughed. 'I should say so!' she said. 'But you won't be able to interview them.'

Sergeant Cole's voice took on a minatory quality. 'I must remind you that this is a murder investigation, Mrs Sarjeant.'

'I'm aware of that, Sergeant,' said Libby, injecting a little ice of her own into the conversation. 'Tonight, not only will the entire cast of *The Hop Pickers* be at the theatre, so will all the crew, members of the press, the Mayor and 200 assorted members of the public.'

There was silence at the other end of the phone. Libby could picture the sergeant desperately trying to think of a way to stop the entire proceedings.

'Tomorrow, then?' he asked eventually.

'Same tomorrow, minus the Mayor and the press,' said Libby, trying not to sound smug. She heard a gusty sigh.

'And the same the rest of the week, I suppose?'

'And twice on Saturday,' smirked Libby, 'and all sold out.'

Sergeant Cole sighed again. 'Perhaps I could trouble you for a list of names and telephone numbers, then, madam?' he said. 'We'll have to get in touch with them all during the day.'

'I'm sorry, Sergeant, but I don't have everyone's numbers. Peter Parker does, though.'

'Does he, now? Thank you very much madam.'

'Sergeant, before you go, does this mean you think there's a connection between Paula's death and our little accidents?'

'I wouldn't call them "little", madam,' replied the sergeant. 'Someone could have been seriously hurt.'

'Or killed.'

'Indeed, madam. Well, I'll – er – leave you to your – er – play.'

Libby thought for a moment. 'Sergeant, I have two complimentary tickets for my – er – play tonight,' she said, 'if you feel you would like to see it. You know – see what's going on.'

There was another short silence. 'That's very kind of you, madam, I'm sure,' he said, sounding vaguely surprised. 'I'll ask the inspector.'

'Oh, I thought you might bring DC Burnham,' said Libby, mischievously.

'Yes, well, we'll have to see won't we, madam,' said Sergeant Cole hurriedly. 'Very kind of you, anyway.'

'No problem,' said Libby, 'I'll leave the tickets at the box office.'

It wasn't until after she'd hung up she realised he hadn't answered her question about the connection between Paula's death and the theatre. Instead, she'd reinforced the idea by suggesting he came to see the play. How dumb could you get.

By half past six, she was a mass of quivering nerve endings. Her best burgundy velvet dress had a mark on it and her hair was even more fly-away than usual. With shaking hands, she dragged on a bottle green satin jacket and wound a green and red scarf artistically round her neck.

'I look like a bloody Christmas tree decoration, but that'll have to do,' she told Sidney as she fell over him at the bottom of the stairs, grabbing at her cape at the same time. 'Wish me luck.'

The atmosphere at the theatre was as charged

as any normal first night would be, without the added tingle factor of it being the opening production, in the presence of various local dignitaries, the press and local radio, and, unknown to anyone else, the police. Libby was interviewed live by an energetic young man whose enthusiasm nevertheless did not extend to actually watching the performance, and she posed with the cast for pictures for the local press, who appeared slightly more interested in the murder than in those still alive. She darted into the dressing room to say good luck at the three minute bell and darted out again in time to escort the Mayor in to the auditorium, after which she took her seat at the back and tried to stop herself from running out of the theatre.

'It's because you've got no control over it now,' said a voice behind her and she looked round to see Ben. He smiled and squeezed her shoulder before moving down the aisle to take a seat with his family. Libby was so stunned she missed the first lines of the play.

At the interval, she dived through the pass door, unwilling to face anybody until afterwards, in case her mounting excitement should be quelled by an incautious remark from some member of the audience.

'It's going brilliantly,' she told an euphoric cast. 'Just keep it up, don't let it slip or rest on your laurels.'

'We're not that dumb, Lib,' said someone, and she felt foolish.

'Here.' Peter put a large whisky in her hand. 'Get that down you, girl, and stop wittering.'

'What about the family?' she asked him. 'Are they enjoying it?'

'No idea.' Peter shrugged. 'I've made a point of avoiding them. Time enough for that later.'

Ben smiled at her again as she came out of the pass door at the end of the interval. Heart thumping, she smiled nervously back and made quickly for her seat just as the lights went up on stage. She noticed Sergeant Cole and DC Burnham in the house manager's seats, which she had ruthlessly wrested from acting-house-manager Peter just before the performance, and hoped they were enjoying themselves and weren't intending to arrest anybody after the final curtain.

The second act started a little hesitantly, but soon got into its stride and Libby found herself marvelling at this company, who had never done anything together before, producing such a professional performance. It seemed, when the lights went down for the final time, that the audience agreed with her, to judge by the storm of applause that broke out. The cast lined up, looked at one another with huge grins and bowed triumphantly.

They were still bowing to a delighted audience when Libby staggered out to the bar and ordered a large scotch from Harry. 'I'll go round the back way to the dressing rooms,' she told him. 'I can't face the crowds yet.'

'Don't blame you, ducks. It'll be all luvvies and darlings, won't it?'

'Well, it will in the dressing room, to be fair,' said Libby, and noticed the auditorium doors opening. 'Right, I'm off.'

The next half hour passed in a daze for Libby. Congratulations were flung about like confetti, sticky moments were relived and gasped over and all the while the Wildes, Parkers, Fishers and Dedhams stood in a group in the foyer and watched impassively.

Eventually, Peter collected Libby firmly by one reluctant arm and dragged her over to the receiving line.

'Well done, Libby.' Ben leaned forward and kissed her cheek and Libby jumped backwards, feeling the colour sweep up into her cheeks. He raised an eyebrow and stepped back.

'Very good, girl,' nodded Hetty gruffly and at this mark of approval, they all joined in, even Millie, Libby noticed. Susan and David smiled vaguely at Libby as though they didn't know quite why they were there, and Gregory sat on one of the uncomfortable plastic chairs and engaged her in polite and intelligent conversation while looking as though he should be in bed. Lenny and Flo stood proudly on the outskirts as though they were responsible for the whole thing. For the first time, she realised James wasn't there. And Sergeant Cole and DS Burnham had long since vanished into the night.

'Very relieved, girl,' whispered Lenny as she passed him to collect another drink from the bar.

'So am I,' she whispered back and wondered briefly if she was ever going to find out what the family secret was – and, indeed, if it had anything to do with the incidents of the past two weeks.

'That girl weren't bad,' said Flo, 'the one who played me. I reckon she were better'n that other one. Younger.'

'Flo!' Several scandalised voices rose in concert.

'I agree.' Everyone looked at Millie in surprise. 'Well, of course, I've lost a daughter-in-law, but she wasn't any good, was she?'

A dreadful little silence fell, while no one looked at anyone else, until David said in a gruff voice: 'I don't know what she was like in the play, Mill, but she was a very nice person.'

'Oh,' said Millie with a grating tinkle of a laugh, 'that's exactly what I meant. Of course.'

Libby looked round for Peter, but he was behind the bar with Harry. She willed him to stay there.

'Didn't know 'er meself,' said Hetty. 'Sorry, and all that, but didn't know 'er.'

'Neither did I, Mum,' said Susan. 'Don't worry about it. David and Ben knew her, though, didn't you?' She turned and looked up at her husband.

'Did you, David?' said Libby. 'I thought you said she wasn't your patient.'

'Used to be,' David said. 'Before she moved.'

'When did she move?' whispered Libby to Ben, as David turned to speak to his mother-in-law.

Ben looked surprised. 'You knew she left. She went to London. Years ago. She was back long before I came back to The Manor.'

'Not recent, then,' said Libby.

Ben laughed. 'Still looking for suspects, Lib?'

'Don't be silly,' she said airily, and wandered away to speak to someone else.

Several times after that she caught Ben's eye and realised that excitement was building in her for quite a different reason. Eventually, Hetty signalled that it was time to go and her heart sank as she saw him collect his coat and shepherd his charges to the door. Reluctantly, she went to say goodbye.

'You'll still be here for a while, won't you?' he said, as she shook hands with David and Susan.

'Yes, I should think so,' she nodded, her heart clambering back up again.

'Good,' he said and disappeared through the glass doors. Libby floated back to her exuberant cast and bought another round of drinks.

It was another hour before the cast and crew began to drift off and still Ben hadn't reappeared. Stephen left with no further offers of escort, but Peter and Harry cashed up the bar and offered to walk her home. Libby managed to put them off, indicating the last few stragglers. She lingered on the pretext of securing the theatre, disappointment seeping unwillingly through her body while she tried to tell herself that perhaps he would come to the cottage if the theatre was closed. And perhaps he wouldn't, she told herself as she collected her bag and cape from the dressing room. It was one thing to come back to a party after dropping off your elderly parents, another to make a clandestine visit to a female in the middle of the night.

She checked that the front doors were locked and began to retrace her steps through the empty theatre, turning off lights as she went. It was as she crossed the stage that she realised that the light in the scenery dock had inexplicably come back on.

'Hallo?' she called hesitantly. There was no answer, just the tapping of ropes and canvas in the breeze. Breeze? She froze. There shouldn't be a breeze. Very slowly, she forced her leaden feet to move towards the stage door.

It was wide open. Libby stood irresolute for a moment before slamming it behind her, not bothering to go back inside to turn the lights off, before she realised that whoever had opened the door could well be out here with her. She peered into the darkness and tried to decide which would be the best way to go. If she had come out of the front doors she would have been on the well-lit drive and could have got as far as Peter and Harry's cottage within a few minutes, but this side was dark and involved a passage through the shrubbery before getting to the front. It would have to be this end of the drive and The Manor.

She ran up the drive, stumbling in the darkness, to the front of The Manor, then, remembering that Ben had said that Hetty didn't lock the kitchen door, she veered round to the side.

'Where are you going?'

The voice seemed to come out of nowhere and Libby was ashamed to hear a small scream break from her own lips.

'Where are you going?' A shape was moving over to her right, moving towards her. 'You can't go towards the huts, you know.'

Libby stopped, her knees trembling.

'Millie?' she said, in a voice that didn't belong to her.

'You can't go to the huts, you know. They're not there. They've put them in the Oast House.'

265

Something was very wrong.

'Have they?' she said, inanely.

'In the Oast House. I've seen them.' Millie was nearer now, standing quite still, hunched in her camel coat.

'Have you just been in there, Millie?'

'Yes. I go to look at them. They shouldn't be in there you know. You,' she took a step nearer and peered at Libby, 'you made them put them in there.'

'They aren't the real ones, Millie. The real ones are way over there. Near the bridge.'

'They aren't the real ones either. She had to put them up, after.'

'After what?'

'Come on. I'll show you where they should be. Then you can put them back.'

Libby thought she wouldn't ever be able to move again as Millie came towards her and grabbed hold of her arm.

'Really, Millie – I don't think–'

Millie simply pulled.

They always say they have amazing strength, mad people, thought Libby wildly, as she was dragged along in Millie's wake. Her foot caught in something and wrenched her ankle, but Millie didn't stop, just kept pulling, while Libby sobbed and panted behind her. As they came onto the fields, it was lighter, but Libby had no idea where they were going, or even in which direction they were heading.

'There.' Millie stopped. 'That's where they should be. There.'

Libby's breath was coming so fast it hurt.

266

'All right, Millie,' she managed. 'We'll put them back. Now I know.'

Millie was looking at her oddly. 'Perhaps I'd better show you why,' she said and moved over to what looked like a recently dug flower bed.

'They don't know I did this, you see. No one ever comes here. No one saw me. I just wanted to make sure.'

Still holding Libby's arm, she bent to pick up a spade lying at the edge of the flower bed.

'You can do it. I'm tired,' she said, and handed Libby the spade.

Libby's first thought was to run, or use the spade as a weapon, but hard on the heels of the thought came the realisation that Millie would grab her or the spade before she'd gone more than a few feet.

'Where?' she asked. Millie pointed. Libby began to dig. It wasn't hard. Millie had obviously been up here very recently. The earth was quite soft. As she dug, she began to wonder what she was digging for. What was buried here, where the old huts had been? She hadn't thought she could get any more frightened, but now her limbs were turning to water, her mind beginning to crack under the strain. She could feel it, feel the screaming inside her head.

It was as the spade suddenly shot downwards and the earth fell away under her feet, that she realised the screaming wasn't inside her head but voices calling. She lost her balance and fell down into the grave. For it was a grave. Her leg was resting on a skull.

Chapter Twenty-four

Libby only had a dim memory of being lifted out of the ground. It seemed a long time, but at last she was being put into some sort of vehicle and bumped slowly towards safety. The bumping made her feel sick, but she managed to take very deep breaths until she was carried inside, when she asked plaintively – and a little desperately – for a bathroom.

She was sitting on the side of a bath, her head resting on the sink, when there was a gentle rap on the door.

'Libby? Are you all right? Can I come in?'

She stood up on shaky legs and opened the door. Ben stood outside, and she realised, from the state of his clothes, that it had been he who carried her in here – to The Manor, she now saw.

'Can you make it in to the sitting room?' he asked, putting both arms round her and holding her like a child.

'I'm sorry I'm so heavy,' said Libby into his sweater, and felt him laugh.

Hetty was sitting by the fire in the sitting room. She seemed to have aged ten years since Libby saw her last.

'There's brandy or tea,' she said, indicating the table, as Ben put Libby tenderly on to the sofa and sat down beside her.

'Both,' he said, and handed Libby a glass.

'I've got to tell you I'm sorry, girl.' Hetty wasn't looking at her, but into the fire.

'It wasn't your fault–' began Libby.

'Oh, yes it was. Start to finish.'

'Mum – Aunt Millie has had a breakdown – that's not your fault.'

'It is, son, it is.'

Ben looked briefly at Libby and then back at his mother.

'Are you sure you wouldn't rather go to bed, Mum? All this has been a bit of a shock...'

'No, son. She might not make any sense, but she was babbling fit to bust when David came to take her away.'

'David?' Libby turned to Ben and was shocked beyond measure at the expression on his face. He nodded.

'Mother called him. It seemed best.'

'He's took her home to Susan for now. They'll look after her. See what's to be done.' Hetty shifted her position so that Libby couldn't see her face.

Libby looked at Ben. 'Do you know what all this is about? Is this why you were trying to persuade me not to go on?'

'I didn't do that, exactly–'

'Well, that's what it seemed like. You and Peter.' Libby took a shaky swallow of her brandy.

'Libby – I'm sorry–' began Ben.

She squinted at him. 'All right, all right. I realise that this has something to do with the family – and solidarity and all that, but how come it only turned up over the last couple of weeks? Why was everyone all for the theatre and the play and

269

everything until then? What happened then? Was it Lenny coming down that sparked it off?'

'In a way.' Ben stood up and walked into the shadows that shrouded the rest of the room away from the bright circle of firelight. 'Peter was already nervous.'

'Yes, I realised that, but I didn't know why.'

'That was Millie and her ghost stories.' Ben came back to look down at her. 'Millie's night-mares had started again–'

'Nightmares?'

Ben glanced at her. 'Sorry, you wouldn't know. Millie used to have nightmares as a child, and she told Peter all about them, just as she used to when he was little. She called them ghost stories. He began to realise...' He broke off. 'Well, then, when Uncle Lenny came down and started doing his "I know something you don't" routine, it sent Millie over the edge.'

'So when did you find out?' Libby's sense of righteous indignation as opposed to bone-melting fear was reinstating itself. 'And why didn't you tell me?'

Ben shrugged. 'Peter told me on Monday night – about Millie's nightmares, I mean. And then–'

'Then there was the fire. Which you found.' Libby finished her brandy and made her eyes water.

'Yes, I did. I gather that you thought I started it.'

'It did cross my mind,' admitted Libby, looking him in the eye but feeling the colour creep up her neck.

'I had been with Peter and Harry. After you left

them. That's what I was going to say before you interrupted me. I was on my way home.'

'Oh', said Libby, deflated. 'Well, what *is* the problem? Why did Millie have this mental breakdown? Don't I have a right to know?'

Ben looked at his mother. Hetty shrugged.

'I'll have to tell you it all, and what you do about it will be up to you. She'll tell now.'

'Oh, God,' said Ben, and sat down next to Libby.

'What I don't understand,' said Libby after a long silence, 'Is why Warburton was buried there? His death wasn't hushed up. Why didn't he have a normal funeral?'

The quality of the silence changed, and Libby found that she was holding her breath. When Hetty spoke, the words seemed to be dragged out of her, from a great distance.

'That wasn't Warburton. That was my father.'

Chapter Twenty-five – 1943

Hetty went into Flo's hut that night. Lillian, pale and drawn, insisted that it was better, Millie and she would be all right. Hetty gave in gratefully and prepared to answer Flo's mother's questions. To her surprise, there weren't any, merely a motherly concern for the huge lump and cut on the back of her head from which blood still trickled sluggishly.

She dreamed, that night. Warburton was coming

271

for her, Warburton was lying on top of her, Father was hitting Greg with a gravestone. She woke up to find Flo bending over her in the half-light from the top of the door.

'Het. Het. Wake up.'

'Wha-a?' Hetty peered up at her friend's shadowed face.

'You was dreaming. You'll wake Mum and Gran.'

'Sorry.' Hetty moved her head and winced.

'Is it your head?' Flo asked sympathetically. 'Fancy a cuppa?'

Hetty sat up and nodded, cautiously.

'Come on outside then.' Flo scrambled over the two older women still snoring on their faggot bed and pushed open the door. Hetty followed, shivering in the dew-soaked greyness that enshrouded the huts. She was still wearing her cotton dress and cardigan, which she drew tightly around her. She watched Flo bustling around lighting the fire, pouring water from the bucket into the kettle and hanging it on the hook.

'Won't be long,' she said, coming to sit beside Hetty on one of the old chairs that lived permanently outside the hut.

'Flo,' Hetty began, pleating her dress between her fingers.

'What?'

'Is it so bad, me seeing Greg?'

Flo shrugged. 'I would've thought it'd be worse for his family than yourn. Seeing as how they think we're filthy hoppers.'

'Greg's family don't. We've all been coming for years. They know what we're like. Carpenter

272

doesn't think that, does he?'

'No,' Flo looked away. 'He's a good man.'

'Has he–?' Hetty hesitated. 'I mean, have you–?'

Flo looked at her, surprised. 'If you mean has he had me on me back, no, he hasn't. He's a gentleman, is Frank.'

'Sorry, Flo.' Hetty shivered. 'It's just that you've always seemed so much more – well, experienced – with men, you know.'

Flo laughed. 'Not that experienced, ducks. Oh, I know what they're like and what I can do to 'em, but I don't want to get caught up the duff, do I?'

Hetty felt her insides turn to water. 'What?' she whispered.

Flo looked into her face closely. 'Having a kid, Het. That's what happens, you know. How do you think they get there? Stands to reason, doesn't it? Something goes in there, and something comes out – nine months later.'

'Always?' Hetty's voice was a thread.

'Not always, no, but you can't take the chance, can you?' Flo got up to stir tea into the boiling kettle. 'Oh, some of 'em do. There's ways, see? To make sure it doesn't happen. But you have to be clever. And I don't want to do it with anybody 'til I feel it's right. Sometimes it feels as though I want to, but I get scared, see?'

'Are you scared with Carpenter?' Hetty was trying to fit this new information into her jigsaw and seeing with awful clarity how well it fitted the empty spaces.

'No, I'm not. He wouldn't try it on, see. Oh, he's kissed me. Asks first, o'course. And some-

273

times I wish he'd sort of, let go, like. But it's better this way. Specially as we've got to go home in a coupla weeks and that'll be the end.'

'Couldn't it go on? Couldn't you stay?'

'Eh?' Flo looked shocked. 'Of course not. Where would I stay?'

Hetty shook her head. 'I don't know. I thought perhaps he might marry you.'

She was surprised to see Flo blush, something that Hetty herself did frequently, but she had never seen happen to Flo.

'Yeah, well. Pigs might fly.' Flo stood up abruptly and rummaged in the box for enamel mugs.

'So why is my dad so set against me and Greg?' Hetty changed the subject.

'Your dad's set against everything, ain't he? I don't know whether it's Greg, or just 'cause you've been doing it with him – could've been anybody. Pride, I'd say.'

'My dad? Pride?' Hetty let out a bitter little laugh. 'That'll be the day.'

'You have been doing it with him, haven't you, Het?' Flo suddenly turned on her, her face serious.

Hetty's blush suffused her whole body. She nodded.

Flo sighed. 'Silly cow. Bad enough with one of the lads back home – but this. And Warburton found out?'

'I think he saw us. The first time–'

'Cor, that was bad luck, wasn't it?' Flo laughed mirthlessly. 'What a bloody mess. How many times you done it?'

Horrified, Hetty shook her head, too embarrassed to speak.

'Come on, Het, once is enough for a kid, but sometimes you get away with it. If you do it a lot – well your odds is against you.'

Hetty felt something inside her shrivel. 'Every day,' she whispered, 'since last week.'

'Gawd.' Flo put her head in her hands. 'Had your monthlies yet?'

Hetty shook her head. 'Not till next week.'

'Well, keep your fingers crossed, then. Not much use keeping your legs crossed now, is there?'

There was no picking on a Sunday. Hetty and Flo went to the mission meeting held on the common by a visiting preacher who clearly thought there was about as much potential in his congregation as in a field of rabbits. The text of his sermon demonstrated his belief that their habits were fairly similar, as Flo remarked. Hetty kept out of the way of her father and her own hut until she saw the men making their way to the lane, which led to the village. Lenny loitered behind, she noticed, then doubled back and panted his way across the common to where she sat at the edge of the hop garden.

'Mum says you can go back, now, Het.'

'Thanks, Lenny.' Hetty stood up stiffly and brushed down her skirt. 'You get off to the pub, then.'

Lenny nodded, and somewhat reluctantly stomped his way back across the common.

'You're a fool, girl, you know that.' Lillian must have heard her coming but didn't look up.

'I'm sorry, Mum.'

'He's not our sort. He's using you – like a whore.'

Hetty winced. 'Mum – he's not.'

'You're seventeen. What do you know about it? More than I thought, I'll allow, but not much.'

'Mum, isn't it natural when you love a person?' Hetty crouched down by her mother's feet. Millie trotted up and put her arms round her neck.

'Love?' Lillian turned hollow eyes on to her elder daughter. 'Love's a joke, Het. It don't mean nothing. It's not real.'

Defeated, Hetty sat back on her heels and watched as her mother stirred the big hopping pot. 'What's Dad going to do?'

'Get drunk. What do you think? I'd make yourself scarce when he gets back. I'll save you some dinner.'

'When's he going back?'

'Later. Soon as Lenny can drag him away. Got to get the train, see?' Lillian stood up and wiped her hands on her apron. 'Bring a chair.' She lifted her own and carried it across to Connie's hut, where Connie, Flo and Flo's mother and grandmother, were already seated, a couple of bottles of stout on the ground before them. Hetty followed slowly with Millie hanging on to her skirt, consumed with embarrassment at facing the combined curiosity of the little group.

In fact, the faces turned towards her were blandly welcoming. Flo made room for her between them and picked up the threads of the conversation almost without a break.

The sound of singing alerted them to the return of the men. Hetty stood up unsteadily, Millie in her arms. The other women got up unhurriedly and began to move in front of her, bending over Connie's hopping pot, shielding her from the eyes

276

of anyone who happened to be looking their way.

The men scattered like a handful of gravel thrown on the ground and Hetty, her view obscured, waited with bated breath.

'They're not here, Het.' Flo turned to her as the other women separated and drifted towards other groups. 'None of them have come back.'

'Dad?' Hetty managed, out of a dry throat.

'Your dad, Lenny and your Uncle Alf. Your mum's gone to ask if anyone's seen them.'

Eventually, Lillian and Connie dished up their meals and Millie, Hetty, Connie and Lillian, Flo and her mother and grandmother sat down to eat them together. They had almost finished when a shout pierced the still afternoon air.

'Mum.'

Everyone turned to see Lenny coming at a staggering run towards them.

'Mum.' He was breathing hard and the smell of drink surrounded him almost visibly.

'Where's your father?' Lillian's face was devoid of expression.

'Don't know. He went off. He wouldn't listen–'

'Sit down, Lenny.' Flo pushed him down into her own chair. 'Get your breath.'

'Warburton was at the pub.' Lenny looked up at Hetty and a ripple went through the assembled women.

'He was getting at Dad. Anyway, he went and Dad started going on about – about–' he hesitated and looked at Hetty again.

'Yes, we know. Get on with it.' Lillian's eyes were fixed on her son's face.

'When we left he said he was going to find

277

Carpenter. We tried to stop him – followed him up to Home Farm.' He stole a quick look at Flo, who kept her eyes down. 'Carpenter wasn't there. So then he just ran off towards the home wood. We lost track of him, so they sent me back here while they carried on looking.'

The women looked at each other. Lillian, whose colour was high, stood up.

'Sorry about this, Connie. If you'll give Lenny his dinner, then I'll go and help them look.'

'I'll come with you, Mum.' Hetty stood up bravely.

'You stay here and look after Millie.' Stay out of trouble, her tone said.

It was nearly dark when they came back. Ted Fisher was not with them. Connie and Hetty dished up overdone stew and vegetables and sat down to watch them eat.

'What you going to do about getting home, then?' Connie asked.

Alf shrugged. 'Dunno. First train in the morning.'

'What's going to happen to your jobs?' Hetty grabbed Lenny's arm. 'You can't afford to lose your jobs.'

'We'll get back in time. Don't worry. The veg lorry goes from the village in the early hours. Uncle Alf – you game for going on that?' Lenny waved his knife at his uncle.

'You get me up, boy, I'll go on the veg lorry.' Alf nodded and returned to his plate of stew.

Hetty wondered how her mother remained so calm during the evening. Lenny and Uncle Alf went back to the pub to see if Ted had returned and the women sat, talking, trying to pretend that things were normal. Millie was put to bed and, at last, Lillian and Hetty were the only two still sitting over the remains of the fire.

'Mum. Hetty.' Lenny's voice came as a stage whisper from somewhere to Hetty's left. 'He came back. He's gone after Warburton.'

'Where's he gone?' Lillian stood up slowly.

'Along the ditch towards the bridge.'

Afterwards, Hetty remembered little of how they made the journey along the bank of the ditch at the edge of the gardens. All she remembered was coming to the bridge and seeing the solitary figure swaying on the wooden bridge, silhouetted against the sky. And her mother's gasping cry as she looked down into the ditch and saw her husband's body face down in the brackish water.

'He came at me.' Warburton's voice was slurred and scared. 'I had to defend meself.' He turned and swayed towards Hetty. 'This is your fault, you bitch.'

Hetty screamed as she smelt the sour breath as he lurched forward and made a grab for her. Somehow, there was a stone in her hand – a big stone – and, somehow, she was hitting him with it. Over and over again. At first his arms went up to shield his head, then he was staggering backwards and then she watched him crumple like a sheet blown off the line, down the bank and into the ditch where he landed half on top of Ted Fisher.

Lenny was screaming at her. She couldn't understand the words and then she felt her mother pulling her away.

'Get him out of the ditch, Lenny.' Lillian sat her down on the bank and shoved her head roughly between her knees. Lenny was gibbering, but Lillian went down into the ditch and helped him drag Ted's body from underneath Warburton's and up the bank.

'What are we going to do?' Hetty was suddenly cold and frightened. Her mind couldn't yet grasp what she had done and she took refuge in Lillian's unfailing common sense.

'We'll bury him. Then no one'll know he was here, so they'll think Warburton was drunk – fell in the ditch. Or done for by one of the travellers.'

'We can't bury him.' Lenny's teeth were chattering. 'Everyone'd see where we'd dug a hole. Anyway, what do we dig it with?'

'Tools in the barn.' Lillian looked down dispassionately at the body of her husband. 'No, we can't bury him out here. Under the hut.'

'What?' Hetty couldn't believe what she'd just heard. She felt as though she was moving in some sort of nightmare where nothing bore any relation to normality.

'Under the hut. Floor's earth. Come on, Lenny, take his top end. Hetty and me'll take a leg each.'

From not remembering much of the outward journey, Hetty remembered every terror-filled second of the return one. She heard Lenny retching behind her, her Mother's laboured breathing and the squelch of her feet in the mud. They kept alongside the ditch and came up behind the huts.

'Go and get the tools, Len. Hetty, you go and get Millie up and get her away.' Lillian stood upright and rubbed her back.

Millie half woke, and Hetty wrapped her in a blanket and carried her outside. Her brain seemed to have closed down now and all she could think of was where she could sit with her heavy burden and how tired she was. The cookhouse was quiet, not many people used it during the day; at night it was the perfect place to sit on the floor and lean her back against the wall.

She awoke with a start to realise that Millie was no longer curled up in the crook of her arm. All the blood in her veins seemed to drain into her feet and she struggled to her feet, her heart hammering.

A glimmer of light showed where Lenny and Lillian were working, which suddenly became brighter. Hetty's heart filled with dread as she ran towards the hut.

Her mother turned on her with a face ablaze with anger and grief as she fell through the door.

'What was you doing letting her get away?'

Millie was clasped in her mother's arms, her little face white and blank.

'Daddy,' she said. 'Daddy.'

Hetty looked down and saw her father's body half covered in earth.

'Christ,' said Lenny.

Chapter Twenty-six

'It didn't turn out the way Mum thought, of course. Everyone thought Dad had killed Warburton, but we couldn't say, see?' Hetty leaned back in her chair, her face still hidden.

'But why?' Ben burst out. 'Why couldn't you have left them both there? No one would have known you had anything to do with it. No one saw you go after them, did they?'

Hetty shrugged. 'I don't rightly know, son. None of us were thinking very straight. Perhaps it would have been better, but one of them couldn't have killed the other and then knocked himself out, could he?'

'Nobody saw you bring the body back?' asked Ben, eventually.

'Not apart from Millie. So you see, it is all my fault. We thought she'd got over it. She stopped having the dreams when she moved back down here with me – funny, that. But this play brought it all back. And then Lenny coming down. He wouldn't have said anything, though. He's just a silly old fool. Liked to tease me about it.'

Libby suddenly found herself disliking Uncle Lenny intensely.

'So she tried to stop the play.'

'Thought it was all going to happen again, I think, poor old girl.'

'And the bridge?' Libby asked.

Hetty shrugged. 'No idea. I suppose it was the photographer. She was taking pictures of all the old places. Millie must have thought she'd find Dad's grave. She wouldn't have. I wouldn't have let her.' Hetty stood up. 'I'd better go and see how your dad is.'

'Does Dad know?' Libby felt Ben's hand tighten on her own.

'No. Didn't tell him at the time, did we? And then after, after the war, well, it would have killed him.'

Ben nodded and she left the room.

'The fire,' said Libby quietly. 'Was that Millie?'

'Yes. She was still there when I arrived. In fact, I saw her before I saw the fire and stopped to see what she was doing. I'd just been listening to Pete's horrific ghost stories, don't forget.'

'Had Millie told him the truth?'

'In a garbled fashion, yes. He told me and we thought she'd got it wrong, of course.' He sighed. 'But she hadn't.'

'So she thought it would come out if we did the play? But how?'

'I can see it, can't you? If a series of events is being replayed in public it stands to reason someone might find out.'

'Well, I have. And what about Susan and David? They'll find out.'

'Yes.'

'Will she be all right?' asked Libby after a while.

'Mum? Or Aunt Millie?'

'Both, I suppose. But I actually meant your mum.'

'I hope so.'

283

'God, what an awful story.' Libby shivered. 'Will you tell her everything will be all right?'

'Will it?' He held her away from him and looked at her.

'We can just forget it all again, can't we? Only the family know.'

'And you.'

'Well, we can pretend, can't we? Like we were going to pretend to be grown-up middle aged people.'

Ben pulled her close to him and Libby tried not to mind that her back felt as if it was breaking.

'What about the play?' she asked, after a muffled moment.

'What about it?'

'Do you want me to cancel it?'

'No. There's absolutely no reason to, now. And it was a great success, wasn't it? We'll make it a memorial to my grandfather.'

'Perhaps we could have a plaque in the theatre. Sort of put a full stop to it. For Hetty's sake.'

Ben kissed her. 'I knew I was right about you.'

'Oh,' said Libby, blushing again.

Then he stood up and pulled her to her feet.

'Can you walk? As far as the front door?'

'I'm only a bit bruised, that's all. And I might have a few nightmares for a bit, I suppose.'

'Then I shall go upstairs and have a quick word with Mum before I drive you home.' He went towards the door, then turned and came back.

'Do you want to get someone to stay with you? Will you be all right on your own?'

Libby sighed. 'I shall be fine. Fran's coming down tomorrow, so it's only tonight.'

'You don't want me to ask David to come out and have a look at you?'

'I thought he was looking after Millie?'

'Susan's there as well, don't forget, and, dull though she may seem, she's been a doctor's wife for years. Very capable woman, my sister.'

'I'm sure she is,' said Libby, 'but I don't need David. As I said, I'm only bruised.'

But it wasn't the bruising or the expected nightmares that kept her awake once she got home, it was Paula's murder.

It was now perfectly clear that Millie had tried to sabotage the play, although Libby still couldn't see her climbing up to cut steel wire, but it was also clear that it had nothing to do with Paula. She wondered briefly if anybody would tell DS Cole or DCI Murray about the events of the evening, but decided that it was in everybody's interest to keep quiet. After all, what good would arresting Hetty do after all this time?

Not, of course, that it mattered to them now. There would be no more incidents, Paula's replacement was, if anything, better than she had been, and, unless the police tried to disrupt the proceedings, as far as the play and the theatre were concerned that was the end of the matter. But, somehow, Libby felt that it wasn't. A mildly malign influence when alive, Paula was still interfering when dead. It was thoroughly un-nerving. After all, if suspicion continued to fall on James, Peter or Harry, or even Ben, the effect would be catastrophic. And Ben had been particularly attentive tonight, thought Libby, turning over with a smile, before drifting into sleep.

285

The nightmares did wake her up after all. Trying to overcome the irrational fear of getting out of bed, she managed to switch on the bedside light and lay listening to the sound of her own heartbeat. Sidney, obviously having noticed the light going on, decided it was breakfast time and began complaining loudly outside the bedroom door. Berating herself for being stupid, Libby slowly swung her legs out of bed and reached for her dressing gown.

Downstairs, light was beginning to filter across the garden and Libby's heart rate slowed to normal. She fed Sidney, put the kettle on the Rayburn and began to go back over the events of the previous night.

Sadly, the triumphant first night performance of *The Hop Pickers* had been totally eclipsed by what had followed. Libby wondered how David and Susan were coping with Millie, and what Peter would have to say about it all. She had a feeling it was going to hit him harder than anybody, even James, who presumably had more to worry about than the past peccadilloes of his family. And, in the cold light of day, with a slightly clearer brain, Ben's attentiveness fell into place as nothing more than a giving and receiving of comfort.

How embarrassed he was going to be this morning, thought Libby, as she poured boiling water into the teapot. She, a stranger, had been made privy to the most intimate and shocking secrets of his family, secrets of which even other members of the family were unaware. She gazed miserably into her mug, telling herself off for being shallow enough to mind, but minding all the same. It appeared that the female psyche remained a perennial teenager despite the slow degeneration of its outer covering. Ever since Ben had walked into the pub that evening two weeks ago, she had reverted to her eighteen-year-old self, plagued with sexual jealousy and insecurity, even, she thought in disgust, in the face of bloody murder.

She poured tea and sat down at the kitchen table. The garden was getting lighter, and Sidney made for the conservatory and his cat-flap. Libby watched him prowl round his territory and wondered if Paula's was a territorial killing. Someone who felt that she was trespassing? But that would mean a woman, and apart from Millie, whom she had never seriously considered, there were no women in the case. Or were there?

'Oh, for goodness' sake,' she said aloud. 'You are *not* Miss Marple.'

Of course there would be disaffected women in Paula's past, though, she thought, as she climbed the stairs to shower and dress. Bound to be with her reputation. She tried to think of any ex-wives or girlfriends she'd heard about, but to tell the truth she hadn't known much about Paula until that night when Ben turned up and Paula started making up to James. She'd known about the relationship with James, but only in a vague sort of way.

And what, she thought, was she supposed to tell Fran? Fran, whom Ben had invited in to their little melange of secrets and lies, and who, either by intuition or clever guesswork, knew a lot more

287

than a stranger ought. She decided she would ask Ben, or if he wasn't speaking to her this morning, Peter.

But when Harry phoned later in the morning, it was clear this would be out of the question.

'He won't be at the theatre tonight, Lib,' said Harry, and Libby could hear the strain in his voice. 'You'll have to cope without us. The caff's full – some of the bookings are for pre-theatre suppers and a couple for afterwards, so I can't be there.'

'Don't worry, I'll do the bar. I'll have to come round and get the float, though.'

'No,' said Harry hastily, 'don't do that. He really doesn't want to see you. He doesn't want to see anybody, but you in particular.'

Libby felt ridiculously hurt, and tried to swallow the lump in her throat. 'Fine,' she managed eventually.

'Come on, Lib,' said Harry, in a softer tone, 'you can understand that, surely? His barmy old bat of a mother nearly does you in, and all over a play wot he wrote. He feels like shit.'

Libby sighed. 'Yes, of course, but he needn't. It's got nothing to do with him.'

'Stoopid old trout, of course it has,' said Harry affectionately. 'Give him time and he'll be back to his obnoxious self. Meanwhile, I'll drop the float round later. Will you be in?'

'I wasn't planning on going anywhere. Fran's coming down tomorrow, but I don't know when. I don't know what to say to her, either.'

'Nothing,' said Harry firmly. 'Just let her watch the play and go home again. We know who was

288

behind the accidents, there won't be any more and Paula's murder is nothing to do with us, so we don't need Mrs Busy-Body Castle any more.'

'That's a bit harsh,' said Libby, suppressing her remarkably similar thoughts.

'I don't know why Ben let her in unless he fancies her.' There was a pause. 'Sorry, Lib.'

'Why're you sorry? Ben and I aren't an item. Good heavens,' she said with a light laugh, 'we're both in our fifties. Much too old for that sort of thing.'

'Never too old,' said Harry. 'See you later.'

Nevertheless, Libby worried about Fran intermittently all day. She was aware of the ambivalence of her feelings; she liked Fran and had quickly achieved a degree of closeness with her, yet she was jealous of her relationship with Ben, from whom she still hadn't heard. Not that she was constantly listening for the phone, of course. And she certainly didn't want to share with Fran any of the events of the previous night, or the details of Hetty's story. When Harry arrived in the early afternoon with the theatre bar float, she tried to find out how much he and Peter knew. All of it, it appeared.

'Ben rang and told us. David phoned to tell Pete he'd got mad Millie last night, and Pete rang The Manor, but Ben was taking you home. He phoned when he got back.' Harry stared moodily out of Libby's kitchen window. 'Bloody awful, isn't it?'

Libby patted his arm. 'Not that bad,' she said. 'It was all a long time ago and it was an accident, anyway.'

'You falling in a pit with an 'eadless corpse? Nah – that was no accident.'

'She hadn't a clue what she was doing, Harry. She only wanted me to dig, not fall in.'

'I'm not so sure. Still, not likely to happen again, is it? Wonder what they'll do with her? She can't stay in that house on her own now, can she?'

'I suppose it'll be up to Peter and James. Do you think she'll be sectioned?'

'Got to be, hasn't she?' Harry looked grim. 'When I think what she's put my Peter through...'

'And James. Don't forget James.'

'He's not gay, is he?'

'Stop asking questions. These are all facts. No, James isn't gay, yes, she'll have to be sectioned, and no, she can't stay in the house. I'm sure when Pete's had a chat with David they'll sort things out.' Libby put out a hand. 'So, where's the float, then?'

'Oh, right.' Harry grinned. 'Got quite carried away. Here.' He delved into a backpack and brought out a large canvas bag. 'Last night's takings have been banked. Just bag the whole lot up and either drop it in to the caff after the show, or bring it home and I'll call round in the morning.'

'I can't drop in tonight if Pete doesn't want to see me.'

'He won't be in the caff, he'll be at home. He doesn't want to see anybody, I said.'

'OK, I'll do that then, and tell you how it went. He'll want to know that.'

'Might cheer him up, although he still thinks it's all his fault for writing the play.'

The performance wasn't quite as sharp as that of the previous night, but Libby was nevertheless pleased with her cast. It felt odd to be in the theatre without Harry, Peter or Ben, especially Ben, she admitted to herself, from whom she'd heard nothing all day, and she was pleased when both audience and cast left reasonably early and she could lock up and go home, after persuading one of the back-stage crew to walk home with her. Puzzled at this unaccustomed nervousness on the part of his redoubtable director, he agreed, and, obviously wondering why she hadn't asked Stephen, waved her off with unflattering haste at the bottom of Allhallow's Lane.

Fran arrived at about half past four the following day. The weather had turned again, and the garden was as warm as high summer, so Libby took tea out under the apple tree.

'So, it went well, then?' Fran took her mug from Libby and leaned back in her chair.

'Very well. Press, pictures and practically a standing ovation. We were delighted.'

'So what went wrong?'

Libby looked up, startled. 'What do you mean, what went wrong?'

'Something did, didn't it? I knew, on Tuesday night. I nearly rang, but decided it was too late.'

Libby looked at her suspiciously. 'I thought you said you didn't...'

'Whatever I said, I knew something was wrong. I keep telling you, sometimes I just know things as though I've been told them, or seen them. I don't trust it, but this time I was sure. It was something to do with you, because I've got closer to you than anybody else down here. I thought at first it was an accident, but obviously…?' She looked a question at Libby, who stared up into the apple tree to avoid her gaze.

'Look, don't tell me if you don't want to, just assure me you're OK.'

Libby bent to stroke Sidney who trotted past on his way to Fran's lap.

'I don't know whether they'd want me to tell you, but you'll just have to keep it quiet,' she said. 'It was Millie who caused the accidents, although I can't see her cutting the steel wire, but anyway, she did the rest because the – er, murder when she was little affected her. When we did the play it sort of unhinged her and she thought it was all happening again.'

Fran looked thoughtful. 'I was under the impression she was only a baby and didn't know anything about it.'

'She was three, I think. And she must have known something, or it wouldn't have given her nightmares.' No way was Libby going to tell Fran Hetty's story. 'Anyway, she broke down completely and David took her away.'

'So what happened to you?'

'Oh.' Libby's thoughts scrabbled round her head like hamsters in a wheel. 'She grabbed me as I was walking home and dragged me off towards the huts. She was so strong! And I fell into a hole.'

There was a short silence. 'A hole,' said Fran.

'Yes.'

'I see.' She looked at Libby for a moment and sighed. 'Well, if you're not going to tell me, you're not. I won't pry.'

'I can't. That's all there is to tell, anyway.' Libby took a gulp of tea.

'OK.' Fran stroked Sidney's head. 'So how's the murder investigation?'

Libby looked up, surprised. 'No idea. DS Cole came to the play on the first night, but I haven't heard from him since. He wanted the names and phone numbers of the entire cast.'

'Going in to her background, then.'

'I assume so. Now we know about Millie and the accidents at least we know nothing's going to happen to us now. It's nothing to do with us.'

'It's to do with the family, though, isn't it?' said Fran.

'Only in so far as Paula went out with James and was in our play.'

'Was pregnant by James. Different thing.'

'Do you think she was?' asked Libby. 'It wouldn't surprise me if the whole thing was a fabrication to trap James.'

'It wouldn't surprise me, either, but I didn't know her, after all.' Fran tickled behind Sidney's ear. 'Are you sure about Millie causing the accidents?'

'I think she admitted it,' said Libby, surprised. 'Although I don't actually think anyone said as much. Why? Don't you?'

'No, I don't.' Fran shifted in her chair. 'That's what Ben brought me down for, and that's one thing I'm sure about. It wasn't Millie.'

Chapter Twenty-seven

Libby was behind the bar washing glasses when Peter came in not long before the interval.

'I thought you weren't coming in tonight,' she said in surprise. 'Harry said...'

'I know, I know. I realised I was being a bit of a drama queen. Sorry, Lib.' He leaned across the bar counter and kissed her cheek.

'Sorry for what? It wasn't your fault I fell down a hole.'

'Yes, it was,' he said with a sigh. 'If I hadn't written the bloody play...'

'Oh, don't talk rubbish. We've been over this dozens of times. You didn't know what had happened, did you?'

'I thought Ben told you? Mum had rambled about something, but I thought she'd got it muddled in her head. She was so young when it all happened.'

'Well, it's all over now, so we can forget about it, can't we?' said Libby briskly, drying a glass and putting it back on a shelf. 'How is she?'

'Still with David and Susan. I offered to take her home with me, but David insisted they kept her. I suppose it makes sense as he's a doctor.' Peter perched on a bar stool. 'But what we do next, I've no idea.'

'Sheltered accommodation?' suggested Libby.

'I don't know if she can cope on her own any

more, even in somewhere like Flo's place. I think it'll have to be an upmarket home for the bewildered like Lenny's. I suppose we'll have to wait and see.'

'Hasn't David told you what he thinks?'

Peter frowned. 'No, he just says leave her with them. I don't know what Susan thinks.'

'Not much, I expect,' said Libby. 'Were Millie and Susan close as they grew up? They're quite close in age, aren't they?'

'Millie was four when Susan was born, so they were brought up more or less as sisters. As far as I can make out, she wasn't too pleased when Susan married David.'

'Oh? Why?'

'No idea.' Peter shrugged. 'Perhaps she wanted him for herself?'

Libby laughed. 'Don't be daft, she must have been married by then.'

'She was, and I was on the way. I bet she wanted to be a bridesmaid and couldn't because of me.'

'Lord, can you imagine your Mum as a nineteen-sixties bridesmaid? I can't.'

'Oh, I can. Just her style.' Peter stood up and stretched. 'Give us a drink, then, you old trout, then I'll relieve you behind the bar.'

But before Libby could reach for a clean glass, the foyer doors swung open. Peter scowled.

'What do you want?' he said.

'Evening, Mr Parker. I just wanted a word. Evening, Mrs Sarjeant.'

'Mr Cole.' Libby looked nervously towards the doors to the auditorium. 'Will you be long?'

'I don't know, madam.' DS Cole turned to Peter. 'It's about Mrs Parker, sir.'

'What about her?'

'DCI Murray needs to ask her some questions, sir, and Doctor Dedham says he can't.'

'That's right. My mother is – er – somewhat confused at the moment. I believe Doctor Dedham has her under sedation.'

'Ah. Senile, is she?' asked Cole.

'Bloody hell! Of course she's not senile! She's only 65.' Peter swung away from the bar and took a deep breath.

'We think she's had some kind of breakdown, Sergeant,' put in Libby. 'That's why she's staying with Doctor and Mrs Dedham.'

'Right. So when did she have this breakdown? Was it recent?'

Peter turned back. 'Does it matter? She's been acting a little strangely for some weeks. It's obviously been building up.'

'Ah,' said the sergeant.

Libby, seeing that Peter was only just holding on to his temper, said 'Would you like to talk somewhere else, Sergeant? The audience will be out here for the interval any minute.'

Peter let out his breath in a rush. 'Come up to The Manor,' he said. 'It's nearest.' He turned and made for the doors.

'Right, sir,' said DS Cole. 'Thank you, madam.'

Libby watched them go with some trepidation. What did the police want with Millie? Surely the police didn't know what had happened the other night?

A burst of clapping indicated the end of the

first act, and one of the first through the auditorium doors was Fran.

'What did you think?' asked Libby, having passed over the wine Fran had pre-ordered.

'Excellent,' said Fran. 'I'll get out of your way.'

'No, that's OK, Fran. Stay here, I can still talk to you in between customers. Most of them pre-ordered like you.'

But Fran shook her head, smiling abstractedly, and moved away from the bar. Libby watched her go over to the big windows which opened onto a tiny terrace for smokers and sit at one of the little metal garden tables. This was worrying. Did Fran really not like *The Hop Pickers,* or had some nasty telepathic thought surfaced in her brain? Libby sighed and turned to her next customer.

Listening to comments made by members of the audience, who had no idea who she was, Libby was gratified to hear a good deal of praise, which distracted her temporarily from worrying about what was happening with Peter and DS Cole, and Fran's unnatural reticence. When the interval bell rang and Fran came to put her glass on the bar, her worries returned.

'What's up, Fran?'

'Nothing. I'm really enjoying it.'

'There's a problem, though, isn't there?'

Fran looked away. 'I'd better go in. I'll see you afterwards.'

That was that then. Libby frowned at Fran's back as she disappeared through the auditorium doors and went to collect glasses.

'Here, I'll do that.' Peter appeared behind her and took the tray from her hands. 'You go and do the washing up.'

'You look more cheerful,' said Libby, as she resumed her place behind the bar.

'They're going to have to get another doctor to have a look at Mum to see if she's fit to be questioned. So she won't be bullied.'

'No, but why do they need to question her? They don't suspect her of Paula's murder, surely?'

'God knows. What worries me is that if they start asking her questions she'll go burbling on about Hetty and Warburton and then we really *will* be in the soup.'

Libby blew thoughtfully on a soapy mass of bubbles. 'Do you remember anyone saying where it happened? Paula, I mean, not Warburton.'

Peter dumped a trayful of glasses in front of her. 'In the car. You know that.'

'No, she was found in the car. Do we know whether she was murdered there?'

'Bloody hell. I never thought of that.' Peter rubbed the end of his nose. 'Well, that'd let my mum out, wouldn't it? If the body was moved.'

'Also,' said Libby slowly, 'it could be that the *car* was moved.'

'We'll 'ave to get you in the force, missus,' grinned Peter, 'but you're right. And that would let my mum out, too. She can't drive. Never learned.'

'Perhaps we ought to find out,' said Libby. 'I mean, they'd know by now. They'd know by – er – lividity, and post thing blood patterns, or something, wouldn't they? The scene of crime people look into all that straight away.'

'I think it's the medical examiner who does that. The post-mortem's been done, I know that much. David said.'

'Well, anyway, they'd know if she was moved or whatever, wouldn't they?'

'I suppose so. What made you think of it?'

'Something Fran said. I hadn't thought of it, either.'

'Fran again.' Peter frowned. 'What did she have to say in the interval?'

'Nothing much. Just said it was good and she'd see me later. A bit odd, really.'

'Hmm.' Peter gave his tray a cursory wipe and set off for more glasses.

By the time the curtain came down, he'd taken Libby's place behind the bar and she was able to slip in at the back and watch the final scene. The reaction, while not as ecstatic as the previous two nights, was enthusiastic and prompted three bows from the beaming cast. Libby heaved a sigh of relief and went back to the bar.

Many compliments later, and Fran was offering to help clear the glasses.

'Nay bother,' said Peter, running hot water into the sink. 'You and Lib get off home. She's done enough for tonight.'

'You sure?' asked Libby, drying her hands on a paper towel.

'Absolutely. Off you go and I'll phone you in the morning.'

Libby and Fran walked down the drive to the High Street in silence.

'Come on, Fran, out with it,' said Libby. 'What's wrong? Was it crap?'

Fran walked along looking at the ground in front of her. 'No, of course it wasn't. I've already told you, it was good.'

'Then what is it? Is something to do with Ben?'

'Why on earth would it be something to do with Ben?' Fran looked up.

'I don't know,' Libby muttered. 'Just wondered.'

'There's nothing between Ben and me, I've told you. No, it's Paula.'

'Paula? The murder?'

'Yes.' Fran sighed. 'It's just one of those facts. I know she wasn't killed where she was found.'

Libby was puzzled. 'We were talking about that earlier, Peter and me. But why should that worry you?' She looked at Fran's averted profile. 'Unless you know who killed her.'

'No, I don't think I do,' said Fran. 'But I'm worried about Millie.'

'So are we. They're getting in a doctor to see if she's fit to be questioned tomorrow. I think we ought to find out who really killed Paula so they don't bother Millie. No sense in upsetting the family all over again.'

'It'll upset the family anyway,' murmured Fran.

'Why? Why do you say that?'

Fran looked uncomfortable. 'Oh, well, you know, James and all that.'

Libby shot her a suspicious look, but said nothing, and they walked the rest of the way back to Allhallow's Lane in silence.

'When are you going back to London?' asked Libby later, as she handed Fran a substantial-looking scotch.

'Tomorrow sometime. Is there anything I can do for you before I go?'

Libby raised her eyebrows. 'No – should there

be? Like what?'

Fran shrugged. 'I don't know. I seem to have been enjoying your hospitality a bit too much.'

'You bought me dinner on Saturday.'

Fran's lips twisted. 'And that wasn't an unqualified success, was it?'

'Oh, come on, water under the bridge and all that.' Libby sat down and took out her cigarettes. 'All these problems have had a good effect on me. I haven't smoked half as much over the last couple of weeks.'

Fran nodded. 'You've had too much else to think about.'

'Certainly have,' said Libby. 'Anyway, tomorrow I'm going to go with Peter to see Millie.'

'Do you think that's wise?'

'Wise? What do you mean? She's Pete's mum. He needs to see how she is.'

Fran looked agitated. 'Will David be there?'

'No idea. Probably at work. But don't worry, we won't upset her. She won't need medical intervention.'

Fran looked at her oddly. 'No,' she said.

'Oh, honestly, you don't think Pete's going to hurt her, do you? How could you?'

'No, no, of course not. I know he loves her.'

Libby was perplexed. 'Then what's the matter?'

Fran shook her head. 'Oh, nothing. Take no notice of me. I'm being pathetic.'

Libby privately agreed, but couldn't help the little niggle of doubt that kept her awake for far too long after she and Fran had gone to bed. Fran hadn't actually demonstrated any startling evidence of psychometry or remote viewing, but

301

Ben's recommendation had carried some weight, and Fran was certainly worried about something. And she still hadn't heard from Ben.

Peter phoned while Libby was having her early morning cup of tea.

'I want to go and see Mum before they get anybody else out there. Are you still coming with me?'

'Do you need me? I'm not dressed yet.'

'No, not really, but you said you wanted to give me moral support.'

'I'll catch you up. I'll keep my mobile on so you can get in touch if you go anywhere else.'

'I'll go and see James after Mum. He's a bit wobbly.'

'I'll catch up with you somewhere, then,' said Libby, and went upstairs to tell Fran and get dressed.

Fran was still disconcertingly edgy this morning, thought Libby as she made her way down Allhallow's Lane in the spring sunshine. She obviously suspected someone but didn't dare say who it was, but whether it was psychic intuition or simple deduction, Libby didn't know. If it was deduction, she reasoned, she should have worked it out herself by now, although perhaps she was too close to all the protagonists to do that.

Blossom decorated the orchard that bordered the lane in pink and white, and Libby could smell the lilac that hung over the vicarage wall. The daffodils were over, and the remains of the tulips bent blowsily in their beds around the horse trough. Spring had well and truly arrived, but it was failing in its duty, thought Libby. It was supposed to cheer people up, to reaffirm life and love. Instead of which, it was insensitively showing off. It should have stayed appropriately wet, windy and depressing. She hadn't even heard from Ben since the debacle of Tuesday night, which added to her own feeling of dejection, and the little niggle of doubt which had kept her awake last night was now turning into a knot of fear somewhere in her stomach.

Chapter Twenty-eight

As she approached the Pink Geranium she saw James coming the other way. He looked drawn and somehow older. She pinned on a determined smile and waved.

'Hi,' he said coming to a halt outside the door.

'How are you?' asked Libby, reaching up to kiss his cheek.

He tried to smile. 'Oh, OK, you know. Supposed to be meeting Pete. He's been to see Mum.'

'I know, I was going to go with him, but he was too early for me. Is he coming here? Shall we go in and beg a coffee from Harry?'

James nodded and knocked on the window. Harry appeared, resplendent in his favourite leather trousers and pink shirt, covered with a long cook's apron.

'Come in, dear hearts,' he said. 'Pete phoned and said he'll be along in a minute. He didn't say you were coming, though, Lib.'

'He knows.' Libby sat down at her favourite table in the window.

'Council of war, is it?' Harry swept aside a newspaper and straightened the cruet.

James just shook his head and collapsed into the chair opposite Libby's. Harry frowned, sighed, and whisked off towards the kitchen. 'Coffee,' he called over his shoulder.

James obviously didn't want to, or couldn't, talk, and Libby didn't know what to say. The silence remained until Harry returned with a cafetiere and mugs.

'Have you eaten this morning, James?' he asked. James looked vaguely surprised and shook his head again.

'When did you last eat?'

'Yesterday sometime. Before the police came round.' James frowned. 'I think.'

'When did they come round?' asked Libby, a cold feeling settling round the knot of fear still resident in her stomach.

'I don't know. Morning, I think. I called Pete.'

'Then I'm going to get you something now,' said Harry, 'even if you don't think you're hungry. You must eat.'

'What did the police want?' said Libby, when Harry had gone back to the kitchen.

'Oh, all sorts of things. All about Paula, and how long we'd been together ... and Mum, and where she was.' James shut his eyes. 'I can't remember.'

Libby pushed down the plunger on the cafetiere. 'They've got to ask questions, James. We want to find out who did it, don't we?'

'Do we?' James gave a small, mirthless laugh. 'I don't think I care. She...' he stopped, looking horrified.

'Caused enough trouble alive? Is that what you were going to say?' Libby poured coffee and pushed one mug towards him.

James flushed. 'No, of course not.' He looked up gratefully as the door opened. 'Here's Pete.'

Peter came in and squeezed his brother's shoulder before sitting down next to him.

'Is that coffee? Thank God for that. Susan hasn't a clue how to make it.' He poured himself a mug and took a scalding mouthful. 'Ow!'

'Serves you right,' said Libby following his lead in trying to lighten the atmosphere. Not, she thought, that it was likely to remain light.

'How is she?' asked James.

'Mum? She seems fine, muddled, and can't understand why she's staying with Susan and David, but otherwise quite bright.' Peter sat back in his chair. 'She's got no memory of what happened the other night, Lib.'

'That's just as well, surely,' said Libby. 'She won't mention it to the police.'

'Why do they want to talk to her, Pete?' James hadn't touched his coffee.

'Haven't a clue. They can't know she had anything to do with the accidents at the theatre.'

'Unless they heard a mention of them when Cole and the other one came to see the play on Tuesday,' said Libby.

'I hadn't thought of that,' said Peter, looking up, 'but even then, they wouldn't know it had anything to do with Mum. Even the cast don't know, and they certainly didn't on Tuesday.'

'So why, then?' James's voice cracked. 'They can't think she...'

'Of course they don't,' Libby said in a rallying tone. 'But we really ought to try and think who might have done, so we can point the police in the right direction.'

'Oh, and they'd take notice, would they?' Peter raised an eyebrow. 'I thought you didn't want to be Miss Marple?'

'I don't. But we know everyone round here better than they do.'

'I bet that's what all the amateur detectives say.' Peter leaned over and patted Libby's arm. 'This isn't a book, Lib. This is real. It's no use speculating, because we don't know anything about what they've found out.'

'Do they know whether she was pregnant?' asked James.

Peter and Libby exchanged looks.

'Don't you think she was, then?' said Libby, with a quick frown as Peter opened his mouth.

'I don't know,' said James miserably. 'She said she was, and she said it was mine, but I don't know.'

'Why would she have lied?' asked Peter.

'I don't know!' James burst out. 'Why would she want to marry me? She didn't love me. Why didn't she go after the other bloke?'

Another silence fell, and Libby made a face at Peter. Harry appeared at the kitchen door and waited.

'What other bloke?' said Peter.

'I don't know. I was sure she was seeing someone else when we broke up and I got the impression he was married. If she was pregnant, I bet it was his and she was trying to get me to take it on.' James put his head in his hands.

Peter nodded at Libby. 'Sounds like it,' he said.

'Why did you go along with it?' said Libby.

James sat back and started playing with his mug. 'Oh, you know. She was – well, she was convincing. I know everybody thought I was a fool, but we were brought up as gentlemen, weren't we, Pete?' He smiled wryly at his brother.

'And look what a gentleman he turned out to be,' said Harry, coming forward and topping up their mugs. 'I'm doing you an omelette, young James. And make sure you eat it.'

'Young James.' Peter patted Harry fondly on the bottom. 'He's older than you are.'

'But so much less mature,' said Harry, and twitched away to the kitchen.

'So did the police ask you about any of this?' said Libby.

'Not in so many words. They didn't tell me anything.'

'Well, perhaps you'll see them this morning at Susan's,' said Peter. 'I said we'd go back when the doctor comes.'

'Oh, he's coming this morning, is he?' said James. 'We'd better go, then.'

'You just stay and eat your omelette or my life won't be worth living,' said Peter, 'then we'll go.'

Libby finished her coffee. 'I'll only be in the way,' she said, 'so I'll go back and see how Fran is. She really enjoyed the play, by the way, Pete.'

'When's she going home?'

'Today, sometime. Why are you so worried about her?' Libby was exasperated.

'She's just butted in, that's all.'

'By invitation. Your cousin asked her, don't forget.'

'Oh, I won't forget that.' Peter looked up at her maliciously. 'And neither can you, can you, sweetie?'

Libby pressed her lips together and picked up her basket.

'While we're on the subject of Fran,' she said, 'she did wonder why we were all so sure your mother caused the accidents. She doesn't think she did.'

Giving James a supportive pat on the arm she opened the door.

'Keep in touch,' she said to the air, and left.

'Morning,' called a voice from across the road, as she turned towards home.

'David!' She stopped and waited for him to cross the road to her side. 'How are things this morning?'

'You mean with Millie?' He ran a hand through his thick hair. 'Not so good.'

'Peter thought she seemed quite bright.'

'Peter? Has he seen her today?'

'Yes, he went up to warn her – and Susan, of course – about the police bringing their doctor to see her.'

David stared. 'What? I didn't know about this.'

'DS Cole came to talk to Peter last night after you said they couldn't interview Millie. They told him then.'

David looked furious. 'Why didn't he tell me?

This is outrageous. They have no right to do this.'

'Well, I think Peter has, as her son,' said Libby doubtfully.

'She's a sick woman,' said David, 'and who knows what she might say to them?'

Libby regarded him thoughtfully, wondering how much he knew of Hetty's story. 'I expect that's why they want a doctor to see her,' she said.

'*I'm* a doctor, for goodness' sake!' David looked ready to erupt. 'Where's Peter?'

'In the Pink Geranium with James,' said Libby. 'Really, David, I don't think you need worry. Millie *is* their mother. They'll look after her.'

David made a sound that sounded suspiciously like "hurrumph", and barged past her into the restaurant. Libby hesitated, torn between going back to see what was going on and a craven desire to keep out of it. Self-preservation got the better of her and she left, making a short detour into the farm shop to buy something for lunch.

'So did you ask about where the body was found?' said Fran, when Libby had finished telling her all about the morning's events.

'Well, no, there was no point. Peter hadn't seen the police, and anyway, why would they tell him?'

'I just think it's important.' Fran kept her eyes down and picked at a lettuce leaf

Libby sighed. 'I'll give Pete a ring after lunch and see if he prised anything out of the inspector, or whoever came with the doctor.'

But Peter sounded even more cheerful when Libby rang him while enjoying a post-lunch cigarette.

'They didn't come,' he said. 'Apparently, Inspector Murray didn't consider it that important, it was only that bloody idiot Cole making mountains out of mudpies.'

'So we were worrying for nothing?'

'Looks like it. Anyway, Mum's off the hook. Funny thing was, David came bursting into the caff just after you went, breathing fire and brimstone about the police questioning her.'

'I know,' said Libby, 'I'd just spoken to him. What was his problem?'

'He thinks Mum's worse than she is. I've told him I'll take responsibility for her, whatever happens, but he's still muttering curses. I never knew he had it in him.'

'Perhaps she was his one true love,' giggled Libby, 'like we said last night.'

'God help them, then,' snorted Peter. 'What a pair.'

Libby relayed this conversation to Fran, who still looked worried.

'And did you find out?' she said.

'Find out? What?'

'Where she was killed.'

'Oh, God, you're not still on about that!' Libby stubbed out her cigarette and stood up. 'No, I didn't ask. The police didn't come to see Millie, so Peter hasn't seen them, either. For goodness' sake, what does it matter?'

Fran looked stubborn. 'It's important,' she said. 'And did you ask them about the accidents?'

'No, I didn't. I told them what you thought and left them to it. Pete didn't mention it just now. I'll ask him later. As there's no reason now for her to be questioned, perhaps he doesn't think it matters.'

'But it does, can't you see? If it wasn't Millie, who was it?'

Suppressing the urge to ask when she was going home, Libby took the lunch crockery out to the kitchen.

'Sorry, Libby.' Fran came up behind her. 'I've been a right pain, haven't I? I'll go and put my things together and get out of your way. I ought to go now, anyway, or I'll get stuck in the rush hour.'

Immediately feeling guilty, Libby turned and smiled. 'You don't have to go yet if you don't want to, Fran. You can even stay tonight, but I'll have to turn you out tomorrow...'

'I know, the children are coming down.' Fran smiled back. 'No, it's fine. I really enjoyed the play, and I hope they find the murderer so you can all get on with your lives.'

'As long as it's not someone we know,' said Libby, 'that's what terrifies me.'

'Do you really think Peter, Harry or James could be a murderer?'

'No, of course I don't.'

'Or Ben?' Fran smiled. 'I'm sure it isn't any of them.'

'Well, that's good, I suppose. But if it isn't them we haven't got any more suspects, have we?'

'I expect the police have,' said Fran. 'And didn't you tell me James thought she'd been having an affair with someone else apart from him?'

'Yes, but who? How will the police find out?'

'They'll have gone through her house and her

belongings with a fine toothcomb, you've seen that on TV. They're bound to find some evidence somewhere. And they'll ask all the other people she knew, not just you lot in the village. Where did she work, for a start?'

'Good heavens!' Libby sat on the edge of the table with a bump. 'Do you know, I haven't the faintest idea.'

'Well, there you are then. Stop worrying.'

'But you're worried. You wanted to know about the accidents, and where she was killed. You must think it's got something to do with us.'

Fran looked away. 'Just a feeling. You know I'm not always right. And I know it isn't Peter, Harry, James or Ben.'

And with that small comfort, she went upstairs to pack.

Chapter Twenty-nine

Libby changed the bed after Fran had gone, and fell over Sidney on the way down the stairs when the phone rang.

'It's me,' said Ben.

'Hi.' Libby took a deep breath to calm her solar plexus.

'Bad news, I'm afraid.'

'Oh, God, what? Millie?'

'No, James.' Ben's voice sounded strained. 'They've arrested him.'

Libby felt the blood drain from her head and

she sat down suddenly on the stairs.

'Arrested him? Why?'

'Why do you think? Actually, I don't think David said arrested, he's just helping with their enquiries.'

'What evidence did they have?'

'How do I know?' said Ben, testily.

'Sorry.' Libby found she was trying hard not to cry. 'Where's Pete? And Millie?'

'Millie's still with Susan and Pete's gone to the police station. Harry's being a little soldier and carrying on in the face of adversity.'

'Don't be so sarcastic,' said Libby sharply. 'I'll go and see if there's anything I can do. I can leave the kids to sort themselves out. They've got keys.'

'I'm sorry, Lib,' said Ben, more gently. 'It's been a bloody awful few days.'

'It has for all of us, Ben,' said Libby. 'I'm very sorry for your family, but I got involved too, and Harry is, after all, Pete's life partner. If he was Pete's wife he'd deserve a bit more sympathy, wouldn't he?'

She heard Ben sigh. 'OK, OK. Sorry. Is Fran still there?'

'No, she's gone. You knew she was coming yesterday, if you wanted to see her, why didn't you come round then? Or come to the theatre?'

'I was busy. I did try and phone you to see how you were.'

'I was here.'

There was a short silence.

'Well, I'm sorry. I don't seem to be able to do anything right.' Libby heard him sigh again.

'Don't worry about it,' she said. 'James is the

one we have to think about now, so stop thinking about yourself. I'm going to the caff.'

Feeling righteously indignant, she put down the phone and went to find paper to write a note for her children who were due to arrive some time that afternoon. She left messages on their mobiles, fed Sidney, flung her cape around her shoulders, picked up her basket and set off. She had no idea what she was going to do, but to sit at home while James was in such a terrible predicament seemed utterly callous.

The Pink Geranium was locked, and when Libby called his mobile, Harry told her he was at home.

'Come on up,' he said. 'You can stop me drinking myself into a stupor.'

Sure enough, he opened the door clutching a brandy balloon at least half full.

'Shall I make some tea?' asked Libby, stepping over the threshold and throwing her cape onto a chair.

'If you don't want to join me,' said Harry, waving his glass dangerously.

'Bit early for me,' said Libby, going in to the kitchen, 'unless *I'd* been drinking since lunchtime.'

'Well, I have. Since Pete came back to the caff, anyway.'

'What happened?' Libby moved the big kettle on to the hotplate and found two of Harry's pretty china mugs.

'Well, you know they decided not to question Pete's mama?'

'Yes, I phoned him just after lunch.'

'So you did.'

'What I don't know is whether he and James actually went back up to see her, and how they found out about the police.'

'Oh, yes, they went up there. And James phoned the police station and they said they weren't coming.'

'Did he ask why?'

'Don't ask me, chuck. I wasn't there. Anyway, Pete comes back all chuffed and we had a drink. There weren't any customers so we were on our own.' Harry put down his glass and fetched milk. 'Then David phoned.'

'David? Where was he?'

'He'd gone home to check on mad Millie and found James being hauled into custody.'

'Christ.' Libby stared at him. 'It doesn't seem possible, does it?'

Harry shook his head and swirled brandy moodily round the glass.

Libby poured water into the mugs and added milk. 'Come on, sit down and tell me the rest.'

When Libby had curled up in her usual chair and Harry had flung himself along the sofa, he sighed and put down the brandy glass.

'Tea, I suppose. I'd better keep a clear head.'

'If you've been drinking since lunchtime that's a non-starter,' said Libby. 'Tell me what happened next.'

'David tried to get the police to tell them what was going on, but all they would say was James was helping them with their enquiries. So he phoned Pete and Ben.'

'Yes, Ben phoned me.'

'And then Pete went mad.'

Libby nodded in sympathy, realising that Harry was actually fighting tears.

'And went to the police station? Did he speak to Millie first?'

'Not much point in that. David said she didn't know what was going on. Apparently, the police knew James was there because he'd phoned to ask where their doctor was. Now honestly, would you do that if you were guilty of anything?'

'Well, you might,' said Libby, 'if you wanted to know what was going on and keep tabs on them.'

'Of course he didn't. Of all the innocents, that James is the worst. Do you remember that night in the pub after rehearsal? When he came in and Paula was all over him? And he couldn't see it, could he?'

'Well, he can see it now,' said Libby. 'He was saying this morning.'

'Bit late, now.' Harry swung his legs to the floor. 'Silly little bugger.'

'Why? You don't think he did it, do you?'

Harry looked up and away quickly. 'No. But I want to know what evidence they've got.'

'In detective stories the amateur sleuth always knows the evidence. Why don't we? We don't even know where she was killed.'

'Or when. Why won't someone tell us?'

'Because if someone lets out that they know a fact not released to the public it means they dunnit,' said Libby, 'so if you said, for instance "Oh, no, guv, that iron, or golf club, or blunt instrument doesn't belong to me," and the police had never said it *was* a blunt instrument or whatever, they've got you. See?'

Harry frowned. 'Well, how does anyone ever solve anything, then?'

'I don't suppose they do. I think it's all in books and television.' Libby sighed. 'I wish we could find out something, though. I'm sure we could help James.'

'What do you think we ought to know, then?' Harry put down his mug and folded his arms.

'Where she was killed. Was it in the car, was the car moved, what was the weapon.'

'David would know.' Harry looked smug.

'He might,' said Libby doubtfully, 'but would he tell us?'

'We can but try.' Harry reached behind him for the phone. 'Here. He's on memory 5.'

'Me? Why can't you ask him?'

'He doesn't approve of me. He's actually quite homophobic, is our cousin David.'

Libby took the phone reluctantly and peered at the keypad. 'OK. Which one do I press first?'

It rang for a long time before Susan answered.

'Dr Dedham's phone,' she said.

'Susan, hello, it's Libby Sarjeant.'

'Hello, Libby. How are you?'

'I'm fine, thanks. How are you? Are you coping with ma – m – Millie?'

'Oh, she's no trouble. Luckily she doesn't realise about James. You know about James?'

'Yes, I do. Shocking, isn't it? Actually, that's why I'm ringing.'

'Oh?'

'Well, obviously, we don't believe for a minute that James did it, so we wondered if there was any

317

clue that perhaps the police hadn't picked up on?'

'Why would I know?' asked Susan.

'David might have seen something, or know whether she was killed in the car. Something like that.'

'I couldn't say, I'm sure,' said Susan coldly. 'Surely you should leave it to the police. They must have some reason for arresting James.'

'They haven't arrested him, have they?' Libby was shocked. 'I thought they'd just taken him in to help with their enquiries.'

'It's the same thing, isn't it? That's what they always say.'

'I don't think it's quite the same. And there's a difference between being arrested and being charged.'

Libby heard a deep voice in the background, and the sound of the mouthpiece being covered, before David spoke.

'What do you want, Libby? Why are you asking questions? The police have got it all in hand.'

'No, they haven't, David.' Libby was getting desperate. 'Surely you don't believe James killed Paula? It's impossible.'

'Someone killed her. I found her.'

'I know, that's why I was asking. Had she been moved? You could have told whether she had, couldn't you?'

'No, of course I couldn't. She had half her head caved in and she was in the driving seat. That's all I saw.'

Libby thought about this. 'Had she been moved?'

'Christ, Libby! I don't know! Forget it.' David almost shouted.

'All right, all right. Sorry. I'll go. I'm just concerned.' Libby made a face at Harry. 'Give my love to Millie.' She waited. 'David? David? Are you there?'

'Rung off, petal. I could hear him from here.' Harry lit a cigarette and threw one at Libby. 'Well, that wasn't much use, was it?'

'At least we know now she was hit on the head and she was in the driving seat, so she must have driven the car to her house.'

Harry thought about this. 'So where was James? I thought he'd moved in with her?'

'Oh, God, of course. I'd forgotten that. So why didn't he realise she was missing?' Libby inhaled a lungful of smoke and coughed. 'I'm going to have to give up.'

'Not right now, dearie. Wrong time. Wait until this is all over.'

Libby sighed. 'If it ever *is* over.'

Her basket began to vibrate against her leg and she fumbled inside to find her mobile and got smoke in her eyes.

'Hello?' she managed finally, squeezing smarting eyes shut.

'Mum? Where are you?'

'Belinda! Darling, I'm sorry I'm not there. Can you cope? We've got a bit of a crisis.'

'I gathered. What's going on?'

Libby gave her daughter a brief outline of the current situation, amid many gasps of outrage and horror, and promised to see her at the theatre later.

'Is Dom there yet?'

'No, Mum, you know what Dom's like. He'll tip up at the last minute. Ad's here, though. He came down with me. He says they'll both bunk down in the living room and I can have the bed.'

After reassuring Belinda that she wasn't in any personal danger (having carefully omitted any reference to her unfortunate encounter with the skull), Libby rang off.

'Belinda and Adam are at Bide-a-Wee. Dominic hasn't arrived yet.' She stubbed out her cigarette. 'I suppose I can't leave them to fend for themselves for too long.'

'Of course you can't. Anyway, you'll have to go behind the bar again tonight, won't you? Pete won't leave the police station while James is still there. And I've got bookings.' Harry reached over and gave Libby's hand a pat. 'It really isn't your problem, petal, no matter how involved with everybody you've become. You could just walk away.'

'Don't be stupid, Harry, of course I couldn't. Even if I didn't love you all, this started with the play. And the play is very much my business – and so is the theatre,' she added gloomily.

The Hop Pickers is a success, isn't it? Well, then.' Harry stood up, bent to give her a quick kiss and swept up mugs and his brandy glass. 'Come on. We'll wash this lot up and then decide what to do next.'

They heard the key in the lock just as Libby was hanging the mugs back on their hooks. Harry rushed past her tossing rubber gloves in his wake.

'James!' Libby surged through the furniture and threw her arms round him. 'Sit down. What happened?'

Peter, emerging from Harry's effusive welcome, answered her.

'If Harry'll give us all a drink, we'll tell you.' He patted Harry on the bottom and sat down next to James on the sofa.

'I'll help you, Harry,' said Libby. 'What do we all want? Pete? James?'

'Your kids'll have to cope for a bit longer, now,' said Harry, as he disregarded everybody's requests and opened a bottle of champagne.

'They won't mind. I'll go straight to the theatre.' Libby looked at her watch. 'Fairly soon.'

With Libby back in her sagging armchair and Harry perched on the arm of the sofa, his arm draped round Peter's shoulders, Peter began his explanation.

'For some reason, the police had never bothered to check where James was the night Paula was killed, and assumed he had been in her cottage.'

'God knows why,' said James wearily. 'If I'd been there, I'd have been there when the circus started, wouldn't I? And surely David knocked on the door? He would have done, wouldn't he?'

'Must have done,' nodded Libby. 'Go on. Except he didn't find her until the next morning. You'd have been at work.'

'Anyway,' continued Peter, 'when they started questioning him they found out he was in London, and hadn't even given up the tenancy on his own house, let alone moved in with Paula.'

'Millie seemed to think you had,' said Libby.

321

'She wanted me to. Very keen on the whole grandchild idea. We hadn't got round to the details.' James put his head in his hands. 'I told you, I didn't know what to think.'

'So what did the police do?' asked Harry.

'Kept on at me a bit, but there was nothing I could tell them, even about the bedspread, so they had to let me go.'

'Bedspread?' said Libby and Harry together.

James looked surprised. 'Yes – didn't you know? She was sitting on a bedspread – or it was in the car. Not quite sure. But that's how they know she wasn't killed there.'

There was a silence while Peter, Harry and Libby all looked at each other.

'There we are then,' said Harry, 'just what we wanted to know.'

'How did you know, James?' asked Libby.

'I didn't, until it came out while they were questioning me. I assumed it was general knowledge.'

'So was she wrapped in the bedspread and then moved, or did it protect the killer, or what? And was she moved, or was the car moved? And where did the bedspread come *from?*' said Libby, getting excited.

'They showed me the bedspread,' said James. 'It was hers. Not from her bed. It was what she called a throw, and she had it over the sofa in the living room.'

'I remember...' Harry began, and then, after a quick look at Peter, stopped. Peter patted his thigh.

'Haven't they got DNA from it?' Libby asked. Harry looked frightened.

'How do I know? Mine could be on it, come to that,' said James. 'Perhaps that's why they pulled me in.'

'In that case,' said Libby robustly, 'they would have pulled in half of Steeple Martin, let alone Canterbury.'

'Oh – and she was pregnant. I had to give a DNA sample.'

There was a shocked silence.

'Well. At least you'll know if it was yours,' said Libby, uncertainly.

Peter and Harry exchanged glances, while James sat back and closed his eyes. Libby surveyed them all for a moment before draining her glass.

'Right,' she said. 'I'd better be off. You can fill me in on any of the details I miss later. But the theatre has to be opened and I'm behind the bar again.'

Harry sprang up. 'Dear heart, you haven't eaten,' he said.

'I had lunch with Fran before she went,' said Libby. 'I'll be fine.'

'I'll save you something in the caff for afterwards. Bring the kinder with you.' Harry flung her cape round her shoulders and kissed her cheek.

'Thank you, Harry.' Libby smiled up at him. 'Look after the boys.'

Chapter Thirty

Libby was surprised to see Peter accompanying her children in to the theatre a little later.

'I thought I ought to make sure they knew the way,' he said, after rapturous greetings had been exchanged and much ceremony employed in escorting them to their seats. 'Just because of our little domestic problem, it doesn't mean they should suffer.'

'As long as James is all right,' said Libby, preparing to wash glasses.

'Not exactly all right, but relieved. He's staying at ours tonight, and said he might come down to the caff later to see you and the children.'

'Well, at least we know a bit more about the circumstances, now. That should help,' said Libby.

'Why would it help? We don't need to know, now, do we? My Mum's off the hook and so is James. They obviously never seriously considered Harry or Ben, so we haven't got to worry any more.'

Libby didn't answer. Now detective fever had gripped her, it was going to be hard to let it go, even if her nearest and dearest were no longer threatened. Especially if Millie wasn't responsible for the accidents. That meant someone was still out there with animosity directed towards – whom? The Family (there it was again, capital letters), the theatre, or Libby herself?

'Come on, Lib, what are you thinking?' Peter came round the bar and began to dry glasses. 'Don't start being nosy just for the sake of it.'

'I know,' sighed Libby. 'I just want to get to the bottom of it. Don't you?'

'No. I don't want anything more to do with it,' said Peter. 'I just want my life to go back to normal. And so should you.'

There was no more opportunity for conversation after that, as Stephen and several members of the back-stage crew drifted in wanting to hear about James's ordeal. Ben appeared during the interval, and after being introduced to Belinda, Dominic and Adam, took them in charge and gave them as much of a guided tour as was possible. To Libby's surprise, just as the audience was going back into the auditorium, David turned up, looking even more harassed than usual.

'David!' said Libby, surprised. 'Are you all right? Can I get you a drink?'

Ben and Peter appeared either side of him.

'Oh, a beer, please,' said David. 'Whatever you've got. What does everybody else want?'

'Give the man a pint, Lib,' said Ben. 'I'll get it. And whatever Pete's having.'

'How's Mum?' said Peter. 'Everything all right?'

'Fine, fine,' said David, taking a grateful swig of his beer. 'James phoned her, but I don't think she realises what's been going on. Very relieved about James, Pete, goes without saying.'

'Thanks,' said Peter, gruffly.

'Libby, sorry I was a bit – er–'

'Grumpy?' suggested Libby.

325

'Rude,' said David with a wry grin. 'I can't stand this police attitude that they can question anybody with impunity.'

'But they can,' said Ben. 'They have to. I know they can seem rather insensitive...'

'Look at the way they hauled poor old James in,' continued David, as if Ben hadn't spoken. 'Just because she was supposed to be expecting his baby.'

'Supposed to be?' said Peter.

There was a short silence. 'I don't know, do I?' said David eventually. 'I only know what's been said. I thought that was the general idea?'

'Do you know the results of the post-mortem, David?' asked Libby. 'Wouldn't they tell you, as a doctor and the person who discovered the body?'

'I haven't asked,' said David huffily. 'I didn't even pronounce her dead. The police surgeon did that.'

'Come on, Lib, it doesn't matter any more,' said Peter. 'Leave it alone.'

Libby sighed and smiled and returned to her washing up. Ben and Peter took David over to one of the tables by the window.

It was just before the end of the play when he came back to Libby at the bar.

'Libby, I think there's something you ought to know,' he said, leaning forward almost conspiratorially.

'Oh? What about?'

'This isn't really the place to talk about it.' He looked briefly over his shoulder to where Ben and Peter still sat at the table.

'Is it Millie?'

'Not exactly. Look, Libby, if I could pop by just to have a word later, perhaps?'

'Sorry David, but later would be about midnight by the time I've closed the bar and the theatre, and I've got my children staying this weekend. They're in there watching now.' Libby didn't mention the planned visit to the Pink Geranium in case David decided to gate-crash.

'Oh, right.' He frowned. 'I really am sorry, but I think it might be – well – urgent. I just don't want to say anything...' Once again, he looked towards Ben and Peter. Which of them he was worried about Libby couldn't tell.

'Shall I pop in to the surgery tomorrow morning?' she asked. 'Or don't you have a surgery on Saturdays?'

'Emergencies only,' said David, 'but I'm often in there catching up on paper-work. If you're sure you don't mind? Only it's been worrying me.'

Intrigued, Libby confirmed that she wouldn't mind at all, and looking more-or-less satisfied, David said goodbye, waved at Ben and Peter and left.

'What was all that about?' asked Peter, bringing their empty glasses over just as a burst of clapping heralded the end of the play.

'He was still apologising,' said Libby. 'He's very concerned about Millie, you know, Pete.'

'I know he is,' sighed Peter. 'He's a good bloke, David. Just a bit dull.'

'What an indictment!' said Ben, coming up behind. 'My poor brother-in-law.'

'Well, he is. Whoops – here we go. Prepare for

more compliments, Lib.'

The doors to the auditorium were hooked back and the audience began to emerge. First to appear were Belinda, Dominic and Adam, who made a concerted rush towards their mother. Peter shooed her out from behind the bar and took her place, and for ten minutes she basked in the admiration of her family, while fielding more compliments from other members of the public.

To her surprise, DCI Murray appeared with a pretty, plump woman clinging to his arm.

'Des Cole said how good it was,' said Murray, holding out a hand and looking embarrassed. 'We were lucky to get tickets.'

'I'm glad you did,' said Libby, delighted. 'Did you enjoy it?'

'Oh, it was lovely,' said the woman, 'much better than the telly.'

'My wife,' introduced DO Murray. 'Loves the theatre. Always going to the one in Canterbury.'

'The Marlowe, you know. I like the musicals,' confided Mrs Murray.

'Well, I'm really pleased you came to see us,' said Libby. 'Do you like our theatre?'

'It's really sweet,' said Mrs Murray. 'Just like a real one.'

Libby heard a variety of smothered snorts from her assembled children and hurried on.

'We'll have to put you on the mailing list, then,' she said, guiding the Murrays to the other end of the bar where a perspex container held the newly printed forms. 'Just fill one of these in and we'll let you know what's coming up. We're hoping to do a pantomime in January.'

'Oh, lovely!' exclaimed Mrs Murray. 'I do love panto. We could bring the grandchildren, Donnie.'

Donnie, glaring at his oblivious wife, muttered what could have been an agreement.

'And I'm so glad you didn't have to question Mrs Parker,' said Libby, turning to him. 'And so are her sons.'

'Ah, well, yes,' mumbled Murray. 'Can't really talk about it, now, of course.'

'No, of course not,' soothed Libby. 'But we're all so grateful that we're out of the picture.'

DCI Murray looked startled. 'I wouldn't quite say that, Mrs Sarjeant.'

'Oh.' Libby felt her stomach sink. So it wasn't over, and now she really would worry about what David was going to tell her. She wished she could talk it over with someone, but it was obviously connected to a member of the family, which precluded everybody as far as she was concerned. Harry, with whom she would normally discuss things, was far too intimately involved. She fleetingly wondered whether to phone Fran, but Fran's rather odd behaviour over the last couple of days decided her against that.

As she said goodbye to the Murrays and began to clear tables, Belinda came up behind her.

'What's up, Mum?' she said, picking up a couple of glasses.

'Nothing, darling.' Libby gave her a bright smile. 'And you don't have to do that. I'll just give Pete a hand and we'll go. Or you can go to Harry's on your own. I won't be long.'

'I'll wait for you. I can dry up or something. The boys can go on. Harry'll love to see them.'

Libby grinned. 'He'll flirt madly with them, you mean. Good job they don't take him seriously.'

As they walked back down the drive a little later, Belinda asked again.

'Something's wrong, Mum. What is it? I thought everything was all right now James was home again?'

'I don't think it'll ever be all right, Bel,' said Libby. 'Murder this close to home is cataclysmic. You question everything and everybody you've held dear, and it leaves this awful sick feeling in your stomach and your head. You feel you want to clap your hands over your ears and run away, like a child.'

Belinda was silent.

'Sorry, that was a bit of an outburst, wasn't it?' Libby tried a laugh, but it didn't sound convincing, even to her.

'It's fine, Mum. You needed to say it to someone, and I guess you can't say it to any of your friends here because they're involved.'

'That's it exactly, Bel. I'm so glad you understand. And now David wants to talk to me about something and won't say what.'

'David? Oh, Doctor David. Wants to talk to you?'

'Yes. He came in this evening and had a drink with Ben and Peter. Then he asked if he could talk to me, but said he couldn't do it then, in front of them. I'm scared, now. I mean, he was the one who found the body. He said earlier he didn't know anything, but he obviously does.'

'Do you think it's something the police don't know?' asked Belinda.

'No idea. The inspector who was here this evening said we weren't all in the clear, so probably not.'

'So, are you going to talk to him?'

'I'm going down to the surgery tomorrow morning. Don't worry, I won't wake you before I go.'

Belinda laughed. 'I'm not so bad now, Mum. I do actually get up before lunchtime. You'll be back before then, won't you? The boys'll want a pint in the pub before we all shoot off.'

'You don't have to go tomorrow, you know,' said Libby. 'You could always come to the after-show party.'

'What, with all the luvvies and in-jokes?' Belinda gave her mother a friendly nudge. 'And who knows who you might get off with?'

'Highly unlikely,' said Libby as they arrived at the door of the Pink Geranium, which was flung open at their approach. 'Oh, hello, Ben.'

By common consent, and partly because Belinda, Dominic and Adam were present, the subject of murder was avoided for the rest of the evening. Occasionally, Libby caught Ben looking at her speculatively, but he made no move to single her out, and she was forced to the conclusion that his attentions on Tuesday night had been, as she suspected, simply to comfort. Not, she reflected moodily as she and the children walked home, that anything much had happened then. Just a couple of cuddles, that's all. In fact, David's revelations could concern Ben, which frightened her even more and made his previous advances slightly sinister.

For once, on going downstairs in the morning, Sidney wasn't lying in wait on the bottom step, but lay squashed blissfully between the two sleeping bags that were all Libby could see of her sons. She picked her way across them and into the kitchen, where Sidney immediately joined her, loudly demanding breakfast.

'Shut up, idiot,' she whispered. 'You'll wake them up. And leave the bread bin alone.'

She took her tea and Sidney's breakfast through to the conservatory and lit the heater. Sidney abandoned her for the great outdoors as soon as he'd cleaned his saucer, and she sat alone, staring into the garden and worrying about what David was going to tell her.

A night's sleep hadn't made her feel any better about things. In fact, if anything, she felt worse. There had been a moment, on waking up, when she felt almost normal, then events crowded in on her, her stomach sank and the black cloud descended, like a fall of coal dust, impossible to clear up.

She managed to have breakfast, shower, dress and leave the house without waking her family, and once again walked down Allhallow's Lane resenting the cheerfulness of spring. The surgery was conveniently placed just round the corner from Maltby Close and the senior citizens who might need it most. Libby found the door un-locked, although the sign said closed, and David behind the reception desk with a pile of buff folders and a gloomy expression.

'Oh, hi,' he said. 'Have you come to save me from all this?'

'I don't know,' said Libby. 'Have I?'

David sighed. 'I hate it. I'm trying to put all my notes on to the computer. Let's have a cup of coffee.'

'I thought you'd have a secretary to do that?' said Libby, following him into a little room at the back with a kettle, a sink and a couple of chairs either side of a battered table.

'I have, and mostly I input as I go along,' said David, filling the kettle, 'but on home visits I have to resort to old-fashioned pen and paper. So it all has to be typed up afterwards, and if I leave it for Sally she gets snowed under.'

'That's very considerate of you. Perhaps you could have a little laptop? Wouldn't that make it easier?' asked Libby, sitting down at the table. 'So what did you want to talk to me about that you couldn't say in front of Ben and Peter?'

David didn't answer until he'd put two mugs of coffee on the table between them.

'Two things, really,' he said, not looking at her. 'The first one – well, I did know Paula.'

'Well, yes,' said Libby, surprised. 'We know you did. Everybody did.'

'Yes, but I knew her better than I let you think.' David wouldn't meet her eyes.

Libby gasped. 'David! You didn't?'

'What?' He looked up, startled. 'Oh, no, of course not. No, but er – when she went away – you know, she – er, well, she sort of – made a pass at me.'

'Really? It doesn't surprise me. How did it come about?'

David's shoulders relaxed. 'She was registered

333

with me then. I wouldn't take her on the list when she came back to the village.'

'Oh, dear.' Libby tried not to smile, but the thought of the upright David being seduced by Paula was really quite funny. 'So what was the other thing?'

'About Millie.'

'Millie? Last night you said it wasn't about Millie.'

'I said not exactly,' said David, pulling at his tie. 'Not *actually* Millie.'

Libby frowned at the tasteful "Sights of Sussex" tea towel draped artistically over the sink. 'What, then?'

'I've had a chance to have a really good look at her over the last few days.'

'I know. That's why you were being so protective of her. You think she's going senile, don't you?'

David winced. 'She's showing signs of early dementia, yes, but basically she's had a sort of minor breakdown. In layman's terms. She'll probably recover, and she might even be able to go back home and live on her own for a while longer.'

'That'll be a relief for the boys,' said Libby. 'So what's the problem?'

'Arthritis.'

'Arthritis?' Libby was surprised. 'She doesn't look as though she's got arthritis.'

'All arthritis doesn't present as bent and crippled,' said David, loftily. 'But if you've got it – ordinary osteo-arthritis, that is – which you probably have, at your age, it does curtail your activities somewhat.'

'Which means?' said Libby, with a sense of foreboding.

'Millie couldn't have cut that steel wire.'

Chapter Thirty-one

I should have expected this, thought Libby, still staring at David as though he'd suddenly grown another head. He looked thoroughly uncomfortable.

'And the bridge?' she said finally.

'No way.' He shook his head. 'Climbing down there and sawing through those planks. Honestly, can you see it?'

'No. I always said I couldn't see her cutting that steel wire. Climbing up into the flies – ridiculous. I think I always knew.'

'Flies?'

'The top of the stage. Where the lighting bars are – that sort of thing. That's where the roof hung before we had the accident.' Libby remembered her coffee and took a sip. It wasn't very good. 'So what *did* she do?'

'The fire. The other incidents gave her the idea.'

'But how much did she know about the other incidents? I can't see Peter rushing off to tell her.'

'Hetty knew. And Lenny. They were bound to tell her.'

'Or someone else,' said Libby, a horrible fear taking hold of her.

'What do you mean, someone else?'

335

'The murderer.'

They sat looking at one another in silence. David had gone pale, Libby noticed, and wondered exactly who he was worried about. She was just worried about everybody.

'Oh, God, this is awful,' she burst out. 'I've got to get back to the children.' She pushed her chair back and stood up. 'David, what are we going to do?'

'Do?' He looked surprised. 'Why?'

'Well, the police don't think the incidents at the theatre are connected to Paula's death. I'm sure now they are.'

He nodded, still looking bewildered.

'So that means the murderer is someone we know, because no one outside would know about the theatre and the bridge, would they?' She took a deep breath. 'Oh, God, I feel sick.'

'But you'd thought of all this before, hadn't you?' said David. 'When you thought Millie had caused the accidents.'

'Yes, but this is worse, somehow. It's confirmed.' She walked to the door. 'Fran knew. She told me it wasn't Millie. Oh, I don't know.'

'Take it easy,' said David, standing up and reaching out a large hand to pat her on the shoulder.

'Tell me,' she said, turning back to face him, 'why did you tell me this? What good's it done? And why didn't you tell the police?'

David looked horrified. 'Why would I do that? It might put someone we know in danger. Besides, they didn't know about Millie in the first place. They only wanted to question her because she was James's mother.'

'So why were you getting in such a state about it?'

'I told you, she's a sick woman, and I don't like the way the police ride roughshod over everybody.'

Libby sighed. There was so much she didn't understand, she just wanted to do what she'd said last night to Belinda, put her hands over her ears and run away.

'Oh, God. I shall have to tell Pete.' She looked up. 'By the way, why didn't you want to say this in front of him and Ben?'

'Because of James, of course. He really is the main suspect, isn't he?'

'Didn't they tell you last night?' said Libby, surprised. 'The police have found out – why they didn't before, I don't know – that he was in London that night, and didn't know anything about the bedspread. Did you know about the bedspread? Well, you must have done, if you found the body, I suppose.'

'Bedspread?' David's mouth was hanging open again. It really didn't suit him.

'Didn't you see it? The police said it was with the body. We didn't know until James told us.'

'No, I didn't see it. It wasn't in the car, I'm sure.' David was looking quite sick, now. 'Where did James say it was?'

'He didn't. As far as I can gather the police just thrust it at him in an evidence bag and asked if he recognised it. I don't know if it was used to move the body or what, but apparently she wasn't killed in the car.'

'Yes, but I found her in the car,' said David. 'In

337

the driver's seat.'

'Well, if she was, she was moved somehow.'

David put his head in his hands. 'God.'

Libby looked down on him. 'I know. It's horrific, isn't it? Now I really must go or the children will think I've been kidnapped. Oh, and David, she *was* pregnant. They told James. He's had to give a DNA sample.'

She left David sitting at the table, his head still in his hands. She felt sorry for him, but there was too much else to think about. She would have to tell Peter and Ben about David's theory and get the theatre checked before tonight's final performance. She was beginning to wish she'd taken more notice of Fran.

On impulse, she knocked at the door of the Pink Geranium on the way past. Harry poked his head out from the back, saw who it was, and came to unlock.

'What's up, petal?'

'Is Pete around?' asked Libby.

'No, he's at home with James. Why?'

'Oh, nothing. I'll call him when I get home.'

Harry frowned. 'Come on, what's going on now?'

'Nothing, I told you. I just need to speak to him before tonight.' Libby smiled brightly. 'See you later.'

She briefly contemplated walking up to The Manor to see if Ben was in, but decided she might as well go home and phone. The children would probably be up by now, making inroads into the contents of her fridge.

Libby stepped into number seventeen and was

immediately assailed by the scent of healthy young male. She opened the curtains and the window in the sitting room, frowned at the sleeping bags discarded like snake skins on the floor and followed the smell of burnt toast into the conservatory.

'Hello, Mum,' said Belinda, waving a slice of toast in one hand and stroking Sidney with the other.

'Morning all,' said Libby. 'Sleep well?'

Belinda nodded and the boys grunted. Satisfied, Libby retreated to the sitting room and picked up the phone.

'Pete, it's me. I've just been to see David, and he told me something rather odd. I'd quite like to talk to you and Ben about it. And James, actually.'

She heard a deep sigh. 'Oh, for goodness' sake, what now?'

'I'm sorry, Pete, it's not my fault this time, honestly. In fact, I still don't really know why David chose to tell me.'

'Didn't you ask him?'

'Well, of course I did, and he gave me some sort of explanation which didn't make sense. He said he was concerned for you and James, I think. Oh, and he didn't know about the bedspread.'

'How can he not have known? The police said it was in the car with her.'

'Oh, don't ask me, I'm beyond it all. But I really do need to speak to you.'

'All right,' Peter sighed again. 'Are you taking your rabble for a pint before they go home, did you say?'

'Yes, in about – ooh,' Libby looked at her

watch, 'about an hour, I should think.'

'So shall I meet you in the pub?'

'I'd rather meet you at the theatre.'

'The theatre? Good lord, haven't you seen enough of that place this week?'

'Trust me,' said Libby. 'I'm going to phone Ben, and I'll go down there as soon as he can open up.'

'If he's around this morning.'

'Oh, no! Don't tell me he's gone somewhere.'

'He was taking Hetty shopping this morning, I know. She wanted to do some food for the party tonight.'

'Oh, well, just you, then. Will I be able to get the keys from The Manor or will you bring yours?'

Peter sighed again. 'I'll bring mine. I'll see you there in about twenty minutes. All right? And this had better be worth it.'

He was right. Gregory Wilde answered the phone breathlessly but courteously. No, neither Hetty nor Ben was there, but he expected them back within the next half hour or so. Could he take a message?

Libby left a message asking Ben to get in touch as soon as he could, and apologising, told her children she would see them in the pub in an hour. She wished they were staying another night, so she could have spent some uninterrupted time with them the next day.

'Oh, Mum, I forgot,' said Belinda, as she was stepping out of the front door. 'Someone called Fran phoned. I told her you'd ring her when you got back.'

340

'I'll have to do it later,' said Libby. 'Did she say anything else?'

'No,' said Belinda, 'but she sounded a bit agitated.'

'Oh, lord.' Libby frowned, wondering whether she should phone Fran before going to the theatre. Thinking Fran was unlikely to point the finger at anyone specifically, she decided against it. She smiled brightly at Belinda. 'I'll tell you about her at the pub. See you later.'

Summer is definitely nearly here, Libby thought, unwrapping her cloak as she trotted down Allhallow's Lane for the second time that morning. It was really quite warm.

Peter was already at the theatre when she got there, and so, to her surprise, was James.

'I need to get out and be normal,' he explained. 'And go back home to the flat, as well.'

'Haven't you got to decide what to do about Millie?' asked Libby.

'Of course we have, but it needn't concern James. I can take care of it as I live in the village,' said Peter.

'Millie's actually one of the reasons I wanted to see you,' said Libby, feeling nervous. Her heart had started bumping away as though she was about to step on stage not knowing the script.

'I might have guessed,' said Peter, glowering at her. 'Go on. What now?'

'David wanted to see me because ... well. He says she didn't cut that wire.'

Peter and James stared at her.

'What?'

'Or the bridge. He says she couldn't have done.

341

She's got arthritis, apparently. I always said I couldn't see her doing that, didn't I?'

'That's good, isn't it?' asked James. 'It means she isn't under suspicion for anything.'

'The police never thought she was behind the accidents. They really didn't pay much attention to them once they realised they didn't have anything to do with Paula.' Libby sat down on one of the little wrought-iron chairs. 'No, I'm afraid it means someone else caused them.'

'So? I'm sorry, I don't understand the urgency.' Peter leaned up against the bar and folded his arms. 'So someone else did them. What are you saying?'

'That person's still about and we don't know who it is,' said Libby.

'And they might not be finished,' said James, obviously catching on.

They all looked at one another.

'And it could be the murderer,' said Peter, slowly.

'David said we'd all thought that before we knew Millie did them,' said Libby.

'Except she didn't,' said James.

'So what are we saying, here?' asked Peter. 'Mum didn't cause the accidents–'

'Except the fire,' put in Libby.

'But not the others, because she's too infirm. So not only did someone else cause them, but that person could be the murderer. Why do we think that?'

'I don't know,' said Libby helplessly. 'I can't remember now.'

'Because the accidents were intended to kill

Paula,' said James.

Libby and Peter looked at him. With growing apprehension, Libby wondered why on earth she'd let herself get involved with this, and remembered belatedly that David had reminded her about James still being the main suspect.

'What makes you say that, Jamie?' asked Peter, in an enviably controlled voice.

'I've been thinking,' said James, sitting down opposite Libby. 'I haven't been involved with the play except on the periphery, and after Paula told me she was pregnant. She was actually scared. She said if someone wanted to hurt her, they knew she would be under that roof, and would have expected her, as one of the principals, to be in the photo-shoot on the bridge and in the huts.'

'But why would someone want to hurt her? And it would have to be someone who knew a lot about the play,' said Libby. 'Oh, God, back to square one.'

'Someone did want to hurt her, didn't they?' said Peter, his eyes fixed ruminatively on the distance. 'And she knew it. Who?'

'Someone she'd had an affair with?' said Libby.

'But why try to kill her? What could be that bad? Just because she might threaten to tell a wife or partner or something?'

'Look,' said James, standing up. 'Nothing's changed, has it? The police are still investigating, and we haven't got their resources, so why don't we just carry on as normal? Even if the murderer is still at large, it doesn't mean to say there will be any more attacks on the theatre. Why on earth should there be? If it was Paula he was after all the time we've nothing to fear, have we?'

Libby felt ashamed for having half-suspected him again, and acknowledged the sense in what he said.

'He's right, Lib,' said Peter. 'We won't have any more trouble.'

'Sorry, I panicked,' said Libby, standing up and feeling foolish. 'David was so worried about it all.'

'That's what I don't understand,' said James.

'Well, at least we know it wasn't your mum, even if we think we know the accidents were directed at Paula. I think he was right to tell us.' Libby fished in her basket for her cigarettes. 'I'm going to pop outside and have a fag before we go, if that's all right.'

Peter grinned at her. 'Feeling foolish, you old trout?'

'No, I'm not. I had to tell you what David said,' said Libby, not meeting his eyes, 'even if I seem to have done nothing but get the wrong end of the stick all through this business. About Ben, Fran, Paula – you name it.'

'Come on, I'll join you in a fag. James, you coming?'

'No, I'll go back and pack if you don't mind. I'll have to get stuff from Mum's as well, so I'd better get on with it. See you, Libby. Thanks for the support.'

'Aren't you coming to the party tonight?'

'Oh, yes, I'd forgotten. Well, I still need to pack. See you later.'

Peter followed Libby into the little courtyard.

'So what's up now?' he said.

'Oh, nothing much. Just wondering who the hell we know who would kill someone and why.' Libby lit her cigarette and sat on a bench.

'That hasn't changed, has it? We've been wondering that for the last week or more.'

'But we know a lot more, now,' said Libby. 'We know about the bedspread. And we know she was pregnant.'

'How does that help?'

'It's another motive.'

'You've lost me.' Peter sat on the bench beside her.

Libby sat thinking for a bit.

'David didn't know about James's alibi,' she said eventually.

'So?'

'Well, I got the impression that he was mostly concerned about James being thought guilty.'

'James is family. He would be.'

'*Thought* guilty. Not actually guilty.'

'Same thing.'

Libby shook her head. 'No, there's something... I just can't put my finger on it.'

'Come on. Your children will be waiting for you in the pub,' said Peter, standing up.

Libby sighed, nodded and put out her cigarette.

All the way to the pub, and throughout the cheerful catching up conversation with her offspring, something niggled at the back of her mind. Ben didn't appear, so either he hadn't returned or Gregory hadn't given him her message. It wasn't until she'd waved the children off in their ramshackle cars that she was able to sit down and think about everything that had happened since

345

last night and rewind the conversation with David from this morning. She was positive something he'd said had given her a clue, but try as she might she couldn't think what it was. Had he talked about the incidents? Well, of course he had, he'd said Millie couldn't have done them. She couldn't have climbed up that ladder to cut the steel wire, and she couldn't have clambered underneath the bridge, nor sawn through the planks, and only someone who knew everything about the production and the photographer's visit could have done either.

So who? No one outside the cast and crew and their intimates. Did she include James in that circle? Yes, he was Peter's brother, but Paula's intimate? Would she have told him everything about the production and the publicity? No, because it wasn't until after the fiasco with the roof that she had told James she was pregnant. So it was someone with a connection to Paula, and it had to be someone they already knew about. Someone who knew about the incidents, when the details hadn't been broadcast by anyone. Especially the details of the sabotaged bridge.

Libby began to come to an appalling conclusion.

Chapter Thirty-two

She had no idea what to do next. Her legs seemed to have turned to water, and she was aware of part of her brain being furious at the disruption of her precious last night. Although, of course, that could go ahead without any of the players in their own particular little tragedy.

Shakily, she stood up. She didn't know whether she should phone the police, which seemed rather presumptuous, and who would listen to her, anyway? Who could she tell? If this really was a detective story, she would go and confront the villain, but in real life all she would get was a denial – and there was always the possibility that she was wrong – or she would be putting her head metaphorically into the lion's mouth. She always got cross when the stupid females did that.

David. Why hadn't she seen it before? He knew all about Paula's murder, about the incidents, and he'd tried to deny knowing anything about the bedspread. He'd even admitted she'd made a pass at him. Was it his baby? And telling her about Millie's inability to cause the incidents at the theatre was so obviously to send her off on the trail of someone else. The only thing Libby couldn't understand was why he'd picked on her to talk to.

So, what was the answer? Ignore it? How on

earth was she to do that? She shook her head, which felt as though it was full of cotton-wool. No, not cotton-wool, moths. Fluttering and beating their little wings against her scalp.

The phone rang. Libby looked at it in horror for so long that the answerphone picked it up.

'Libby, it's Fran.'

Libby snatched up the receiver. 'Fran,' she said shakily. 'Thank God it's you.'

'What's happened?' said Fran sharply. 'Are you all right? Have they ... have they found out?'

'I don't know,' said Libby, relieved, 'but I think I have.'

'Of course it was obvious once I put it all together,' she said, after telling Fran how she'd come to her conclusion, 'but I still don't know why.'

'I'm not entirely sure you're right. Something doesn't feel – anyway, it's something to do with both James and Paula. I don't know what. I tried to warn you.'

'Yes, you did, I see that now. Why didn't you tell me then?'

'How could I? It was only one of my feelings, and everyone had been so dismissive of those – even you, in a way.'

'Yes,' sighed Libby, 'I'm sorry. Anyway, what do I do now? It's the last night party tonight.'

'I wouldn't worry about it. If you've worked it out, be sure the police have, and they've got all their sophisticated forensic stuff. There are bound to be traces.'

'So I just carry on regardless? How will I do that? Everyone's going to be there tonight. I can't

348

face them.'

'Yes, you can. After all, the police have had plenty of time to do their tests. I expect they've got results now.'

'Not from James's DNA test. That was only done the day before yesterday. Don't they take weeks?'

'Not weeks. Anyway, that doesn't matter now, does it?'

'No, I suppose it doesn't.' Libby sighed again. 'So you think I ought to let well alone?'

'I do. Will you be all right? Do you want – no, I don't suppose you do.'

'Do I want you to come down? Yes, I do, but the family are going to close ranks on this, so perhaps not. I might come up to London next week, though. Stay with Belinda. I could see you then?'

'Just ring me. Anytime. And now you'd better go and get ready for your big night out.'

How Libby got through the afternoon she had no idea. She let the answerphone pick up messages from Peter, Harry and Ben, none of which sounded as though there was anything wrong, so she guessed no arrest had been made, but when she arrived at the theatre none of them had arrived.

'Libby?' Stephen came up behind her.

'Hi.' Libby tried to smile. 'All ready for the big night?'

'Just about. How about you? You don't look too happy.'

'Well, no. It's all this – you know – business.'

'Paula business, or accidents business?'

'Both,' Libby sighed. 'Pete's Mum didn't cause

349

the incidents, and I can't think why we even considered that she had, really, so someone else did, and that person could well be the murderer. Unless it was the passing tramp theory.'

'I've always hated that,' said Stephen, perching on the edge of one of the little iron tables. 'You always get it in TV mysteries, where the family and friends say it must have been an escaped convict or something.'

'When it couldn't possibly have been,' Libby nodded, 'absolutely. Anyway...' Her voice trailed off as she realised what she was about to let slip.

'Anyway? What? Don't tell me you know who this person is?'

'Of course not.' Libby swallowed hard and tried another smile. 'Oh, God, look at the time. I'd better get on.'

Quelling the now familiar churning in her stomach, Libby opened up the bar, wondering how she'd get on without a float, and fielded questions from the company as to the whereabouts of Peter. It was with relief that she saw Harry come through the glass doors just as the audience were going in to the auditorium, and then she saw his face.

She waited until the foyer was clear, went round the bar and put her arms round him.

'Are they all right?' she asked.

Harry held her away from him. 'How did you know?'

'I don't really. I just saw your face,' she said.

He sat down on a bar stool. 'What a bloody mess,' he said tiredly. 'I can't believe he'd do it.'

Libby stepped back and took a deep breath.

350

'David,' she said.

Harry looked up and nodded.

'I worked it out,' said Libby. 'And he was the one who found the body – that's always suspect, isn't it?'

Harry rubbed a hand over his face and frowned. 'You don't know, then?'

'Don't know what, Harry? Has he been arrested?'

Harry's face crumpled. 'No, Lib. He's dead.'

Libby felt the room spinning and sat down abruptly on a stool, gripping tightly to the edge of the bar counter.

'Susan found him in the surgery,' Harry went on. 'He'd taken some kind of massive overdose. He didn't go home for lunch, so she went looking for him.'

'Oh, God.' Libby put her hand to her mouth. 'Was it after I saw him this morning?'

'I don't know. We knew you'd been there, so we all rang you this afternoon to see if he'd said where he might be. We thought he'd been called out to an emergency.'

'My God, poor Susan. And Millie? Where's Millie?'

'James has taken her back to Steeple Farm. Susan's gone to Hetty's.'

'Did he leave a note?'

'I think so. Pete and Ben are at The Manor. I left Donna in charge at the caff.' He stood up with an effort. 'Come on, we've got a bar to run.'

Somehow, they got through the evening. To Libby's surprise, Hetty's food had been delivered, and once they had set it out and served the over-exuberant last night crowd, Libby quietly handed over the bar and theatre keys to Stephen, who took one look at her face and asked no questions.

'Come back to ours,' said Harry. 'Pete'll come back there, and at least we'll know what's going on. Unless you want to go home?'

'No, I'll come back with you,' said Libby, shivering. 'I couldn't bear to be on my own and not know.'

It was after two o'clock when Peter came home, surprisingly followed by Ben. Harry poured them all large whiskies and when Libby offered to leave them, Ben came and sat on the arm of her chair.

'No,' he said, 'you've been in on this since the beginning. It's only right you should know all about it.'

'She knew,' said Harry. 'She worked it out.'

'Oh, not about the suicide,' said Libby hastily, 'but about David causing the accidents and – you know – Paula.'

Peter hadn't said a word. Now he looked up, his face haggard. 'He didn't cause the accidents,' he said.

Libby looked from Ben to Peter, then at Harry, who shrugged imperceptibly.

'David was Paula's father.'

Libby knew her mouth was hanging open, but didn't seem to have the ability to shut it.

'You remember we said there had been a rumour about him coming to the country to get away from a woman?' Harry and Libby nodded. 'Well, he did. Paula's Mum. Then, several years later, after he'd married Susan, she tracked him down.'

'And moved here? What did she hope to gain by that? Did she think he would leave Susan for her?' asked Libby, at last finding her voice.

'No, I don't think so. She merely wanted support for herself and her daughter. She wasn't terribly healthy.'

'Flo said she was delicate,' murmured Libby.

'So why did he kill himself?' asked Harry. 'Because she was pregnant? Did he know that?'

'Oh, yes, he knew.' Peter sounded grim.

'Oh, God,' gasped Libby. 'It wasn't his?'

'No, that's one sin he seems *not* to have committed,' said Ben.

'Eh?' said Harry.

'Incest,' said Peter.

The silence hummed around them as the truth began to dawn on Libby and Harry.

'James,' said Harry at last.

Peter nodded. 'Apparently my little brother is only my half-brother.'

'Millie and he...' Libby gulped. 'And we joked.'

'We were right. Remember I said my Mum wasn't too pleased when Susan married David? Well, when he first arrived they started an affair.'

'David and Millie?' Harry said disbelievingly.

Peter nodded. 'Then he broke it off because he wanted to get married and settle down, but they resumed it later. It seems just as young Jamie turned up, so did Paula and her mother.'

'But Paula didn't know he was her father?' said Libby.

'Oh, she already knew he was her father. He told her that before she moved to London, after her mother died.'

353

'He said she made a pass at him,' said Libby.

'I expect that's why he told her,' said Ben. 'And from then on she had a hold over him.'

'Is that why he killed her?'

They all looked at her with varying expressions of shock on their faces.

'He didn't kill her,' said Ben.

Libby looked from one to another in confusion. 'Then why did he kill himself? I thought...'

'You got it wrong again, dearheart,' said Peter, 'or is this your friend Fran's idea?'

'No.' Libby was blushing furiously now. 'She said she didn't feel it was entirely right.'

'Well, bully for her.' Peter swallowed the remainder of his whisky in one gulp and held it out to Harry, who took it silently and refilled it.

Ben put his arm round her shoulders. 'David was an honourable man, and the thought of the pain he'd caused was eating away at him. She told him she was pregnant, and when he found her body he was convinced it would all come out.'

'Well, he made sure of that, didn't he?'

'Why didn't he tell James?' asked Harry. 'He had a right to know, if anyone did.'

'Can you imagine going up to someone and saying "You know that girl you've just got pregnant? Well she's your sister." It's like that old song,' said Ben.

'"*That girl is your sister but your Mummy don't know*,"' muttered Libby.

'Something like that. David was too ashamed, and I suppose when he found her dead he was relieved and worried all at once. He said in his note he couldn't bear the pain he would cause those he loved when the truth was known.'

Peter laughed. 'Silly sod. No one would have known about it if he'd kept quiet. Except Milady Snoop over there putting two and two together and making five.'

'I'm sorry.' Libby couldn't think of anything else to say. She'd never felt so humiliated or ashamed in her life.

Peter leaned over and patted her on the knee. 'Don't worry about it, you old trout. He wanted to talk to you this morning because he genuinely thought someone else was behind the accidents and Paula's death. You just misinterpreted it.'

'I feel awful,' she said in a small voice.

'Join the club,' said Peter.

'So we still don't know who...?' said Harry.

'Apparently not. When they get all the DNA analysis back they might know who killed her, but whether that's the same person behind the accidents is another matter.'

'And whether they've got a sample of the murderer's DNA, presumably,' said Libby.

'They haven't got mine,' said Peter, 'or Harry's, have they?'

'They've never asked me,' said Harry. 'Did they ask you, Ben?'

Ben shook his head. 'Does that mean we've never been serious suspects?'

They looked at one another.

'Probably not, then,' said Libby. 'We really don't know much about police investigations, do we?'

Ben was frowning. 'Pete, did your dad think James was his?'

'Yes, apparently he did. Well, at least, I never heard anything...'

'Well, you wouldn't, would you?' said Ben reasonably.

'And what about Susan?' asked Libby. 'Did she know?'

'I don't think so.' Ben frowned. 'David didn't think she did, in any event. That was one of the things in his note. How much it would hurt her when she found out.'

'Pity they didn't think of that thirty-five years ago,' said Peter.

Ben looked at Harry. 'Can I leave him with you, now?' he said quietly.

Harry nodded. 'I'll look after him.'

Ben stood up. 'Come on, then, Libby. I'll see you home.'

'Will they be all right, do you think?' asked Libby, as they walked down the High Street, her arm tucked protectively into Ben's.

'Harry'll look after Pete, and Peter will look after James and his mother. He might not like what she did, but she's still his mother.'

'And your poor sister. What about her?'

'I don't know.' Ben sighed. 'She'll stay with my parents, I suppose, but she's hardly going to want to see any of the Parkers, is she?'

'What I can't understand is why, after talking to me this morning, he suddenly decided to kill himself. Was it something I said?'

'I've no idea, Lib, but don't start blaming yourself. He obviously wanted to talk to you particularly, and I would guess he already had it in mind to – well, to do what he did, but wanted

356

to make sure we knew about Millie.'

'Then why tell *me*?' asked Libby. 'Why not tell Pete, or even you? Why *me*?'

'Perhaps he thought we'd see through him – perhaps we were too close.'

'God what a mess,' said Libby, unconsciously echoing Harry.

Ben squeezed her arm. 'Don't have nightmares, Lib. We'll get over it.'

She looked at him as they turned into Allhallow's Lane. 'I can't help the nightmares, Ben. I just hope the rest of you don't get them.'

He stopped, and Libby was aware of the silence of the night around them. He ran a finger down the side of her face and she shivered.

'Are we all right again, now?' he asked.

Libby looked at him for a long time without saying anything. Finally, she said, 'If I knew why we haven't been all right, I might say yes. But I don't.'

Ben looked down. 'My fault. I got so muddled about the family, and I felt you were interfering.'

'Oh, yes, that came over loud and clear. What I couldn't understand is why you brought Fran in. If I was interfering, what was she doing?'

'I suppose I thought, as a complete outsider, she might be able to clear a few things up so we could forget about them, then she could just disappear back where she came from.'

'But you see her for work. How could she disappear? Anyway, I thought you fancied her.'

Ben looked up and grinned. 'Yes, I thought you did. Well, I don't. Tell you who does, though,' he added, looking thoughtful.

'Who?'

'Your Stephen. You'll have to watch him.'

'Stephen? Really? How do you know?'

'He asked about her. Seemed very interested. And he's left you alone, hasn't he?'

Libby sighed. 'Yes, he has. In fact, when he walked me home the other night he told me he knew I wasn't interested, but hoped we could stay friends, sort of thing.'

'There you are. He's transferred his affections.'

'Just as well, although I don't see much future in it, with her in London and him down here.'

'I did offer to pass on his phone number. I wouldn't give out hers, obviously.'

'What did he say?'

'Oh, he was all for it. Land line and mobile. He really is a nice bloke, you know, Lib.'

Libby sighed again. 'I know. Just terribly boring. I feel bad about bringing him over here now. He must have taken it as a sign that I fancied him.'

'You'd think by the time we reached our age we'd have grown out of all that sort of behaviour, wouldn't you?' said Ben.

'That was exactly what I've been thinking these last two weeks,' exclaimed Libby.

'Have you? Why?' Ben moved a fraction closer.

'Oh, you know.' Libby felt the now familiar blush creeping up her neck. 'Well, you do know, you annoying man. Perfectly well.' She turned and began to walk up Allhallow's Lane. 'And I'm not going to ask you in tonight, either. I think you need to get back to the bosom of your family. You're going to have an absolutely bloody time over the next few weeks, and Susan's got to live with it for the rest of her life. Your poor sister.'

It was Ben's turn to sigh. 'I know. But I think Pete's going to have a bad time, too. I blame Millie more than David in all this, and he's going to have to live with that. Mind you, so's James.'

'I wonder if they will put her in a home, now?'

'David said he thought she might be able to live on her own for a while longer.'

'Sheltered housing, then?'

'But not here. Not in Maltby Close.'

'No, that would be a bit much, wouldn't it?'

They stopped outside Libby's door.

'I'm sorry if anything I've done or said contributed to any of this,' said Libby in a muffled voice, as Ben pulled her close to him.

'Don't be daft. If anyone's to blame, it's Pete for the play and me for the theatre. And now, shut up.'

He shut her up more effectively than ever before, and, by the time he let her go, Libby's legs were threatening to give way completely.

'I'll ring you in the morning,' he said. 'Sorry the last night turned out so badly.'

'I'd forgotten about that,' said Libby, surprised. 'Good lord!'

But when she got in to bed a little later, she remembered. Remembered the cast, high on success, wondering why she'd left them in their hour of glory. Thank God for Stephen, who had so obviously understood and who would have smoothed things over as he had done throughout the last difficult weeks. You never had to tell him twice, and he had used his initiative more than once on her behalf. So he got a little annoyed

359

with her sometimes? Well, you couldn't blame him, thought Libby sleepily. Just hope Fran doesn't find him as boring as I do...

Chapter Thirty-three

On Sunday morning Libby woke to an overcast sky and a sense of foreboding. As she hadn't been at the after-show party she had no idea what arrangements had been made for the "get out" at the theatre, or whether Stephen had arranged to strike the set that day or leave it until everyone had got their breath back. She assumed the cast would arrive at some time to collect personal items, and she had told them at the start they would be required to pack up costumes and props and clean the dressing rooms, so she only hoped someone had thought fit to remind them of it last night. Stephen would have, she was sure.

She decided ten o'clock seemed an appropriate time to go, but when she phoned Stephen at nine-thirty to check, there was no reply. Either he had already left, or he'd stayed over last night with someone in the village, which seemed a likelier explanation. Wrapping her cloak around her and jamming an ancient sou'wester on her head, she said goodbye to Sidney and plunged out into the rain. Damp flakes of blossom blew into her face and made the path slippery and, despite the rain, she soon became overheated inside the cape. All of which had the effect of keeping her mind off the events of yesterday, so when she finally made it up the drive to the theatre and saw Stephen coming towards her with an expression of the utmost compassion on his face, it all hit her with renewed force and she was hard put to it not to burst into tears.

'Don't worry, Lib,' he said, putting an arm round her shoulders and giving her a squeeze. 'I told them all to be here as early as possible this morning, and we did some of it last night, so there's hardly anything to do.'

'How much do you know?' Libby asked, turning to face him.

'Only that David's dead. Harry told me last night. None of the family will be here today. I'm surprised to see you, frankly.'

Libby sighed. 'One of us had to be here,' she said, 'and I'm not family, after all.'

'As good as,' said Stephen wryly.

Libby turned to go in to the theatre. 'Not at all,' she said.

Emma, coming out with an armful of costumes, stopped in front of them.

'We're so sorry to hear about David, Lib,' she said. 'Is it – I mean, we wondered...'

'Anything to do with Paula's death, she means,' said Stephen.

'Not as far as I know,' said Libby, 'but I don't really *know* anything. Thanks, anyway.'

Emma's sentiments were repeated by almost everybody as Libby wandered round the building feeling redundant. The small back-stage crew just smiled at her and carried on taking down flats, and wrenching nails out of wood. She stood staring up into the flies, wondering yet again how anyone could have got up there and cut the steel wire. And why. All the speculation about the family, and which of them wanted the play to be stopped was at an end with Hetty's revelations, and the tragedy of David's death was really nothing to do with it at all. The accidents were a complete mystery, now, just as they had been from the first. Libby just wanted to forget it all and move on. Which reminded her, she was going to try and get up to London to see Fran and stay with Belinda. She was just reaching into her basket for her mobile, having remembered it for once, when it began to ring.

'Libby, it's Fran.'

'I was just trying to ring you,' said Libby, 'how spooky.'

'No, not spooky. What happened yesterday?'

Libby paused, not really wanting to tell Fran over the phone.

'Something happened. I had this terrible dream. Come on, Lib. What happened?'

'What was your dream?' asked Libby, cautiously.

'I'm not going to tell you in case it has nothing to do with anything,' said Fran, sounding irritable.

Libby moved away from the wings out on to the middle of the stage. 'David's dead,' she said as quietly as she could.

'What?' Fran gasped. *'David?'*

'That wasn't your dream, then?'

'No ... oh, God, how dreadful. Was he – was he – er, killed?'

'He committed suicide,' said Libby.

There was a silence. 'Then it was true,' said

Fran finally.

'What was?'

'Do you remember me saying it was something to do with Paula and James? Well, it was, wasn't it?'

'Yes, but...'

'Don't tell me now. You're on your mobile, so it's obviously not convenient, so ring me when you get home, will you? It's important.'

'Fran, if it's important, you must tell me now.'

'I can't, Libby. I'll tell you later.'

Libby looked at the phone in bewilderment.

'What's up?' said Stephen, climbing on to the stage and wiping his hands on a disgusting-looking piece of cloth.

'Nothing,' said Libby, 'it was just Fran. I'll ring her back at home.'

'Oh, Fran.' Stephen looked down at his feet. 'Did Ben give her my number, do you know?'

'No idea. He told me he was going to.'

'How do you think she'd react?'

'I don't know, Stephen. I hardly know her. She just said she needs to talk to me.'

'Her psychic thing, is it?'

'How do you know?' said Libby in surprise.

'Oh, word gets around,' said Stephen, looking uncomfortable.

'Yes, but how?' said Libby suspiciously.

'Oh, Libby. You know how much gossip there is around am-dram.'

'Don't use that awful name,' shuddered Libby.

'Don't be so pernickety,' said Stephen, his eyes narrowing. 'You can be a real pain, sometimes, Libby.'

Libby looked up, startled. 'Sorry, I'm sure,' she said. 'I'll go, then. I'm not needed here, and I can come in at any time to collect anything I've forgotten.'

'Your own little domain, isn't it? Just what you've always wanted.'

'Stephen! What on earth are you talking about?'

'Oh, nothing. Forget I said it,' said Stephen, turning into the wings. 'I'll give you a ring.'

Libby set off down the drive feeling disquieted. The change in Stephen's manner from when he greeted her to just now was disconcerting, and she wondered how many of her cast and crew had felt the same about her. Was she a bossy old cow with megalomaniac and despotic tendencies?

At the bottom of the drive she hesitated, wondering whether to call on Peter and Harry, who surely wouldn't be opening the restaurant today, or leave them alone until they wanted to speak to her. If ever.

However, as she walked past the Pink Geranium, she was surprised to be hailed by a muffled shout from inside. Harry waved her to the door.

'I didn't think you'd be open,' said Libby, as she stepped inside.

'Got bookings, and Donna can't cope on her own after last night. We used up all the emergency staff. Anyway, Pete's gone over to his mum's. They're all in a bit of state.'

'Hardly surprising. I wonder if they'll ever recover?'

'Want a coffee or something? I could do with a break from chopping veg,' said Harry, sniffing his long elegant fingers and making a face.

'Lovely. Shall I do it?'

'No, you sit there and put your feet up. I'd just made a pot.'

Harry came back from the kitchen with the coffee, mugs and an ashtray. 'So, reckon we're going back to our outsider status, then?'

'You and me against the Family?' Libby looked up at him. 'Probably. They're going to have so much to deal with, aren't they?'

Harry offered cigarettes. 'And all we can do is offer hands to hold or shoulders to cry on.'

'Well, at least we don't have to worry about Paula's murderer being in the family now.'

'No?' Harry raised his eyebrows. 'What about Susan?'

'Susan?' Libby was horrified. 'For God's sake, Harry, you can't believe that.'

'If she knew about Paula and James and realised that the whole thing would come out if they got married, how do you think she'd have felt? Especially as she and David had no children, and he had two from two different mothers, one of them being her own aunt.'

'I suppose so,' said Libby doubtfully, 'but surely she'd realise that with Paula dead it would all come out anyway.'

'Not if it was in the heat of the moment,' said Harry, taking a sip of coffee.

'But the body was moved, wasn't it? In the bedspread. Susan couldn't have done that. Besides, if it was the heat of the moment she'd have hit David, not Paula.'

'Not if she'd known for a long time and kept it

quiet. She had a position to keep up, didn't she?'

'Oh, this is rubbish,' said Libby. 'Of course it wasn't Susan. And she couldn't have rigged the accidents, either, and it looks now as if they had something to do with Paula rather than the play.'

'Well, start looking for who could have done them, then,' said Harry. 'Now that some of the wood's been cleared from the trees. Opportunity and all that. And don't start saying you're not Miss Marple. We've heard that before, and you're still worrying away at it.'

'Oh, gosh, yes. That reminds me,' said Libby, standing up and stubbing out her cigarette. 'Fran called and I said I'd phone her back when I got home.'

'More psychic stuff?'

'I don't know, Harry. But even if she doesn't quite believe it herself, she does come out with some extraordinary things. If she's got something to say, I need to hear it.'

'All right, don't bristle up at me.' Harry stood up and gave her a kiss. 'I'll ring you later and if we're still out in the cold perhaps we can have a drink together or something.'

Feeling a bit better, Libby hurried along the High Street towards Allhallow's Lane, and was surprised on turning the corner to see Stephen coming towards her.

'There you are,' he called. 'I'd just about given up.'

'What's the matter?' asked Libby, drawing level with him.

'I wanted to apologise. I shouldn't have said what I did. I suppose things have got to me more than I thought.' Stephen wouldn't meet her eyes.

'You had me worried,' said Libby. 'I thought I'd turned into an ogre.'

'No more than most directors.' Stephen turned his head and grinned. 'Anyway, we've more or less finished at the theatre. Want to come and see?'

'No, I don't. I've had enough of the theatre for a while, thank you very much. Anyway, Fran's expecting me to call her, so I'd better get home.'

'With no strings – I could make the tea while you phone her?'

'Did I invite you for tea?' Libby smiled.

'Yes, but not today. I'm just taking it up today, that's all.' Stephen smiled back.

'Oh, go on, then. Just be careful of Sidney.'

Sidney, however, retreated upstairs in a huff, thoroughly fed up that his house was yet again being invaded by Others.

Libby lit the fire, although it wasn't really cold, just depressingly gloomy and wet, and showed Stephen where things were in the kitchen before dialling Fran's number.

'At last. What have you been doing?'

'The get out. Well, I wasn't exactly, but it was being done.'

'So tell me what's happened. From the beginning.'

Libby told her, perching on the arm of the armchair nearest the window and staring out at the rain reducing the green to a quagmire. The blossom from the hawthorn drifted wetly down into slush-like drifts.

'I said it was to do with Paula and James, didn't

367

I?' said Fran, when she'd finished.

'But the murder wasn't. Unless Harry's right, and it was Susan.'

'No, it was David who was coming through so strongly to me. And I said I thought you were wrong.'

'Yes, you did. And I feel bad about going to see him.'

'He asked you to. But I still don't see why it was you he wanted to talk to.'

Libby sighed. 'Either everyone wants to talk to me or nobody does.'

'Well, I wanted to tell you about my dream. It's all to do with opportunity.'

'That's what Harry said,' said Libby. 'Who had the opportunity?'

'Not just for the murder,' said Fran, 'but the accidents.'

'And did you see who it was?'

'I didn't actually see, but it was easy to work it out.'

'Is it?' Libby frowned. Opportunity. For the accidents. For the murder. Not just opportunity, but the means. She heard Stephen come into the room behind her.

'Can't find any sugar, Lib,' he said.

'Libby!' Fran's voice was sharp in her ear. 'Libby, be careful.'

And of course, it all became clear.

Chapter Thirty-four

'Libby? Have you got any sugar?'

Libby slowly turned towards him. 'In the cocoa tin by the sink,' she said.

'OK.' Stephen went back into the kitchen. 'Libby!' Fran was almost shouting.

'It's OK, Fran,' said Libby shakily. 'I've got it. I think.'

'Is he there? I can feel him.'

'Yes, he's here. Are you sure it's him?'

'Well, as sure as I can be. It feels like it. Call the police.'

'How can I? When he's in front of me?'

'I'll call them, then,' said Fran. 'Keep him talking.' She rang off.

The blood was pounding in Libby's head and she thought she might faint. As Stephen came back in to the room, triumphant with two mugs and the cocoa tin, she slipped off the arm and onto the seat of the chair. What do I say? she thought.

'Sugar?' he asked, holding up a spoon.

'No, thanks.' Libby reached out to take a mug and hoped she wouldn't spill it.

'So did Fran want to know about David?' Stephen sat back in Libby's cane chair, which creaked. She wanted to tell him to mind his own business but didn't dare. Instead, she nodded. He looked so normal, in his jumper and jeans and Cat boots, his pleasant face smiling an enquiry.

'Did she think he'd murdered Paula?'

'No, she didn't. In fact, that's what she said to me yesterday, when I thought he might have done.'

Libby took a sip of scalding tea, which Stephen had obviously made by pouring boiling water on to a teabag, and then taking it out too soon. She squashed an instinctive grimace.

'Do the police think he did it?' asked Stephen.

'I've no idea,' said Libby. 'Will they have to investigate his death?'

'Oh, yes. Didn't your friends tell you? They will have been called. Was there a note?'

'I believe so,' said Libby, unwilling to reveal any more family business. 'But I don't know why he would have killed Paula.'

'Well, he was her father, wasn't he?' said Stephen, and Libby nearly fell off the chair. 'Oh, sorry, didn't you know?' Stephen took a sip of tea, keeping his eyes on Libby's horrified ones.

'How – how did you know?'

For a moment Stephen looked disconcerted. Then he shrugged. 'Oh, she told me,' he said.

'She did? I didn't think you knew her that well.'

'I told you I knew her. When I told you she was a p.t. and you knew what it meant.' He laughed.

'So you did.' Libby took a deep breath and put down her mug. 'I didn't realise you knew who her father was, though. I certainly didn't.'

Luckily, Stephen didn't question her as to whether she had known before he told her.

'And why would he kill his own daughter, any-

370

way? Not just to stop her telling anyone, surely. After all, she'd already told you.'

'I don't know,' said Stephen. 'Anyway, he didn't, did he?'

'No,' said Libby, 'and he couldn't have been responsible for the accidents, either.'

'The accidents?' Was she imagining things, or was Stephen looking wary?

'Well, yes. Apparently they think the accidents were first attempts to kill her.' Libby looked down into her mug.

'Rubbish. She wasn't even at the bridge.'

'No. That's very puzzling, actually. And even if she had been there, how would anyone be certain she would be the one to fall off?'

'Frightener.'

'Oh, yes! That's what James said. He said she thought someone was out to get her, or frighten her, at least. You think she was right?'

This time she was certain Stephen looked wary. 'It's the only explanation, isn't it?'

'I suppose so. And David was hardly the build to go scrambling up ladders or underneath bridges, was he? And I don't suppose he had wire-cutters or anything. I can't believe we thought Millie could have done it.' She took a deep breath. 'It must have been someone with opportunity. And a very good reason.'

'I expect there were a lot of men with a good reason,' said Stephen, keeping his eyes on Libby's. 'But I would have thought it was a spur of the moment thing.'

'Really?'

Stephen's eyes moved to the window and Libby

turned her head. A dark car had just drawn up outside, and as she watched she saw DCI Murray get out of the passenger side. Stephen stood up and a wave of relief washed through Libby, leaving her quite light-headed.

'It looks as though you've got company, Lib,' he said. 'Still under suspicion, eh? I'd better leave you to it.'

Libby stood up and caught DS Cole's eye as he peered through the window. He nodded briefly as there came a sharp rap on the front door. Across on the green two patrol cars had pulled up silently, but with their ominous blue lights signalling trouble. Stephen was pulling on his coat and looked up. 'You're in more of a mess than I thought,' he said, his eyes going quickly from the front door to the kitchen.

Without a word, Libby made a dive for the front door, but Stephen was before her, grabbing her wrist as she reached for the latch. Throwing her to the floor he turned and made his way as quickly as he could through the assault course of the front room. Libby managed to get to her knees and open the door, but before anyone could do anything, Sidney took a hand. Streaking down the stairs and over the furniture in a single bound, he was in amongst Stephen's feet before DCI Murray had even stepped over Libby.

The language, Stephen's and Sidney's, was appalling. Torn between hysterical laughter and feeble tears, Libby watched from the floor as DS Cole gently assisted Stephen to his feet and suggested he might like to accompany him to the station. Little DC Burnham appeared nervously as Stephen was ushered firmly out of the door, without even glancing at Libby, and helped her to her feet.

'No caution?' asked Libby shakily, looking out of the window to where Stephen was being helped into the back seat of one of the patrol cars.

'No, we haven't arrested him yet,' said DCI Murray. 'Now, Miss er – Mrs–'

'Sarjeant,' said Libby weakly, 'with a J.'

'Ah, yes. Well, now, DC Burnham, could we have some tea, do you think?'

DC Burnham paused on the edge of rebellion.

'Oh, yes, I'd love a proper cup,' said Libby. 'Stephen had just made some, but it was awful. Here, I'll do it.'

'No, madam, you sit there,' said DC Burnham, softening. 'I'll make a proper pot, shall I?'

'Do you feel up to a few questions, madam?' asked DCI Murray, creaking in to the cane chair. Sidney reappeared, his fur still standing on end, and came to investigate, ready to repel all boarders.

'Yes, I'm fine,' said Libby, although she knew she wasn't. 'Did Fran phone you?'

'Mrs Castle? Yes, she did.'

'I can't believe you came just because she said she thought I was with the murderer.'

DCI Murray smiled. 'But when she said exactly who you was with – I mean, who was with you – well, we thought we'd better come.'

'You mean, you knew it was Stephen?'

'We had our suspicions, madam.'

'But, how?'

DC Burnham came in with a tray she'd

373

unearthed from somewhere and the cups left out since Millie's visit.

'Mr Pringle had every opportunity to cut the steel wire at your theatre, he knew in advance about the visit of the photographer, and he had arranged to meet the deceased on the night of her death.'

'I didn't know that!' gasped Libby.

'No, madam, you wouldn't.' DCI Murray took a tea cup and looked at her solemnly over the rim. 'He was the father of her child, you know.'

'You had his DNA?'

'Oh, yes, madam.'

'I didn't even know you'd interviewed him,' said Libby, shaking her head.

'Well, madam, you would only see the parts of the investigation that involved you, or that any of your friends told you. And they told you plenty. You were all becoming a bit of a nuisance.'

'But not Stephen. He didn't tell us anything. Will you tell us why? When it's over? Will he confess?'

DC Burnham leaned forward. 'The baby was his, and his DNA was found on the bedspread, and all over her house and car. He wasn't very careful. He'd be better admitting it.'

'What about motive?' asked Libby. 'Was it jealousy?'

'Probably,' said DCI Murray, 'but we're not over-concerned with why, madam. Just who, how and when. And Mr Pringle is the who, he had the means for the how, and was available for the when. I can tell you that he and the deceased had been having a relationship for some time. At least a couple of years, apparently.'

'He did say he knew her,' said Libby, relieved to find the shaking was getting less. 'But I thought it was just a passing acquaintance. But wait a minute – he was married up until a year or so ago.'

'Yes, madam. So his wife told us.' DCI Murray looked smug. 'Another woman was apparently the cause of their split.'

'Paula!'

'It would seem so, from evidence found at her house. Yes. He was very careless.' He leant forward conspiratorially, ignoring DC Burnham's disapproving expression. 'It appears the young lady fell against the marble fireplace.'

'So it was an accident?'

DCI Murray nodded. 'In a way. I doubt if she fell there all by herself, though.'

'So what about the bedspread?'

'The throw? We think he wrapped her up in it and put her in her car, intending to drive it away. I think the fire sirens scared him off. He certainly didn't bother to clear away any evidence from inside the house, and there was plenty.' He sat back, looking pleased with himself. 'He'd never have got away with it.'

Ten minutes later, after assuring themselves she wasn't a quivering wreck, the police presence left and Libby went straight to the phone. While she was still explaining things to Fran and thanking her for her prompt action there was a heavy pounding on the front door.

Ben, Peter and Harry crowded into the room overwhelming her with hugs, kisses and, from

Harry, a large bottle of scotch.

When she'd sorted them all out, found seats for them all, pacified a now furious Sidney and found glasses for the scotch, she slumped into the cane chair and began to explain.

'So he must have been seeing Paula for months,' said Peter, when Libby finally ran out of steam.

'While she was still seeing James, certainly. Before that weekend when she said they'd conceived.'

'It was years, according to DCI Murray,' said Libby.

'That was why he agreed to come over here and stage manage,' said Harry, with the air of one who has had a light bulb moment.

Libby nodded. 'And I thought he fancied me. That'll teach me.'

'He went to some trouble to make it look as though he did,' said Ben, patting her hand. 'I was very jealous.'

'You old bugger, you weren't,' said Peter. 'You knew the old trout didn't fancy him back.'

'So what exactly did Fran say?' asked Harry.

'She told me yesterday she didn't think I was right about David, but today she said she'd had this dream about opportunity. And that made me think about what you'd said. And Stephen was right here when she was telling me, and suddenly I realised. He was the only one who had the opportunity to cut the wire, he knew who would be underneath it, or not, and he knew about the photographer coming.'

'Do you remember I couldn't get hold of either Paula or him that night I phoned everybody?'

376

said Peter. 'I suppose they were together.'

'Maybe, and then when he got home there would have been this message. She must have already told him about the baby and her intention to snaffle James,' said Ben.

'So he decided to frighten her again. He almost admitted that to me,' said Libby, shuddering and causing three willing hands to vie with each other to top up her scotch.

'The fire, of course, that must have diverted attention away from him up at Lendle Lane,' mused Harry.

'I would have thought it would have been the opposite,' said Ben. 'More people around the village late at night.'

'I don't suppose he intended to kill her, he probably just lost his temper. We still don't really know how she was killed, do we?' said Peter.

'She hit her head on the fireplace.' Libby shuddered again, and Ben heaved himself over to sit on the arm of the cane chair to put his arm round her. The chair uttered a protesting creak and Sidney swore from underneath it. 'DCI Murray said he thought it was an accident, but Stephen panicked. And the fire engines disturbed him, like Ben said.'

'There you are then,' said Peter, 'spur of the moment, I would have thought, then he drove back and collected the bedspread to wrap her in to make it look as though ... oh, no, she was left in her car.'

'He had to use something of hers rather than his, or something from his car, or wherever he killed her, so it didn't link back to him,' said

Harry. 'Hey, I'm getting good at this.'

The other three looked at him with disapproval. 'Sorry,' he said.

'I don't think it was that well thought out,' said Libby. 'The police think he wrapped her in the bedspread to move her. That's all there was to it. What I don't understand is why David didn't see it.'

'He'd just found his daughter dead,' said Ben gently. 'I don't suppose he was seeing or thinking straight.'

'We actually suggested Stephen right at the beginning, didn't we?' said Libby. 'He was the obvious one for cutting the wire.'

'But we didn't know he knew Paula. How could we have done?' said Peter.

Libby shook her head. 'We couldn't. I was surprised when he admitted it to me the other day.'

'Do you know what's so awful?' said Ben, absentmindedly stroking Libby's hair.

'All of it?' said Libby, squirming slightly.

'No, the fact that it wasn't James's baby and David committed suicide for nothing.'

'If only he'd waited,' said Harry.

'It would still have come out about him being the father of both of them, and he was really worried about that, as well. Incest does *not* go down well in village life.' Peter swallowed the last of the whisky in his glass and stood up. 'Come along, pet. Let's leave these two to recover from all the traumas. And you've got some prepping up to do while I go and tell the rest of the family.'

When they'd gone, Ben threw a log on the fire and sat down opposite Libby.

'All right now?' he asked softly.

'I don't think I shall ever be all right again,' said Libby, with a shaky laugh.

'I don't suppose you were ever in any danger,' said Ben.

'No, I don't think he thought I knew anything, although he did begin to look a bit wary when I mentioned a couple of things which obviously struck chords. I just can't believe how calm he was. He only lost it right at the last minute when he saw the police cars.'

'And Sidney saved the day,' said Ben. 'Your Onlie Protector.'

Libby reached a hand down to pat Sidney's tail, which was all she could reach.

'So, nightmares over?' Ben stood up and took her hands.

'I don't suppose so.' Libby looked at their clasped hands. 'I really don't know how anybody gets over anything like this. All those people in books who shrug it off and go on to the next murder without a backward glance. I shall have nightmares for ages.'

Ben pulled her to her feet. 'You'd better feed Sidney,' he said.

'Why?' said Libby, leaning gratefully against him.

'Because, purely on account of the nightmares, of course, I'm going to take you upstairs, no more arguing, and put you to bed.'

'Just me?' she asked, looking up at him.

'Just us,' he said.

Libby smiled and kissed him.

'I'd like that,' she said.

The publishers hope that this book has given you enjoyable reading. Large Print Books are especially designed to be as easy to see and hold as possible. If you wish a complete list of our books please ask at your local library or write directly to:

Magna Large Print Books
Magna House, Long Preston,
Skipton, North Yorkshire.
BD23 4ND

This Large Print Book for the partially sighted, who cannot read normal print, is published under the auspices of

THE ULVERSCROFT FOUNDATION